CLAIMED
BY

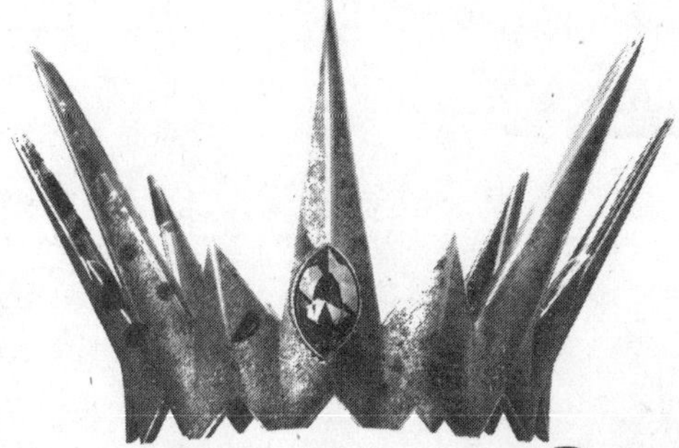

SHADOW
AND
BLOOD

CLAIMED BY

SHADOW AND BLOOD

JEN L. GREY

ANYA

Anya
An Imprint of Meredith Wild LLC

Cover Design by Covers By Juan

Paperback ISBN: 979-8-88953-202-6

CHAPTER ONE

A bitter smell filled my nose, and my stomach roiled. The sound of heavy, frantic footsteps rushing away pulled at my consciousness, but when I tried to open my eyes, the world spun, and bile inched up my throat.

What the hell? Had I drunk too much? *Ember, what's going on?* I tried to pack link to my older sister. But then I noticed that the warmth of our pack link bond was muted ... and everything crashed back over me—being kidnapped and swept into another realm, then thrown into deadly bridal trials where contestants didn't hesitate to murder each other in an attempt to survive and gain favor with both the Shadow and Aureline councils to wed the Shadow Prince.

Vad.

At the ball, he'd asked me to be his queen.

The breeze shifted, and the floral perfume of lilies mixed with the coppery tang of blood. The scent was so strong I could taste it.

It was still nighttime. I was on the ground, one arm outstretched. I tried to move my hand, but it wouldn't budge. My fingers seemed to be wrapped around a wooden handle. Thick liquid soaked my gown, hot near my hand and sleeve but cooling as it reached my chest and side, and a strange arm was wrapped around me, cold fingers pressed to my shoulder.

Adrenaline pumped through my veins, burning off some of the haze, and I finally managed to open my eyes.

My stomach dropped.

In the shadows of what I thought might be a garden, King Merrick lay beside me, dressed in his black royal surcoat with silver embellishments. I lay next to him with my hand ...

Oh Fate. No.

My fingers were wrapped around the handle of a ... a *dagger* that was lodged in his chest, left of center, barely shy of his heart.

A strangled scream ripped from me.

What the *fuck*?

"Help! The king needs help!" I shouted. I tried to push myself up, my bare feet scrabbling on the slick stone, but I got no traction. Instead, I slid in the blood that coated my entire side.

My heart twisted. I had to put pressure on his wound. The blade needed to remain in place until a physician could oversee its removal, or it could worsen the bleeding and his condition.

I placed my free hand against the marble, needing extra help to get onto my knees. As I rose, a sickening squelch sounded, and my other hand pulled out the dagger like it was attached to me. My heart dropped into my stomach.

And then the entire nightmare came to light.

Dark blood spurted from the gaping wound and poured onto the pathway. A sharp hiss escaped the king's chest, wet and wrong, like something tearing open.

The king's dark blue eyes met mine, and my throat tightened. He was in even worse shape than I had feared.

Eyes glassy and lips pale, he lifted a hand and dropped it to his chest like he was beckoning me to come near. I dropped to my knees beside him and lowered my head, just as his tongue ran over his lips as if they were parched. His next breath came with a horrible sucking sound, as if air was being pulled through his wound. Blood trickled from the corners of his mouth. "L-l-lilies," he gurgled weakly.

A scream tore through me as I pressed my free palm over his wound. Despite the pressure, my wolf ears picked up on his weakening heart. As if Fate were taunting me, thick blood pulsed against my hand, slower and slower, and not due to the pressure.

I tried to drop the dagger so I could better help the king, but my fingers remained wrapped around the handle. A weird, smooth, dark rope bound it to my hand. It looked like it was made of ordinary fibers, but it felt like a snake, and when I tried to shake it off, a prickling and pinching sensation at every point of contact consumed me.

My heart nearly stopped. This *had* to be some sort of awful nightmare. One I needed to wake from.

My wolf within surged forward, sensing danger. She was right, though I couldn't panic. I needed to stay as calm as possible.

Breathing through my mouth, I studied the dagger. It was half the length of my forearm, the metal blade slick with blood and with faint traces of iridescent green on the blade.

The strange black cord around my hand turned iridescent, then gray, then faded. The dagger clattered to the blood-soaked ground and splattered in an arc of thick red droplets.

Footsteps pounded again, this time coming toward me.

I whimpered as my vision blurred. "Please, hold on. They're almost here." His face had gone deathly pale, but his eyes remained fixed on me as he tried again to form words. His fingers twitched like he wanted to communicate but couldn't. Nothing but rasping breaths escaped him.

I pressed both hands firmly against his chest as I leaned in.

His lips parted, but his throat worked uselessly. Another breath rattled from him, shallow and ragged.

"No," I whispered. My arms trembled, but I didn't move. I could still make out the faint pulses of his heart. Tears spilled down my cheeks. "Hold on."

The footsteps were louder now. Voices echoed behind me, but I couldn't make out the words. I didn't dare look away. Blood was smeared over the front of my gown, thick and clinging. My knees burned where they'd hit the stone, and my hands ached from how hard I was pressing.

He was still breathing. Barely. Just barely. "Help! He needs help," I sobbed.

Guards flanked me and seized me by the arms. Their black armor chilled my skin as they hauled me back, ripping my hands from the king's chest.

No. Now there was no pressure on his wound. I thrashed against them and got free, then dropped back beside him and put my hands back on his chest.

Once again, strong hands gripped my arms, the fingers digging hard into my skin. The guards ripped me backward away from the king once more.

"Save him! Someone stabbed him. His heart is barely beating. Save him, please!" I jerked, trying to break free once more.

The heartbeat became no more than a soft, fading thrum, yet each beat cut deep. He'd have had a better chance of living if I hadn't pulled the dagger out. Accident or not, it didn't matter.

Vomit burned my throat. "He needs a physician *now*!" My voice broke.

Heavy footsteps thundered closer, then halted. I looked up and saw ... Vad. Dark hair streaming wildly over his shoulders, he stared down at his father. That inexplicable tug in my chest intensified, but I fought it. My pulse quickened as terror sickened me. What would he do to me? Whoever had framed me had given me no hope of an alibi.

His head snapped up, and his rage-filled, storm-gray eyes locked with mine. A knot formed in my throat as the world slowed around us. His sculpted jaw clenched, and a muscle jumped. "Stop!" He stepped forward, then fell to his knees. His voice was hoarse. "Stop, let her go. Briar! Guards, unhand her *now.* Let her speak. Briar, what happened?"

His words snarled in my head, tangling in a mass of rage and confusion. I wanted to tell him that I'd found his father like this, beg him not to hate me, but I didn't have a chance. I tried harder to break free, but the guards continued to drag me away.

My bare feet scraped the marble, slipping in the cold, congealing blood as if it were oil. The air smelled bitter and bloody, and a cloying scent covered the perfume of the lilies.

The pool of Vad's father's blood was so large that it was mere inches from reaching Vad's feet despite the space between them. Vad tried to clamber to his feet, staggering, and stretched out his hands, either toward me or the king, as the guards continued to pull me away.

Two figures resembling reapers materialized from the shadows and crossed in front of Vad, one robed in dark gray and one in light. Council members.

The light gray reaper placed a hand on Vad's shoulder, holding him back. Vad sneered and took in a shaky breath.

A sob ripped from my chest. The guards dragged me to the edge of the garden, and Vad's wild gaze snapped from the council members back to me. His eyes darkened.

My heart shattered more than I'd ever imagined possible. Of course. Why wouldn't he think I'd done it? Whoever had killed the king had set me up perfectly.

Dark shadows slicked from the guards' hands, and cold

magic brushed my skin. Shadows thickened around me. My lungs froze. What the hell were they doing? The sensation was similar to what it felt like when the other bride contestants and I had been portaled to our trials through the sigil of the Shadow Kingdom, but only marble was below us now.

"I need to talk to her, right now," Vad screamed, and the world swirled in grays.

All at once, the gray disappeared, and my feet grated against a coarse stone floor. My nostrils burned from the horrible stench of mold, rot, and blood.

The guards heaved me forward with a grip so tight that the metal of their armor pinched my skin. I had no clue where these twatwaffles were taking me, but if I went there, I'd likely wind up dead or severely injured.

I thrashed, struggling to break free, my wolf howling in my head. I tried to yank their gloves off and break through the metal, but nothing bothered them. They didn't miss a step.

The joints were the weakest points of their gauntlets, but I couldn't get a good grip.

A strange new warmth within me flared, and my skin prickled.

Fae magic.

My skin crawled, and I yelped, staring at my arms, expecting them to be covered in bugs. They were bare. Yet the sensation intensified, and I jerked around, trying to stop the feeling. Where were the bugs coming from? I couldn't see anything but a broad hall with dark stone walls, greasy sputtering torches, and a jagged stone ceiling.

The torchlight cast sickly shadows over the walls, making the prison feel alive. Somewhere behind me, water dripped in a slow, almost deliberate rhythm. Chains rattled erratically, and strangled cries followed each clang. Heavy thuds echoed, accompanied by deep-throated screams.

One of the guards chuckled. "If you don't share everything, your future will be nothing but crying and screaming like the others."

I swallowed hard, realizing what was going on.

Torture.

What sort of sick hell was this place?

A sour taste filled my mouth. "I'll tell you everything I know. Someone stabbed the king. It wasn't me—"

"Silence." The guard on my left struck the back of my neck with what I thought was the flat of his palm. "We have no time to waste on lies."

The edges of my vision darkened, and acid burned the back of my throat. I wanted to say more, but I wasn't stupid. They viewed me as guilty, and I couldn't blame them. Someone had staged me perfectly, like a puppet with strings. I'd done exactly what they'd wanted.

We reached a heavy iron gate that groaned on its hinges as it opened. I stumbled again, my knees buckling, but the guards jerked me upright and threw me into the center of the chamber.

I fell onto my knees, blinding pain shooting through my limbs. I swallowed a whimper, not wanting to give these assholes any pleasure in what they'd done. Instead, I bit the inside of my cheek, trying to focus my attention away from my neck, feet, and knees, and forced myself to stand upright.

Two more guards with wings extended strode out of the shadows as if they'd been waiting for me.

"You can leave," the taller of the new guards commanded.

The first two turned to depart, and I had a sudden, urgent thought. I yelled, "Rhielle! She's injured. Someone should check on her."

One of them looked over his shoulder at me, and the tall new guard spat, "Leave. Now."

These new guards wore dark gray armor instead of black

and hoods that obscured their faces entirely, not even showing the light of their eyes. Their heavy armor was identical metal over leather, except for the crests at the center of their chests and the emblems on the backs of their gloves. One had a shadow wolf, a sword, and a three-pronged rune. The other had a dragon, a mace, and a circle around a triangle.

The guards who'd brought me here hurried off, leaving me alone with these two, who screamed small-dick energy. Still, they had to care about the king. Surely.

"Please, whoever killed the king might try to hurt Prince Vad. I swear it wasn't me. You have to catch whoever it was, or else—"

The guard directly in front of me struck me across the face. My head jerked to the side, and my jaw throbbed as my lips stung. Tears burned my eyes, but I blinked them back.

"You don't speak unless you're spoken to." His voice, low and harsh, grated on my ears. He wiped the back of his glove on my ruined dress.

My blood slicked the wolf, sword, and rune on the back of his glove, which glistened like it had been stamped with deep crimson ink. I swallowed more blood and bit back another sob as my wolf growled within me. I touched my lips and winced at the wetness seeping into my mouth.

They shoved me against the nearest wall and groped me roughly, searching for weapons. I gritted my teeth and took a ragged breath. I couldn't show weakness in front of them, but I also had to acknowledge that they were certain I'd killed their king. Once I explained, I hoped to Fate they'd listen.

I held in a laugh. I must be in a desperate situation to be calling on Fate to help me.

An image of the dying king flashed into my mind, and the little bit of humor died.

Vad thought I'd killed his father. Worse, the king was dead, or near it. It had been a perfect setup. When I closed my eyes, Vad's gaze burned into my soul. That rage. That hate. My chest tightened in response, and I wanted to scream ... as if I needed more of that. Fate had already decided to fuck with me. Now I'd been framed for murder. Was I ever going to return home to my sister, Ember?

Who would do this?

Was it Kaylen? My fingers dug into porous stone, and a growl rose in my throat just from thinking of my fellow bride candidate's smug face. It had to have been her.

The guards finished searching me and jerked me into a single chair sitting in the center of the cell. They bound me with coarse rope that burned and itched as soon as it touched my flesh. The flaming tattoo on my upper right hand flared beneath the fibers, writhing and pulsing as if it were trying to fly away.

If only I could fly.

The guards snapped the ropes extra tight, securing loops to my ankles and wrists and the legs of the chair. Then they fell back, stepping out of my line of sight. More screams echoed in the distance, along with pleas for mercy. A shudder coursed through me, and sickening dread pooled in my stomach. I glanced around the cell.

In one corner, there were cupboards and a table that almost blended into the darkness. From this angle, I caught the glint of metal implements and polished stone on its surface. My gut twisted.

I was facing a wall. The door was probably behind me, and I guessed that was where the guards had gone to stand. Having my back to them made me snarl. Every twitch and breath and even the absence of any sound made the dread stronger. They could do anything to me, and I wouldn't know until it happened.

Steady footsteps reached my ears. I tensed, and my wolf

growled. The burning from the rope intensified as another prisoner's scream pierced the air. Then the cell door scraped open with a loud, grating whine.

The soft swish of heavy fabric and a light metallic clicking sound merged with the footsteps, growing steadily closer to my left. The scents of rotted greens, pepper, and steel struck my nostrils.

My heart raced faster, and the ropes burned even more.

A shadow moved to my right. I kept my gaze to the left, though, because with the fae magic here, I trusted my ears more than my sight.

A tall man in a dark gray robe leaned into my narrow range of vision. He frowned as if disappointed I hadn't been fooled. I straightened my back, my heart lurching.

Never had I seen a more off-putting fae. He was thin and angular, with dull green eyes, and his sharp features tightened with a cruel smile as he looked me up and down and circled me, hands steepled. His fingers were sheathed in silver claw rings, delicately filigreed at the base like jewelry, but tapering into long, razor-sharp points that gleamed in the torchlight like polished blades. Each one curved just slightly inward, and they clicked softly as he moved and tapped them against one another.

I glared, trying not to imagine how easily he could cut me with those.

His sleek silver hair was bound with a single band, and the ponytail slid over his shoulder, moving as if it were solid. He gripped my chin between his thumb and forefinger, his pointed nails almost cutting into my skin. "So this is the king's assassin. Such a delightfully wretched creature. Your visit here will last only as long as it takes you to answer our questions. Answer honestly, and you'll be out of here with minimal difficulty. Fail to do so, and your stay will stretch across days. Maybe weeks.

Maybe more, depending on how long your body and mind hold out."

My tongue grew thick in my mouth, and my throat tightened. Blood still trickled from my lips, but I straightened my shoulders and stared at him, unblinking.

He flashed me an unnerving grin, revealing far-too-perfect teeth. "Let's start with something simple. Why did you kill the king?"

I narrowed my eyes at him and lifted my chin. "I didn't kill the king."

His grin broadened. His perfectly manicured brows lifted, and he clicked his tongue. "Oh ..." He chuckled darkly. "Wrong answer, my dear." He wrenched my head back at an awkward angle, then lifted his left hand and pointed a claw directly at one of my eyes. A cruel smile twisted his thin lips, and he traced a line in the air and then flicked the tip of the claw at the edge of my bloodied lip. "But I'm not worried. Everyone here eventually tells the truth precisely as they should. You won't be any different. It's just a matter of time.

"Now ... let's try that again. Why did you kill the king? Or shall I hurt you further?"

Chapter Two

Vad

My magic exploded inside me, ready to burn down the entire realm. Anyone who wanted to keep Briar from me would die a gruesome and painful death by my hand.

The two Shadow guards dragging Briar away through my mother's garden would be the first targets, and their deaths would be more gruesome, thanks to the way they were ignoring the demands of their reigning prince and future king.

The way they were manhandling her as if she were a criminal ensured that no compassion would be given to them as I took their lives.

I clenched my hands and stumbled forward, my stomach twisting in a way I'd never experienced before. The world spun, and my limbs grew heavy. My body burned, and I tried to make my legs rush toward her. I took in her long purple and ivory skirt, wet with blood and leaving a long dark streak behind her that seemed to reflect the golden branches woven into the gown's design. One entire side was drenched in crimson, suggesting she'd been lying near my father as he died. I could only imagine what horrors she'd witnessed. Tears poured from her gorgeous jade-green eyes as she stared at me, begging for my help.

Yet, I couldn't get to her. My legs weakened further, and the ground became unsteady. This sudden sickness must be due to my father not transferring his power to me. But I had to fecking save her! The way they were treating her—their future *queen*—was abominable.

Two council members stepped in front of me, blocking my path. The man whose lighter gray robe signified he was Aureline Fae gripped my shoulder.

My blood warmed, and the cold of the magic intensified, trying to take control of my body once more. But there was no quenching this rage, and I tugged harder at my Shadow magic. "I order you to get out of my way!" I snarled.

"Your Highness." The dark-gray-cloaked Shadow Fae council member lifted both hands. "I understand your anger, but the woman committed this crime while participating as a contestant to become the Shadow Queen. This matter falls under Fate's purview and thus is a matter for the Aureline to handle. Not us. The Shadow Kingdom will have justice for your father's death in time."

The garden closed in on me, and a shudder shot through my spine.

Father.

My gaze darted to where his corpse lay beside the marble fountain in the silvery moonlight, just beyond the moon lilies my mother had once planted. My hands balled into fists. This should not have happened. Where were his guards? And even without guards, the enchantments in the garden should have protected him. My mind fought to understand it all.

A horrible, sickly-sweet odor masked the lilies and merged with the scents of blood and death.

He was dead.

And they were trying to take Briar from me.

I couldn't lose them both.

I most certainly could not lose *her.*

Bile rose in the back of my throat, and the world spun. The once vibrant red water in the fountain had turned murky pink. My father ... was gone, and our magic would weaken unless it became fully vested in me. We were vulnerable. My chest tightened so hard I couldn't catch a breath.

Loss poured through me and hollowed me out. He'd been murdered, and whoever was behind this had set up Briar to take the blame. That was the only reasonable explanation—because I *knew* her, and she would never do this to him or me. How many people were part of this conspiracy?

Someone wanted to destroy my family and legacy. They'd put our entire kingdom at risk. I took a ragged breath and commanded, "Get out of my way."

Another sharper sob ripped my attention back to Briar. Our eyes locked, and the pain and terror in her glassy green irises cut through me deeper than a blade. The two guards held her tightly, the one on the left curling his hand and summoning a portal. Dark and light gray wisps swirled around them.

I shoved through the council members, but the gray had already swallowed her. Two guards in light gray armor suddenly appeared and grabbed my arms like the guards had done to Briar.

"Release me this instant. I need to talk to Briar right now!" My demand turned into a scream. My shadow powers flared, and my wings shot out. My magic faltered before surging in sputters. The strange surges weakened my knees, but I continued to form my shadows into weapons.

Crackling energy curled from my fingernails and turned into dark claws ready to rip them apart. I'd tear them all to pieces and hang their corpses on the outer walls for defying me.

Two more guards surged forward, and the Aureline guard lifted his hand. Moonlight flashed over something in his palm.

Red seared my vision, and stinging pain flashed over my face.

Aureline magic.

Bitterness coated my tongue, and my strength cracked as the power sapped me beyond that single blow.

My knees and hands struck the marble pathway, but I refused to stay in a weakened position, so I thrust myself to my feet. One of the guards struck me back down.

The Aureline council member leaned down. His light-blue eyes blazed as he said, "Remember your place."

Remember my place. Feck that. He needed to remember his.

I refused to allow some council that wasn't of my kingdom to punish me. The Aureline Council members were only to get involved if the balance in our realm was at risk. At this moment, none of that was happening. Just the horrible assassination of the Shadow King, but his heir was here and able to take the crown.

Pure rage sparked through my veins, and the pain receded to a dull ache. I slammed my hands down, shadows surging, and shoved upward, sending both guards and the council member sprawling as my shadows tore loose. My magic lashed out, jagged and wild, slicing across the guards in black arcs, cutting clean through the first guard's chest plate. He stumbled backward, breath catching as the council member skidded across the marble. Even when he slid out of reach of my magic, he screeched like my shadows were harming him.

The other set of shadow tendrils whipped around the guard who'd struck me, plowing into the back of his knees and making them buckle. I caught him by the arm, and he stared, wide-eyed, as I ripped off his mask and drove my fist into his face. Bone cracked beneath my knuckles, and hot blood spattered across my skin.

But it still wasn't enough.

More guards hurried in with horrified expressions.

A strange clarity settled over me as I drew back my fist for another blow. No. Not now. Not yet. The Aureline Fae were considered the protectors of Nytheria, their word said to echo Fate itself. If I openly opposed them, it would be seen as rebellion against Fate, and the other kingdoms might unite against me. Even if this was the only traitor among the Shadow Council, they could sway the others to declare me unfit, sever my bloodline, and seek a new heir to rule the Shadow Kingdom and safeguard its magic.

I swallowed the bitter words clawing up my throat. I couldn't lose sight of my purpose. Briar. I had to free Briar. If I lost control or seemed unstable, I'd lose any chance of helping her.

Slowly, I straightened, wings flexing and unfurling behind me like a ragged-edged storm. The council member cowered at my feet, having slid so far on the marble that my shadows hadn't touched him.

"My place?" My voice came out low, even, edged in chilling shadows. "I am the prince of the Shadow Fae. Heir to this throne. Son of the slain king. Rightful bearer of this kingdom's magic." My claws flexed at my sides, slow, deliberate. Inside, my pulse hammered, and my strength flickered. My shadows had barely reached six feet, and the restoration of their strength flagged within me in a sickening spiral. "It is my place to speak to the suspects and investigate a crime committed on *my* lands."

I squared my stance as I continued. "I have allowed you to exercise your due rights in oversight of the bridal competition. But disrespect in my court will not go unanswered. Lay another hand or incantation on me, and I will tear it from your wrist and wear it as a trophy."

No one moved. The air itself seemed to hold its breath. Even the torches burned quieter, shadows shrinking back as if they, too, feared me. I had to be strategic. The Aureline guard had struck me, and the Shadow Council member had not even flinched. Nor had the two dark-garbed guards dragging Briar away paused when I'd demanded to be allowed to speak with her. Those Shadow guards would learn a lesson about disobeying their future king soon enough.

I shook my head, trying to clear the sluggishness away. I'd been careless and forgotten that the best way to deal with threats was the political way—the fae way.

This was why I hadn't wanted to fall in love. The emotion tangled logic and reasoning, making people irrational and brash. It had put the people I loved in danger. But no more. I wouldn't let these fecking bastards win ... so I'd play their game for now.

Fingers curling against the marble, I breathed deep. How many Shadow Fae were involved in this? That Shadow Council member clearly was, but that didn't mean the entire Shadow Guard was corrupt. Otherwise, they'd have taken over.

Amid roiling nausea and the aching hole in my chest, my flesh prickled with warnings. I let my gaze drift over every face in the garden. "Make no mistake. I am grieving. I am furious. And I will soon be coronated." My lips twisted into something cold, sharp. "When I am, I will remember all that happens here." I fixed my gaze then on the Aureline Council member who had struggled to his feet. "See to it that justice is done, but do not make the mistake of disrespecting me again."

I ignored my throbbing jaw and spat out a mouthful of blood. Everyone here was an enemy, but these enemies wouldn't realize how much they'd fecked up until they felt their own lifeblood draining from their veins.

"Have you lost your fecking mind? Did you just strike the prince? My future king!" Footsteps pounded to my side, and a feathered wing brushed my back before snapping away.

I turned my head. Thalen's brows quirked over his rageful amber eyes. All playfulness had vanished.

I gave a small shake of my head, trying to communicate, *Not now. We don't fight now.*

Whoever was behind my father's death didn't yet have the political or military support to overthrow the royal family, or they wouldn't have staged the murder. But if I acted like an insane fool, they could claim I was no longer fit to rule. It was an unusual tactic, and I had heard of it happening only once in the past few centuries, in another kingdom. But these were clearly unusual times.

I held up my hand. "It was no matter. I pushed the council member and slipped."

Thalen's eyes narrowed. He set his hands on his waist, the white feathers of his displayed wings moving faintly in the breeze. "Funny how that—"

"It *is* no matter." I fixed him with a sterner gaze, willing him to understand. For all his teasing, Thalen was an excellent fighter, and anger blazed through him. "The Aureline Council is here because my father was murdered." Another spasm cut through me, but I adjusted my stance.

Light drained from Thalen's eyes, and he ran a hand through his shaggy ash-blond hair. "I heard ... I heard screaming and yelling." His throat bobbed. "I ... Rhielle is near death. Myantha saw that her door was open, and some of the guards were missing. She came to get me when she couldn't find Briar. Rhielle is with the physicians now."

I set my hands on my hips. Another wave of sickness crashed over me and made my head spin.

Members of the Shadow Guard entered the garden, shouting for someone to call more guards and a physician. It was futile for them to send for extra help; Father was already dead. But I remained silent and kept my focus on Thalen.

"Briar was found beside my father's body. She is being investigated by the Aureline Council for murder." Forcing the words out felt like blades across my tongue, but I spoke them with an icy calm.

Thalen paled. He started to shake his head, but I shot him another stern look. He stiffened and straightened his shoulders, then nodded.

The council members studied me, arms at their sides and heads slightly tilted in opposite directions. Beneath their hoods, I glimpsed their faces. Both had furrowed brows and pinched mouths. The Aureline Council member in light gray had sharp blue eyes and dark freckles across his nose. Freckles were unusual among fae, so he'd be easy to locate. The Shadow Council member had one gray eye and one blue eye. His left hand had a scar that hooked from the back of his hand to the inside of his wrist.

They seemed surprised and slightly disappointed.

Good.

I would treat the matter as if I had made a small error. Nothing more would be said aloud. Dignity would remain intact, and honor would require no further response.

"Justice will be done." My fingers dug into my black belt. "I will not stand in the way of it, nor will anyone in this kingdom or another. The wrongdoers will be brought to justice." Despite the sheer hate burning in my veins, I fixed my gaze on both council members. "My father's body must be prepared for burial, and the dagger that was used to kill him will be taken for the ceremony. If you require further examination, you will speak with me. I trust this is acceptable, as we are honoring the requirements of each kingdom?"

The two council members exchanged a look and pressed their lips firmly together. They had no choice but to honor my request since I was behaving rationally. They hadn't expected that.

I tilted my chin and cleared my throat, urging an answer.

The Shadow Council member nodded. "Of course, Your Highness."

"Good." I turned my attention to the guards nearing us. "Search the garden and the perimeter. A suspect has been taken, but search for anyone else who may be involved. I doubt it was just one individual. Leave no stone unturned, and if I sense even a hint of negligence, the repercussions will be serious for all involved."

Out of the corner of my eye, I noticed the two council members glance at each other as if they were uneasy. A muscle in the Shadow Council member's jaw ticked as the Aureline Council member shifted his weight.

More footsteps sounded in rapid succession. Finbar, the head of the Shadow Guard, appeared, followed by more soldiers. His honey-gold skin had gone pale as ash, and his dull brown hair was disheveled, evidence that his glamour was slipping.

I angled to face him and commanded, "Report." As head of the entire guard, he was so busy that I didn't often see him. My father had insisted on overseeing all security matters involving the palace. The last time I'd worked with this man directly, we'd quelled an insurgency.

"Your Highness." He bowed his head and struck his fist over his heart. "I regret to inform you that the entirety of the king's personal guard assigned to protect him during this event has been assassinated. And the royal guards stationed in the guest wing were enchanted. One of the contestants has been grievously injured and is comatose."

My blood curdled. How deep did this plot go? We were dealing with multiple enemies, perhaps dozens. Could it be the entire Aureline Council? Add in the enchanted guard, and our situation was even clearer.

Then I remembered ... Finbar's younger brother Ruar had been one of my father's guards this night. "All four?"

He gave a tight nod, and the muscles in his jaw trembled. "Yes, Your Highness."

That had to be why his glamour was slipping—he was mourning his brother as well as the king. He had vouched for his brother to take that role six months ago.

I wasn't the only one to suffer loss this night. "It is impossible for one individual to have been the cause of all this death in such a short time span, and to successfully kill and enchant such well-trained royal guards. We will find all involved in this treacherous scheme and ensure they receive the *appropriate* punishment." No one could claim Briar had been responsible for all that. She didn't have fae magic, and she couldn't have been in more than one place simultaneously. She also lacked contacts within our kingdom.

Finbar offered another nod, though his expression remained masked.

I wasn't fully certain I could trust him or anyone I didn't already know well.

Despite his stoic expression, his slate blue eyes darkened, letting me know that this was hitting him almost as hard as me. "If you require my life, I accept your judgment. If you allow me to keep it, I will dedicate it to finding all involved in this atrocity and bring them to the blades of justice and Fate."

It was an old tradition that, if the king was murdered, the captain of the guard would be executed for failing to protect the king. However, the tradition was useless when it came to practical purposes. Maybe I couldn't fully trust him, but making a change now would only add more chaos.

I met his gaze, unblinking, and studied his face. "Your life is mine. To my knowledge, you have done nothing that prevents you from continuing to serve. Demanding your life at this time would accomplish nothing."

Stepping closer to him, I stretched my wings, ensuring they were on display for all to see. I wouldn't lower my voice—everyone needed to hear this—but I arranged myself so that the councilman and Thalen could see my expression. "What happened tonight is a violation of all we hold dear and a horror that will stain our kingdom's existence for eternity. All those involved with the enactment of these travesties will suffer a thousand times over. Their names will be blotted from any honorable mention, and they will be made into objects of scorn and derision. None will escape my rage or the horrors I will inflict upon them."

My heart wanted to lurch from my chest, but I took a heavy breath. Going on an immediate killing spree would only aid them in proving I was unfit to lead. I'd do this smartly and let them sweat, unsure of when I might strike.

I turned and saw my father's body once more. A spasm shuddered through me, and my chest tightened so hard I couldn't draw a full breath. For a moment, I felt like a child again, weak, small, and incapable of changing even one thing for the better.

It was worse than when I'd lost my mother. Then, despite my father's grief, he had ruled. He'd overseen the investigation and tracked down her murderers. Though he never felt that he had learned the full truth behind her death, he had exposed several people who had been unquestionably guilty of conspiring to kill her.

Not so long ago, I'd called him a failure for becoming distant from Elara and me, for withdrawing from most public matters in the kingdom, and for letting his life revolve around Mother's death. I hadn't understood the full weight of what he carried ... until now.

I wished I could take those words back. He had lost the

love of his life and had two constant reminders of her memory—Elara and me.

Now my goals were to find whoever was behind this and avenge my father, and to rule with Briar by my side for all eternity. To do that, I had to locate people who had information on this conspiracy and torture, if not murder them. The only thing holding me together was that I would get Briar back one way or the other. She needed me to free her from whatever horrific prison they'd taken her to and to avenge her for whatever cruelties they'd set upon her, and I craved her body and presence. No one would ever keep us apart again ... not even Fate herself.

"Your Highness, are you well?" Finbar asked, bringing me back to the present.

I lifted my chin. "Yes, why?"

"I sent for Sekondel the hexwright to examine the guest hall and all the guards, to ensure that this does not happen again, unless you have someone else you would like to have serve in that role?"

Sekondel was a decent woman. Faithful in her duties and skilled in magic of all sorts. I had perhaps missed more of what he had said. "Is there a reason she would be seen as unfit for such a task?"

"No, Your Highness."

I drew in a steadying breath. "Then she will do. If anything, send for a second hexwright to offer another perspective. Perhaps Haude or Sterenn." I raised my hand before anyone could ask me anything else. "Give me a moment to pay my last respects to my father before his burial."

Everyone nodded, and even the council members stepped back. Only Thalen remained at my side, motionless.

I strode on weak legs to the lifeless husk that was my father and knelt beside him. The cold marble bit into my knees, and the congealing blood soaked into the fabric. That smell of fading life, metallic blood, and sweet lilies swirled around me, tethering me here when I wanted to vanish and track down Briar.

Thalen knelt beside me, his head down. His shaggy, silver-white hair hung over his face.

I reached out and closed my father's eyes. Already, his flesh was cooler than it should be, all traces of heat fleeing as life already had. I prayed there was some measure of mercy that allowed him to now be with my mother. He'd never stopped loving her.

Apparently, he hadn't stopped loving me either.

Not that that would have kept him from criticizing me now. I could hear his voice in my mind. *Why are you wasting time over my corpse? It's for the worms now. Head up. Shoulders back. Spine straight. Now. Handle this. Don't shame me.*

I lifted my head, and the world spun to the point I wasn't sure I could get to my feet. But staying here and shaming my father's legacy wasn't an option.

I had to rise to convey strength, authority, and calm, despite what had happened. But my legs still felt like jelly.

Panic sank its claws into my chest. My beloved had been taken from me. My father had been murdered. How long before they moved against Elara and my friends? Or me? If I did not make the right choices, my kingdom would collapse, and our magic would fail. I couldn't act rashly.

Spiraling would accomplish nothing. I had to focus on getting Briar back first and foremost. That would eliminate all the other problems, and it was what my heart wanted most. *Hold fast, my love. Hold fast, and know I'm coming for you.*

A sour taste filled my mouth. I had to play this game.

But when I set my hand against the stone to help myself rise, I noticed something odd.

The button on the inside of my father's surcoat was missing.

Strange. Especially since Father had always ensured he was immaculate in his royal clothing.

This particular button was intended to keep his surcoat aligned, but its placement meant it wouldn't be easily torn off during a struggle. And there was hardly any evidence of a struggle here. No rips or tears marred his garments except at the point of the dagger blow. There wasn't even a shredded thread or cut embroidery along the hem and lapels.

I climbed to my feet and turned, then stilled. Five death attendants had arrived. They stood a few feet away, waiting for me to finish paying my respects. I hadn't heard them, but that was to be expected—they moved like shadows. They wore long dark-gray robes with blue lining and soft hoods that shrouded the upper halves of their faces. A shadow beast medallion hung around their necks, the beast himself shown with his head down and his crimson eyes closed in mourning for the fallen.

The four behind the leader each held an unlit golden thurible strung with two long gold chains and an onyx handle. If they had followed tradition, each one would have already been filled with incense, and they would light them as soon as the king's death was confirmed.

My heart clenched. I remembered the scents of black myrrh and white copal, thick and smoky with earth and wood. My mother's face flashed into my mind, along with the scent of her floral perfume. Her soft, dark-gray eyes had always been so gentle, and even when she'd scolded me, she'd never lost that tenderness.

The incense had masked all other scents so well that I hadn't smelled anything else during the grieving rituals for my mother, and now it would do the same for my father. In some respects, it was a blessing to no longer smell death and blood, but there had been something haunting in the once familiar scent of my mother being erased, just as my father's would be as well.

The leader stepped forward, hands clasped, the long flowing sleeves covering all but his fingertips. "As one song ends, another begins. Their memory endures within us and beyond as one shadow merges with the other and the new legacy begins. His name will forever be commemorated in the Hallowed Hall. May Fate guide his spirit to eternal peace with his beloved. We stand at the service of the new ruler of the Shadow Kingdom." He bowed his head and lifted his hands. On his wrists were black tattoos of crossed daggers.

My throat tightened, and unshed tears burned my eyes. I dipped my head forward. "So shall it be, and may there be peace." There would be no peace for me ... at least, not yet.

The attendants behind him spoke one after the other in solemn voices. "So shall it be, and may you find peace in his memory."

I exchanged a few more words with Finbar about what was to be done and left him to give orders. More and more people had gathered. Servants and stewards asked for guidance. I answered them but kept my gaze fixed on the death attendants. They knelt beside my father and examined him with great care, adjusting his garments and taking his pulse.

The leader lifted his hands and cupped them together as the other four presented the thuribles, holding them by their tapered bases rather than the onyx handles. A dark-blue flame appeared between the leader's palms, and he lowered them to the mouth of each thurible in turn. One by one, the incense within smoldered. Dark, fragrant smoke rose. It cut through the sickly sweetness almost at once, and all bowed their heads.

I had to make plans. I needed to be the one to inform my sister, and I didn't want her to see him like this. Thank Fate, she must not have heard anything. But was it safe to leave my father's body here? What if there was evidence we had missed? The death attendants would put my father's body in a safe and secure place, which should preserve any additional evidence. But could they be trusted?

Thalen moved closer to me and glanced around before nudging my elbow. "I call the one with the dagger tattoos Broodfather Bladeface."

I lifted an eyebrow, but my shoulders slackened a bit with relief—he knew we needed to be subtle about our suspicions.

He lifted his shoulder and then said even softer, "*My* Chaos would like him. He's very perceptive. I'd trust him to throw blades at my face any day. I actually did, twice."

His Chaos? He'd damn well better not be talking about Briar.

My shoulders tightened, but I ignored the anger. I couldn't lose focus, and this was Thalen's way of informing me that we could trust Cahmin, Head of the Death Attendants.

Though I didn't appreciate him using Briar that way, at least I knew we could go find Elara and a place where we could speak plainly with each other.

Thalen canted his head and looked me dead in the eye. "Nothing like knowing you can trust a man not to stab you in the face." He gave me that small, sly smile that he used when telling me a secret.

The smoke from the golden thuribles soon reached us, and Cahmin strode toward us, smoke swirling behind him.

He inclined his head toward me and folded his hands. "We would ask that all depart so that we may prepare the king's body for internment and the mourning rituals. Your Highness, do you have any requests?"

"Preserve everything. Let no one near the body without my permission." The words sounded so cold as they left my lips. But that was who I had to be now, even though it felt as if my realm were vanishing from under my feet.

My attendants arrived as Finbar assured me that the new guards had been sent to the guest hall to protect the other contestants, and the hexwrights would ensure all enchantments had been removed except those permitted for our safety. I then sent one of my attendants to personally inform Vyraetos of the Shadow Council of what had happened. We had to ensure that the magic of the Shadow Kingdom vested in me properly before the disruptions in the magic spread to the entire kingdom. The murky pink fountain water was a warning sign. Usually, magic would be transferred from one ruler to the next at the coronation, but there had to be a contingency for situations involving assassinations and accidents.

Thalen and I left the garden, Thalen's wings tucked snug against his back and his gaze guarded. Desolate weeping and soft cries from servants punctuated the air as we passed from the main hall and made our way to the royal family quarters. As we walked past the competitors' hallway, I noted that all the doors were closed and guards stood outside them.

Passing through the great double doors into our private area was like entering a world entirely separate from the chaos of the rest of the palace. The air was still and calm, smelling of my spiced cologne, Elara's soft floral perfume, and Father's juniper soap. My insides clenched, and my vision blurred again with unshed tears. Father's scent would fade, just as the peace in this place would soon be shattered.

After a few more steps inside, when we were away from everyone, Thalen cut his eyes at me and raked a hand through his hair. "I assume we both know there's no fecking way Briar is in any way responsible for your father's death?"

"Of course not. Don't be an imbecile. Someone framed her." I turned and crossed my arms.

He twitched a shoulder, and his silver-white wings

loosened. "Of course. Though it's obvious who. *My* Copper Chaos wouldn't kill anyone who didn't deserve it, and—"

I saw red. We were alone and safe, and all my anger and pain channeled toward him. "She isn't *yours*!" I snapped and lunged at him.

His eyes lost their spark, and he stumbled back a few feet. He needed to learn, along with everyone else, that Briar was mine, and mine alone.

"Don't ever call her *your* Copper Chaos again." My shadows hesitated half a breath, then exploded out of my back and along my wings.

CHAPTER THREE

My vision tunneled as shadows writhed and twisted, forming whip-fast tendrils that reached for Thalen's throat.

He ducked, his wings tucking tight as he rolled backward. "Whoa, easy there, you big bellend—"

One of my shadow tendrils curled around his shoulder and neck and snapped him back against the wall. I grabbed him by the arms, blood thundering in my ears. "*She is not* your *Chaos*! Never call her that again. She is *mine*!" My magic faltered, flickering like a sputtering candle flame before surging again. My knees threatened to buckle, my stomach souring even more, but my physical grip on him didn't weaken.

Face pale, he lifted his hands. "Understood. I was only trying to tease you, but I should've known better. That's my fault, and I'll stop this instant."

I slackened my grip on his arms slightly.

He let out a shaky breath. "Briar is *yours*. I never thought she was anyone else's. She doesn't belong with anyone but you, and I'd bet your best vintage of moon whiskey she feels the same. Put the fangs, claws, and shadows away. *Please*. I'm sorry. I won't say it again ..." Then he mumbled, "At least, not today."

"I heard that," I gritted out as my chest heaved. I couldn't get enough breath to fill my lungs. The shadows tightened again before releasing and vanishing like smoke into the floor.

I let Thalen go and stepped back as I tried to push back against the enormity of the grief crushing me and suffocating my thoughts. At least, the jealousy felt like sickening fire, providing heat and an urgent clarity. A tendril of fear curled through me, bringing even more ice. It had been years since I'd lost control to the point that my shadows behaved like this. I was unraveling, and I had to bring myself back in. Otherwise, Briar could pay the price.

Adjusting his shirt, Thalen slumped against the wall. "We both know nothing clears your head as much as rage ... to a point. Add on Briar, and that wasn't thoughtful of me at all." He straightened and rolled his shoulders like he'd had the wind knocked out of him.

Thalen knew that, when I lost my temper, my Shadow magic reacted. That was what he'd done to me whenever we sparred, and one time, in a shadow rage, I'd accidentally knocked him off the edge of the labyrinth wall. Sometimes I despised how glib he was in the face of danger, but considering what we were up against, his resilience and hardiness would come in handy.

He smirked. "You sure you're finished, or do you need to take another swing at my ribs for closure? Maybe smash my face into the wall for good measure? Get some more of that rage out of your system and get in balance?"

"Call her yours again, and I will." I snapped my surcoat back into place and straightened my sleeves. My body thrummed with warning. The longer Briar stayed with my betrayers ...

Acid burned my throat, and I stopped my thoughts from continuing. If I imagined what they were doing to Briar, I'd lose the control I needed to truly save her.

Thalen bit his bottom lip. "Maybe we can use that display

as our secret weapon. We get to the prison, and then you go berserk like that and worse. They won't stand a chance. Assuming you can keep it under control for now and then act completely feral."

My lungs ached. I couldn't get enough air. My magic thrashed beneath my skin as if it wanted to shred through flesh and bone and couldn't find its balance. I choked it back. The last thing I needed to do was destroy half the damn corridor, but each time my thoughts returned to her, the rage boiled up. My stomach threatened to empty at the thought of her screaming in the dark while I stood here, helpless.

Every single one of them would pay in blood and agony.

My hands curled into fists again, and I dug my nails into my palms until the skin split and blood welled. But even that couldn't ground me.

I slammed my fist against the black marble wall at my side, and a hairline crack split up the stone and behind a gold-framed painting of a peace signing. My breath snagged in my throat as my lungs constricted.

Thalen approached from the side. "Don't disappear into your grief and sorrow now. You know we're going to get her back. Of course, when I say 'we,' I mean you, and I'll help. Nothing's going to change that, and they're going to pay for what they did. What I was saying before is that we can trust Broodface. Even if the Aureline Council is up to something treacherous, and it isn't just one or two of them with the Shadow Council, he won't let them interfere. He takes his duties personally."

The anger still coiled within me, threatening to drown me in its heat just as the grief wanted to sink me into a void I'd never escape. But Thalen was right. We *were* going to get Briar back. "And Captain Finbar? Do you know more about him? His brother Ruar died tonight. Can he be trusted too?" To my knowledge, he'd never done anything even slightly questionable in his service.

I started walking again, dreading telling Elara what had happened.

Thalen followed. "So far as I know, yes. And I know how to make sure of that too. Leave it to me. I'll make sure you get *your* Copper Chaos back. Though we should probably figure out what I can call her to let you know I'm talking about her without mentioning her name."

"Yes, we need something. But we've got to find out which Aureline prison they've taken her to." I dragged my hand through my hair, then turned to face him. "Can you do something for me?"

He lifted his shoulders and spread his hands. "Anything."

"Find the guards who took her away." I swiftly described both of the lower court guards with every detail I could remember. "See if you can get one of them alone. The Aurelines won't let anyone who isn't avowed to their service remain there long, so they probably sent them back as soon as they delivered her."

Thalen's expression had gone hard, and his eyebrow tweaked up. "You want one or both?"

I'd love to make both disappear. But restraint was essential. If I didn't hold myself together, I'd lose everything. "One. And only if you can ensure no one notices he'll be missed. This can't come back on us. We don't want to raise suspicions. But if you find both, learn whatever you can. They'll be dealt with in time."

Thalen cracked his knuckles and winked at me. His wings twitched as if they were in on the joke. "No one will suspect a thing. I'll have a servant bring you black currant wine as soon as I find one and get him down in the onyx cellar."

"Good. No one can know we're doing this though," I reminded him sternly.

"I'll be as silent as a shadow. Well, a real shadow. Not yours when they're going insane." Thalen tapped his hand to his brow and darted away.

I sighed and continued to walk in silence down the black marble hall, my footsteps growing heavier and heavier. The gold embellishments now seemed dull, the delicate painting of the portraits faded. Color was no longer bright. Everything was miserable, and I balanced on a knife's edge of self-control. Even as I forced myself to stay calm, the storm that brimmed within me intensified, wild and ferocious, craving the blood of my enemies and longing to hold my Briar. My shadows prickled within my consciousness, begging me to unleash them and let them feast on the blood of anyone who hurt her.

What were those fiends doing to her? If they hurt her—feck, they'd taken her from me. They were all dead men walking. But if they hurt her beyond taking her from me, I'd make sure they suffered ten times as much as she had. My fingers twitched at my sides.

I passed the juncture of the hall and turned toward Elara's rooms. Was she even awake? My stomach sank as I imagined tears welling in her dark-blue eyes, which were so like Father's. The hour was late, and she tired easily. Maybe she'd already gone to bed. Part of me just wanted to get it over with, but my dread grew. This would shatter her world.

The faintest line of light shone beneath the dark embossed door, likely from one of the lamps that was always lit in case of an emergency. Over the years, she had endured many.

Her bedroom door clicked open, and my other best friend, Silus, stepped out.

My brow arched, and my spine stiffened.

His charcoal surcoat was straight but slightly mussed, the fine black fabric rumpled near the collar. The deep cobalt cravat had been loosened, and the top button of his shirt was undone.

His brow lifted like a mirror of mine when he saw me approaching. "Physician Tai just departed a few minutes ago." He stood with his arms at his sides, but his posture was unusually tense. His throat bobbed. "Elara began to feel quite ill, but she's resting now. She managed to get through one of the dances before she was too exhausted and had to leave the ball. Her condition is worsening. Physician Morlo will examine her in the morning unless there's an emergency in the night."

His words struck like blows to my heart. "How long has she been ill tonight? How bad is it?" I braced my hands against my belt. Had Father's passing made it worse?

"It started shortly after you left."

He didn't mention Briar, and I narrowed my eyes.

"She was fine and wanted to dance, but then she started feeling worse and couldn't draw strength from the shadows. She tried to come back alone, but I insisted on escorting her. By the time we got here, she was struggling to breathe, and her glamour had faltered, so I sent for the physician. Physician Tai said Elara's condition is worsening but rest is the best thing for her. After Tai gave her a draught, she seemed to calm and remained peaceful."

The timeline didn't match up with Father's death and the removal of his power, and the resulting instability of our kingdom's power, for it to be the sole source of her decline. Had someone tried to hurt Elara, or was it bad timing—or connected in another way? "Why didn't you tell me what was happening?" I demanded, taking a step forward.

"You were with Briar." Though he said the words in that quiet tone, his jaw tightened. I could guess what he was implying.

I lifted my chin, the muscles clenching and ticking beneath my skin. "You should have informed me. Is she sleeping now?"

As he nodded, his arms remained straight at his sides, and

he did not move from the door. A small frown creased his brow. His polished boots bunched the thick gold and black rug that ran the length of the hallway until he smoothed it back into place with his right foot. "Yes. And she should continue to rest. Physician Tai ensured the nightmares would not trouble her, but if you wake her, she won't be able to rest at all. Why ... what's happened?"

The question hung in the air like a door blade poised to drop. I couldn't avoid it any longer, though speaking it aloud would make it real in a way that threatened to shatter what little control I'd managed to claw back.

"Father is dead." The words came out flat, emotionless. It was the only way I could say them without my voice cracking. "Murdered in the garden."

Silus's throat bobbed, but his lips stayed pressed in a tight line. When he finally spoke, his voice was barely above a whisper. "How?"

"A dagger to the heart. His personal guard was slaughtered, and the guards in the guest wing were enchanted." I forced myself to continue despite my throat trying to close. "Briar was found beside his body. The Aureline Council has taken her into custody and is claiming jurisdiction."

His expression shifted from shock to something harder. His dark, feathered wings tensed as if preparing to unfurl. "She was found beside his body?" His voice dropped low, dangerous. "Of course she was. An outsider who can turn into a shadow beast—" he spat the words as his lips curled "—who appears from nowhere, and now the king—your father—is dead? And you can't see what's right in front of you?"

The accusation slammed into me like a physical blow. My shadows erupted without warning, coiling around my arms and spreading across the floor like spilled ink. "Be careful how you speak of my beloved and your future queen, Silus."

"No." He stepped forward, away from Elara's door, his usual calm shattered. "I warned you this would happen. That she was unpredictable and dangerous. Your father lies dead, and you defend this woman? She bewitched you, made you weak, made you blind—"

"Enough!" The word tore from my chest as my wings flared and my shadows lashed out, scoring deep grooves in the marble walls. The temperature in the corridor plummeted, frost spreading from where I stood as my magic surged and waned, then surged again. Nausea cut into my stomach like blades. I was losing control, and I didn't care. "You dare accuse her?"

Silus's wings snapped fully open, the charcoal feathers catching what little light remained in the corridor. His face had tightened into cold calculation mixed with barely restrained fury. "I dare speak the truth you refuse to see," he growled. "Even if she didn't wield the blade herself, your father is dead because of her. Because of what she represents. Because of what you were planning to do for her. And now Elara suffers because of her as well."

My spine locked. "What are you implying?" My shadows coiled and spiraled, threatening to explode out again. "Speak plainly."

Silus met my gaze. "You were going to defy them all. The Shadow Council, the Aureline Council—you were going to choose her. A beast changer with no fae magic, no lineage, no right to our throne. Just like your father did when he chose your mother, a woman without noble blood. Do you really think that the councils would allow that without consequence? Your father suspected there was more to your mother's death than it seemed. Her death was a warning, plain and simple. Your father defied Fate and the councils to marry your mother, and now you're planning to do the same. Do you think whoever is behind this will stop here? That they won't use your decision to prove you're not fit to rule when you come apart because you can't have the one you want? That they won't go further and destroy Elara as well? How dare you cast aside your duty to this kingdom and your true family in favor of some common—"

Red exploded around my eyes. I seized his throat, hauled him forward, and then slammed him backward into the wall. A heavy *thwack* resounded, and his leg clipped an ornate black and gold vase that spun and crashed. Porcelain exploded across the floor in a thousand glittering shards.

"You *dare* to speak of my family and Briar in such a manner?" I snarled, my shadows erupting from every surface, wild and uncontrolled. They lashed out and scored deep gouges in the walls, shredding portraits, tearing through rugs, and grating across marble. One of my own tendrils whipped across my face and sliced my cheek.

Silus's hands flew up to grip my wrists. His dark eyes bored into mine with an intensity that matched my own fury. "I dare because someone has to," he choked out. "Your father is dead. Elara grows weaker by the day. And you—you're so consumed by this outsider that you can't see the knife aimed at your own throat!"

"She is not responsible!" I snarled. "And I will *kill* anyone who claims she is, including you."

"It doesn't matter!" Silus strained to speak as my fingers squeezed tighter. "They're either using her to destroy you or sending you a warning. Either way, your enemies will destroy everything!"

"Not if I destroy them first." My shadows swirled. I wanted to crush his windpipe, to watch the light fade from his eyes for daring to speak ill of Briar and invoking my mother's death.

His hands tightened on my wrists. A thousand memories flashed through my mind of all the time Silus, Thalen, and I had spent together as friends. The first time Thalen discovered moon whiskey and brought it to where we were playing beyond the fountain, when we all drank until our heads spun and we vomited in the lilies and ferns. The many times we had sparred and challenged one another as we felt out our different powers and learned to parry and strike using earth or shadow or air or just the basic fae magic and combat skills. The one time we'd gotten stranded because we'd slipped through the veil and had to use our skills to survive despite being children in a hostile wilderness.

The three of us had been inseparable. But that was not how it was now.

Cold descended upon me, but those memories stayed my hand. I thought of Briar. She wouldn't want me to do this, for my own sake and to spare me future regrets, not for Silus's safety.

Releasing Silus, I stepped back, my blood still vibrating with rage. My shadows trembled, ready to attack, but they, too, obeyed me. "Get out of my sight and stay out of my way. I will be civil with you in public for my sister's sake and her feelings for you, and I will not speak of this freely unless I must. But if you ever speak against Briar again, I will rip out your throat and feed it to the shadow beasts."

Silus slumped and then flung his arm up to grip the wall and steady himself. He massaged his throat as he stared at me, his brows drawn up and pain in his eyes. "All I want is—"

"I know what you want, but you're wrong about Briar, and I will prove it to you. My focus is on saving her, making her my queen, protecting my family, and saving this kingdom. As your prince and, soon, your king, I will not tolerate any more disrespect. Now go."

His jaw clenched. Then he bowed his head. "As you say, Your Highness." He strode away, his posture rigid.

I remained motionless at Elara's door, grateful she slept so deeply that she hadn't heard our confrontation. Though I did not want anyone else to tell her about Father, I couldn't bring myself to wake her. Instead, I traced a shadow sigil on her door to alert me when she opened it, and I strengthened all the protections that were currently in place around her room and the royal family's wing. I'd check on her in the morning. Tonight, she could get her rest. There would likely be many sleepless nights after this. At least, while she rested, she would be in the shadows and drawing up her strength.

I turned back down the hall, my head pounding. Sleep would not come to me tonight. Not unless I took something, and I couldn't risk dulling my senses right now. Instead of going to my own room, I continued to the observatory.

What if I had insisted Briar stay in the observatory with me and wait? Told her that she belonged in my chambers even if I had to leave for a while? I hated myself for not insisting. Stubborn as she was, I should have protected her. And these fiends were trying to use her against me.

The heavy, dark door loomed over me, the coiled markings etched into the stone seeming to judge me almost as harshly as I judged myself. Here, I'd be able to plan and determine the best course for returning Briar to my side, crowning her my queen, and protecting my family.

I turned the handle and pressed the door open. It yielded easily, but then I froze, catching the scent of dried blood, smoky vetiver, and charred balsam. Three dark-gray-robed figures stood in the center of the observatory near my telescope.

My wings flared, and my shoulders tensed. "What are you doing in my private sanctum?" I demanded. This wasn't the complete Shadow Council, and I had certainly not approved anyone coming here.

Vyraetos stepped forward, his withered hands unmistakable as he pressed them palm to palm. "Your Highness, we must speak. Immediately."

Chapter Four

BRIAR

My heart galloped as fear tried to strangle me, but I refused to look away from the fae's dead eyes. The corner of my lips stung where he'd dug in his claw, but I forced myself not to react.

He wanted me to be afraid and to beg, but I would *never.* My wolf snarled inside, inching forward, readying for whatever head-twatwaffle had in store.

No.

Twatwaffles were the guards who'd brought me here. This man had more of an edge and was sadistic. Henceforth, I'd call him Douchewaffle.

I hung my head. I was channeling my inner Thalen, but I needed an outlet that didn't involve crying.

"No answer results in the same punishment as the wrong one," Douchewaffle rasped with a crooked smile.

His previous questions echoed in my head. *Why did you kill the king? Or shall I hurt you further?* No matter what I said, he'd torture me, even if I lied and said I did it. "I would *never* harm the king, so do what you want to me." I set my jaw, knowing that pretty soon I'd be in so much pain I'd wish I were dead.

A humorless smile pressed across his lips. "You have never been a visitor to these sacred halls, so allow me to introduce myself. I am Colm Ainle, Chief Interrogator. I recommend you cooperate in this matter. Failure to do so will result in exceptionally uncomfortable results for you. These interrogation chambers boast many rooms that excel at loosening the tongues of those who think themselves above it. Why not save yourself the agony of it all and confess?"

"Well, I'm Briar, and there's nothing I need to confess. I didn't kill the king, but whoever did is still out there, so you're wasting your time, focusing on the wrong person instead of hunting down the people involved."

He swiftly lifted his hand and moved it toward me as if to strike me. My body tensed, but before I could flinch away, my wolf snarled and took enough control to hold me in place.

Douchewaffle scowled before he schooled his expression.

I gritted my teeth, hating that I'd almost given the bastard what he wanted. The warmth that had taken residence within me flared, matching the pulsing of the butterfly-flame wings of the tattoo on top of my hand. Fate had placed the tattoo to mark me for the bridal competition. Had it also marked me for this too?

The ropes dug into my wrists, which was a blessing in disguise. When he tortured me, I would focus on that pain instead of whatever he was doing to me.

His hand stopped just in front of my face.

Tilting my chin upward, I didn't break eye contact with him.

Lips twisting into a cruel smirk, he chuckled. "Cheeky. Now that's a trait I will enjoy breaking. I don't actually have to lay a finger on you to make you talk, and you will talk, my dear."

"I'm happy to talk, but I refuse to lie." There was no way I'd admit to something I didn't do, especially killing the king. I'd rather die by torture than have Vad hear that I admitted to hurting someone he loved. I wouldn't break, for him and for myself.

His eyes narrowed, and he cocked his head, studying me with a clinical expression. "I'm merely asking for the truth that I need to hear and for information about your so-called shadow-beast changing ability, among other things. And, most importantly, your confession regarding the king's assassination. Start wherever you like, or ..." He held up his hands, and this time, smoke smoldered from his fingertips, and the claws turned gold, then silver, then dull gray as before.

Streams of gray resembling dying gasps of a fire licked from his skin and stank like an acrid combination of burning hair and rot, as if he'd pulled magic right out of a corpse. The space between us folded inward, choking off air, pressing heat and cold into the same unbearable point.

His cold laughter echoed in my skull. "It only gets worse from here."

I pressed my lips together firmly, refusing to give him the satisfaction of another sound. My wolf snarled, and the strange, warm magic inside me sputtered before diminishing. A lump formed in my throat, and I blinked back the tears burning my eyes.

The air wavered like a mirage, and the lines of the room blurred. All of a sudden, my body seemed to be ripping apart. Nausea lurched in my stomach, and the worst physical agony I'd ever experienced lanced through me.

Just when I thought I couldn't handle any more of it, the pain eased.

My breathing turned ragged, but I refused to let him know how much he'd harmed me. I channeled my sister and did the very thing I knew she'd do to anyone trying to break her—I raised my head and met his eyes.

He wrinkled his nose, and then pain shot through me again, as if the bits that had been torn apart were slamming into each other and trying to fit themselves back together. Acid burned my throat as my breath constricted and my wolf howled.

He tilted his head and rocked back on his heels. "Why did you kill the king?" He tapped his fingers in the air, and with each movement, something seemed to slice into my lungs. I bit the inside of my mouth to prevent the cries trying to leave my body.

"Confession is good for the soul. So, why waste both of our time? Tell me what I want to hear." He lowered his face in front of mine, his rank breath striking my nostrils as he spoke slowly. "You probably think you're being quite brave, but let me be clear—this is *only* the *beginning*. It gets worse from here unless you cooperate. You don't have to say much. Admitting that you did kill the king will be sufficient to keep this from escalating."

My muscles clenched tight as I struggled against the painful bindings digging into my skin. I channeled the fae version of the profanity. "Feck you!" Each word took so much effort that my head spun.

His eyebrows flicked upward, and he stepped back. He traced a finger through the air in a languid motion and then flicked it at my chest. "You're delaying. We all know you killed him." The scent of eggs and sulfur slammed into me, and this time, it wasn't from his breath.

My heart skipped a beat. Either he didn't truly know whether or not I was the murderer, or he knew I wasn't but wanted to frame me. Either way, he'd just lied.

Just as I opened my mouth to confront him, the oxygen in the air seemed to thin, and my head spun. My lungs burned as if covered with acid, and I gasped, but nothing filled them. The invisible blades twisted deeper, slicing through my thoughts until I couldn't tell the ceiling from the floor.

My wolf surged forward, lending me strength, her presence a warm barrier between my consciousness and the torture. Her howls echoed inside me. Ember's face flashed into my mind, and I drew comfort and strength from the memory of her. Screams of agony joined the howls, pulling Ember away from me. The yips and howls sounded like the cries I'd heard months ago, when Ember's and my family pack had been slaughtered.

This didn't make sense. My new pack and I had defeated the vampires. But then I noticed I was in our home pack neighborhood, surrounded by the corpses of all the loved ones I'd left behind to die during the first vampire attack, ending with Dad and Mom.

My wolf whimpered as guilt and torment spread like dirt being thrown on top of me.

"Tragedy always follows you, doesn't it? You aren't the one who does the saving, but you are the one who causes the problems."

Once again, the scent of the lie hit me, adding to my misery.

Douchewaffle's voice slithered against my skin. "You killed the king. Let me help you remember."

The scent thickened—another lie.

Heat exploded behind my eyes, and I watched myself standing between the fountain and King Merrick in the garden. He scowled at me and gestured with a gnarled hand, and I yelled at him. The words were vague, and I knew I had never spoken them. I caught *vicious* and *competition*. Then a dagger flashed in my hand, and the king fell back a step, his eyes widening with alarm. I lunged at him and plunged the dagger into his chest.

Then the image faded, leaving me back in the present.

No!

That wasn't real.

None of that happened.

Douchewaffle had to be using some sort of fae magic to convince me that I *had* killed the king.

I clenched my eyes shut tighter. Pain sliced through me again and pulsed in my veins. A scream tore out of me as I writhed and struggled while my wolf howled and surged forward, trying to help me break free.

We had to escape.

I had to tell Vad I hadn't done this and get back to Ember.

Vad.

The dark expression he'd worn as he'd watched me being dragged off to prison flashed in my mind. His stormy gray eyes had radiated a mixture of pure rage, confusion, and grief.

"Tell me what you see." Douchewaffle's breath puffed against my cheek.

I forced my eyes open, and tears streamed down my cheeks. "A creepy dumbass standing in front of me." My voice shook, but I wasn't going to let him win anything more than I could help.

"You think you're so brave and cute. But I'm done holding back."

He curled his fingers in front of my face, and my entire body tightened. All the horrible feelings began to build again, like floodwaters behind a dam that refused to let down.

Horrible things circled in my head. My pack destroyed. Vad's hatred growing with his belief that I'd murdered his father. Thalen turning on me because the truth was too hard to believe. And then the false image of the king scowling at me returned.

This time, I smelled the blood and the light scent of lilies mixed with an overly sweet scent of something else. It filled my nose and wedged deep, pulling me into the moment. The king swayed on his feet, then fell back. And I saw myself spring forward with that dagger glinting in the moonlight a second before I stabbed him in the chest. Blood sprayed my purple and ivory gown, but I remained beside him and whispered something to him.

"What did you try to forget?" Douchewaffle whispered in my ear. "Tell me what really happened. Tell me what you see."

My mind spun as I tried to block the image. But the way the garden had smelled remained. The moonlight had cut across the path like a smooth blade, while the fountain waters had flowed red. It looked so *real*. It would have been so easy for the king to slip. The stones nearest the fountain were slick with the spray of the water ... or had we not been that close?

A sickening jolt of doubt jarred me, but my wolf snarled, helping me push the made-up memory out of my brain. "The last day my sister and I ran together in animal form before I was forced to come here," I spat out.

The dark walls of the interrogation room wavered back into view. The rancid scent of my lie filled my nose, but Douchewaffle stood there, jaw clenched.

Sweat pooled on my brow. "It was a lovely day."

He cupped one clawed hand along his ear. "Is that a tremor I hear? If it was a good day, then why are you crying and in pain? All I am asking is that you tell me what you see."

"The sun is shining, and my pack is in animal form." I opened my eyes, remembering the last run we'd taken before all hell had broken loose. I concentrated on the memory, shoving out the one he had been attempting to implement with magic.

He gave me a false smile, then pressed his two fingers together and curled them against his palm.

Sharp pain lanced through me once more, aching as if my ribs had cracked and reformed. I bit back an agonized scream and sucked in another breath.

"No lies. I know when I'm being lied to."

So do I. Each time he tried to tell me that I had, in fact, killed the king, I could smell the lie.

Again and again, he plunged me into that horrifying

space, the deaths and torments of those I loved worsening and becoming more real. And each time he forced me to watch the king die by my hand, the moment became more real. My senses sharpened, and I was closer and closer to the vision of myself until I was staring down at the king through my own eyes with the dagger in my hand rather than watching from outside my body. I felt it all: the tight rage as I demanded to know who he thought he was to allow these horrific competitions, the dampness of the fountain's spray, the pressure of his flesh as it yielded beneath the blade, the heat of his blood, and the horrible sucking sound when I drew the blade back.

Lilies. The king had said *Lilies* in the garden, and the one in this vision hadn't. He'd said nothing and managed only to make that horrible gurgle.

I grabbed onto that memory. This wasn't real. Each time Douchewaffle showed me the false scene, I went over all the parts of it that were wrong. If the king had fallen, he would have had a head wound. My hand had been bound to the knife by rope when I'd woken beside him.

"Tell me what happened," he whispered. "Just a few short sentences, and I'll give you a break."

I clenched my jaw and summoned every ounce of strength I had left. "I already told you—I didn't kill the king. I see Ember and my pack running in the woods." This was part of what grounded me too—to answer the same way as before, even though the sulfur made me nauseous and caused my head to throb even more.

"Is that what you see?" His eyebrow arched, and there was something cruelly playful about the way he spoke. "All I have asked is for you to tell me what you see. I am not asking you what happened anymore."

I wanted to spit at him, but I didn't have enough saliva in my mouth. Instead, I shook my head and glared at him. My wolf paced anxiously within me, hackles raised.

He hummed as he stepped back. "Do not think your strength will serve you. If anything, all it will accomplish is bringing you more suffering."

A snarky response rose at the back of my mind, but my mouth was too dry to say it. So I said what I could, something I had heard Thalen and others say hundreds of times. "Go jump in the void."

He smiled, and the ice of it froze his murky eyes. "Far stronger than you have broken within these walls. It's only a matter of time, and we have that in abundance. No one is coming to help you. The prince has cut you off. The next time you see him will be at your execution or internment, if the Aureline Council decides that you should not suffer a simple death."

Those words stabbed me like poisonous blades. Cold spread through me as I envisioned seeing Vad again in those circumstances. My heart pinched so tight I couldn't breathe.

He stepped back and motioned to someone behind me. The door scraped open, and heavy footsteps strode toward me. His dull eyes slid once more to my face, and that sickening smile curled the edges of his almost nonexistent lips. "I think you're ready for a little soak. If you survive until tomorrow, we'll resume our conversation. And if I am not satisfied, I will put you in a very special place—a place so quiet you'll hear your own blood flow. No one has managed to stay in there more than five hours without going insane. Sometimes sooner. I'll keep you in there at least three hours. Maybe longer. If you don't like that idea, I'd recommend you take very, very deep breaths while you're soaking." He guffawed as the gray-armored guards appeared on either side of me. They stooped and unfastened my bonds.

My wolf surged forward, longing to spring toward the door

and run free. But my feet and wrists throbbed and stung as pins and needles exploded through them. When I tried to stand, I crumpled, barely able to break my fall.

With annoyed grunts, the guards hauled me through the door and into the hallway. My legs dragged behind me like wet sandbags. The spinning in my head intensified, and my wolf tried to push forward again to help me move, but everything felt heavy and wrong. Down the hall we went, past three more doors. Then the guard with the bear engraved on the back of his glove shoved a metal door open.

The stench hit even before they pulled me over the threshold. Rot. Mold. Rusted iron and something worse—something dead and long forgotten. This room held more of a chill than the hallway, the walls slick and the air damp like a basement after a flood. In the center sat a container of black, stale water.

Knowing I needed to get out of here as quickly as possible, I lifted my legs, allowing the two guards to carry my entire weight, and kicked out. My rubbery limbs didn't obey. I missed the guard on my left completely and managed to knee the guard to my right in his thigh.

The one I hit grunted and glanced at the other guard. They both shoved me backward and let go of my arms, and I slammed onto my back on the stone floor. My head and elbow cracked against the stone, and pain exploded in my lower back. After all the mental torture, I could only groan hoarsely.

I pulled strength from my wolf and clawed at the stone, trying to scramble away. But the two guards grabbed me again even harder. I punched out with my right hand, missing the guard I'd hit in the thigh but managing to clip the other guard's helmet. Pain radiated up my arm. Before I could jerk back, Thigh Guard's fist crashed into my ribs, and I collapsed.

The world dulled, and my blood thundered in my ears.

Thigh Guard fisted my hair and hauled me to the edge of a massive tub. Panting and uncoordinated, I dug my feet against the stone again and tried to pull back as the horrid scent of the water hit me—sulfur. It smelled almost identical but somehow stronger than what a person smelled of when they lied.

I could *not* bathe in that.

I scrabbled against the floor, the bottoms of my feet now so raw it felt as if they'd been skinned, but my efforts did nothing.

Thigh Guard yanked harder on my head, and tears spilled down my cheeks. They tossed me into the tub as I screamed.

My entire body submerged in the nasty water.

My head went under, and the world darkened. Water filled my mouth, tasting worse than it smelled—like rotten eggs, rust, and disgusting lake water. My stomach roiled. The water filled my ears, and my lungs burned as I fought to hold my breath.

Douchewaffle's taunt echoed in my mind. *Worse is waiting for you, so just inhale.* Fuck him! I dug my metaphorical heels in again and fought as the burn intensified. I wasn't going to die in this place. Not smelling like this, and not right now.

My ears buzzed, and the pressure had become almost unbearable when hands gripped my shoulders and yanked me upward.

Cold air hit my face as my head rose inches above the water. I gagged and choked, spluttering foul liquid. My stomach finally lurched, and I leaned over the edge of the tub and vomited disgusting water and bile. I hadn't eaten in over twelve hours. Some of the liquid hit both the guards' boots, and my wolf pranced a tad at the little bit of justice we'd served.

I spat out more water and glared at them even through the pieces of hair that clung to my face. They didn't look like doing this affected them at all. Their eyes—cold blue and icy green—portrayed not even a fragment of emotion.

As I took a deep breath, they shoved me under again, and

I sucked some water into my lungs.

The nightmare resumed, and it seemed never-ending. They held me under until my lungs throbbed and my throat spasmed ... until I felt death right at my door.

My wolf cried, but she was as helpless to fight back as I was.

I didn't know how many times they did it. Time turned liquid like the water. I floated somewhere between pain and nothing, and they didn't ask me anything. It was just a constant cycle of shoving me under that filthy water until I thought I'd drown, then ripping me back out, letting me breathe for a too-short moment, and shoving me back down. I clawed my hands bloody as I raked them across the rough stone. Each time they brought me back up, I sucked in agonizing breaths and choked on the water until they forced me under again.

Finally, they lifted me from the tub and flung me away. My butt hit the floor hard, and cold air whooshed around my body. Pain exploded everywhere: my lungs, my butt, and my head. I dropped to one side, the stone scratching my arm. I barely had the strength left to hack up the foul water.

I choked and gasped for breath, vomiting again as the guards picked me up by the arms once more. At a steady pace, they carried me between them out of the room. My feet dragged on the rough rocks, and the sharp points scraped the tops. As much as it stung, each time I tried to lift them, they hit the floor once again.

Fear burned within me as raw as my throat and lungs. Where were they taking me?

Other pairs of guards were escorting prisoners through the hall, their strides unrelenting and their boots scuffing upon the stone.

Two of them held a woman with tangled blonde hair by the elbows, her knees scraping the ground as she sobbed.

Another man with purple hair tried to walk between his

guards, but he stumbled, and one of the guards backhanded him. Blood exploded from the man's mouth and sprayed a dark wall. A third prisoner wore black, shroud-like attire that covered him from head to toe. He left behind a blood trail that seeped into the porous rock.

A loud scuffing in the hallway to my right drew my attention. A high-pitched male voice said, "I can't keep doing this. It's too much. I don't deserve this. She's had enough."

My head threatened to implode. I had to remember that they weren't torturing only me. I looked up as two guards pulled the man down a cross path. The prisoner's long gray shirt hung in tatters from the neck, and his arms were bare and bruised. His haunting, sunken blue eyes had large bags beneath them.

Several long, bleeding gouges marked the skin of his shoulders. It looked as if needles and tubes had been shoved under his skin and then ripped away. Silver streaked his filthy chestnut brown hair, which had large, matted clumps that didn't hide bald patches forming at the sides. "I can't keep doing this." His voice trembled, and his heels left a trail of blood that glistened in the torchlight. "I won't."

"It isn't like you have a choice," said the guard on his left.

The guard on his right shook him as they continued through the main hall. "You'll stay here till you die or you cease to be useful. And if you cease to be useful, you'll die too. So enjoy breathing while you can."

I twisted my head to try to see him better. Something about him held my attention. His soft pleas faded as the guards dragged him out of sight.

The guards holding me pulled me into another long, dark hall. The oppressive scents of blood and rot choked me, growing stronger with each step. Fewer torches sputtered in their dark, oily holders, and the pools of orange-gold light were separated by rivers of darkness. Screams and pleas for mercy echoed around us like a storm. My own throat was raw from screaming, and every inch of my body ached.

I tried to keep track of our turns in case I ever got free, but they began to blur in my mind.

Finally, we entered a dark, low-ceilinged room with only a single sputtering torch on the far wall. Aside from the heavy metal door that slid on creaking hinges, the only thing in the room was a dark hole in the floor. The smell of mildew, sulfur, and rot worsened and stung the inside of my nose.

"Enjoy your accommodations. They aren't quite as nice as the guest hall of the Shadow Palace, but you'll make do." Thigh Guy chuckled.

Of course, he'd be enjoying this.

They dragged me to the edge of the hole and heaved me forward. Icy panic clawed through my veins as I reached for the edge and tried to gain traction. But they laughed louder and shoved me into that stinking dark hole as if I were nothing more than a bag of trash.

I swallowed a scream, not wanting to give them even more satisfaction, and plummeted through the darkness until I struck stone. The impact drove what little breath I had left from my lungs. I lay there, bleeding and aching, unable to stand. Pain spiraled outward from my shoulder and hip where I'd struck the unforgiving ground.

Rolling onto my back, I stared up at the distant circle of dim light above. The metal door clanged shut, and heavy footsteps retreated.

Thanks to my wolf, my eyes adjusted swiftly. I made out the shadowy contours of my prison. It was at least a twelve-foot drop from the jagged opening above me, and that appeared to be the only entrance or exit. The rest was a pit.

Water trickled down the stone wall on the far side and collected in murky puddles. A pile of what might once have been hay sat in one corner near some bones. Skulls, ribs, and thigh bones stood out from the rest, and my stomach roiled once more.

These had to be fae bones.

My blood turned colder than the air. They could abandon me here, and no one would ever know where I was.

Something skittered across my hand. I jerked away, biting back another scream as a beetle the size of my thumb disappeared into a crack in the floor.

My wolf whined, pressing against the edges of my consciousness. I drew on her for strength, but despair clutched my heart, and I couldn't stop my tears from falling.

Was this what Fate had in mind for me all along? For me to fall in love when I'd known it was a mistake, and then get framed for murder and left to rot away in a filthy hole, far from everyone I loved? My wolf nudged me. I offered what comfort I could, but it was next to nothing. The shadows deepened as I became more aware of the cold and the aches in my flesh and bones.

I pulled my knees to my chest, ignoring the sharp pain that radiated through my body. "If this was your plan," I whispered hoarsely to Fate, "it's a cruel one." After the slaughter of my family pack, I should've known she despised me. Tonight was just the icing on the cake.

I reached for my pack links and found nothing but one very faint warm spot. Fate, I missed Ember, but I was so glad she wasn't living in this hell with me right now.

A shimmering light flashed through my shut eyes, so much that I cracked my eyelids and winced. A bright circle of blue-white started small and slowly widened, like water spreading in a pool. The light pulsed and expanded, swirling into a circular pattern that grew more defined with each passing second.

"What the—" I eased back, wondering what sort of new

hell they were bringing upon me.

CHAPTER FIVE

Rage exploded within me, and grief for the loss of Father and Briar stung painfully. My chest threatened to implode.

One of my hands remained on the door, and my wings trembled with tension as they remained flared behind me. I scanned the observatory's black marble walls and the wooden shelves lining them to see if any of the books, charts, parchment rolls, crystals, and skulls were out of place. The gold-framed telescope was still in the center of the generously sized room, the table next to it still holding my crystals, lenses for stargazing, and notes. The two black couches in one corner of the room were vacant. The only things out of place were the three Shadow Council members standing before me in full dark gray robes.

If they wanted a fight, I'd give them one. But I had to let them play their hand so I wouldn't come across as irrational and give them justification for deposing me.

My Shadow magic flared, not wanting to be contained, fanning the flames of my rage even higher. I pictured Briar's face, reminding myself that I was doing this for *her.* I had to pretend to stay in line and seem willing to hear what they had to say ... for now.

Vyraetos pressed his hands together. "With all due respect,

Your Highness, this is a matter that would be best handled in private." He bowed his head and gestured toward the still-open door.

Despite my concerns, curiosity got the best of me. I closed the door. The lock clicked into place, and I had to remind myself I couldn't be in too much imminent danger here. My observatory had multiple spells and sigils woven into it for my protection and the protection of those I loved, and it was one of the worst places for an ambush.

My shadows itched for blood and violence, and my wings pulsed. If Vyraetos and these other two fragile council members wanted to test my strength, I would happily show them my might and deal with the corpses later.

I strode over to them. The heavy woven hoods hid their faces, and the two council members standing behind Vyraetos kept their hands folded before themselves but tucked into their sleeves, hiding any tattoos or scars that might identify them.

I didn't have time for games or wasting time, so I commanded, "Speak."

Vyraetos lowered his hood. His gray hair was disheveled as if he had dressed in haste. The dark circles beneath his gray eyes spoke to many sleepless nights, and he looked even more ancient than he had the last time I'd seen him. "First, we extend our deepest sympathies for the loss of your noble father. He was a good man and a good leader, and though the Shadow Council did not always see eye to eye with him, he still held our respect."

My chest tightened with greater fervor, shortening my breaths and hollowing me out. *This* was why I'd been determined to not love anyone else. It weakened me, and I despised that feeling above all others.

I gave Vyraetos a curt nod. "Such statements hardly require that you invade my personal sanctum at this hour and without notice."

"It is not the only reason for our presence here or this subterfuge." Vyraetos kept his gaze locked with mine. Though his gray eyes were clouded from his age and exposure to harsh elements, there was a sharpness in them that reminded me of an ancient guardian owl. "Times have become dire, Your Highness. Your father did not pass his power or the crown to you before his death, and the magic of our kingdom is more unstable and tenuous than ever, especially given our tensions with the Aureline Council. We need to strengthen and stabilize what remains of the bond so that you can endure until the crowning of your queen."

My gaze narrowed in on him, and I stepped closer. "What tensions? Speak plainly." The Shadow Council's duty was to the kingdom as a whole, not to my family and line, but my father had trusted Vyraetos, and Vyraetos had shown more discretion and wisdom during the bridal competition than I had expected. I remembered that he had warned the others that Kaylen was not likely to be a good ruler because she lacked discretion in her ruthlessness. But that didn't mean he would support my choosing Briar over Rhielle, who was the general favorite among the Shadow Council.

Vyraetos exchanged a glance with the hooded councilor on his left and then the one on his right. He motioned toward their hoods, and they both pulled back the heavy fabric, revealing council members Laro and Melnani. Melnani was a little taller than Laro, with an aquiline nose, hollow cheeks, and silver hair so pale it was almost white. She wore it slicked flat to her scalp and braided down her back. Laro was thicker, and his left cheek was a latticework of scars with a shadow beast tattoo darkening the right side of his jaw and throat. His steel gray hair was cut short except for a section in the back long enough to form a single braid down the back. His violet eyes had narrow pupils that were more snakelike than fae, unlike Melnani, whose eyes were so dark it was impossible to tell where pupil ended and iris began.

Both bowed their heads.

Inclining his head toward me, Vyraetos dropped his arms and gestured again to Laro and Melnani. "You may speak freely in front of my two associates. There are others within the Shadow Council whom I trust only in most matters, but these two I trust implicitly. This conversation must remain entirely secret. I suspect you will want to tell your own inner circle, but do so only if you are certain it will not spread beyond them.

"Our situation is perilous. As I mentioned, tensions between our council and the Aureline have worsened, and there is a new faction within the Aurelines that has split them. This situation is not the first conflict we have had with them, but it is building up to be the worst. The two councils must work together to conduct these competitions, and we rely on the larger Aureline Council as well as the Aureline High Council, which is over them, to interpret Fate's will in matters even beyond selecting the trials and the order." He canted his head as he made this point. "We have concluded that there are some within the Aureline who are planning a coup. The assassination of your father has at least temporarily eliminated Briar from the competition, and the attack on Rhielle has also at least temporarily eliminated her."

I gritted my teeth as my heart ached all the more. "Briar did *not* kill my father." I watched him for any trace of a reaction.

"No, she did not," Vyraetos said it as plainly as if stating water was red and the night was dark.

Laro and Melnani both nodded as if they were one.

"If she were to continue through the trials, Fate would not strike her down; of that I am certain." Vyraetos pressed his lips together. "This wasn't simply an assassination. It was a warning. It is apparent from the most basic of assessments that there are multiple individuals involved in this scheme. They are signaling what they are capable of, and they are maneuvering their chosen bride into position. They will urge us to resume the bridal competition tomorrow, and then to have the wedding as soon as one wins, to ensure that the magic of the Shadow Kingdom does not become untethered.

"Kaylen is the Aureline Council's favorite, though they are not unanimous. However, if the magic of our kingdom is seen to be at stake and Rhielle remains unconscious, then many members of the Shadow Council may be persuaded to vote for Kaylen. Despite being uncertain that Kaylen is directly involved, we think it likely, and if the power of this kingdom is seen to be weakening, then far more will support her than will trust you."

My mouth dried, and my hands fisted. Of course Kaylen was involved in all this. She was ruthless and vile, and they had confirmed my worst fears.

I gritted out, "I will delay the competition and the wedding. There is no way that fecking woman will become my queen." Though I could not recall all the formalities, I would have only one queen, and I had chosen. Even if Briar had never existed, I wouldn't have accepted Kaylen.

"You are permitted to delay the trials within reason." Though Vyraetos said this calmly, there was an edge to his voice that advised caution. "But if enough of the Shadow Council become concerned about the stability of our kingdom's magic, then they may move to depose you for either instability or weakness. The three of us would certainly oppose that, but we are not enough. The weakening of the magic itself would easily convince any arbiter asked to settle the dispute that action must be taken."

I met his gaze without blinking. "At least one on the Shadow Council is in league with the Aureline Council faction. One of you was in the garden with a younger member of the Aureline Council, and the lower court guards who took Briar away did not heed my orders. That means they have some direct measure of influence beyond simply wanting to see our kingdom's magic stabilized."

"We are aware, though we do not yet know who is involved," Vyraetos responded. "We will uncover all who are part of this conspiracy. But what I'm proposing is that you permit us to buy you time."

"And how would you accomplish that?" I folded my arms.

Vyraetos exchanged an almost imperceptible glance with Melnani. "Tonight, we will vest the Shadow magic in you. It is the only way to ensure the connection does not unravel and leave the kingdom vulnerable to outside manipulation. But it will last for only a limited time, and the pain will be ... excruciating."

Laro and Melnani glanced at each other, hesitation seeping into the lines of their faces.

I remained motionless. "How much time will it buy me?" I didn't fully trust them, as this could be a trap. But if they could strengthen my magic, it would help me delay the third trial. I still felt weak and tired, which didn't bode well for getting Briar back.

"Six days, perhaps. Maybe seven, if Fate favors us." His gaze drifted over me as if evaluating me once more to determine if I was strong enough. "But it could be as short as three days. We won't know for certain until the vesting is completed, and this magic can be capricious."

In my current condition, I might not be able to push off the final trial for more than a day. Three days would be a blessing from Fate.

Melnani leaned forward slightly. "You have enemies, Your Highness. There are many who have the ear of the Shadow

Council, as well as some on the Shadow Council who do not trust your judgment. If you do this, you must not let them see you falter or that you suffer. You must project strength and composure at all times."

Her voice scraped over my ears, reminding me of every moment when I had nearly lost control. Especially tonight. "I will not falter." And I wouldn't. I didn't care about pain, or risk, or the slow rot that might consume me from within if something went diabolically wrong. If the ritual gave me six days—feck, if it bought me only three days—I would find Briar and drag her out of whatever Aurelian prison they had put her in. I would take whatever pain or torment was required gladly, even if it splintered me to dust in the end, so long as I saved her. "Can any of you tell me where they took Briar? The Shadow Council has connections with the other kingdoms' councils, so I would presume it is a simple inquiry."

The three exchanged glances. Melnani's mouth twitched, and Laro stared at me without blinking.

Vyraetos lifted his wrinkled hands as if helpless. "Ordinarily, yes. But this night, when we spoke to our friends and allies outside our council, we learned that the Aureline Council is treating this assassination with more care and intensity than when the Ignis King and the Terran Queen passed under similar circumstances. They are not permitting even some Aureline council members to know where she is."

"My father is the one who was murdered. I have the right to face the accused."

"You do, but if you do not know where she's being held, they can delay you from seeing her. We will do all we can to ensure you are able to speak with her as soon as possible. I have renewed my request, and Melnani and Laro have done the same. But ... if I may offer one piece of counsel—do not acknowledge how deeply you long for Briar, or in any way signal your intent to make her your queen."

Vyraetos did not even ask me if I intended to make Briar my queen. He understood. "My focus is on justice for my father." I spoke the words with flat conviction. "What else do we need to do to continue this .... vestment process?"

Vyraetos dipped his head. "Come with us. We must make haste. The loyal members of the Shadow Council have assembled. But first, Your Highness, I must warn you that this process is not without risk. Connecting to the raw power of the Shadow Realm after the previous king failed to transfer it may destroy your mind, or even take your life. You will have to endure with great strength and a formidable will to survive.

"The alternative is to delay until the magic weakens and hope that Rhielle awakens in time to participate in the final trial, or another bride comes forward to displace Kaylen as the favorite."

My stomach twisted, and bile crept up my throat. The horrid taste spread over my tongue. There was no real choice in this matter. They could not ask for a better cover to assassinate me. What choice was left to me though? There did not seem to be much chance of rescuing Briar within less than a day. "What are my odds?" I asked.

Vyraetos did not flinch. "At best, it is an equal chance of success to failure."

"Realistically, based on what you know of me and what has already happened."

"Perhaps a one in four chance, Your Highness," he said. "It's impossible to say for certain, but you have been under great strain and are already weakened due to your father's death."

I clenched my jaw, inwardly cursing the wretchedness of the situation. Even having a few hours' delay would be better than nothing. But having more time could give my plan a chance to actually succeed, and Briar would be safe.

"What assurances do I have that this is not a trap?" I lifted my chin and stared at the three of them. If I went with them, I'd have to go alone. Silus wasn't an option, and Thalen was investigating the guards involved with Briar's imprisonment. Could I trust any of my personal guards? Involving more people in this matter would make it more likely that our enemies could discover our plan. I had to be wise.

Vyraetos inclined his head once more and pressed a hand over his heart. His Shadow magic flared in dark swirls around his shoulders and away from his chest, making itself more apparent while leaving his heart vulnerable, as was custom in vows such as this. "I swear it on my own life and on the lives of my children and their children that no harm shall come to you by my hand. Should any within the chamber seek to do you ill, I will fight at your side with my own lifeblood and power."

Laro and Melnani mirrored his pose. Their magic was not so potent, and Melnani's seemed more silver while Laro's was more charcoal. But they uttered the same words.

It was more than I'd expected. If any of them proved treacherous, then their entire line would suffer.

"Very well. Should things go wrong, I ask that you extend your vow then to these matters—look after my sister, and find a way to transfer the throne to her if possible. And if that is not possible, ensure that she is provided for and kept safe from any who might harm her. See to it that Briar is rescued and returned to her home on Earth. She is innocent of all that has been levied against her, and she does not deserve to suffer." One consolation was that, if I died, the Aurelines would likely not be as determined to hold her. They would no longer need to keep her from becoming queen. They'd probably keep up the show of a trial, but they'd be more receptive to a compromise. At least, I hoped so because she was an uncertainty here with her connections and magic.

My heart panged. I didn't understand why Fate would be so cruel as to select someone I had a life-altering connection with to be framed for killing my father and dragged away for his murder. I wanted to protect her, and the best way to do that was to become as strong as possible so that no one would question my decisions. If I could get Briar to safety, then my death would have purpose.

Eyes stinging, I blinked back tears. I hadn't wanted love, and now that death was at our door—hers or mine—I could finally imagine the life I could have with Briar.

Vyraetos's shadows again swept around his shoulders and away from his chest, and his words brought me back to reality. "My vow is so extended. As you have said it, so shall it be."

Laro and Melnani did the same.

With a grim nod, I drew in a deep breath. "You have my gratitude and respect. I will go with you."

Vyraetos turned his palm upward once more, and gray and black wisps swept out of his hand and around us. My head spun, and my stomach lurched as the shadows spun around me. The cold, comforting tendrils pressed against my body, joining my own magic and tightening to the point that I couldn't tell where they ended and I began. My strength surged as the magic pulsed through my veins.

The sharp tang of magic burned my nostrils, and my stomach lurched. Without a second thought, I brought Briar's face into my mind to keep me grounded. I pictured her running, her vivid green eyes sparkling with life and mischief, her wild light-copper hair flying in all directions, and her perfect body soft and curved just right for holding.

My heart shattered, hating that she was in danger and not beside me now. *Damn you, Fate, you won't keep her from me!*

Soon, the realm steadied, and a cavern with chiseled black stone walls that was unmistakably beneath the palace came into view. The colder air bit my skin, and the faintest drip of crimson mineral-laden water echoed around a single ring of dark-gray hooded figures, who stood shoulder to shoulder around the perimeter of a pool. Their faces were hidden, their hands folded and hidden within their sleeves. There were about twenty in total, a little more than three-quarters of the full Shadow Council.

In the center of the cavern sat a pedestal of raw obsidian. It jutted up from the floor as if it had grown there. Perched atop it was a polished black orb larger than my own skull. Dark purple light pulsed within it amid churning swirls of shadow, dull and flat.

Vyraetos, Laro, and Melnani materialized near me, their robes fluttering with residual magic. Laro and Melnani at once fell back, and the ring of council members shifted to accommodate them. Vyraetos remained motionless, drawing the swirling darkness back into himself.

The walls glistened with veins of liquid silver, as if the rock itself were bleeding. A memory of my last moment with Father sprang forward. He'd been trembling, and he'd looked so weak. Not like the man I'd always known. Pain gouged my insides, but I forced my breathing to steady.

It was deathly silent, and my skin prickled with caution. I forced emotions away. Projecting my strength and focus was vital.

As my heartbeat steadied, I picked up on more sounds: low breaths and the faint rustling of fabric. Thick, cold magic pressed upon me, stealing my breath. I'd never been this weak. The air seemed unable to reach my lungs.

I looked upward at a high, vaulted ceiling and a cloud of darkness that spun in lazy vortices, tendrils occasionally sloughing off to drift down and vanish before reaching the floor.

My shadows stretched into the darkness and circled the

pedestal, licking up to the sphere and tasting the raw power of its fluctuations. It was like trying to put my hand into an uneven waterfall. My spine stiffened instinctively. After my father's passing, I had known that the magic would not be so potent and would seem unsteady compared to its usual flow, but actually tasting that weakness had bile creeping up the back of my throat. The power made every nerve in my body thrum. It was a disconcerting sensation that worsened my fatigue and nausea.

Vyraetos moved to the other side of the pedestal and hovered his weathered hands over the sphere. The dull purple light flickered beneath his fingertips, signaling that it, too, had been weakened by my father's death. The other council members stepped forward and formed a tighter circle around us, their breathing synchronizing into an eerie rhythm that made the hair on my neck rise and was more sensation than sound.

Raising his hands, Vyraetos said, "In light of the treacherous betrayal that has led to King Merrick's untimely demise, it is incumbent upon us to ensure the protection of our realm's magic. All present are in agreement about our course."

"Vest the power in King Merrick's heir. Vest the power in Prince Vad." The assembled members spoke as one, their voices hazy amidst the power of the chamber.

The tang in the air intensified, becoming more like the scent of lightning and storms surging among fires.

Vyraetos turned his gaze upon me, his voice a low rumble. "When I indicate it, place your hands on the orb, then endure."

My fingers twitched as I inclined my head. The weight and burn of the magic already had my knees wanting to buckle. Trials and tests of endurance were among my least favorite in this kingdom, but this would prove whether I was still fit to lead. My stomach twisted in anticipation, and my nerves sang as I braced for the pain. I closed my eyes, pulling Briar into my mind once again. Just the thought of her helped me stand stronger.

Vyraetos hummed a low note. The other members joined in, and the air vibrated with their voices. "The eternal night embraces us. Ancient Fate is summoned. Behold this, the son of a king who was wrongly slain. Shadows bear witness to this, son of our magic, protector of our kingdom, chosen by Fate."

My skin prickled, and my muscles tightened. The tension in the chamber rose with each breath. Then Vyraetos gestured toward me.

Stomach heaving, I placed my hands on the dark orb, fingers splayed across the surface. The stone was almost feverishly hot, and power thrummed through it like a massive heartbeat while the shadows churned above.

Vyraetos spread his arms wide as the council members continued to hum. "Vest in him the fullness of power. Vest in him the fullness of the shadows."

The orb heated more, seeming to burn my flesh, but I kept my hands steady and set my jaw. My blood pumped faster as the shadows above began to twist like a cyclone. The dull purple light flickered more as if the magic itself taunted me.

Briar.

I have to remember Briar.

The council members chanted, "Vest in him, vest in him," as Vyraetos continued.

"Prince of Shadows, Prince of Night, receive the weight, measure, strength, and depth of our hallowed powers."

The weak light in the orb pulsed, and the shadows above me descended in thick, writhing streams.

Then the first shadow struck and pierced my chest like a chilled onyx spear, severing bone and sinew as it cut into my heart. My shadows flared protectively, trying to force the first shadow tendril away. I gritted my teeth and locked my stance to keep from bowing forward as the shadow yanked me downward and a heavy buzzing filled my ears.

The second shadow struck, this one driving into my left shoulder and slicing all the way to my wing. My breaths shallowed, and my jaw clenched until my teeth ached. Intense heat and vicious cold seared through me. I'd never experienced pain like this.

This is for Briar. Hold on to that.

I needed time to rescue Briar. Time to seek vengeance. Time to protect what remained of my family and my kingdom.

The humming of the council members continued as the vibrations from the magic intensified.

My gaze darted upward again in time to see the third shadow shoot toward me. Light and darkness exploded in front of my eyes as the icy tendril pierced my right shoulder. My wings flared and twitched as agony splintered through me.

Another shadow punctured my temple and drove through my mind, igniting memories and thoughts with blinding clarity. *Briar.* I called her face in my memory again and held on tight. I focused on the taste of her lips and the heat of her body against mine, gripping the orb tighter and leaning forward to brace myself, and then a fourth, fifth, and sixth shadow sank into my spine, my stomach, and my skull.

A strained grunt escaped my lips, but my jaw remained shut. Sweat poured down my brow. Pain saturated my consciousness and swallowed me whole. Not one point on my body was free of this torment. Screams of agony sealed in my throat and chest, trying to rip out of me, and yet depriving me of the very breath I needed.

A seventh shadow tendril appeared in front of my face, then speared me through the eyes. Heat, cold, and darkness exploded over my face and through my mind. Everything vanished, and I fell into the void.

CHAPTER SIX

The orb ignited within my grasp.

The skin on my hands melted, and the frigid coldness of the Shadow magic pressed even harder upon me. My lungs stopped working, and the ground spun. I closed my eyes and tried to keep Briar's face foremost in my mind. She was the final vision I wanted to see before death.

The dull purple light of the orb flashed through my eyelids, blocking her face from me and reminding me that I was a failure to my father, my sister, Briar, and my kingdom. When I opened my eyes, crimson water was seeping over the orb and turning pink.

The message was clear.

I had failed.

I'd marred my family's entire legacy.

No. *No.* It couldn't end like this. I refused to give up when the threats against Briar, my family, and kingdom were so strong.

The fire beneath my hands ebbed, and icy agony spiraled through my veins and drove away every trace of warmth. The magic wanted to suck me away from consciousness and drag me the rest of the way into the bottomless depths.

No. I was doing this to gain more time, not less. Death wasn't a consequence I was willing to face. I had to survive and be as powerful as possible; otherwise, this was all pointless.

I gripped the now frozen orb tighter, barely feeling it in my palms. Shadows poured into me, and my own shadows couldn't fight them off any longer. My heart slowed, and the shadows coiled around me, making me feel as if I were suffocating. I grunted as my knees hit the ground with a painful *bang*. My fingers slipped, almost releasing the orb, and I screamed as I dug my fingertips back into the stone. The urge to let go and vanish into the darkness pressed against me.

Images blazed through my mind: Father's iron grip on my shoulder as he demanded I show strength, the set of his jaw when he saw Mother's body placed in the marble crypt with her hands folded over the bouquet of death blossoms on her chest, the first night Elara awoke screaming, clutching her chest and shaking with terror when the illness set upon her, and Briar—my Briar—grinning and covered in blackberry trifle and daring me to join in the fun.

The last memory made my heart skip a beat.

Briar made all this suffering worth it, and I clung to that memory. Every image of the people I loved strengthened me, even as the shadows sought to rend me apart and the council's voices climbed to a deep booming rhythm.

Get through this. Fecking void, you have to get through this. And yet, the orb drank from my life force greedily, and the void promised peace and safety. It'd be so easy to let go, but what would that mean for Briar?

I couldn't die, not until I saw she was safe with my own two eyes.

I wouldn't give up or be manipulated into losing. I wouldn't be owned. I wouldn't accept any queen but one, and I would carry her from that forsaken prison myself.

The shadows spiraled around me, and the frigid agony continued to build. I clenched my hands and jaw even tighter, biting down so hard my own teeth might crack. And suddenly, torment, ice, and darkness surrounded me.

My chest seized, and I screamed internally, *I refuse to die!*

Deep within my soul, something clicked into place. My lungs expanded and filled with clean air once more, and my shadows eased, as if both my shadows and the source recognized one another and were at peace. The agony ebbed, and I opened my eyes to find that my sight had returned.

A sob built in my chest as my shadows surrounded me. They didn't grip me from within as tightly as they had just a day before. The light within the orb had gone from dull to a rich, deep purple, and thrummed more evenly.

I swallowed the cry. This was the miracle I'd asked for, and I wouldn't complain. However, the return of the kingdom's magic wouldn't last long. Time was ticking once more.

I opened my mouth to speak, but it was too dry, and the words wouldn't form. I swallowed hard and glanced at the council surrounding me.

All but Vyraetos dropped to their knees and bowed their heads. Their long hoods draped forward, but this time, they spread out their hands and turned them so that the palms faced me. "The power is vested in King Vad. The power of the Shadow King is now seated."

Vyraetos strode around the pedestal and stopped in front of me. I straightened slowly and squared my shoulders, my wings twitching. Remnants of pain cut through my veins, aching and pulsing with each breath and heartbeat.

He bowed his head and then also lowered himself to his knees. "The fullness of our kingdom's magic now rests within you. It will hold for at least three days, perhaps up to seven. May Fate guide you as you seek the answers you need, and may your bride bring you great strength and further balance this power when the bond is sealed."

I nodded, then I stood and took two steps away from the black pedestal. Shadows spiraled over my arms, wings, and chest. The scent of scorched ozone, cold rock, and fresh blood hung in the air, and I focused on keeping my feet steady beneath me and my spine straight, the silent weight of the council's eyes a pressure on me. Even now, power lashed wildly at the edges of my awareness, tearing at the boundaries of the realm and merging where I started and it began. The notion didn't terrify me as much as it should have. For a heartbeat, I almost welcomed it. I was so *tired* of holding back.

The room seemed smaller than before, shimmering with energy, and my body felt exhausted. I needed to be alone before I collapsed in front of everyone. My legs were shaking, and my head was pounding. I gestured for the council to stand.

Vyraetos pressed his hands palm to palm. "We serve the Shadow Kingdom and its ruler." The others rose and echoed his words.

I was fortunate that, in this case, they viewed the interests of both my rule and the Shadow Kingdom as being in alignment. Removing me from power would now be more complicated, though when the magic weakened, such a removal would become simpler.

I lowered my head, and the room spun. Still, I cleared my throat and spoke steadily. "And I shall do all within my power to preserve and protect our kingdom." It was the right response, even if the truth was that the kingdom was not so high in my priorities as my family and, most of all, Briar.

Vyraetos shifted his gaze over me. "If I might be so bold as to suggest it, Your Highness, I recommend you return to your chambers and rest for a few hours. The vesting process leaves the body and mind taxed. The morning will bring with it more conflicts that will require your attention, and we still need to prepare for the formal coronation for the benefit of the kingdom."

I bit back a bitter laugh, steeling my expression as I gave a curt nod. Sleep was the last thing I'd be getting, but they didn't need to know that. I couldn't rest until Briar was safe. I suspected that what I had just gone through was nothing compared to what my enemies were doing to her.

I exchanged a few more cursory notes with Vyraetos and then called the shadows to transport me back to the observatory. There were so many plans I needed to make, but first, I needed to see if Thalen had located either guard.

As the observatory appeared around me, I stumbled forward, my legs hitting the edge of one of the couches. Luckily, there were no unexpected visitors this time, so I took a moment to catch my breath.

The air still held the charge of magic but also a tinge of fresher, lighter air from the hall, as if someone had just been here moments before.

Someone other than me.

Muscles tensing and shadows flaring out, I glanced around the chamber past the golden telescope and back to the black couches and—there, on the center table between the couches, sat a large crystal flagon of black currant wine. The signal. Thalen had found at least one of the guards and gotten him to the onyx cellar.

My blood surged with delight at the thought of wreaking vengeance on one of the bastards who had dared to touch my beloved. After what I'd endured, if it couldn't be Briar sitting here waiting for me, this was exactly what I needed to see. *Fate bless you, Thalen.*

I called my shadows, the cool tendrils stirring within me just as my knees gave way and I almost dropped to the ground once again.

I snarled, disgust seeping through me at how physically weak I was, but I had to remember the cause. I had gained enough power to give me more time to fix this mess, and I needed to rest, but time would run out quickly. I needed to push through and free Briar.

Saving my strength, I walked toward the back staircase in the eastern wing of the royal quarters. The heavy diagonal door guarding it slid open on soundless hinges to reveal a narrow passage of the gouged rock, the stairs so narrow that barely half my foot fit on one at a time. My shadows urged me down into the depths, which gave me a little surge of energy.

Traces of quartz made the onyx walls glimmer even without torchlight, and my eyes adjusted to the darkness ... not that I needed them to. I'd walked this way so many times I knew the path by heart. My shadows slid along the walls, and I kept my wings folded tight against my back.

The staircase twisted four times in a tight spiral before opening into the tunnel of coarse-cut stone. Nothing had been polished or sanded, but some of the roughness of the stone floor had been worn away over time. I suspected my sparring, training, games, and youthful endeavors had added a fair bit of wear over the decades, and my footsteps were silent now.

I caught the tang of blood. No sounds stirred, but most likely, Thalen had taken special care for that and created a circle of silence. The faint thrum of Sylvan magic pushed against my ears. My own shadows could mute sounds as well, especially if I focused them, but Sylvan silencing magic was especially powerful because it commanded the very air itself.

Around the next bend of the narrow passage, I reached the entry to another staircase and glimpsed pale light beneath the reinforced metal door. It yielded to my touch as the magic of the guard sigils recognized me.

The onyx cellar was a large, low-ceilinged room of rough-hewn stone and diagonal stone cubicles for storage. In the center of the room, in a chair, sat a prisoner with his hands bound behind his back by spindles of thick wire, head lolling as if he'd just been struck. The prisoner's ankles were lashed to the chair's legs with the same material, and livid bruising around his extremities made it clear that he was far from comfortable. Thick bolts screwed the feet of the chair into the stone floor to prevent him from toppling it and escaping.

Blood trickled from the corners of the prisoner's lips, and a pile of armor lay by the western wall, stacked haphazardly next to cubicles that previous royals had used for storing special vintages.

Across the room, Thalen leaned against the wall, his amber eyes bright and sharp. His gaze slid to mine, and he gave a small nod as if to confirm it was one of the guards who had taken Briar.

I smirked. Now I could release some of the anger I'd been trying to hide.

When the guard saw me, he started to speak, but not a peep reached my ears.

Smart, Thalen.

I couldn't spot the markings of the circle of silence, but Thalen used to love to brag about his skills until he learned hard lessons in discretion. The last time I'd seen him utilize this kind of magic was years ago, during a wilderness conflict against cursed beasts that had stalked us by our heartbeats, and he'd left traces of the circle in the packed earth. Apparently, he'd been practicing.

The Sylvan magic prickled and chaffed my own as I neared the guard. Two steps closer, and his pained moans became audible.

"What have I done to displease you, Your Highness?" The

guard's shoulders twitched. "I have done nothing to harm you or your father."

I circled him slowly, not looking at him as I took in the onyx cellar. Thalen would have prepared everything, but I wanted to ensure all was well myself. Dark metal brackets fastened to the stone walls held low torches, creating enough pools of amber light to brighten most of the floor.

My shadows slid along the walls like a second consciousness, drinking in every sensation and detail. I held my wings out but relaxed, my spine straight, though I almost stumbled as I reached Thalen.

He quirked an eyebrow, not missing that I wasn't well. He remained quiet, but I knew he'd address the matter with me later.

"No one is aware you took him?" I leaned back on my feet, trying to hide my near fall.

Thalen's mouth flicked upward in a crooked smile that didn't show his teeth. "It's hard to scream for help when you don't have breath." His posture remained loose, and his wings hung lazily, his white feathers nearly brushing the floor. But anyone who believed he was relaxed was a fool. "The circle is reinforced. No one will hear anything now that he has his breath back."

"I have done nothing wrong," the man cut in, voice shaking and pitching higher.

Crossing to the bound man, I rested my hands on my belt and spread my wings wide. "What is your name?"

"I am Deln of Ilnon, a faithful servant of the Shadow Kingdom and to you, Your Highness. I have never done anything to harm the kingdom or the royal family, I swear," he rasped. Blood dribbled from his mouth.

I chuckled darkly. "A faithful servant who failed to listen or even acknowledge his prince when he was told to bring the

Earth woman back?" It felt wrong to speak of Briar in such cold terms, but it would feel even more wrong to speak of my feelings for her to this cringing failure of a man. "Why did you not heed my orders?"

"I—It wasn't me!" Deln started, but his gaze snapped to Thalen, and he cringed.

Thalen fluttered his fingertips, and small wind blades formed near Deln's face, hanging in the air as they waited for his instruction. "We've already talked about lying." One of the tiny wind blades darted just up to his lips as if ready to dive in and carve the lie off his tongue.

I kept my own expression neutral as I stared Deln down, unblinking. "Why did you not heed my order? It was clearly stated multiple times."

Deln's jaw worked. The small wind blades remained still in the air before him.

I circled him once more, my boots scraping on the coarse stone. "Only one order was given. Mine. And you defied it. Blatantly. Neither you nor your fellow guard even flinched, and you worked as one."

"Your Highness, I—"

"Vow the truth." I stopped in front of him, and my shadows spiraled closer. They crept up the legs of the chairs. "Vow on your life and on the lives of those whom you cherish that you will speak only the truth."

His face paled. His tongue flicked at his lips. It wasn't considered good conduct to demand a vow for something like this. The magic always took its toll, and if the vow was not given willingly, my magic would compel it at a cost to me. How much strength that would require depended on the will of the person being interrogated, but I could already tell I'd be able to rip through this man's like wet paper, even in my current state. Still, the price of it would make me physically weaker.

If this got me closer to freeing Briar, I'd take the cost. I would get to her, even if I couldn't stand or walk and had to crawl. She was worth it all.

I lowered my face to his, staring him down as my blood boiled. "Vow now that only the truth will cross your lips, or I'll let Thalen hook those wind blades back in your mouth and cut out every lie, spoken and thought."

His blue eyes widened, and sweat rolled down his bruised brow. "Your Highness—"

The nearest of the tiny blades shot forward and cut a line just inside his cheek. He jolted back, blood blossoming from the wound and spilling over his lip.

"Oops," Thalen said. "Were you about to make the vow or protest?"

Deln's throat bobbed, his gaze darting frantically between Thalen and me. He licked his cracked lips before focusing on me. He cleared his throat. "I-I vow upon my own life that I will speak only the truth."

"Vow it on your life and on something that would cause you pain. Otherwise, your words mean nothing to me," I growled. My shadows lifted as they spread and darkened like streams of ink pouring into once-clear red waters, and the air chilled around us. My breath frosted in his face, yet within me, an inferno raged, coiling tighter and tighter.

"I vow it on my life and on my children's lives," he murmured.

I raised an eyebrow and dropped my hand hard against his shoulder. My shadow claws pressed against the nailbeds, itching to emerge and puncture his flesh. "Your children aren't here. I don't even know if you have any children, and you wouldn't be the first who was willing to pass pain to his children to save his own skin. I reject that vow. Vow to speak the truth on your life and to your great, agonizing suffering. That seems like it would be the most impactful to you."

His throat bobbed again, and his mouth moved wordlessly.

I squeezed his shoulders and let my claws emerge. They cut into the ecru fabric of his tunic, the points pressing deeper with each breath I took. "Arguing would be a very bad choice. Anything other than the vow I require will result in even more pain and suffering. Is that what you want?" My eyebrow twitched upward as I dared him to defy me again.

Thalen watched with his fingers tensed, ready to send more of the wind blades shooting forward.

Deln whimpered and stiffened, his breath shuddering in his chest. Sweat had darkened the collar of his shirt. "I vow it," he gasped. "I vow it on my life, and to my great ... agonizing ... suffering, if I do not speak the truth."

There. It was done. Reluctantly, but binding nonetheless.

His suffering didn't concern me. My anger and hatred would push me through until Briar was free, and this bastard was as guilty as he was a dead man walking. He had dragged my beloved away and put her in the hands of my enemy, who would no doubt use torture to force her to admit to something she hadn't done. But first, I would make him acknowledge every scrap of truth. "You are one of the two guards who seized my beloved, are you not?"

He nodded slowly. My shadows curled back closer to me while remaining within his line of sight, a reminder that, beyond the vow, I would inflict great pain upon him if he crossed me. "Y-yes. I was, but we—" He stopped short.

I gripped his shoulder tighter. "You what? Were you going to tell me you didn't mean to hurt her? That you didn't mean any harm? Then you realized it was a lie. You can't say you didn't mean her any harm because that isn't true."

"He doesn't give a damn about Briar." Thalen made the tiny blades dance. Two of the blades became hooks as his magic transformed them. "When I asked him, he called her a scaffing bitch and a copper-haired whore. I overheard him saying that no one would mourn her. Very strong opinions on the future queen. Treasonous opinions."

With each word Thalen spoke, my blood seared hotter and hotter, thundering in my ears. My shadows flared, and my wings tensed, intensifying the darkness. The need to kill and seek vengeance pulsed within me, and my mind flashed up images of this man dead on the floor with his throat ripped out and his spine snapped. Acid rose in my throat along with the hatred.

"It was—it was—" He strained as the impacts of the vow pressed against him and the lie he debated speaking into existence pained him.

"Why would you call her such things?" I spoke each word with piercing clarity and hoped that the terror was already ripping him apart.

He squirmed in the chair, and the wood squeaked. He couldn't get any traction with his feet, and his fingers twitched.

"Well?"

He paled even more, his complexion now like parchment paper. A vein in his temple throbbed. "One of the Aureline Council members instructed us to be prepared in case we were summoned, and we were told to stay close. He said that we were to take a prisoner away immediately, no matter what else was said."

"Who told you this?" I demanded as my claws cut deeper into his skin. Blood blossomed along his shoulders, and he began to stink of fear.

"I—I couldn't see his face, but he was one of the younger members. He wore gray leather gloves. Maybe sealskin. There was nothing notable about him."

"Was he in the garden with us?" I didn't loosen my grip,

but I didn't push my claws deeper either.

"M-maybe? I don't know. I swear I don't know." He winced as if preparing for a blow.

"What about the Shadow Council member who was with him?"

"I don't know him either." Deln stared up at me with white-rimmed eyes, his pulse thundering in that vein. "I don't know any of their names. No one ever gave them. The council member just told us to come to the northern entrance of the garden because there would be a situation."

"When did you receive this instruction?" I demanded.

"Perhaps an hour before midnight. Maybe a little after. I don't know the exact time."

"Were you on duty?"

"Preparing to start at the second watch." His breathing turned labored. "He said that we were to report at the garden's entrance and be prepared for the signal." He tensed and leaned in, trying to ease the pressure on his shoulder from my claws and grip. "The signal came through a voidglass coin. Two flashes of light."

"Was there talk of Briar before this?" I released his shoulder and slowly walked around him again. My shadows branched off, three morphing into sharp spear-like formations and posing themselves at his jugular, the base of his throat, and along that throbbing vein.

His jaw worked. "Y-yes." Another nervous swallow and tightening of his body spoke as plainly as his words.

I returned to stand before him again and spoke in a low tone. "And what was said of her?"

"I want it to be clear that I didn't say this—the Aureline Council member said that she was a ruinous wretch and that her existence was a blight upon every fae realm, and she had to be removed for the good of all fae."

"Was there ever more than one council member present?" I seethed.

"Not that I saw."

"Were you aware of any others involved?"

He moistened his lips again. "Th-there are several, based on what they said. I overheard some conversations. They said Vyraetos was a fool and would lead the Shadow Kingdom to its doom, but his disappearance would be too suspicious. And they said Briar was ... a death trap for our people here. The Aureline Council is divided."

Nothing new there. I crossed my arms as I stared down at him. "What reason was given for their hatred of Briar?" My shadows brandished in front of him, two turning into slick, sleek blades.

"She isn't one of us. She isn't fae." He stumbled over the words. "Now, please let me go. I'm sorry for not heeding your order, but I swear I will be—"

I jammed my hand over his mouth as I leaned closer. My fingers dug into his cheeks. "Briar is your future queen. And you betrayed her as much as you did me and my father, your king. You were a part of his assassination. So do not *dare* to speak of loyalty now."

He trembled violently, and it would have been so easy to snap his neck in that breath. But there was one more thing I needed to know. "What prison did you take her to?" I moved my hand so he could speak, though I still gripped his face.

A low, panicked groan rose in his throat, and his muscles tightened. Of all the things I had asked, this was the one he most wanted to avoid. Probably because he had been bound in some way to hide it, or because he had been threatened with grave consequences if he spoke.

And that made sense.

After all, the Aurelines could not deny the visit of a ruler for whom they were conducting an investigation without good reason, and there was no good reason to deny me in this case. But they could hide the name of the prison and delay my reaching her, as Vyraetos had warned. Formal inquiries could take days.

I released his face and stepped back. Then I clasped my arms behind my back and set my shadows to split and rear before him in dozens of needle-like blades that glistened as if coated in venom. "Answer me, Deln, or these shadows will enter your veins and drag the truth from you."

"Your Highness, *please*—" He strained back, but the chair remained bolted to the stone even though the wood creaked under his weight.

"Answer me!" My rage flared hotter and choked me. This worm planned to withhold the location. My stomach twisted, and the power that flared through me intensified beyond what I had ever experienced. Three of the needle-like shadows plunged into him, one in each shoulder and one in the center of his chest. His body convulsed, and he screamed in agony.

My shadows sliced deeper, piercing into his veins in ways that would maximize pain without risking his life. "I am more than happy to cut the truth out of you, and my associate has already identified your partner in this crime. So you are not essential." Two more of my shadows plunged into his chest. I only guided them with general will as I let my Shadow magic take control. The heat of his blood was nothing compared to the ice of my shadows, the piercing precision of my magic spreading beneath his skin like liquid frost. His eyes rolled back, and saliva pooled at the corners of his mouth, mixing with the blood.

I drew the shadows back and left behind wounds that looked deceptively small. Letting him die now would be a waste—one I would enjoy but couldn't afford. Not yet.

He gasped and sobbed through the pain. "Don't make me answer, please!"

I struck him across the face, disgusted with his plea. He was one of the people responsible for Briar's abduction. She was probably being tortured far worse than this, and she didn't deserve one moment of pain or fear. "Answer. This is your last chance." I grabbed him by the face, my claws emerging and digging into his cheeks as I swept my shadows up. Two pierced him in the chest as he screeched. Veins bulged along his neck, and he twisted back as far as he could. I let another two shadow needles lance through him, just under his ribs on either side.

The chair jolted, wood shuddering beneath his spasms, but I gave him no relief. He deserved nothing but pain, and a vicious need to hurt him more blossomed within me. If I knew what Briar was suffering, I'd make him endure the same. But as I didn't know, I let my imagination and shadows guide me.

"Last chance," I snarled. A single needle of a shadow curled up over his face and stopped over his eye.

His pupils widened. "Firellan's Spine!" The words tore out of his mouth as he sobbed brokenly.

My spine locked, and I almost snapped his neck.

Chapter Seven

I scuffled back as the light intensified, carving out a perfect circle in the middle of my prison. I attempted to get away from this new threat, but my body wasn't cooperating, and my raw hands struggled to find traction.

Still, I managed to move back several feet as the edges solidified, creating what could only be another damn portal. Where the fuck were they taking me now? I should've known they wouldn't leave me alone to heal.

My wolf eased forward, her hackles raised, but then a familiar scent hit my nose—lilac, rose, lavender, and wet earth.

Could it be my many-greats-grandfather?

My chest expanded in hope, but I squashed it. He hadn't wanted me to be taken by the fae. I wasn't sure what that meant, but this wasn't going to be a welcome-to-the-official-fae-family conversation.

The portal stopped expanding. I couldn't see through to the other side. My heart pounded and then nearly stopped when Many-Greats-Grandfather said, "You shouldn't have fought me when I tried to save you from all this."

Despite being bloody, smelly, beaten, and weak, his attitude annoyed me so much that I managed to roll my eyes. *That* was what he wanted to say to me? I told you so? Why bother at all? "Yeah, you sure told me. Are we done?"

"Do not take that tone with me," he said. "You should have listened to me, but you did not. Now here you are."

I folded my arms as a shudder cut through me. My whole body ached, and my lungs burned. He hadn't stepped through the portal, and the flickering circle was still open, but not low enough that I would be able to easily reach it. "Did you come here to gloat?"

"No, and we don't have much time. I told Ember and Ryker you were ... safe, more or less. We're working on a way to get you home. Ember wanted me to let you know that you aren't alone, and you aren't forgotten."

My heart clenched, even as my annoyance with him forced me to swallow that he considered *this* safe. "Are they okay?"

"They're fine. Worried for you, of course. We will find a way to get you home though. You just have to remain alive."

I rolled my eyes again since I seemed to have just enough energy for that. "Oh, good to know. I was considering dying just for spite."

He continued as if I hadn't said anything. "Whatever you do, you must not wed the Shadow Prince."

I flinched as if he'd struck me. It wasn't as if Vad wanted to marry me now. As far as he knew, I had murdered his dad. His storm-cold eyes bored into me even in memory, his gaze filled with rage and grief, the sound of his roar echoing in my mind as he demanded they bring me back.

"Not only that, but you must not tell *anyone* of your Aureline heritage. Both those things are imperative."

"You didn't tell me the Aurelines were so ..." *What was the right word?* "Evil." Pangs of fear and grief stabbed through me while betrayal curdled my soul. I tensed further, digging my fingernails into my bruised arms.

"Some are, yes, but not all, I assure you." He sighed.

He seemed to have run out of words. "Why shouldn't I marry the Shadow Prince, and why can't I tell anyone of my lineage?"

Something cracked on the other side of the portal, and the sound of footsteps scuffing on stone came through. "People are coming. I can't stay. Remember my words. Do not, under *any* circumstances, marry the Shadow Prince or tell anyone of your Aureline heritage. I'll return when I can. Be brave, child. You are stronger than you realize, and you will not fall to these monsters. Fate will bring us through."

Before I could respond, the portal snapped shut with a faint pop. The prison plunged back into cold darkness, leaving me alone with my pain and the stink of my own blood amid the filth and damp. I wanted to scream. No matter what, I never got any answers.

When I called on my wolf to strengthen my vision, bile inched up in my throat. Layered with filth, algae, and mold, this disgusting pit was an unholy grave for all those who had been trapped here. Above me, jagged stalactites cut down from the ceiling, droplets of silver water forming and dripping into pools. Several of the stalactites appeared to have broken off, and I dropped my gaze to find that they had fallen onto the ground.

Bones of what I assumed must be captives who had been here before me jutted out from a pile of hay that was not simply moldy but stirring with life. Slick black beetles slid among the discolored flakes, and ridged white worms writhed in the thin layer of muck at the edges.

Shuddering, I drew my focus inward.

Fate sucked.

My skin crawled, and my chest ached so painfully I had to blink back the tears. At least Ember and Ryker were safe and trying to figure out a way to save me.

My shoulders drooped with shame. They shouldn't have to get involved with fae matters, and even if they did, they didn't have the right magic to make rescue a possibility.

Hell, Many-Greats-Grandfather couldn't even get me out through that portal, and something had stopped him from reaching out to me sooner. It must not be easy for him to communicate like that, and he *lived* in this realm.

I placed my forehead on my knees, which throbbed from where I'd scraped them during my near-drowning. I grimaced and straightened, replaying all that had happened. The *real* version, not Douchewaffle's false vision that still wavered at the edges of my mind, trying to catch my attention.

No. I wouldn't let these bastards win. My wolf snarled threateningly as I pushed the false memories out of my mind, leaving me with the horrific-enough truth.

She pushed forward, wanting to shift into wolf form. At first, I resisted. With how bad my injuries were, it would be risky to shift. With the way my feet and hands were ripped apart, the stretching of my skin and body could tear worse, making the wounds horrible. Although ... if they didn't tear worse, the magic surge would heal me.

And I needed a chance to get out of here.

I stopped holding her back. My wolf surged forward, desperate to use her senses to find a way out. My skin tingled as the fur tried to sprout, but then everything halted. My wolf pushed harder, but there was ... a wall.

Something pressed hard against my skin, causing even the tingle to ebb. There had to be some sort of magic in here.

My wolf jerked back like something had harmed her. And the truth crashed hard on me.

I couldn't shift, so there was no way to heal myself.

My bottom lip quivered, and I tried like hell not to break down, but it was so damn hard.

Drip.

I had lost *everything*, and I wasn't even being dramatic.

Drip. Drip.

The slow, irregular dripping of the water grew louder with each drop. If I didn't get myself under control, I might die from the noise alone.

A muted sound caught my attention, so faint I'd almost missed it. I urged my wolf again to help me hear. After a few more minutes of dripping, the sound again filtered into the room—a faint whimper followed by a deep sob or scream. The masculine noise resembled the cry of someone who'd screamed himself raw with despair. The hoarse voice held a vaguely familiar tone, as if I might have heard it before.

The sound grew louder, as if he were on the other side of the wall and drawing closer to me from some room beyond.

Too weak to stand, I crawled toward the sound, wincing as my bruised and bloodied knees scraped against the rough floor. The dripping continued and pelted my body, and my hands grew slick with blood.

My stomach knotted. With all this water, the structure of the cave could be compromised, which meant I had to be *very* careful.

I approached the part of the wall where the crying seemed loudest. The voice drew closer, along with a soft plopping sound, as if he were dragging himself. Then it stopped, and the cries grew more muffled, desperate, and aching.

I bit my lip and pressed my hands against the wall. My open wounds stung, but I needed the support to help locate the source of the sound. Maybe there was an opening in the wall or some way to more directly communicate.

Taking a deep breath, I closed my eyes and focused on the man's breathing and whimpers instead of my own torment. My wolf took charge, and I ran my fingers over the wall and felt

... a divot. I paused, listening. This was where the sound was coming from. I opened my eyes and found a vertical crack that ran from the top of the wall down to the floor. It was fingertip width, and when I peered through it, on the other side, I could make out a shivering, dark form.

I moved to change my view and realized he was curled up with his head lowered and his fingers thrust into his shaggy, greasy chestnut hair. His ragged gray shirt was soaking wet and clung to his form, leaving his bruised and battered arms bare.

"Are you okay?" I whispered hoarsely. I flinched. *What a dumbass question, Briar.* I wanted to bang my head against the wall. But what else could I ask? None of us was all right, but saying hello or good evening would have felt contrived.

The crying stopped, and the man lowered his shoulders and lifted his head. "Who's asking?"

Even though I could see only about an inch of him at any time, I made out tunneling needle marks on his flesh near his collarbone and the front of his chest.

He was one of the prisoners I'd seen in the hall. The one who had said he couldn't keep doing this.

Inhaling shakily, I wanted to give him hope, but even the time I'd been here had started feeling like eternity, and I already had the sense that there would be no escaping. "Someone who heard your cries earlier and wishes like the void to get out of this place."

He tipped his head back and looked at the crack sidelong, managing a hoarse croaking laugh. "I am sorry we find ourselves alike in this state. Are they feeding one of those traitors from your lifeblood as well?"

"Feeding?" My fingers curled tight against my palms, digging into already raw flesh. I ignored my discomfort and leaned closer to the crack. "What does that mean? Is that included in their tortures?" Even if I didn't know exactly what it meant, it sounded horrible.

The tip of his tongue darted out and moistened his cracked lips. "Both my blood and my magic are compatible with whoever they're feeding. When she needs more magic to replenish herself, they drain blood and magic from me. They'll continue doing it to me until I cease to exist." His breaths grew more ragged. "We're all dead already. It's just a matter of how we get there in the end."

"Who is 'she'?" I pressed closer to the crack. Something skittered across my hand, and I jerked back. An aching blade of pain spiraled through my body as it protested the movement, and a grunt escaped me.

He tipped his head back, and the wall blocked my view of him. "I've never seen her. She takes my life but has never deigned to see me. All I know is that two members of the Aureline Council are involved in this. Probably more. What of you? Why are you here?"

I rubbed my hand, still feeling the scratchy legs of whatever had run across it. Was there any point in keeping secrets from him? I wanted to tell him just to remind myself of the truth and push away the false memories further. "They think I killed the Shadow King. But I didn't. I was framed. They've been trying to put fake memories in my head and change my perception of what happened while pretending they're getting a confession."

"Ahhh, the tender mercies of Colm." His voice shuddered, as if he'd tried to laugh and failed. "Be careful with him. As careful as you can be. He'll twist everything you think you know. But you can hold out. Just ... hold on to the truth. Tell yourself what you must remember over and over again for as long as you can." He scoffed, but his voice sounded even more strained, as if he was verging on breaking into some combination of hysterical laughter and sobs. "What do they call you?"

"Briar," I said softly. "What about you?"

"I was Elias. I suppose you can still call me that."

Was. I shuddered. He'd pretty much acknowledged that he was never going to be the same person again. My throat tightened as I tried not to contemplate what might happen to me if I had to stay here much longer. If I had to endure days like this for an extended amount of time, there was no doubt I'd be feeling the same way. I might be determined to persevere, but everyone had their breaking point.

"It's so cold." He wrapped his bony arms around himself, and the veins near his chest throbbed along the dark tubular bruising. "It's always so cold. They don't even have to use much heat to torture you with temperature later. And there's a point where the cold burns too." He dipped his head forward into my view. "You have to hold on to every good memory you have, Briar. Especially if they take you to the Whispering Veins."

"The Whispering Veins?" Goosebumps prickled across my arms, and the temperature seemed to drop several degrees. As bad as today had been, somehow I knew that what Colm had in store for me would get far worse.

He lifted a hand and traced a design in the air. "It's this tall, narrow chamber. There are spikes on one wall at uneven intervals and of irregular sizes. Sharp enough to wound and maim but not enough to kill. Believe me, I've tried to die there. It's arranged in such a way that it's as silent as death. So silent that your ears strain for any sound, and you can hear your own blood as it pumps through your veins. Your mind and body become starved for any sort of stimulus because it's pure darkness. Not even shadow sight can grant you vision in that place. Time becomes even more meaningless, and the air starts to hurt. But then ... even worse, sometimes void vermin slip inside. They've cast spells so you can't hear the vermin when they approach. The only way you know they're there is when they're on you ... clawing, biting ..." He doubled over, hugging himself tighter.

I could make out half his face through the crack now. His silver eyes blazed as he continued, “I tried to escape once, and they locked me in there, but Colm had them attach the draining tubes to my veins while I was in that wretched place. I could hear my life draining from me, and he said he had half a mind to just let it spill out until I met my end. I was a fool to think he’d ever have that kind of mercy. Still ...”

“That’s awful, and to go through it alone ...” I trailed off because words were useless. It didn’t change a damn thing.

His eyes took on a stormy edge, the rawness of his horror like looking in a mirror. Bile rose along the back of my throat.

Elias struck his palm against the wall and came so close that I could see only a sliver of him through the crack. “Colm will take you there. If he’s trying to break your mind and force you to confess, he’ll trap you in that space and keep you there until you pray for torture. If you can’t escape, then kill yourself the first chance you get. But not on the spikes. They’re enchanted. They’ll wound you, but never enough to kill you.” He laughed darkly and flinched back while covering his face. “Don’t let them take you there. Don’t!”

My breath hitched, and I lurched back, even though he couldn’t possibly touch me. His struggling gasps turned into frantic sobs as he dropped down to the wet ground of the cell. He lay there, trembling and holding his head. “You can’t go in there, Briar. You can’t. If they can’t break your body, they’ll break your mind. And sometimes, they do both. Do whatever it takes so you don’t go in there.” His voice became a series of muffled wails as he gripped his head tighter.

I swallowed hard as panic ripped through me. My lungs couldn’t fill with oxygen. Leaning forward again, I pressed my hands against the wall, searching for a weakness or a bigger crack that I could use to get the hell out of here.

"Any chance you know how to get out of this place?" It wasn't as if I could just tell Colm *Nope, the Whispering Veins is a no-go for me.* And as for escape, I'd have to get out of this cell first, then figure out the rest. "We could work together."

He dragged the back of his hand over his face. Blood trickled from his cracked lips. "Don't waste your time on me. If you get a chance to go, leave me. I have days left at most. As long as they don't put you in Whispering Veins, you'll make it a couple weeks at least. If they do, you've got days at most before your mind is gone."

His words punched me in the gut. "You tried to escape before, and it didn't work. What didn't work about it?"

"I attempted to make it to the tunnels. Used to be able to command stones to move, but here they're charmed in most places. Didn't see the sigils. They hide them under stones and masks." His voice shook. "They have so many spells and sigils, we can't see that they don't worry about our attempts. Is anyone looking for you? If they can find a way in, you might have a chance. Your best hope, meanwhile, is to find a natural indentation, a tunnel, a crevice, and hide there when things get bad. They'll send someone in to get you if you don't come out, but it's better than being out in the open cell. Especially when the shaking starts."

My heart sank. Many-Greats-Grandfather said he and Ember were working on rescuing me, but who knew how long that would take.

If only Vad or Thalen was trying to find me ... My heart skipped as I wished that were true.

But I knew better.

Having hope was stupid. Vad thought I'd killed his father. He'd want me to pay for that.

I swallowed a whimper, and my eyes welled with tears. Vad *must* be thinking of me like that. I closed my eyes and drew in a shaky breath.

No. I wasn't going down that road. There was no time to think of what had been ruined. I had to find a way out of here and save myself.

"What happens in the cell? What makes it shake?" Was my cell like his? There didn't seem to be any crevice or tunnel or formation on mine.

He whimpered. "I don't know. Sometimes, the entire cave system this prison is built in shakes, and stalactites will crash to the ground, killing anyone in their path. Either the guards cut these chambers out of the rock, or the spaces opened on their own. Who knows? But the guards don't do anything to make them safer. This tunnel is part of my cell. I stay in here because it's harder for them to reach me, and there aren't any stalactites. No chance of getting out though."

The broken stalactites now made sense. I glanced over my shoulder and counted at least ten that had fallen in here. Holy shit. I had to get out! This was equivalent to sitting in a minefield.

"Come on, Elias," I said, trying to force strength into my voice. "Let's figure something out. How long do we have before they come to get you?" *And how long before they come to get me?*

He muttered something, but his voice remained muffled, and it didn't sound like he'd answered me. I forced myself to my feet and nearly dropped to my knees again due to my wobbly legs.

My feet burned and ached, and blood wetted my every step. But I was going to find something in this pit that I could use to escape. Based on the number of bones lying around, at least five fae had died down here. There were five skulls scattered about this space and many more bones strewn in the hay. None of the femurs or rib bones looked strong enough to withstand more than scraping the algae and mold or stirring up the muck. They were demineralized and cracked, making them useless for digging my way out. I picked one up, and it fell apart. The others weren't in any better condition, and accidentally stepping on one made it crumble.

There were more cracks in the walls and floor, so dark I couldn't see much beyond them. The consistent dripping of the water confirmed that I'd be in a lot of trouble if there were ever a flood.

A scorpion scuttled out of a crack and vanished beneath the pile of rotting hay. The cell opening they'd pushed me through was over twelve feet above me. Even jumping didn't get me close. At least not yet. There weren't enough loose rocks to create even a crude platform.

Elias continued to moan, but the words had become less garbled. "No way out if no one's looking for you too. If you disappear, you're gone. No way through."

I froze. His words were poisoning my mind, but I wasn't going to let that stop me. I needed to redirect his thoughts, as much for him as for my own well-being. "Tell me something about yourself."

"Can't take any more. They're not looking for me. Gone. Drained forever."

If he was right that Colm and his minions were so confident in their spellwork that they assumed no one could get out, I could use that to my advantage.

I pressed my palm against the stone wall, trying to find any purchase, any weakness. Cold claws of panic stabbed my chest. "If there's anything they missed, I'll find it. There has to be a way out."

Elias's sobs quieted and were replaced by a hollow chuckle. "They don't miss anything. That's what they do. They find every weakness, every crack in your armor, and they exploit it until there's nothing left of you."

I gritted my teeth. My wolf paced restlessly, pushing me to find a way out. If only Ember was here. She'd know exactly what to do.

I shook the thought away. Fortunately, my sister was safe on Earth. "Tell me who they're keeping alive with your blood, then. What do you know about her?"

"Not much. No one is looking." His voice moved as if he were trying to stand. "Ironic, isn't it? She won't die, but I will. Then they'll find someone else."

I stepped on a loose stone, and as I put my weight down, it shifted, and I twisted my ankle. Chest heaving, I held back a whimper, not wanting to freak out Elias any more than he already was. I couldn't stop just because I'd gotten another injury, so I hobbled around the cell until my ankle swelled up and I could barely feel the bottoms of my feet.

My fingers burned from pressing so hard against the icy stone and the trickling water. My body felt heavier, and my clothes were almost entirely drenched.

Did having someone looking for me count if they weren't in this realm? Did Many-Greats-Grandfather really understand the issues of this place? I couldn't help but wonder if he truly understood the dire situation I was in.

He might wait too long to try to do something about my situation.

No. I couldn't let my thoughts become negative. That wouldn't help anything. I knew my sister, and she'd keep looking unless she physically couldn't any longer. I needed to channel her strength and determination.

There had to be a way out.

I wasn't sure how long I'd been looking. Time moved weirdly, with no light to indicate its passing. I glanced down and saw blood trickling from under my feet. I was in worse shape than I realized, which meant I'd been exploring the cell for longer than I thought.

The ground began to tremble, and Elias whimpered, "It's time."

I opened my mouth to ask what he meant, but the entire cave shook around me, so hard that my ankle and feet gave out. I dropped hard on my butt and looked up just in time to realize that all my pain was about to be over.

I was going to die.

Chapter Eight

"Firellan's Spine?" I demanded. It was the smallest of the prisons but the most vicious, the one where they sent political dissidents, hardened criminals, and vicious traitors. The tortures and punishments they inflicted in that place—

I snapped my shadows back and released Deln. He dropped as low as he could in the seat, his limbs bruised and his fingers twitching as he spluttered. Blood dripped from his cheeks and covered his shirt.

Only a small measure of satisfaction pulsed within me to see it. Nothing would compare to when Briar was back in my arms and the true murderers of my father were punished along with anyone who had dared to lay a hand on her. The chill that spread within me urged me to resolve this swiftly so that I could go to her.

"What do we do with him now?" Thalen asked, though his tone suggested he knew what would ultimately happen and simply wondered about the method. He dissolved the tiny wind blades and straightened, but his face had gone paler than usual, likely because he, too, knew what that prison meant.

My eyes narrowed at the gasping wretch. "One more question." I held up a finger as I stepped toward him. "Did you enjoy hurting Briar?"

His gaze lifted to mine, and his face twisted in response, blood trickling from his mouth as he whimpered. He wanted to lie. I could practically see the rusted gears of his mind spinning as he tried to come to an answer that would be true and yet not reveal this. But there was none. I let the silence sit, my shadows and wings bristling. His silence was as good as a confession.

My shadows shot out once more with only one internal command: tear. With stunning precision, they shot into him and pierced his heart and lungs. He convulsed and spasmed, blood spilling like water onto the stone.

My shadows drew back, but the hollowness in me remained. This wretch's death had done little to sate me. Urgency coiled tighter in my chest as I straightened my shoulders. "Deal with his body. Make sure no one finds him. We'll deal with the second one later, when his disappearance won't be as likely to be noticed."

Thalen swiped his hand through the air. The previously invisible circle around the chair and Deln flared into view, and then the lines binding it thickened. "I know nothing is going to keep you from going to Firellan's Spine, but as sure as the void is dark, you aren't going in there alone. The body won't go anywhere. We mask the door, and I go with you."

My chest tightened, a mixture of irritation and gratitude cutting through me. For all his goofiness and ridiculousness, Thalen was a relentless ally. "If you can keep up, fine. Not wasting time arguing with you." I strode toward the door, my boots splashing in the blood. The room spun for a moment, but there was no stopping what happened next.

Hold on, Briar, I'm coming for you.

Thalen followed half a step behind me. By taking the back halls in the palace, we avoided risking more delays. Most of the servants, attendants, and others who would be awake at this time were in other corridors. We moved toward the Receiving Hall, knowing that we needed to use the hallways to get to the prison fast. I couldn't show weakness until I returned, or I'd risk all the kingdoms learning of my dire situation.

We entered the Receiving Hall, a chamber where each kingdom's sigils glowed in the walls. The large shadow beast sigil set into the center of the floor was second in size only to the one in the throne room. Six tall, narrow stone arches stood at the back of the enormous room, each with a set of three marble stairs and a small platform leading up to it and flanked by the banners of the kingdom the archway allowed access to. A pair of Shadow guards stood on either side of each entrance, with a single messenger from each kingdom represented on the right. The guards stood at attention, postures rigid and halberds or spears clasped firmly in their right hands. The messengers were alert but more casual in their poses, at least until they noticed me.

Clad in dark gray robes with a multi-colored belt fastened at his waist, Buldan, the Shadow messenger on duty, stiffened. Panic flashed in his purple eyes, as if he thought he'd been caught failing in a task. His peaked cap almost slid off his slick, dark hair before he straightened his shoulders. He crossed to me, drove his arm across his chest, and bowed his head. "Your Highness, the traditional notices have already been sent, but the leaders have not had time to organize their response beyond the initial extension of regrets."

I brushed that aside, not caring about the gifts or words the other leaders would send. "Hold your station, Buldan. That's not why I'm here. Stay alert." I spoke harshly, with no hint of weakness.

They all stared at me, the guards still at attention but waiting for any command I might utter. The Ignis messenger looked as if she were considering saying something, and the

Aquen messenger's brow furrowed before he schooled his expression into neutrality like the Sylvan and Terran faes. The Aureline messenger, a young woman I did not recall seeing before, studied me with sharp yet hooded slate eyes, her arms clasped at the back of her pale gray robe.

My footsteps echoed in the hall as I strode toward her. She stepped to the bottom of the three stairs that led up to her archway.

She bowed her head with deliberate slowness, her long hazel braid sliding over her shoulder with the movement. "Your Highness, how may the Aureline serve you?" When she straightened, she folded her hands before her, her fingers in perfect alignment.

Did this woman know the truth of what her people had done? No guilt shone in her eyes, and the deliberate slowness of her movements might simply be from anxiety in trying to perform to perfection. "I have business to conduct in Firellan's Spine," I said firmly.

Thalen stopped to the right of me, one hand resting on the dagger at his side.

The messenger hesitated for a breath, then bowed at the waist. "Of course. We are eager to serve. May I inquire what business this might be?"

"You may not. Either grant me access, or provide a reason that it cannot be done." My wings twitched, and I suppressed the urge to growl. Glaring would have to suffice. Now that I was out here again, I had to project the same controlled but stern demeanor that was essential.

Her fingers curled into her palms before she nodded and stepped back. She turned to the archway and approached it. Though I couldn't see anything through the archway beyond the shimmering light that gave the space between an effect similar to frosted glass, she could hear whoever was on the other side. They spoke in hushed tones for a moment before she pressed her fingertips to the right side of the archway and drew a runic pattern. The archway shimmered, and she stepped away.

I turned to look at my own guards and the other messengers who were present. "If I have not returned within two hours' time from the perspective of this hall, follow inquiry and retrieval protocols."

Time sometimes passed at different rates in these places. Prisons often had distortions, which made it easier for them to torture prisoners and keep them unbalanced. But if the Aurelines tried to pull any dirty tricks on me, they'd have to deal with my people making matters far worse for them.

Passing through the archway was as simple as passing through any doorway except for the slight rushing sensation that made my stomach spin and my knees wobble for half a step. The brightness surrounded me, harder to see through than the darkness, and when I emerged and blinked it away, I found myself in the cold, dark halls of Firellan's Spine.

My boots scraped uncomfortably against the coarse, dark floor, and a horrid stench of decomposing plant matter, old blood, fresh blood, and spoiled food surrounded me. Low screams and throaty cries cut through my ears, searing into my soul. I wanted to vomit, and bile crept up my throat. None of those voices was Briar's, thank whatever sliver of mercy Fate had for that. But what soured my stomach even more was that Briar was here, and I had no way of knowing how long it had been from her perspective, if they had altered her awareness of time.

Thalen braced his hands on his waist. His white wings spread out as if searching for any hint of danger or of Briar.

Two Aureline guards stood at attention on either side of the archway, their pale gray armor glistening in the low torchlight.

They stared straight ahead without acknowledging me, but a slim man whom I had almost missed in the shadows stepped forward. He bowed his head. "Your Highness, how may I be of service?"

"I wish to speak with Chief Interrogator Colm Ainle regarding the prisoner Briar in the matter of my father's assassination." I fixed the smaller male with a sharp gaze and gave a dismissive wave of my hand, not allowing him to ask further questions. Thalen stopped just behind me and folded his arms, his expression stoic.

The messenger opened his mouth to question me, but I glared at him and arched an eyebrow. He fell back, bowed, and then scuttled away. Within minutes, the soft, steady footsteps of another individual reached my ears. Colm, if I were to guess. He carried with him a particular stench that made my nostrils flare. As he rounded the corner, he at once inclined his head in the minimal showing of respect. Blood stained the coarse fabric of his gray robes. *Briar's blood.* I recognized her scent at once, the ginger and cinnamon notes especially strong in the murk of this place.

My insides lurched, and fire spiked within me. As my shadows tensed, I restrained them. Adrenaline pumped through my body, pushing away the physical fatigue left from the vesting ceremony.

Patience.

Calm.

I had to remain in control, evaluate the situation, and determine an appropriate response that would get Briar out of here without dooming her and plunging us into war. I resisted the urge to curl my hands into fists and kept my claws sheathed. It was getting harder now that my Shadow magic had intensified and my self-control had frayed, but for Briar, I could do this. There would be plenty of time for vengeance later.

Colm stopped before me, hands laced before himself. "Your Highness, what an unexpected surprise, especially after the events of this night. My sincere condolences for the untimely and vicious loss of your father. Is there some manner in which I may be of service?"

I met his gaze with the same iciness. "I have come to speak with the assassin." The words curdled on my tongue, sickening as I forced them out.

His brows rose sharply, and his eyes widened. "Your Highness, this is most unusual—"

"It is my right under the shared law to confront the alleged killer of my father." As I spoke, I took care to keep my words clipped and cold, not permitting any trace of passion to rise. Yet just saying them made me burn and ache with the need to destroy those who had dared take Briar from me. This man almost assuredly had something to do with it and had harmed her. I'd heard rumors about him. Though he was one of the heads of the prison itself, he was also its primary interrogator and someone who enjoyed torture.

I couldn't wait to end him publicly and with Briar's help.

Men like him made my skin crawl, and my claws itched to rip out his throat as much as my shadows longed to tear him apart. Thalen shifted his weight back, and though he remained as stoic as Silus in this moment, I knew he felt the same way.

Colm inclined his head once more, and he forced a far too thin smile. "Of course, though one might wonder how it is that you believed it was appropriate to come here."

"Was her location supposed to be a secret?" I feigned ignorance. "Curious. Regardless of whatever lapses there are in your customs, I am here now. It is my right to see her. I know she is here. I smell her blood on you."

His jaw clicked as he clenched his teeth. The flash of a grimace vanished in an instant. I could tell he was weighing the risks of lies and refusal, and though my guts churned and every feeling part of me screamed against it, I had to play the part of the cold Shadow ruler to perfection.

I canted my head, looked him in the eye unblinking, and allowed my wings to flex. "I am certain you have done your due diligence in extracting answers from her recalcitrant little mouth." Each word was bitter, a poison within my soul. I wanted to vomit, and the acid that burned along the back of my throat made it all the worse. But I would lie, cheat, murder, and steal to get her back. "I've heard praise of your work and skill over the years. I am certain it was well earned."

"It is my art form," he said with another shallow nod. His gaze flicked over me, narrowing as he considered this, likely gauging my sincerity. "There is great joy in convincing a wretch to speak truly. Especially in the pursuit of justice."

"Yes." I offered a cold, flat smile. "Retributive justice is rewarding in its own right, and I wish to speak with the one who killed my father." Those words were the foulest I had ever spoken, and my blood thundered in my ears simply from saying them.

Colm frowned even more. He pressed his palms together and let his metal ring claws touch one another. "Your Highness, allow me to be blunt. I am surprised to see you here. If I understand the situation, you actually preferred this bride to any of the others. Surely being here causes you great distress. Do you hope to reconcile with her?"

I scoffed and set my hands on my belt as I curled my upper lip. "My mother was murdered by outsiders. My father as well. What tolerance do you expect me to have? All I have asked of Fate is a strong bride. You can ask any of my advisors."

Thalen spoke up from behind me. "He's said it many times with great fervor and sincerity."

"Still ..." Colm tapped his claws against one another. "I

cannot recommend that you speak with this wanton wretch."

"Why? I intend to look her in the eyes and demand answers. If anything, I would like her brought back to the Shadow dungeons so my own people may participate in her punishment." Oh, how I wanted to seize this man by the throat and beat him within an inch of his life. Then I'd let Briar finish him off, if she wanted to, or allow her the pleasure of watching me do it. The only thing close to satisfying now was setting him up for his doom. Whatever made my queen happy and soothed the injustices and harms. "Justice must be served, and sooner rather than later."

The four lines on Colm's brow deepened. He pressed his palms tighter against one another. "Your Highness, we have not yet extracted a confession. We do not yet know if she had accomplices, though I am certain she did, or whether there were plans beyond this assassination."

"Trivialities." I arched my eyebrow and fixed him with a steely gaze as my murderous desire rose. "I presume you are aware of my people's traditions with regard to justice. Surely you do not intend to deprive my people of this? I am aware that the Aureline Council oversees the bridal competition and, as such, is claiming priority in the investigation, but I must insist that the Shadow Kingdom also have its due. My people must see justice done."

"But of course, *Your Highness*." The ice in his tone became more apparent, and his unusual emphasis on my title hinted at his suspicion that I had been made king. Most likely, he had picked up on the strengthening of my power. "These matters cannot be rushed." He gestured for me to follow him and signaled to the guards at the end of the hall. They vanished with the heavy click of armored boots on rough rock. "I do not think it wise to transfer her back to the Shadow Kingdom until we have completed our interrogations. Given all that must be done, I assume you would rather direct your attention elsewhere. After all, you must choose your bride, prepare for your coronation, and mend your kingdom."

I had to walk a careful line here, as did he. The Aurelines had no king and were ruled by their council. Colm assuredly had influence among them, and I had to play this horrific game. "I appreciate your counsel, Chief Interrogator. But surely you can understand my position. I do not want to take a queen or be coronated while the assassin draws breath. My kingdom requires closure. My father's blood cries out for vengeance from beyond the grave."

"You intend to execute her before the coronation?" His lips pressed into a tight line.

"Is there a reason it should not be so?" I demanded. "Some have even suggested forcing her to compete in the final trial to allow Fate to decide how she dies." I wanted to wash my mouth out from the sour taste that filled it from speaking of Briar so vilely.

Thalen tucked his wings down as he passed beneath a particularly low stalactite. "I fancy that option, personally. Let Fate end her. Fate loves dramatic ends. We could even allow the entire kingdom to watch."

"They do say that Fate will strike down any who participates in a trial after harming the royal family of the one whom the bride was to wed," Colm said slowly. "But there are risks."

"It does not need to be determined now, but I will expect an answer soon. For now, I wish to look into the eyes of the one who killed my father and demand my own answers. I will speak with you afterward when I am ready to finalize my requests." That was the closest I could bring myself to a compromise, and my mind was already spinning with how I could get Briar out of this place. The rough stone hall we walked down stretched on and on in an endless nightmare of side halls, every step punctuated by piercing wails and mournful groans.

Colm's stride was unhurried, as if he had all the time in the world and relished making us walk through every tormenting moment, watching and testing for weakness while letting us see what a labyrinth this place was, despite allegedly being one of the smaller prisons. Aside from the tension in Thalen's jaw and shoulders, he maneuvered his way through as if this were a walk in a willow-ringed meadow at night.

We entered a broad room with a single door, every wall inside slick with something that looked faintly like old blood but stank of mold and rust. A single plank table and four chairs sat in the back, along with an oil lamp, some parchment, an inkwell, and a quill. A few small knick-knacks adorned the shelves, along with some stout jars filled with viscous potions. As far as meeting places went, this was drab and unpleasant and clearly intended to discourage lingering.

Colm stopped in front of the table and gestured to the chairs. "I can send for refreshments if you wish, but we were not anticipating guests at this hour."

"No refreshments will be necessary. All I require is to speak with that woman."

Another nod, and he stepped back. "Of course." He left the room.

My heart tightened within my chest as my energy coiled deeper. *Lash out. Strike him. Break his neck. Rend his bones.*

No. No. Calm. Patience. Play the game. Set up every piece to prepare for the final takedown.

I set my jaw as I heard the soft shuffle of footsteps and the heavier tramp of boots. But it was that familiar tug in the center of my chest that told me everything I needed to know.

CHAPTER NINE

A stalactite right above me cracked and dropped, barreling toward my head.

My wolf surged forward, taking control and rolling my body to the right. My side and achy knees hit coarse stone and blinded me with pain. I yelped and flinched, waiting for the agony.

A *crash* sounded to my left, and the ground shook underneath me as I landed hard on my butt. Wet pieces of stone hit my face and arms, stinging worse than a bee ever could, and then there was silence.

I sat, stunned, adrenaline edging out most of the pain. But when warm liquid oozed down my face and cheeks, I came back to reality.

I was bleeding.

The room spun, and my lungs screamed. I inhaled choppily, desperate for oxygen, and blinked. Fresh tears streamed down my dirty face, no doubt mixing with the blood and dirt.

Even being kidnapped on Earth seemed like a luxury stay compared to this.

Elias hadn't exaggerated about keeping track of time. It was impossible here, and I hadn't even been subjected to the horrible torture chamber he'd described.

I could have been here for mere hours, days, or even weeks. I had no way to gauge it, but I had to hold on and wait for Ember and my pack to find me.

A grinding noise made me freeze. My gaze shot up as the heavy metal door above me scraped open. Desperately, I wiped my tears from my face and jumped to my throbbing feet, refusing to let the guards know I'd been crying.

Light flooded in, and my wolf surged forward. The sudden hit of light after being in the dark for who knew how long caught me off guard, and I stumbled back down to my knees.

Heavy footsteps approached the edge of the hole, and two guards without masks under their helmets appeared. The closest was a square-jawed man with a scar over his left eyebrow. He barked, "Stand back."

I straightened, trying like hell to ignore the sharp ripping sensation of skin and bone peeling apart in my feet and stand as confidently as possible.

The one who'd spoken held a thick rope coiled in one hand and tossed one end down to the floor, where it landed in the center of a puddle with a wet *slap*.

He smirked and looked at me in a way that made me uncertain if his dick or the rope held his attention. "Grab hold," he commanded, and chuckled low in his throat as he glanced at his friend.

Of course, they'd be like this. The small-dick energy in the cave was damn near suffocating. "I'm'a pass. I'll just stay right here." And I meant every word. I'd rather stay in this pit than touch or do anything they wanted me to. I wouldn't give up and begin obeying.

Fuck that.

And *fuck* this place.

"I'm fine if you want to be difficult." Scar Eye winked.

The torchlight caught on the jagged blue-purple scar over his eyebrow. It dipped down to his eyelid. "You being obedient or as unpredictable as a phoenix will bring me joy in different ways."

His innuendos were purposeful, and I realized that, even here, men were sexist.

Maybe some would find that familiarity comforting, but not me.

My wolf snarled in my head, and her hackles rose. "Haven't you heard? If you push me too far, I bite." I'd done that to Kaylen during the first trial after she'd stabbed Arielle, the first friend I'd made here and someone I'd wanted to protect, in the back. I'd been in wolf form, and I hadn't hesitated to bite the bitch. I wasn't above doing it here and now.

I might be their prisoner, but I'd make sure they suffered along with me.

"These ropes contain magical bindings. Are you certain you want to do this the hard way?" The second guard leaned back and sighed. He was heavier set, with craggy wrinkle lines around his dull blue eyes and over his brow. Leaning forward, he rested his gloved hands on his belt. Both Crag Face and Scar Eye had a red mark on the cuff of their right glove. It looked like a chalice. "All you're doing is encouraging him."

That settled hard into my bones. I didn't want to *encourage* him, but he'd made it clear that being obedient would have the same effect. Maybe I could give him a taste of medicine he'd never had before.

I forced my bottom lip to quiver, despite my wolf snarling at the weakness I was showing. At the end of the day, night, or whatever the hell the time was, I was at their mercy. If they wanted to play games with me, I'd return the favor.

"This is your last chance to take the rope of your own volition." Scar Eye jerked the rope, making it *slap* again.

Water hit my face, and I clenched my hands, causing the

blood to ooze even faster. I might not be able to kill him, but I would get some revenge.

"You're just taking me somewhere to torture me more. Why should I willingly hand myself over to you?" I could guess that they'd be taking me to the Whispering Veins.

"We're going to have someone tend to your wounds." Crag Face sounded gruffer than before. "There's too much for us to look forward to, so we can't have you getting sick and dying too fast."

There was no stench of a lie, and my stomach soured even more. They wanted to heal me so they could hurt me all over again.

The fae were savage.

Ever since I'd been kidnapped, I'd witnessed the fae hurting each other and killing anyone they deemed a threat or competition.

Earth didn't seem quite as cruel anymore. Sure, we had some people like that, but the majority were decent. Here, most of the fae seemed to be vicious ... at least, many of the ones I'd been around were.

I glanced over my shoulder at Elias's crack in the wall. He'd gone silent.

My heartbeat quickened a little. The guards expected me to be too injured to do any harm. Maybe this could be my opportunity to escape? If my wolf helped me, maybe I could break free and hide until Many-Greats-Grandfather located me again.

I stepped forward, and agony ripped through my feet and legs. I didn't hold back my wince as I slowly moved toward the rope.

"Good girl," Scar Eye sneered. "Be careful, but hurry. I don't want to miss mealtime."

Just mealtime. No other term.

They must be doing that on purpose so we'd have no concept of time. Assholes.

Hoping I could make him late, I didn't pick up my pace. Instead, I let out all my grunts of pain, which echoed and mixed with the drips of water.

Both guards crossed their arms, and Scar Eye smirked. Crag Face huffed.

My blood boiled, and my wolf snarled low and threatening. I gritted my teeth, trying to keep myself under control.

I'd make them both pay.

But not *yet*. The timing had to be perfect.

As soon as I reached the wet rope, the first guard whipped it into the water again. It splashed me all over, but my body was already freezing and covered in water, so it didn't make a difference.

Still, the rudeness alone had me itching to fight them now.

No. I had to be smart. If I acted too soon, I wouldn't have a chance in hell.

"Grab the fecking rope," Crag Face snarled, seeming unamused by the first guard's antics. He shot the other fae an annoyed look, his wrinkles deepening with his scowl.

This time, I eagerly grabbed the rope and swallowed my whimper as my raw flesh burned. Blood slicked my hands on the already wet rope, and I couldn't get a firm grip. I was about to wrap it around my wrists instead, but Scar Eye jerked the rope upward.

The rope sliced through my already raw skin, and I whimpered. Everything in me screamed for me to release it, but then I'd have to start the entire process over.

I wrapped my legs around the rope to prevent myself from slipping further. My eyes burned from unshed tears, but I blinked them back, needing my vision to be clear.

As soon as I cleared the top, rough hands seized my arms

so hard I'd have bruises. The two guards dragged me across the stone floor, my already raw feet feeling as if the rest of my skin was being raked off like cheese against a grater.

"I can walk," I said sternly.

"Shut up," Crag Face growled and yanked harder.

But Scar Eye threw his free hand in front of the second guard, causing him to halt.

"If she wants to walk, we should let her. If she can't keep up, we can use the rope as a whip until she goes fast enough."

Crag Face grunted. "You're wasting time. We have our orders."

"She's going to the doctor. She'll be fine. They won't ever know." Scar Eye smiled widely.

Though it was the last thing I wanted to do, I let out a yelp as I climbed to my feet, hoping they wouldn't see me as threatening at all.

"Fine. But we can't take forever."

"I agree." Scar Eye spun and rolled up the rope, leaving the end piece out so he could smack me.

I whimpered, and the first guard jerked the rope so it would hit me on the side.

This might be my only chance. My heart raced as my wolf pushed ahead, lending me her strength. I caught the rope and, despite feeling as if my hand were about to be ripped in two, yanked back.

Scar Eye's eyes widened as he fell forward. Crag Face ran the five feet between us and grabbed my wrist. I dropped the rope as he jerked me toward his body, and I opened my mouth on instinct. I didn't have time to shift, but that didn't mean I couldn't bite. His eyes widened, and he started to reach for his dagger.

I opened my mouth wide and sank my teeth into his nose. His sickly sweet blood filled my mouth, making me want to gag, but I held on tight.

He grunted as my teeth sank even deeper. Something struck the bottom of my chin, causing my jaws to clench harder, allowing my teeth to cut entirely through the cartilage. His other hand fisted the hair on the back of my head and yanked me backward, and I spat his nose and blood from my mouth.

I tried to grab his shoulders but snagged his arms instead. Blood made his already slick metal armor impossible to hold on to, and I slid backward until my butt hit the ground. My shoulders and head followed, banging the floor. My ears rang, and the world spun so hard that I couldn't tell which way was up.

A glint of metal caught my attention before something rammed into my ribs. I yelped, unable to stop myself from crying out as pain blinded me and my lungs stopped working. I turned onto my side, not wanting him to hit me again.

"You stupid fecking bitch," Crag Face bellowed and kicked at me once more. I winced, expecting the same radiating pain, but it fell short. It hurt, but nothing like my side.

Bile inched up my throat, and I couldn't fill my lungs.

"Get off me!" Crag Face yelled thunderously. "The bitch has to die."

"Stop." Scar Eye's cocky demeanor had vanished, and panic made his voice shrill. "Master Ainle wants her in the best health possible for the Whispering Veins. Even though she deserves it, think about what could happen to *us*."

"She bit off my *nose*," Crag Face gritted out. "She has to pay!"

"Then we'll have to pay for not obeying Master Ainle. Think about your family. His punishments won't stop with just us."

A sour taste filled my mouth, and my lungs burned. Even the guards feared Colm Ainle. Lovely.

"Fine," Crag Face snarled. "Tie her up again. The wench can't be trusted."

"Now *that* I agree with," the first guard replied, and strong arms pushed me forward.

I choked as my front was pressed into the floor. A foot stepped on my back, and I wanted to buck it off, but I couldn't move. Everything hurt, and I was too dizzy to get a sense of where everyone was.

My ribs ached, and the edges of my vision darkened as the guard continued to put pressure on me and tied my hands behind my back. Just when I thought I might die that way, my body was jerked upward by the rope.

The world swirled, but I managed to see blood running down Crag Face's hand as he clutched where his nose had once been. Warm liquid dripped from him onto my chest.

I swayed, and my knees buckled.

"We don't have time for this." Scar Eye hoisted me over his shoulders like a sack of potatoes, my lower ribs balancing on his shoulder. It was enough to keep additional pressure on my lungs and make the blood rush to my head even faster.

"I'll follow you and make sure she doesn't try something else," Crag Face rasped.

They hauled me through twisting corridors, my head spinning with pain and my ears ringing louder than ever before, blood dripping from my chin and toward my forehead and hair. And my lungs still weren't working. Black dots darted through my vision as I took in ragged gasps that felt like they didn't contain any oxygen.

Finally, they shoved me through a wooden door into a small room with a finished stone floor. The sharp scents of herbs and alcohol stung my nostrils.

A thin fae woman with ashen skin and hollow eyes stood beside a stone table. She wore a plain gray smock, and her hands were stained with what looked like traces of blood and dirt. She must be the doctor, or the equivalent in this place.

"Put her there," she instructed, pointing, her voice flat.

The guards heaved me into a sitting position on the table with more force than necessary. My hip banged against the stone, sending fresh jolts of pain through my already tortured body. I bit back a cry, determined not to give them the satisfaction.

"Leave us," the doctor said, not bothering to look at the guards.

"Orders are to stay," Scar Eye grunted. "This one's the king killer. Not that she's confessed yet."

I despised these people and everything they stood for. The corruption here was just as bad as, if not worse than, it was on Earth. These people were desperate for me to be their scapegoat. I opened my mouth to pop off a retort, but I didn't have enough oxygen to even whisper.

"You think I don't know that?" the doctor snapped. She clicked her tongue as she rolled her eyes. "You think Master Ainle hasn't been excruciatingly clear about how she is to be prepared? She's got to be in better than decent health if she's going into the Whispering Veins, especially if he wants her in there in the next hour."

The next *hour*? No. Fate was a scaffing bitch. I struggled to control my breathing as my chest tightened.

"And I need aid as well." Crag Face stood on the other side of me.

"You'll have to wait until after *her*." The doctor exhaled loudly. "Orders were given, and *she* is the *priority*. I won't have Master Ainle coming down on me. You won't bleed out in the next half hour, so grab a towel and call in a replacement."

Scar Eye scoffed as he folded his thick arms over his broad chest. "Just get it done."

Elias's warnings clawed back into my mind—silence so profound you could hear your own blood pumping, darkness so complete even shadow sight failed, void vermin that attacked without warning. My hands trembled ... or at least I thought they did. Who knew at this point?

I wouldn't let them see my terror.

I flattened my palms against the stone and forced myself to take a slow breath. Then I scanned the room for anything I could use. It was a simple space, with numerous cupboards and counters filling most of the walls. Medical supplies lined the shelves—jars of herbs, rolls of bandages, and cups of tools. Probably scalpels in the one clay cup on the second shelf over the nearest counter. If I could reach one of those scalpels, or even just that jar ...

I had to try to escape. It might be my only way to get out with my sanity.

The guards positioned themselves between me and the door, their eyes tracking my every movement. Crag Eyes now had a towel pressed against the wound on his face, and he stared at me with so much hatred that I shivered. Scar Eye went to the door and bellowed for another guard to come at once.

The doctor stood in front of me, blocking my view of most of the supplies. Even if I managed to grab something, I'd be stopped in seconds.

"Don't even think about it." The doctor put a finger into my face and narrowed her eyes. "You try escaping or even fighting, and I'll carve a pain sigil on you that'll keep you writhing till dawn." She scoffed and turned away, then rummaged through the supplies on the counter nearest the table, muttering under her breath. When she turned back, she held a clay jar full of a murky brown liquid that smelled like rotting vegetation, vinegar, and spoiled meat. My stomach churned.

"Drink this," she commanded, thrusting it toward my face.

"All of it."

I hesitated, eyeing the viscous fluid. Tiny black specks that looked like dead gnats were floating in it.

"It prevents infection," she said flatly. "Makes you more resistant to the elements. Doesn't do much for the pain, but it'll help you live to see a few more weeks. No bad side effects other than the taste. Can't say the same for the tortures Ainle has lined up for you."

The guards chuckled.

I took the jar with shaking hands. There was no scent of sulfur to reveal the doctor was lying. Small comfort. *Fuck them all.* I hated them. If I could, I'd rip them apart.

I raised the jar to my lips, my breath steadying a little. The first sip hit my tongue, and bitter and slimy liquid swiftly filled my mouth.

My throat convulsed as I fought against my body's natural instinct to reject the foul concoction.

"All of it," the doctor repeated, her eyes cold and unblinking.

Each swallow was worse than the last. The liquid crawled down my throat, coating it with a film that made me want to claw at my neck. My stomach lurched. Breathing through my nose, I willed myself not to vomit.

"Keep drinking," Scar Eye barked, taking a threatening step forward.

I glared at him over the rim of the jar and forced down another mouthful. My eyes watered as the sludge hit my empty stomach like a stone. The last few swallows were pure torture, each one bringing me closer to retching. When I'd finally drained the jar, I had to press my fist against my mouth to keep from spewing it all back up. Tears sprang to my eyes, but I refused to let them fall.

The doctor snatched the jar from my hands with a sneer. "At least you can follow simple instructions." She turned away, set the jar down with a sharp clack, and reached for another container on the shelf. She returned with a shallow jar filled with a pale green paste that smelled of mint and something sharper, more medicinal. Grunting, she grabbed one of my ankles and yanked my foot up. The sudden movement sent pain shooting up my leg, and I bit my lip to keep from crying out.

"Hold still," she muttered as she began slathering the salve onto my raw, bleeding foot.

The paste burned like fire at first contact, and I couldn't stop the hiss that escaped my clenched teeth. My wolf snarled, wanting to rip the woman's arm off, but I forced myself to remain still. The burning sensation gradually gave way to an odd numbness that spread from my soles up through my ankles.

"What is that?" I rasped.

"Something to keep you from bleeding out before they're done with you," she replied without looking up. Her fingers dug in, pressing the salve deep into my wounds. "Can't have you getting infected before you make your confession. 'Specially not if you're going into the Whispering Veins. Might even heal you for good if you have enough magic in your veins. Healthier you are going into the Whispering Veins, better the torture. Not as much to focus on aside from the looming madness and silence, until suddenly there's too much."

The doctor continued methodically treating my wounds, applying the burning paste to the cuts on my legs, hands, arms, and chin with the same clinical detachment.

"Stop flinching," she snapped when I jerked away from her touch on a particularly raw scrape along my forearm. "The more you move, the longer this takes. And my time is valuable."

She grabbed my chin roughly and turned my face to examine the cut at the corner of my mouth where Douchewaffle had dug in his claw. Her fingers pressed painfully against my bruised jaw as she dabbed the paste onto the wound. Healing always hurt, but this woman seemed to delight in her painful efficiency and offered no comfort. Not that she would to me.

Finally finished, the doctor moved away to replace her supplies. I rubbed my arm, my thumb pressing against one of the bruises. It still ached, but it no longer felt quite so fresh. Somehow, that vile concoction had settled, and my feet no longer burned as much. Small improvements. I cast another look around the room, hoping to spot some tool I could reach without the guards spotting me. There was nothing within arm's reach.

Another guard entered. He had narrow gray eyes and a large reddish nose that had obviously been broken several times. A clawed vine tattoo curled beneath his chin and straggled down his throat into his armor. He jerked his chin toward the doorway, and Crag Face strode out, still pressing the towel to his nose.

Claw Tattoo had a dull orange mark on his gloves that resembled a mirror. He took up a position near Scar Eye, and the two whispered briefly. Claw Tattoo raised an eyebrow at something Scar Eye said, then muttered something that made Scar Eye grunt. How articulate.

Another ten or fifteen minutes passed, uncomfortable and unpleasant. The doctor wiped her hands on a stained cloth and stepped back. "Done. She'll live long enough for whatever Master Ainle has planned, and a fair bit longer than she'll want." She turned away as if I were nothing more than a broken piece of furniture she'd glued together.

"Time to go," Scar Eye growled, reaching for my arm.

I jerked back, then gripped my stomach. "Wait," I blurted. "I feel sick. That medicine ..." I clutched my stomach, doubling over. "I think I'm going to—"

"Save it," Claw Tattoo snapped, grabbing my other arm. "Master Ainle doesn't like to be kept waiting, and you deserve everything you get after what you did."

My wolf surged forward, desperate and snarling, as they hauled me off the table. My feet hit the floor, and though the salve had numbed the worst of the pain, I still staggered.

The door burst open with a bang that made us all jump. A thin fae with disheveled hair and wild eyes stood in the doorway. His chest heaved, and he was pale, as if he'd seen some indescribable horror. "Oh, thank Fate. I feared you'd already taken her. Master Ainle demands to see the prisoner immediately in the receiving room. Do not delay. And put on your masks."

Scar Eye scoffed. "Fine." Both guards put the dark masks on over their faces and seized my arms, their fingers digging into my flesh as they hauled me out of the room. My feet skidded against the stone floor, the numbness from the salve making it impossible to gain proper footing.

"Move faster," Scar Eye snarled, yanking me forward.

"I would if I could feel my feet," I snapped back.

Claw Tattoo struck me across the back of the head. Stars exploded in front of my eyes, and I staggered forward.

"What's this about?" Claw Tattoo grumbled. "We were supposed to take her straight to the Veins."

"Don't ask me. I know as much as you," Scar Eye replied. "But I'm not questioning Ainle's orders."

I struggled weakly against their grip, my mind racing. What did Douchewaffle want now? Another round of torture before the Whispering Veins? And why did they have to put their masks back on? My wolf paced anxiously within me, sensing something was different.

We turned down a corridor I hadn't seen before, wider and better lit than the others. The guards' boots echoed against the coarse stone, and my own feet made sick, slapping sounds as they dragged me along. The salve made my steps uncertain, and I skidded more than once, earning rough jerks from my captors.

They dragged me down another hall and shoved the door open.

"Get in there," Scar Eye growled, shoving me so hard I stumbled several steps into the room before catching myself. A sharp tug in my chest sent chills down my spine, and my stomach knotted. Even before I lifted my head, I knew who was there, and he wasn't here to help.

CHAPTER TEN

The tugging in my chest took control while desire and need soared through me. I wanted to run to the fecking door. My wings twitched, and my legs wanted to move, but I forced them to remain still. I inhaled, deep and slow, trying to settle myself as Briar drew near.

"She close?" Thalen murmured from beside me, tucking his wings tightly into his back and smirking.

I opened my mouth to respond, but the heavy wooden door swung open and banged against the coarse stone wall.

The dim oil lamp on the plank table rattled, and two masked guards entered, holding someone between them.

No. Not *someone*.

Briar.

Seeing the harm they'd done to her stabbed like a dagger into my heart.

Cuts, bruises, and scrapes marred nearly every inch of her pale, bare flesh. Dark circles had sunk under her wide jade eyes, making me desperate to let my shadows loose and shred her tormentors apart.

She had done *nothing* wrong. She was too good for this realm. Feck, she was too good for me. I didn't deserve her. But

Fate had marked her, brought her here to meet me, and I would never let her go.

A part of me had *known* they would torture her, but an even bigger part had hoped I was wrong. Seeing her in this condition gutted me.

The pungent odor of healing salve and the slick streaks on her arms and legs told me they had treated her, which meant her condition had likely been far worse than it was now. Mud and slime clung to her limbs and clothes. Her dress was ragged and stained, not a trace of white remaining, and there was a split in her chin as if she'd been hit. They'd bound her wrists together with rope, and I knew that made the way they were holding her arms especially uncomfortable.

Who had done this to her?

I would kill them all slowly and wretchedly, watching their magic drain into oblivion with a huge smile on my face.

My shadows flared out as if to separate her from the bastards restraining her, but I pulled them back and braced my stance. A few shadowy tendrils brushed her feet. It was the only way I could touch her and show some sort of affection.

Her legs shifted a little, like she'd felt it, but the guards held her still.

Never in my life had I understood how being within a few feet of someone could still feel like there was an entire realm between us. Knowing that I couldn't help Briar right now had my blood thawing and my rage pulsing.

Her shoulders tightened, and she drew back as if caught between alarm, confusion, and caution. The guards gripped her arms even more tightly, at awkward angles.

"Don't struggle," one of them snarled. "Or I'll draw the ropes so tight that they'll fracture your bones, and we'll hold you at the breaks."

My hands clenched at my sides. Thalen inched forward too,

his gaze cold and calculating as it was when he was preparing to eliminate threats.

Briar closed her eyes, and her face tensed for a second before she opened them and looked right at me.

A *zing* pulsed into me. My lungs froze, and my back straightened. My entire body burned with the need to crush her to me and shield her with my wings. I wanted to take her to safety, clean her in a warm tub, mend her wounds, then lie down beside her and kiss her lips softly while drinking in her ginger and cinnamon scent.

But no.

Despite being the Shadow King, I had to stand here like some daft fool, playing politics and setting the pieces of her eventual rescue in motion while she wavered before me, barely able to stand. I narrowed my eyes and examined her, wanting to document every mark, bruise, and injury that had been inflicted upon her by *them*.

A fire beast mark marred her cheek, along with a small half-imprint of what looked like a chalice.

Insignia markings.

Someone had struck her in the face, and they had not held back, given the blows had left such deep imprints. The red of the cut in her chin was darker than some of the others, suggesting that it had happened recently.

All those who had harmed her and killed my father would be served a death ten times worse than what they'd inflicted. I'd cut them to pieces and let the life drain from them as my queen watched. She could join me in their execution if she liked. The one who'd marked her face would be left for the end, to show everyone what happened when they touch my beloved.

The stench of this place filled my nostrils, and the hollow ache within my chest expanded.

Colm appeared, stepping forward with his arms clasped

behind his back, and barked out, "What are you doing here, Selvan? You and Oathfeln weren't paired for duty. There are protocols to be followed." The claws on his fingertips twitched.

The guard with the dull orange marker on his glove bowed but still held Briar tight, his metal fingers digging into her flesh. He shook her. "This one bit Elr's nose off. He needed treatment."

Pride flared through me as I fought to keep the corners of my lips from lifting. That was my Briar. Not backing down even in a void-cursed place like this. She had the spirit of a shadow beast. But what would they do to her? Men like Colm didn't like to be shown up, and these guards needed little reason to be cruel.

A chill cut through me as I realized that, if Briar had bitten through the guard's nose, he hadn't been wearing his mask. And if he wasn't wearing his mask, it meant either her guards had become exceptionally sloppy in their protocols, or they believed she would die before leaving the prison.

A muscle in my jaw jumped as I ground my teeth. I would make this work. I was already searching for the solution. Everyone had a weakness, including Colm.

Thalen shifted beside me. Though I did not look at him, I had no doubt he had the same concern.

Colm's breath hissed through his teeth. "A wretched little human bit off Elr's nose?" He shook his head. "I am disappointed that he was so lax that he permitted that to happen. His punishment will be swift and severe."

Briar's upper lip curled with contempt, and her hands remained balled into fists, fingers pressed over slick red cuts that were probably not bleeding because of the salve.

Colm faced me and canted his head. His murky eyes glinted as he offered a faint smile. "Perhaps Your Highness would like to see how we handle a prisoner's insolence?"

My shadows stretched farther along the mottled walls,

aching and thrumming within me as the flame of the oil lamp sputtered and hissed. Beating this man's face in and shattering every bone in his body would send us hurtling into open war with the other kingdoms. I was okay with that if I could get Briar out safely, but this wasn't my kingdom. I didn't have the manpower to do it, but I'd be fecking damned if I was going to stand by and actually *watch* them torture my beloved.

I narrowed my eyes and sneered. "Do you think I care that a prisoner harmed one of your guards? If he was so careless as to allow a wounded and smaller female to get the upper hand, he was being more than a little careless and deserved it. This is so disappointing. I thought you only employed the best."

"Perhaps ..." Colm's brow furrowed. "But such conduct cannot go unpunished on either side."

I took two steps closer to him. "Are you saying that the nose of one of your careless guards is more important than the business of the royal Shadow Fae?"

Colm straightened his shoulders. "Not at all, Your Highness, but—"

I pointed at her with a sharp gesture. "Do you understand how this impacts justice? She looks like a wreck, all banged up, bruised, and bloodied. If she is to stand before my people and my people are to have justice, then she cannot be harmed further. She must be whole and relatively well for the suffering and punishment to show its full effect. The assassin of a king must suffer publicly, and the punishment must be brutal, clear, and slow in its execution. I am here to determine which punishment is most fitting and to look into the eyes of the one who destroyed my father." My right hand curled, the claws pricking the inside of my palm as I stared into his eyes. The claws of my left hand dug into my thigh as I fought to stay calm. I hated how this must sound to Briar, but if I wanted Colm to believe me, Briar had to remain clueless.

Colm sized me up with a sharp gaze, then straightened his shoulders and pressed his palms together. "I see."

His expression did not suggest he agreed, and I knew I had to walk a fine line if I was going to convince him. Suspicion was standard, and he wasn't convinced that I hated her.

Refusing to look away, I gave a curt nod. "Good. Now, I would speak with this woman in private." I braced my hands against my belt and stared at him unblinking.

"Don't fret. I'll be here with him." Thalen crossed his arms.

Colm's expression remained as guarded as before. He looked between Briar and me, his dull green eyes hard as granite and his ornamental claws pressed point for point against one another. His throat bobbed, and a fleeting image of me snapping his neck with my shadows emerged in my thoughts.

Eagerness to do that settled hard over me.

Patience. Not just yet. You have to play this with care.

The tension in his body was the only real indicator of his strain. He pressed his palms more tightly together. "Your Highness, please forgive me, but I cannot permit the request. The wretch has yet to confess how she managed to accomplish the assassination, and though we have taken every precaution, I cannot, in good conscience, permit you to be left alone with her, even with a member of your own guard."

Huffing, Thalen chuckled. "Even with just one guard, I guarantee you that when we leave, there will be no missing extremities. Not so much as an ear or a fingertip."

Scowling, Colm lifted his chin. "This is the first time anything like that has ever happened. There is no need for concern. It won't happen again. Nonetheless, with no confession, I can't allow a private conversation."

I wanted to choke him. To rip each claw ring off his hand and impale them in his fingertips, but I gritted my teeth instead. They'd probably have a way to listen to our conversation regardless, though I'd have happily risked it. I couldn't stand the hostile eyes on Briar. I wanted to sweep her close, brush the matted hair from her face, and whisper vows of vengeance and devotion. For now, I had to hope that she would understand the truth that lurked beneath the surface and that we all had a role to play.

I inclined my head at Colm's words, pretending to consider them. "Very well. I suppose it makes little difference in the end." I turned my attention to Briar.

The oil lamp flickered, and the foul air in the room pressed far too close. She met my gaze with a mix of defiance and fear. If she knew I was bluffing, she gave no sign. In truth, she likely believed I did hate her. My shadow stroked her ankle beneath the hem of her stained skirt, and she shivered.

My heart shattered into even smaller pieces. *It wasn't your fault. I know it wasn't you. I'm going to save you.*

If only she could hear my thoughts. All the things I longed to tell her.

Wishing was for fools.

I had never dreamed of finding someone whom I would love, let alone someone my sister and father both approved of as well. And these bastards had stolen her from me.

With every ounce of self-control, I hardened my voice. "Speak, woman, and tell me what happened."

She looked down her nose, and her lips trembled. Her copper hair was all tangled, plastered and matted to her skull. "I did not kill him. I went to Rhielle's room because I saw the door was open, and then someone attacked me—"

"Lies," Colm growled. Venom dripped from that single word as he stepped closer to her.

Her teeth bared as she shook her head. She fixed him with a gaze so murderous I knew she'd bite off his nose if she had the chance. "*You're* the one who's lying."

"She is a liar," Colm continued. "You should not trust a word she says. I have looked into her mind, and I have seen the truth."

I lifted one hand and kept my focus trained on her. When I spoke, my voice was hard as steel. "I want to hear *her* words on this matter. Even if they are lies. Lies abound in this place."

"What would you expect in a prison of traitors?" Thalen asked with a cold smile.

Briar's face twisted, and her knuckles whitened as she curled her hands into fists. "I am not a liar or a traitor! I woke up next to the king. Some magic had been used to bind his dagger to my hand, but they had already stabbed him! I didn't know it was attached when I pulled my hand away. I tried to stop the bleeding. All he said was 'lilies.' That's all! Then the guards were there. I swear I didn't kill him. How could you think so little of me that you would believe I'd do this? It doesn't even make sense." Her gaze fell to Thalen. "Please. I've been framed. I didn't do this! I would never—I would never kill someone innocent."

Thalen kept his stance firm, his expression like ice. One wing twitched. "Justice will not be avoided. Whatever aid is due will be granted, and the guilty will suffer. Simple as that, Briar. Can't be any other way."

Her expression fell, and her gaze dropped. Only the slight increase in Thalen's wing twitching told me how much saying that had ripped him apart inside.

"A very clever lie." Colm sneered at her. "You don't see the king as innocent. After all, he was the ruler of the people who forcibly removed you from your home. While most would understand that Fate led you to take part in this competition as an example to the others, you are too small-minded and self-important to allow for such a thing."

"That's not true. I know it wasn't his choice. It's tradition—

and culture." Briar's voice hitched, and she turned her focus once more to me. "Please believe me. You know me. I would *never* have killed your father. Why would I kill him? He was so kind to me last night, and you heard what he said about me. And beyond that, I would never hurt him because I know how much he means to you. I'd never do anything to hurt you in any way or form. Please, believe me. I—I love you." Her words trembled in the air, and she looked at me as if the whole world might shatter if I didn't believe her.

I clenched my jaw and bit my tongue until I tasted blood to hold back the words I so desperately wanted to speak. My shadows flared against the wall, and the room's temperature dropped in response.

With great effort, I kept my gaze fixed upon her. "Do not say that again. For a declaration of love to be spoken in a place such as this is profane. For it to be said now ..." I forced out a sound as close to disgust as I could manage.

It was enough. I might as well have struck her or stabbed her myself as she blanched, and the light in her eyes flickered. A few tears leaked down her cheeks. "Is Rhielle all right?" she asked, her voice shaking.

"She is resting in the physician's care." I used the coldest tone I could manage. "I will be looking in on her shortly after I return."

"Your associates were unable to kill her," Colm said in that smug, icy tone.

"I didn't try to kill her, and I don't have any associates." She balled her fists.

"She breathes and rests now. I will go to see her after I leave here." And after I spoke with Elara.

"And he'll see Kaylen as well. Seems Fate has made quite a lot clear." Thalen lifted his shoulders in a cold shrug.

I barely suppressed a shudder of revulsion. He'd been right

to make that comment. If I wanted to sell this, I had to look as if I were open to Kaylen being my bride. "Yes. Quite clear."

Briar tensed and firmed her lips into a tight line. Her brow furrowed. She knew how I felt about Kaylen.

Colm *hmmm*ed as if considering my words.

I returned my focus to Briar. The look in her eyes was almost too much to bear. And I was about to make it worse. "Can you give me any explanation as to why you would kill my father?"

Her voice shook. "I didn't kill him." She emphasized each word.

Shaking my head, I scoffed and turned my gaze from her. "I don't have time for this."

"Take her away." Colm waved lazily.

The guard with the red marker cleared his throat. "Back to her cell or to the Whispering Veins?"

Briar stiffened. She struggled in the guards' grips, but they held her firmly in place.

My blood chilled. I knew that place. They were going to put *her* in *there*? I faced Colm more fully, hands braced at my belt and my eyebrow arched with all the imperious annoyance I could manage. I would not tolerate any further harm to her, mentally or physically. This ended now. "I am certain there has been a misunderstanding."

Colm's eyebrow lifted as well. If looks could kill, that guard would have been dead. "I do not see what has been misunderstood. She will not be further harmed physically. That is already quite the compromise."

"Was I not exceptionally clear that the assassin must stand before the Shadow Fae and give an account and be punished? The Whispering Veins drive people to babbling madness. There is no way to know when her mind will break. What good is her public punishment and execution if she is a babbling wretch who is unaware of the price she is paying?"

"I assure you that breaking her mind is in no one's interest. We simply seek to extract a confession." He spread his hands apart.

Unblinking, I spread out my wings. "I am not familiar with all of your methods, but let me be clear—anything that might result in death or insanity is too much. The Whispering Veins must not be utilized. In the interests of shared cooperation and justice, I forbid it."

I didn't dare look at her, but my mind spun. Would she forgive me for this? My stomach soured. I would get her out and make everyone feel my wrath. The innocent would feel the chill of my magic, and the ones I deemed guilty would die.

Thalen studied her with an uncharacteristic frown. The natural silver-white of his wings had taken on a muddier gold color at the tips as they reflected the dull torchlight. Our shadows stretched long against the walls, and mine ached all the more with the urge to tear Colm to pieces and fold Briar close. Playing this game was growing harder every moment, and time wasn't doing either of us favors. I needed to address this and return to tell Elara and find the people to help me free Briar.

Colm's eyebrow arched more sharply. "Matters of interrogation fall entirely in my purview, Your Highness. I am more than willing to offer some concessions, as I have done, but—"

"My understanding is that you were to determine whether the bridal candidates had been harmed or the selection tampered with, and you were seeking a confession from her as a favor to my people, for which we are exceptionally grateful. But I will be direct with you. Her confession means nothing to me. I have all the evidence I require, starting with the corpse of my father. There is no further point in interrogations. And I would prefer any further suffering of hers to be used as an example."

Colm kept his palms pressed together, claws lined up. "There is still the matter of her conspirators."

"What words can be spoken in this place that could be trusted?" I turned my focus to Briar then, willing her to understand what I was saying. Her gaze was hard as stone, every muscle in her body locked. Just standing likely hurt her, and neither my words nor my presence was bringing her comfort. "What happened in that garden was unprecedented deception, and great loss has come about because of it." My mind spun as I struggled to come up with a statement that would fool Colm and soothe Briar. "Someone was trying to rig the bridal competition, but Fate cannot be denied. Nor will my father be denied justice."

Colm cleared his throat and started to offer another objection, but I held his gaze and cut him off again. "My people deserve closure. If she comes before them looking like an unhealthy sack of bones, all scraped and bruised, then seeing the devastation that will come from the Shadow Fae sentencing will be far less impactful. The same is true of her mind. If, in those final moments, she is capable of providing a true and honest confession, it will do far more for the people if it is clear she is physically whole rather than her rundown appearance creating the lingering doubt that she was forced to confess under torture. No, the truth of her guilt is known. And justice will be served."

The faintest hint of a sob escaped Briar's lips, and I steeled myself to avoid looking at her. Thalen's expression wavered, and his brow creased deeper.

Colm scowled as well, though his eyebrow arched in a way that suggested he was intrigued. "So you do intend to execute her publicly and painfully?"

The words soured on my tongue, but I could prepare this

first part of my plan imminently upon my return. I would have Colm make the ideal execution for himself, and he'd be none the wiser until it was too late. "Preparations are already underway. The bridal competition will resume its last test within the week, and the wedding shall happen along with all other formalities. So, as far as I am concerned, the first act of my new bride and the queen of the Shadow Fae will be to preside over the execution of the assassin and any others involved. Seems a fitting way to conclude the wedding and prepare for the celebration. Perhaps we'll even hold the execution during the celebration."

"Your bride will participate in the execution or simply watch?" Colm's eyes brightened as he canted his head.

"If she wishes. I haven't yet settled on the method. Something appropriate that lies within her talents, if she wishes it. My queen will have my full support in this matter."

"Assuming one of the two top contenders of the competition is the final winner, then either one would certainly happily and ferociously destroy the assassin," Colm said in a far milder tone than I expected. A cruel smirk tugged at the corners of his mouth. The plan was working. At least this phase of it. "I have not had the pleasure of meeting either yet, but I am certain Fate will choose well."

Briar's nostrils flared as if she smelled something especially horrid. Her eyes widened briefly.

What was that about? I scowled. Something in Colm's statement had caused a reaction. Perhaps just distaste or mistrust. Either way, Colm was falling into my trap, proving he had some sort of vested interest.

Colm continued, "May I ask what execution methods are being considered?"

I twitched my shoulders as I considered this question. Perhaps I could maneuver things even more to my advantage. "I am considering the possibilities. The Bleeding Bloom, the

Thirteen Mutilations, the Iron Coffin. Perhaps a new one. Force the assassin to become a beast, and let her be hunted for all to see, followed by something appropriate." My stomach churned as if I were speaking of Briar's death, even though my plan was the furthest thing from it.

One of the guards chuckled while the other grunted.

A slow, cruel smile spread over Colm's mouth. "Oh, how deliciously archaic. Your great-grandfather was the last to inflict the Bleeding Bloom and the Thirteen Mutilations on a traitor, I believe. I didn't see it myself, of course, but I have heard of both. Those dark crystals blossoming from the accused's veins, eyes, and mouth? Excruciating. Perhaps you could make that one of the Thirteen Mutilations? I believe you have the option to choose which horrors are visited upon the guilty."

Despite my distaste, I gave a curt nod. Time to set the plan in place and bait the trap. "A distinct possibility, though my final choice will be made upon learning what my bride prefers. I realize that I have asked a great deal of you, and that you are exceptionally skilled in interrogation and torture. But perhaps I can offer you this concession. I want my father's murderer to suffer beyond reason and for that suffering to be done in a public display to serve as a warning. Would you be willing to assist me in ensuring the public punishment and execution are appropriate for this task?"

Colm's eyes widened, and he hesitated a breath. Then he bowed his head and tapped the claws of his steepled hands together. "It would be an honor, Your Highness."

"Excellent. I will expect you to come to the palace at your earliest opportunity since I'm sure your *guards* can handle her in your absence. I'll assign a guard to you to ensure you receive all you require, and I will instruct my own interrogator and executioner to cooperate with you fully.

"I would also appreciate a list of all procedures performed

upon her and by whom, to commemorate it in the record. The assassin and all allies will be made an example that will ring out for all time. You needn't worry about torturing Briar further." I forced myself to look at her.

When I saw how she was looking at me now, her jaw tight and her eyes watery, my stomach somersaulted. My mouth went dry, and my throat thickened.

I masked the tremor in my voice with a sneer. "Without her knowledge of the exact suffering that awaits, her imagination will torment her well beyond anything that could be done." And soon after this, I would press him to make an additional concession and let her be moved to the Shadow Kingdom, or at least to better quarters. But he had to be handled with care, or else he might move her to a different prison and further obstruct the rescue.

Colm's nostrils flared, and he scoffed. "I do not fully agree, but I am aware that the suffering of the Thirteen Mutilations is all the greater the healthier the victim is. As far as those who are involved, that will be added to the record. It is our privilege to be able to participate in justice and to provide support in this most difficult of times." His cruel satisfaction and entitled smugness were nearly unbearable.

I drew my shadows back in, including the one that was trying to curl alongside Briar's shadow and hold her. They'd been creeping closer to her without my notice. The curling, claw-like tendrils looked ominous, and she did not yet know that they wanted to comfort her as much as I did.

"Is there anything else you require, Your Highness?" Colm's posture relaxed, and the warmest smile I'd ever seen on his face curved his almost nonexistent lips.

"One more thing before I take my leave." I drew in a steadying breath and fixed my gaze once more on Briar. Her face had gone pale, and her lips trembled ever so slightly. More tears brimmed in her eyes.

All I could hope was that Briar would understand why I had to do this—if not now, then in time. I wanted her to know that I would burn everything down, walk away from my kingdom, do whatever it took for her to be by my side for eternity. But if I played this wrong, she would die horrifically in this place. I had to get her out of here without letting them hurt her more. I would free her within a day or two, and I'd grovel happily for the rest of my existence if she'd allow it.

"Understand that I will not rest until justice is served. My father's murder will be avenged, and all who have done harm in this plot shall pay tenfold. You said that I knew you, but I ask now whether *you* know *me*. If you truly consider my words, I'll believe that you do, and that you know I am disgusted and enraged at what has transpired."

Briar flinched but didn't look away, though she blinked faster. A few tears rolled down her cheeks. One day, she might think back on this and realize what I was actually saying, but today, my heart broke at the betrayal and grief shining in her eyes. I forced myself to draw in my shadows and straighten my wings.

I strode toward the door, Thalen close behind. We had to get out of here before I lost all control. *Soon, Briar. Soon. I swear it. Soon, I will make all this right.*

The soft rustle of fabric stirred the air, and then her voice reached me in a tone more soft and broken than I had ever heard it. "Vad ..."

I shouldn't have stopped. I needed to keep going, but my feet refused to obey. Fate, what was she going to say? I couldn't let her break me.

CHAPTER ELEVEN

BRIAR

My wolf howled in agony as I watched Vad walk away. Restrained and unable to go after him, I wished like hell that I could get him to believe me. Part of me flared with anger that he hadn't given me the benefit of the doubt before casting judgment, but even the anger was laced with grief, and tears blurred my vision.

"Please," I broke out as he stopped.

Stomach churning, I waited to see what he would do next. I hadn't anticipated him standing at the heavy wooden door with his back to me, its broad expanse eclipsing the flicker of torchlight on the wall.

Vad's wings arched, trembling at the edges and merging with the shadows. His hand hovered above the metal door handle, fingers splayed. His shadows swirled around my feet like a caress, or like he was fighting not to jerk me upside down. The hollow ache within me chilled me more than his magic, but now that I was in a room where magic wasn't bound, the strange warmth of my new magic flared.

Scar Eye snarled. "How dare you speak to the prince in such a familiar manner?" Out of the corner of my eye, armor flashed toward my face. I braced and turned to shield myself.

But the blow didn't come.

"Was I not clear?" Vad demanded in a cold, low voice. "She is not to be harmed so that she may be ready to face true judgment and suffer for her guilt."

My head lurched upward. A long, thin shadow had coiled around Scar Eye's fist and held his arm back. The metal frosted beneath the shadow's grip as Scar Eye winced and his breath came in harsh pants.

Vad's shadows tightened. "Do you not think I am capable of defending my own honor?"

Thalen had taken a step toward us as well. His eyes flashed with anger, and for a moment, I saw the Thalen I'd known before, when he'd protected me while teasing me back at the castle. He smoothed the emotion back into his stony expression.

"There is no need for concern, Your Highness. We are more than capable of punishing her appropriately for that disrespect." Colm spoke with clipped words as the two guards gripped me even tighter.

Reality hit me so hard that my legs almost gave way. I couldn't even say his name? I barely noticed the dull aching of my wrists, bound together too tightly and held at an awkward angle with my elbows drawn out and my stance unsteady.

"Take her away," Colm commanded. "We will ensure her punishment is appropriate without causing harm to the future plans."

Claw Tattoo jerked me, and I whimpered before I could stop myself. My wolf grew restless inside me, wanting to break free and get to Vad. But I couldn't, not like this. All that would accomplish was hurting myself.

He didn't want me anyway.

Vad's hand curled into a fist, and his shadow curled even tighter along Scar Eye's wrist and bent his arm back. "No," Vad said. "I will deal with her in private, and I will measure out the appropriate punishment."

Thalen released a tight breath, and his gaze darted between Vad and me.

I sucked in a shaky breath, trembling so hard I had to clench my teeth. For the first time since I'd met Vad, I wasn't sure I wanted to be alone with him. A chill ran down my spine.

Colm's brow lifted. "I beg your pardon, Your Highness?"

With eyes the color of a raging storm, Vad looked past me at Colm. He stalked the few paces back, wings flaring. The shadow tendril that caressed my ankle remained in the pool of shadows and squeezed my bare foot tighter. It lingered over the cuts and scrapes, providing relief with its coolness.

Colm straightened his shoulders and pressed his palms together. Those merciless claw tips of his clacked against one another.

Head inclined forward, Vad loomed over him with his shadows and wings flared out. "This woman disrespected me. It is not your place to punish her. It is mine." He pointed in my direction but didn't glance at me. "It's my *right* to punish her for what she's done. *Alone.*"

My head spun, and my chest constricted painfully. Vad not only hated me, but he wanted Colm to plan my death, and he also wanted to hurt me himself for speaking his name.

Smile vanishing, Colm blinked. The corners of his eyes tightened.

Thalen remained near the door, his thumbs looped in his belt as he avoided my gaze. The guards at my side tensed, and their hands tightened enough to intensify my discomfort.

"I assure you, we can provide more than appropriate repercussions for her actions." Colm sucked in a deep breath, puffing out his chest.

"I have no doubt you can." Vad's face tightened. "But this was done to *me*, and it's within my rights to punish her as I see fit. Are you trying to disrespect my position as she did? Am I now to punish you both?"

Colm's breathing quickened, but it seemed to come from far away, like he wasn't in the same room as I was. It was as if I were separated from them, even though I stood right there.

"Of course not, Your Highness. It is simply—" Colm started, and Vad lifted one hand and leaned closer, the shadows around him darkening. Scar Eye winced as the shadow holding him bent his arm back, but he didn't let go of me.

Thalen scoffed then crossed his arms. "The High Aureline Council should be at the palace when we return. I'm sure they'd *love* to learn what happened here."

Colm's entire body stiffened. He glanced between Vad and Scar Eye. "The prince is correct. He should punish her as he sees fit. Release her, and we'll step outside while he deals with her insolence."

My fingers dug into my palms as the guards grunted and released their hold on me. The shadow tendril retreated from Scar Eye's arm. He shook it out and gripped it to his chest.

My heart galloped painfully. I still couldn't comprehend Vad hurting me willingly. Worse, his believing so readily that I'd killed his father made me want to scream into the void.

"Want us to bind her to the wall?" Claw Tattoo's fingers pinched my arm even harder.

"Not unless the prince commands it," Colm responded.

"No. If she harms me, I deserve it." Vad scoffed and looked at me.

I froze as his gaze raked over me. Heat coiled in my stomach while pain strangled me. The way his eyes drank me in still set me ablaze, and I hated myself for that. Except ... that shadow of his still held on to my leg, hidden from sight, caressing me. My stomach knotted. Was he playing games with me?

Claw Tattoo and Scar Eye exchanged a look and then

released me. Scar Eye shoved me in the back, causing my hips and knees to unlock as my balance shifted. Panic surged through me, and I started to fall.

The cold, slick shadow on my leg curled tighter and slid higher along my calf. Still hidden by my ragged, stained skirt, his shadow supported me enough to help me regain my balance without anyone seeing.

My heart raced faster as I straightened and held my bound wrists before myself. Maybe he was saving me so he could have the pleasure of destroying me more thoroughly himself. Could it be that horrifically simple? The fae worked like that, but I'd thought Vad was different.

My wolf whined as if she didn't believe that. I wasn't sure I did either, but doubt clung to me, cold and as uncomfortable as my clothing.

The guards strode away in a single row, and Colm moved toward the door as well. "If you require aid, please do not hesitate to call out, Your Highness. We will be just beyond the door." He inclined his head forward.

I kept my eyes fixed on Vad, but he remained focused on the door, as did Thalen. Vad's hands stayed braced on his belt, his index finger tapping against the leather.

Thalen's hands twitched at his sides, and he spread his silver-white wings. He gave a grim nod in Colm's direction, though Colm didn't seem to notice.

The heavy door clicked shut behind Colm. The guards' footsteps echoed their departure, heavy and deliberate. The air seemed to thicken with the horrible smells of rot, sweat, mold, and blood.

Vad said nothing. Part of me wanted to die, and yet I also wanted to hear him tell me to my face that he didn't believe me and that he believed I murdered his father. I wanted to experience the real man behind his princely facade.

The tendril around my calf pulsed with a soft energy. I looked down and tried to lift my foot. The shadow moved, not holding me prisoner but simply flowing with me.

Nothing made sense anymore.

The temperature in the room dropped, and my breath frosted. The darkness in the shadows intensified. I looked back up in time to see the ghost of a cocky smile on Thalen's lips as he turned his hands palms up, and then a blur of pure darkness as Vad lunged at me. His shadows ripped up beneath me and lifted me off the filthy stone.

I yanked at my rope, needing to fight. But my wrists were still tied tightly. My wolf snarled, determined to not die at the hands of the man I loved without being able to fight back.

A panicked cry slipped out before Vad thrust me against the wall, one hand at my throat and the other over my mouth. I kicked and flailed as best I could amidst the tangle of his cold shadows, and I braced myself for bone-jarring agony. But the shadows rose with me, cradling my legs and holding me up. They even swept under my feet to keep me from striking my bruised toes and heels against the wall.

What was this? What was he doing? Was this some mind game?

His claws pressed on my skin as he leaned against me, his warm, smoky leather scent filling my senses and almost overpowering the horrid stench of this place.

The pressure should have knocked the breath from my lungs or cracked something, but instead, the darkness underneath me kept me cushioned, strangely buoyant, so that my dignity took the brunt of the hit. My heels dangled a few inches above the ground, my toes wrapped in his shadows and kept immobile. The icy grip of his fingers dug in, careful but unyielding.

"I—" I started, but before I could say more, he placed his

mouth against my ear and whispered huskily, "Don't be afraid, Briar. I love you, and I know you didn't do this. None of this is your fault. I'm sorry I can't save you yet, but I will. The plan is already in motion, and we will kill anyone who does or has done you harm."

My heart raced faster, and I cut my eyes to him. His own storm-gray eyes softened, though there was something desperate and wild in them.

He loved me? That was the last thing I'd expected to hear during this encounter.

For a moment, the world consisted solely of the warmth of his lips at my ear and the trembling thrill of his body caging mine. If I focused on his scent, everything else faded away.

My mouth fell open against his fingers, and I whispered, "Vad?"

"Look scared." Vad kissed the tip of my ear and added, "They have to believe that I'm harming and threatening you, and they might be able to see in here somehow, so ... try to look more afraid." His hot breath tickled my ear, and I bit back a near-hysterical giggle.

All this hell was worth it as long as he believed me and didn't hate me. I forced my eyes to widen and twisted my features into a fearful mask.

"Good girl," he whispered. "I don't know how long before Thalen's and my magic tips them off, so we must do this swiftly. My shadows will leave marks on you like bruising, but they won't hurt you—it will just feel quite cold. It's going to be all right, Briar," he whispered as his broad chest pressed against mine and his heart thundered. "Forgive me for all I said. I have to play this infernal game to get you out of here, or they will kill you. I have to make them believe this is real, but trust me, Briar. I will not know peace until you are safe." His hand over my mouth didn't move, but the palm at my throat eased. His thumb caressed my lower lip for a breath, and heat sang through my veins. Shadows reached up and coiled around my throat. "You must stay strong. Heal as fast as you can. And be ready. I *will* get you out of here. I'm just not certain when."

His words rolled over me like a tidal wave. Slowly, it all started to make sense. For once, the desperate part of me that had dared to hope had been proven right. I'd scented no lies on him, but he had been careful with his words. So like a fae! But there was one lie I needed to address. I shook my head, realizing I didn't know how much time we had.

A shudder passed through me as his shadows stroked my throat. "Kaylen or Rhielle. Colm knows one of them, and I'm betting it's Kaylen."

One eyebrow tweaked up before he steeled his expression and cast a swift glance over his shoulder. "You're certain?"

"Yeah. I smelled his lie," I whispered back. His hand was still at my throat, his claws lightly pressed against me. When had he gotten claws like this? They must be part of his Shadow magic, or he'd hidden them from me. They weren't just ornamental claw tips that sat on the tops of his fingers, like Colm's. These were actual claws, and my wolf loved it.

"Really ..." His eyebrow tweaked higher, and a smile pulled more at my mouth. "How?"

"It's a wolf shifter thing I can tell you about later. Also, there's a prisoner here they're taking blood and magic from to feed someone. I don't know who they're feeding, but his name is Elias. Can you save him too?"

"Not even two minutes with me, and you want me to do a favor for a stranger?" He clicked his tongue, but there was a small curl at his lips that suggested he wasn't annoyed. "I can't guarantee anything. All that matters to me is getting you out. But we'll see about this Elias. Can you tell me anything else about him?"

"He's been tortured badly, and he's a Terran Fae. Shaggy chestnut hair. Four tattoos on his throat and chest—they look like bear claws. He's in bad shape. I don't think anyone is supposed to know he's here."

Vad's stance shifted, though he didn't loosen his grip on me. "That's forbidden. Not that it likely matters in this place. I'll see what I can learn. More importantly, I'm getting you out of here."

"Thank you," I whispered. "And thank Fate you believed me. I love you, Vad."

The corners of his mouth curled up more, and he kissed my ear once more. "I love you with all I am, and I wish I could tell you so much more, but we don't have time. Know that I'm going to bind Colm to a vow, and I'm going to have him help me plan the instruments of his own destruction along with all those responsible for framing you and killing my father. If you want to kill him, I will prepare him for you. I meant every word I said about letting my queen choose the final course. Anyone who hurts you, remember them. I will let you bathe in their blood before my whole kingdom as I proclaim your innocence and my adoration. And if you cannot forgive me, I understand. But know that, regardless, I will get you to safety and clear your name."

The door crashed open, the wood rebounding hard enough to rattle the lamp on the table. Scar Eye and Claw Tattoo entered again at a run, daggers drawn. "Liar! You betrayed the trust of our leader," Scar Eye shouted.

They charged straight at Vad.

CHAPTER TWELVE

I gritted my teeth, and my fangs protruded. I'd never forget the voice of the man who wanted to punch Briar.

The guards' rapid footsteps thundered into the room, causing me to press my body harder against Briar's. I wasn't ready for our time to be over. It wasn't enough. Feck, it'd never be enough.

I'd known they'd come barging in sooner or later, and I was furious that I couldn't just take her with me. But that would make them more determined to kill her.

Fortunately, if I let her go, I'd be acting as if I'd done something wrong, so I stayed pressed against her body, cherishing the buzzing sensation that thrummed between us. I kept one hand at her throat and the other over her mouth. Her eyes widened and cut toward the guards.

Feck these bastards.

"Daggers," Thalen muttered, and a flash of white in the corner of my eyes indicated he'd spread out his wings.

Without turning my head, I unleashed my shadows. My magic rushed out, eager to protect Briar and me. One tendril made contact with someone, and I jerked it down. A weight fell forward, and a loud *clank* rang out, and then a shirring sound, like something had slid away.

Briar whimpered and struggled against my hold, and Thalen's wings flapped just as something sharp scraped between my shoulder blades. The thick leather of my surcoat, along with the protective symbols woven into it, kept the weapon from doing much more than pinching my skin.

All it had taken was a moment of distraction to nearly get stabbed in the back.

Another shadow tendril shot out behind me but found no purchase.

"How dare you attack the heir of the Shadow King?" Thalen spat.

I turned my head slowly and glared at the guard who'd attacked me, now struggling in Thalen's hold. Of course, it was Oathfeln. The bastard was pretty much begging me to kill him. He'd tried to punch my beloved, and now he'd rushed in here, cutting our time together short. Even if all he'd done was interrupt us, I'd have wanted him dead or at least maimed. I would give almost anything to be able to cradle Briar against me and have my shadows bring her comfort.

Selvan lay where my shadow had yanked him down, still wrapped in the tendril.

My hands remained at Briar's mouth and throat. "Let him loose, Thalen. I'll handle both of them."

Obeying, Thalen released Oathfeln and moved to stand by the wall behind me. My shadows immediately bound Oathfeln's wrists, and the air chilled further. My shadows dragged both men to the opposite side of the room, their boots scraping the floor. Thalen snagged Selvan's dagger, and I tightened the shadows so hard that Oathfeln's dagger dropped from his hand and clattered out of reach.

Briar whimpered beneath my hand and jerked her head sideways as if my grip was hurting her. Smart. She was playing along, though it required little acting—her face was already streaked with tears, grime, and blood, and her body trembled from cold and exhaustion. I kept her pressed firmly to the wall, letting my weight pin her while my shadows cushioned her. For show, I flexed my hand on Briar's throat and gave a mock squeeze.

Both guards struck the far wall and crashed to their knees with wet groans, shadows binding their arms and yanking their chins up. The shadows constricted especially hard around Oathfeln, twisting around his throat and forcing him to arch so much that his entire body would snap if I willed it. He shuddered as my shadows squeezed his windpipe tight enough that he couldn't even croak. Selvan's veins bulged, and his lips strained in a silent scream.

"Did you truly think rushing into a room in which the Shadow Prince is executing his judgment and attacking him was wise?" I asked in a cold, flat tone. More shadow tendrils flared up in the inky darkness, my shadows covering almost the entirety of the floor now, ensuring anyone who entered would be vulnerable to them.

"What is all this commotion—" Colm appeared in the doorway with his hands already pressed palm to palm and claw tip to claw tip. He scanned the room, his eyes widening briefly as he took in the scene. When he saw his guards kneeling on the slick stone floor, bound with shadows, his nostrils flared, and his jaw tightened. He did not step far enough into the room to cross my shadows but instead remained just beneath the stone archway.

"Were you eavesdropping on us when I explicitly said not to?" I lifted my chin and sneered.

"They shouldn't have been." Colm grimaced. "I was tending to other matters."

"Then your training of your men leaves much to be

desired." I spoke slowly, ensuring he understood each word. "Are you in the habit of permitting such flagrant abuses and violations? This may well be considered an act of war." I could treat it as such, but offering that little bit of room for negotiation meant I could set the rest of my plan into motion.

Thalen scoffed. "Apparently so. Imagine the scandal if they had succeeded. Another death. Another assassination. One might think the harsh treatment of Briar is a ruse to cover up the fact that you were involved in the king's assassination too." He remained still, though I knew he was prepared if things went poorly. His circle of silence had vanished as well, disappearing into the natural muting and chill of my shadows.

Colm's expression soured, and he bowed his head. "Not at all. Not at all, Your Highness." These guards had shamed him—unless they could offer some good excuse for attacking me, and there was none. "I am certain they thought they had good cause, though it is likely that this is a misunderstanding."

"Let them defend themselves then." I loosed Selvan, and he collapsed and clutched at his throat.

I kept Oathfeln pinned, ensuring that the chill of my shadows intensified and that his position was as excruciatingly uncomfortable as possible. "Speak," I growled.

Colm nodded, but his posture remained tense. His lack of confidence confirmed that he had not ordered them to enter, and the nervous energy in his manner broke through his typical calm.

Selvan struggled to his knees, his leather trousers creaking. He pointed at Oathfeln. "He said the prince is still in love with her."

"In love with her?" I barked. For good measure, I intensified the shadows around Briar as well as Selvan and Oathfeln, and she gave a muffled cry while they grunted and cried out. Making sure the shadows beneath her skirt still held up her legs, I wrapped more shadows around her throat and pretended to choke her.

I made no such pretense with the guards. "You are suggesting that I am in love with the assassin who murdered my father and king?"

"Oathfeln saw ..." Selvan whimpered. His hand continued to work at his throat.

Oathfeln grimaced as he fought for breath. "You—you weren't torturing her. You were leaning against her and caressing her ... with your shadows."

"You think this looks like affection?" I tightened my shadows on him. A surge of nausea passed through me, and my head spun, warning signs of my powers starting to strain.

I'd been using too much magic, and it was already weakening. The fact that I was not in Shadow territory made my energy drain all the faster.

I needed to wrap this up without giving any sign of weakness. The tension in Oathfeln's arms and shoulders had to be nearing their breaking point. "You think my shadows are warm and cuddly? Do you feel *safe* and *loved* in them?" I sneered these last words, and Briar offered a muffled protest.

Colm's lips pressed into a tight line. "Do you have any other evidence?" He hadn't asked me to release Oathfeln, and he had stepped back a whole pace, as if that would keep him from my shadow's grasp if I decided to restrain him. His jaw was clenched so tight I marveled I didn't hear his teeth cracking.

I'd make sure I heard it when I killed him.

All in due time.

Oathfeln turned his white-rimmed eyes toward Colm and pleaded, "I know he loves her. I—swear—"

His lack of impulse control was to my benefit. I cut my eyes at Colm. "You expect me to accept this wretch's interpretation of my interrogation and permit him to stab me in the back while

I am your guest? Not only your guest, but the heir apparent of the Shadow King himself."

Composure fracturing, Colm pressed his hands tighter together. "There is no excuse, Your Highness. This matter will be handled appropriately. I give you my word."

I lifted a hand. "Your guard has shown himself untrustworthy twice. Under fae law, his life is forfeit ... or do you have another interpretation? Your High Council is arriving soon to speak with me on the matter of my father's assassination. I'm sure they'll be deeply concerned to hear that there was an attack upon the heir apparent."

"No!" Oathfeln shook his head. "It's—"

But my shadows sealed his mouth tight, and he ended on a whimper.

Keeping his head down, Selvan remained on his knees.

"I am aware of the law." Colm's throat bobbed, and he bowed.

Good. Then he was aware of his options. Even the allegation looked bad for someone like Colm, who was an interrogator and overseer of the imprisonment of some of the most dangerous fae and those who simply needed to disappear.

"His life is yours to do with as you choose," he added.

My eyebrows shot upward while Oathfeln jerked his head from side to side and struggled to break free.

Though I had expected a concession, I hadn't expected him to freely offer *this*. But Colm was ruthless. Sacrificing a bad guard who had unequivocally endangered the entire prison and interrogation system was an easy choice. And this fool of a guard had also allowed Briar to bite off the nose of his partner. His indiscretions could result in far more eyes on this place.

Colm was being quite rational, which left me with an even better opportunity. I could leverage the guard's actions and inform the Aureline Council, and an investigation could be launched to pressure Colm. But this guard had harmed Briar, and I had an opportunity to avenge what was mine. I already had a plan to pressure Colm. Oathfeln's death would eliminate at least one person who had and would continue to harm her.

I kept my hand at Briar's throat, and my gaze seared into Colm. Even after I made him take the vow, his guards might cause issues. All of those vows of protection could be easily undone by one person stupid enough to not obey. My gut warned me that, if I left him alive, Oathfeln would be a particular problem. I'd have preferred to draw out his suffering, but Briar had bitten off his partner's nose, and he had tried to strike her after being told not to. Then, of course, he had tried to stab me.

I inclined my head slightly to Colm. "Then his life is forfeit for this crime."

I tightened my shadows around him with suffocating strength. A helpless gurgle escaped his lips, and they turned blue, every tendon in his neck pulled taut. His ribs creaked, and his spine arched, his legs kicking, boots scraping across stone as he writhed in the hold of the magic.

Colm's eyes widened slightly before he steeled his expression.

Briar tensed. I despised making her uncomfortable, but this had to be done.

However, my shadows continued to support her. I moved my head, pretending I wanted a better view of Oathfeln so she didn't have to see yet another violent death.

Oathfeln's fingers clawed at the air, twitching helplessly, his arms still twisted behind his back. Half the shadows wrapped around him pulled down, and the other half pulled up. The tension built as his eyes bugged out. Then his spine and neck snapped with a heavy, wet *crack,* and he folded in half like a snapped branch in flood waters.

Another pang of nausea passed through me, twisting in my guts. Gritting my teeth, I bit back the urge to snap all my shadows back in. Fatigue burned my eyes, and a dull ringing sounded in my ears. Time to wrap this up and pray that not much more would be needed for my demonstration.

My shadows flung Oathfeln across the room. His body crunched against the opposite stone wall and then slid down into the pool of shadows. I turned my focus back to Colm. "At least here, justice has been done, though I admit I would have preferred something more prolonged and arduous, given the nature of his crime."

Colm tipped his chin up and tapped his claw tips together. "You are far more ... proactive than I expected, Your Highness. Certainly more so than your father."

I gave him a tight, cold smile, though my limbs were numb from the overuse of my borrowed magic. Not much left. I'd probably shortened my time a day or two by using so much.

I folded my shadows inward to keep the edges from flickering. "You Aurelines are bound to neutrality. I am of the shadows, and I am at home in chaos, darkness, and pain."

"Your reign will be most intriguing to see unfold, Your Highness."

I didn't acknowledge him as I turned my focus back to Briar. "As for this one, she is exactly what I thought," I said. It was a careful matter of trickery to hold her in this way, and I feared hurting her if I held her too tightly or at too awkward an angle, especially with my control wavering. "No mercy will be shown in this matter.

"The only reason I do not make you scream is because the screams I intend to draw from you will be far longer and louder than any I would hear now from your weary throat. But cross me, and ..." I clenched my shadows tighter around her like a strong embrace, and she gave a strangled cry in response. "I don't think more needs to be said."

Every cell in my body screamed not to release her, but I steeled my breath and forced my hand from her mouth ... and dropped her. Her arms flailed, and she shrieked. My shadows struck the ground, mimicking the sound of flesh striking stone. She let out a squeak of protest and ducked her head. Her matted copper hair slid over her shoulders and tickled my shadows. I left the one shadow tendril curled along her ankle and up her calf. "Do you understand me?"

She nodded and flinched. She seemed small and fragile, as if an errant wind might break her. She clutched her throat protectively, shielding the reddened skin. I flinched inwardly at the sight of my marks on her, not knowing whether they caused pain, nor being able to kiss them away.

I couldn't focus on that now. I drew my shadows in like a rippling tide of ink and fog. Another spasm of nausea swept over me, but I squared my shoulders. There could be no outward signs of weakness. Not now.

I fixed Colm with a stern gaze and gestured at Briar. "I need to execute someone who is strong and cunning. I need my people to see her at her best and watch the murderer be taken out by my strength." I inwardly smirked, knowing that she would not only be seen in her best health but as their queen. "She is too thin, too injured, and appears weak. See to it that she is fed with non-moldy bread and given better clothing so the elements will not harm her. If food poisoning, illness, or another element eliminates her, I will treat the matter as if justice has been denied my kingdom and respond with the full force of our law."

"Of course. We will ensure she is fed and clothed. She will be well prepared when it is time for justice." Colm eyed her and stepped farther into the room now that my shadows no longer covered the floor. Not that it would take long for me to seize him.

I conserved my energy, knowing better than to press my luck.

"Good. We do not want anyone to pity her. And right now, well ... look at her." I wrinkled my nose in disgust. "Let her dread her death, not welcome it."

Colm clicked his tongue. "Yes, she is pathetic, Your Highness."

Selvan stood on shaky legs and groped for his dagger. Oathfeln's mangled corpse lay in a grisly pile, blood and spittle leaking from his mouth. An unpleasant sight and a stark warning.

I pointed at Briar and rasped, "And you will not give these men any further trouble, else I will return and determine what can be risked in the preparations for your execution and what manner of pain should be added to your demise. Do you understand?"

She nodded meekly, keeping her eyes averted from me.

In that moment, she seemed a ghost of herself, and it hurt to see her weak and not fighting. But she'd made my job easier, and soon, I'd lay out the second half.

I turned to Thalen and nodded. He gave a quick nod in return, understanding it was time to leave.

The floor seemed to shift under my feet, and searing pain lanced through my skull.

I blinked hard, forcing my expression to remain impassive. To Colm, I commanded, "See to it that your remaining guards understand what is at stake. My people will not be denied their justice. I have vowed it, and it is the only way there will be peace."

"As you wish, Your Highness." Colm bowed, his claw tips clicking together. His tone was simpering, but I could feel the dark edges of his anger.

Fortunately, that wasn't going to be an issue for long. I knew precisely how to handle him and further separate him from the Aurelines.

I strode beyond the doorway as Colm moved to Selvan and spoke with him.

I heard his mumbles, informing Selvan about getting Briar food and suitable attire while Briar huddled, quivering, in the back of the room.

Did I hurt her? My heart throbbed, and bile inched up my throat. I'd tried to be careful with her while making my anger believable. I'd wanted to check in with her and take care of her, but there was too much at stake. The yank in my chest toward her almost had my legs moving. But if I misstepped now, then all of this would have been for naught.

The room seemed to close in on me. We had to get out of here so we could get her back to me sooner.

Taking a ragged breath, I whispered to Thalen, "Return to the entry point and retrieve the merlinite orb from my chambers. It's on the second shelf in an onyx setting. Place the orb in one of the polished boxes. Then bring it here."

Thalen curled his fingers to further hide our voices from anyone listening. "That orb was your mother's, wasn't it? It was part of a set shared with your father. Isn't it quite powerful?" His normally warm amber eyes turned dark, and I could almost see his mind swirling. "It's irreplaceable."

So is Briar. "Leave and get it *now.*"

CHAPTER THIRTEEN

"You realize that, with time, focus, and exposure, the orb will enhance Colm's powers." Thalen bit his bottom lip, and the corners of his eyes tightened. "Why in the void would you want that? Imagine the other people he might harm."

"I don't care. He agreed not to harm her, and he won't be able to hurt her when this is through. He won't have them long enough to do much."

Thalen's brow creased, and I knew he understood I referenced Briar. "Should I bring your father's as well? Those two orbs work in tandem."

They did. The labradorite orb had been my father's, and he'd given it to me shortly after Mother passed. Using the merlinite alone was dangerous, but I didn't much care about Colm's safety. "No. We may need the second for another favor."

Thalen's jaw clenched, and he tilted his head, staring into my eyes. His look was uncharacteristically serious. His right wing twitched again. "What about Elara? The orbs belonged to her parents, too."

She'd be upset and wounded that I hadn't conferred with her. But I was the king, and even though I didn't want to upset her, Briar's safety came before *everything,* even my sister's feelings.

I ignored the guilt that weighed on my shoulders. "We have other mementos and symbolic items with which we can mourn them both. She will understand. Regardless, it is *my* choice." The vow I was about to demand of Colm was significant, and I had to offer something that could entice him to compromise whatever his position was with the people who wanted Briar to disappear.

The mastermind behind the assassination of my father had almost assuredly offered Colm something potent and tangible to get Colm to handle Briar. And I couldn't risk Colm doing something that would make the others in this conspiracy lash out at Briar in more dangerous ways. They still had to think their plan was working. We had to catch everyone who was involved in this sordid scheme and be strategic about how we connected them. They couldn't become suspicious.

Thalen drew in a deep breath. "I'd have to leave you alone."

"For a brief time." It was hard to anticipate how long it would take. Time passed differently here, and there were spells and incantations to further warp the passage of time in certain places within the prison as well.

"You have no idea how long I'll be gone. It could be an hour or a matter of minutes, and you saw what those two guards did." He leaned in closer, and his eyes flashed in challenge. "You can't take on everyone if they turn on you—"

"This is an order from your king," I snapped, unblinking. "Use your magic to move faster if you're so concerned, but do not trouble me with excuses."

Huffing, Thalen gave a stern nod. "Try not to die while I'm gone, all right?" His usual levity splintered, but he darted away, his silver-white wings folded tight against his back.

I kept my pose controlled and at ease, hands braced at my belt and wings spread. My shadows hugged the wall, where I kept them, and I fought my urge to wrap them around Briar.

"Your guard leaves you unattended?" Colm's brow furrowed.

I offered him a thin smile. "I sent him to retrieve a gift. Despite all that has happened, I feel that skills such as yours should be given their full due. He will meet us at the portal to the Shadow Palace Receiving Hall."

Eyes sparking, Colm straightened. "Your Highness, a gift is not required. I am simply a tool for justice."

"Is a gift truly a gift if it is required?" I arched my brow. "I think you and I are in agreement in this matter. We both understand how imperative justice is." I strode to him and placed a hand on his narrow shoulder. "And Selvan, the last guard standing, understands that he and every other guard in this place must abide by what we have discussed, or they will be forced to endure the full wrath of the Shadow King?"

"It has been made explicitly clear, Your Highness." Colm's voice carried an undercurrent of warning. He clasped his hands behind his back and squared his shoulders.

I'd danced at the edge of insult, but I could navigate my response without going too far. With an outward smirk, I forced myself to turn away from Briar.

Even though this was his domain, I gestured for Colm to follow me. "Walk with me. I have never seen a dungeon set up quite like yours. How long have you managed this place? Disciplinary matters with those few guards aside, it seems as if you have quite the efficient organization."

"Indeed, we do." Colm's shoulders relaxed a touch as we headed toward the hallway.

I struggled to focus, even as I glanced at Briar, hoping she would meet my eyes for one more second.

As if Fate had listened, Briar glanced up, eyes shiny with unshed tears. My heart fractured, and even though I had to keep my stoic expression, I stepped into a shadow and allowed my magic to dart out once more, caressing her foot and calf to secretly tell her I loved her the best I could.

That brief second wasn't enough, but I had to lead Colm away to solidify my plan. I tensed my wings, trying to ground myself. Briar's ultimate safety had to be my top priority.

Forcing myself into the present, I listened raptly, parsing Colm's words for anything that might help my plan while taking note of the layout in case that plan failed and I needed to know my way around to get Briar out.

We made our way through the broad passages, our footsteps echoing against the stone and our pace unhurried. I kept my shadows coiled close, conserving their strength while maintaining the appearance of control. Every muscle in my body ached with fatigue, but I kept my spine straight and my strides steady. Over the distant screams and moans that filtered through the heavy air, Colm spoke of the prison and its history and purpose.

By the time we reached the portal through which Thalen and I had entered, Thalen had returned. He carried the box with both hands, his steps precise and his expression stoic.

"Ah. Excellent." I took the box from Thalen and presented it to Colm. The warm resinous scent filled my lungs, bright and rich with notes of citrus and myrrh, reminding me of better times and the many hours I had spent with my mother in the observatory, searching the sky. I had no doubt that, if Mother hadn't died, she would have approved of my plan ... and would have worried ceaselessly until Briar was safe.

Lips pursed, Colm waited for an explanation.

"Since you will soon be assisting me in preparing our dungeons and our executions, I want you to have something of the Shadow Kingdom. You may find it useful in your own endeavors, as I am certain you are also an individual who is constantly seeking to improve himself."

Thalen remained just behind me, and though I couldn't see him, I could feel his concern.

Colm took the box and passed his clawed fingertips along the open lock. The metal clicked softly, and he lifted the lid. His eyes widened, and he exhaled. "This is ... unexpectedly generous." He cradled the polished red-brown wood with one hand and dipped the other in to caress the orb's surface. "Merlinite?"

His tender gesture made my skin crawl. I hated how he touched what had belonged to my mother, but this had to be done. Briar's life was worth everything to me.

"Merlinite carved from a single block and imbued with Shadow magic, though one does not have to wield Shadow magic to work with it." For a time, he would begin to build his powers, but I had to remember that this man would not see the rising of the next full moon. I could deal with my own unease and even my sister's rage if it meant Briar would be safe.

Colm's face transformed into a huge smile, and his delight, even as he tried to hide it, confirmed that this was going to work. This was the key to getting everything else set in place.

"It is a powerful stone. I can feel its energy even here. You have honored me greatly." He placed his palm over it as his gaze sharpened.

If he pushed too hard to tap into the power of the orb to strengthen his own magic and did not take proper precautions, his magic could weaken and be more susceptible to overextension and could perhaps even injure him. Father had always warned me that tapping into Shadow magic could sneak up on a person faster than any of the other magics in the realm and leave them weakened and vulnerable. With a powerful enough channel, such as with the vesting, it could even cause death.

The merlinite orb wasn't powerful enough to kill, but

if Colm overused it, it could cause debilitating injuries and sap his magical strength for days. I could only hope he'd be foolish and overeager enough to overlook the danger during his exploration. It would be an added benefit if he did.

Colm was used to the balance and flow of Aureline magic. Shadow magic had no such balance.

Thalen arched an eyebrow as Colm continued to examine the orb. He rolled his eyes before asking Colm, "Shall we leave you alone with it?"

I shot Thalen a chastising look before returning my focus to Colm. "I am pleased that you appreciate the gift."

Colm didn't acknowledge Thalen's quip. "This will allow me to craft far more horrifying tortures and methods of interrogation that can be unleashed at your coronation. Indeed, it will enhance my skills of persuasion significantly."

Of course he would use it for torture. "I expect nothing less. The execution after the coronation will be spoken of for centuries to come, but ... there is one favor I must ask to ensure that all goes to plan."

Colm dragged his gaze from the orb to me. His fingers stilled on its surface. Despite my pretense, a gift this powerful didn't come without at least one favor required in its wake. "And what might that be, Your Highness?"

I stared at him. Asking for a leader such as Colm to take a vow was a risky thing, but the man's ego made him somewhat easy to manipulate. My wings pulsed as the shadow energy within me ached to emerge again. "I wish for you to speak a binding vow that you will do no harm to Briar in any fashion until the time of her formal execution in the Shadow Kingdom's formal court."

After receiving a gift, it was discourteous to deny a favor. Especially to a ruler, and a grieving one at that. He could return the gift with claims of not being worthy of such an honor. But

Colm wanted the merlinite orb. A man like him could enhance his powers with weeks of dedicated focus in harnessing its energies ... assuming he lived that long.

And he wouldn't.

"You wish me to make a binding vow over something to which I have already pledged?" Colm's thin eyebrow arched. "The satisfaction of seeing such a wretched life brought low before the public of the Shadow Kingdom after a wedding and a coronation is more than incentive enough for me to keep her alive. To be permitted to participate in the grand and lavish proceedings that will lead to her excruciating demise is likewise a great honor."

"If it is of no consequence and falls in line so well with your intent, then there's no reason not to make the vow." Thalen lifted one shoulder as he flashed Colm a crooked smile. "Sounds like everyone wins."

Colm's lips pressed into a tighter line. "It is not about intent."

I raised a hand and channeled a more calm and somber tone. "Of course. It is not that I don't trust you, but both your guards intruded, and one attempted to stab me in the back." I savored this leverage. Though my plan hadn't relied on it before, it certainly made it easier now. "One is dead, yes, but the other entered as well in violation of standard hospitality for even the most common visitor, let alone royalty. This is about ensuring that I have done all within my power to bring my people the justice they deserve. I do not fear your actions in this, but I fear the recklessness of some of your men. As their leader, you answer for them as I answer for mine. And when I speak with the Shadow Council, they will ask me if a vow was given. I may not yet be king, but I must do my due diligence as a wise ruler would. Surely you understand."

The shadows from the torches spaced evenly on the

pockmarked wall loomed darker, subtly responding to me.

Colm's gaze moved from me back to the polished orb that lay in the center of the black velvet. "Of course, Your Highness. I vow on my own life that no harm will come to Briar from me until the day of her formal execution in the Shadow King's formal court. May painful death take me if I violate this vow." He tilted his head as his clawed fingertips tapped the side of the box. Greed sparked in his murky green eyes.

A good start, but I noticed the omission. I shook my head. "Not quite enough. As I said, the issue is not simply that you oversee these men but that they must be held to account. You said most are not so undisciplined, but the guards that I have seen were driven by emotion and barbarism. My instructions could not have been any clearer before, and yet they disobeyed. They seemed little more than animals, and I cannot trust their judgment, so there must be greater clarity. Now, I do not blame you for your men's errors as a reflection of your personal character. You can only work with the tools you are provided. The Aurelines are renowned for their balance and wisdom. As I have seen the level of your wisdom, I know you can control them so long as you have the right tools. But it would be a great favor for you to grant me this assurance."

This was the true test. His jaw worked, and I could practically hear his thoughts spinning over whether the power to be gained from this orb over time was enough to offset whatever else he'd been promised.

I let the silence sit heavy between us and made no move to take the box. But my shadows coiled tighter within me, urging me to set them free. Another wave of nausea cut through me. I needed to get home—no. To the palace. It wasn't home without Briar.

Eyes narrowing, Colm seemed to be contemplating the cost. Then, pressing his claw tips against the wooden box, he dipped his head forward. "Very well. I extend my vow and so swear it on my own life and power that neither I nor my guards nor anyone in my employ or supervision shall cause any harm to Briar until her execution in the Shadow King's formal court. Should any harm come to her because of that, may my death be painful and slow."

Thalen cut his eyes at me. He didn't need to say a word for me to know he was worried that Colm had so swiftly agreed. It caused me a tinge of concern as well, but I accepted his vow with a slight incline of my head. "I hope you will soon visit my palace so that we may begin the preparations. Briar will be transported to our prison as soon as arrangements can be made." I needed to ensure whoever was guarding her did not fall prey to an attack, as the guard had the night before. Ironically, until I got this sorted out, she might be safer here than in my own kingdom's prison.

"It will be my honor to serve in this fashion." Colm bowed deeper.

Final pleasantries aside, I forced myself to push back through the portal to the Receiving Hall. Each step I took farther away from Briar seemed to slice through my heart, but I needed to go back to put my plans into action.

In the hall, my own messenger hurried to me with missives ranging from condolences to offers of aid to gifts, and an update on the Aureline High Council.

"A few of the High Council arrived." Buldan rushed the words out as he bowed at the waist. "The rest will arrive soon. We have placed them in the guest hall beyond the hall housing the bridal candidates. Is that satisfactory?"

"It is." My mind spun and ached at the thought of all I had to accomplish before I could bring Briar back. The height of the candles near the door indicated we were nearing the dawn hour. Elara would wake soon, and I had to talk with her before any of the servants did. The morning after a feast or celebration, she generally slept until noon, but I doubted that would be the case today. Her own magic had likely sensed Father's passing, and I didn't want to risk her being alone and confused when she woke. I could wait in her gathering room while I worked on the rest of my plans.

Thalen strode along beside me, saying nothing until we reached the high double doors of the royal family quarters. The familiar black and gold marbled walls soothed me after the harshness of the prison.

But then reality slammed into me, and my knees almost buckled.

Briar was still there and not with *me*.

My stomach soured, and the pleasant scents of incense, smoke, leather, and cologne seemed to mock my memory of the rot and filth that surrounded her.

Thalen prodded me as we passed a gold-framed painting that depicted one of my ancestors standing before the red river that flowed beneath our palace. "You do know you're going to need to sleep sooner rather than later."

I couldn't rest until I had Briar in my arms, brought my father's killers to justice, and got the orb back. "I'll sleep when I'm dead." The statement came out more like a growl than I intended.

"Yeah, well, that might be sooner than you think. And I'm not imagining it. Your shadows are getting a lot more aggressive and decisive. Are you even fully in control of them?" His wings twitched as he scanned me up and down.

I shook my head, scoffing. It was hard to explain how they had transformed in the past hour. The magic that had poured into me from the vesting was still chaotic. It was like I embodied the ocean, and though I was aware of the shadows, they also seemed to have their own will. Part of me suspected that, even if I hadn't willed it, they would have gone to Briar's defense anyway.

Something about her called to me in a way no one else had. Maybe it was the unusual nature of how the Shadow magic had been vested in me, but it felt as if Briar had awakened something far deeper than just love. "I am in control."

"Color me cautious." He folded his arms as we reached the intersection where the hall branched toward the family quarters. He stopped short when I turned toward Elara's rooms. "She won't be up for hours. Go rest, and you can talk with her when you wake. I'll find Silus and wait with him in case she rises early."

I shook my head and continued toward her door. "No. I don't want anyone else to tell her. It's a difficult and confusing situation. She deserves to hear it from me, including why I'm doing some of the things I'm doing." I loved my sister and wouldn't risk hurting her in this manner. The explanation about the orb would have been hard enough without it coming on top of the tragedy of our father's passing.

The golden veins in the obsidian walls caught the low light of the torches, creating a peaceful atmosphere at odds with the turmoil inside me. Despite Father's murder and the chaos that had erupted, this hall remained unchanged—serene, dignified, eternal.

"You can wait with me if you wish," I conceded, too exhausted to argue. "But when Elara wakes, I need to speak with her alone. This news ... it should come from me, without an audience."

Thalen nodded, his silver curls catching the light. "I'll behave, Your Royal Moodiness. I promise not to make any jokes or quips that will make your life worse. I will offer only the ones that make your life better."

"So you'll be silent then? Somehow, I find that unlikely." I shot him a doubting glance.

As we neared Elara's chambers, a sound caught my ear. I held up a hand to stop Thalen from responding as I stopped in front of her door.

Dread pooled in my gut. Someone was crying.

Elara.

No.

I clenched my hands. Had someone told her, or was she having a premonition? Maybe she'd had another nightmare or woken in pain? Not that I wished her more suffering, but ...

My throat thickened as I held my hand over the ornate handle. I'd hoped to have more time to prepare what I wanted to say. But ... there was no time.

I pressed the door open and stepped inside.

Elara sat on her embossed indigo settee, her shoulders hunched, her slender frame looking more fragile than I'd ever seen it. Her long black hair hung loose around her face, and her glamour flickered like a dying candle before it stabilized. For a moment, under the wavering illusion, I glimpsed the gauntness of her cheeks and the heaviness of the shadows under her eyes. Her ivory skin looked patchy.

Beside her stood Silus, one hand resting protectively on her shoulder, his usually stoic expression etched with sadness and concern. He looked up as I entered, his dark eyes meeting mine with a solemn hardness.

The bastard must have told her. I took a step toward her. "Elara ..."

Tears glinted on her cheeks in the golden torchlight as she turned away from me. Her shoulders trembled as she tried to choke back sobs.

"You need to go. She doesn't want to see you." Silus moved in front of Elara, blocking her from my view. He wrinkled his nose in disgust.

Had he really just told me to leave?

Chapter Fourteen

My wings flexed and then snapped against my back, but for Elara's sake, I bit back what I wanted to say and do to Silus. I didn't want to upset my sister more than he already had.

Inhaling, I smelled jasmine and night roses with a hint of a sharp medicinal tang from the twilight bonsais that adorned numerous shelves and small tables in my sister's room. Not even those scents could calm my guilt over her learning of our father's death from someone other than me, nor my anger at Silus's betrayal.

I stepped forward onto the thick indigo rug. "Elara, we need to talk." I would make it abundantly clear that I didn't need *his* permission to speak to my sister.

Silus's jaw tightened, and he edged closer to her. He looked to her as if silently asking if she wanted him to remain.

But Elara had her head bowed and was weeping into her hands. Teardrops stained her blue velvet dressing gown, and her left foot had slipped out of its matching blue slipper.

Thalen cleared his throat and jerked his head toward the door. "Silus, care to walk with me to pick out some wine? I think we could all use a drink right now. Feck, probably for the next several days."

"You get the wine. I'm not leaving Elara." Silus folded his arms over his chest as his charcoal-feathered wings twitched.

The feck he wouldn't. He didn't get to come here and give orders when I was the king's heir and his ruler. He'd woken her up to tell her about our father dying, and now *this*? I wanted to strangle him, but I couldn't risk upsetting Elara more. "I think—"

"It's all right." Elara scrubbed her face and drew in a ragged breath. "No one has to leave or stay. It's ..." More tears brimmed in her dark-blue eyes.

A sharp familiarity cut through me as I realized how much her eyes and other features were like a feminine version of Father's. The hollowness in my chest intensified.

She wiped her cheeks again. "Is he really dead? And Briar was involved?"

My wings and shadows bristled. Normally, I was grateful that Silus looked out for her, but he'd gone too far. Informing her of our father's death and the circumstances was *not* his place. The fact that the bastard couldn't have waited until I returned made me realize he needed to learn what was.

Silus nodded. The way he held himself, stiff in his navy surcoat, made it clear he had no regrets about telling her. He had barely moved an inch from her side, and now he was glaring at me with clear challenge, as if to assert that he was here to protect Elara.

With her health and at this hour, she should have been resting. But no. He'd had to wake her and tell her about Father and Briar before I got back. It would have cost him nothing to grant me that small amount of time. I wasn't only her brother; I was now the leader of this family and soon to be her king. That came with responsibilities. "Father was murdered. Briar didn't kill him or participate in planning his assassination."

"I didn't say that she did." Silus straightened. "I said she was involved in his death, most likely as a pawn. Her presence at a minimum led to someone attacking us. If she had not been here, none of this would have happened."

"Didn't realize you'd become a psychic in these past hours." Thalen snorted. "Who exactly blessed you with this newfound second sight? Whoever it is has you playing the buffoon quite well."

Silus glared. "Can you prove me wrong?"

"In time, regarding Briar, most definitely," Thalen responded. "I fear you will only see it once you stop being an ignorant sniffling flightling. You act as if she's an Aureline contestant."

"Please, don't fight. And he *knows* she's *not* Aureline. Fate would never allow that and risk us losing our magic." Elara's shoulders shook harder, and she pressed her trembling hands to her face. "I can't deal with more arguments and all of us being divided."

The sight of my little sister's pain struck me harder than a physical blow. I crossed over and knelt beside her settee so that I was closer to her eye level.

Silus reached for my arm, and my shadows snapped out and loomed over him in threatening barbs. He didn't get to tell me not to comfort my sister.

He jerked back in shock as my shadows separated into multiple tendrils, obviously far stronger and more ominous than they'd been earlier this very night. If that wasn't a sufficient warning, I didn't know what was.

His lips pressed into a sharp line, and the skin around his eyes tightened, but he pulled back. His gaze shifted to Thalen, who lifted his shoulders in a shrug as if to say, *If you cross him now, you get what you get.*

This wasn't the time or the place to confront Silus fully. I'd deal with him later. Right now, I needed to take care of my little sister.

The silence in the room grew weighted, interrupted only by Elara's futile struggle to stop crying.

She wiped at her eyes repeatedly, sniffed, and scrubbed her face, but more sobs wracked her. "I don't understand," she gasped. "Why would anyone do this? Why would they kill him in Mother's garden? He was on good terms with all the other kingdoms!"

I brushed the dark hair back from her face. "Father's murder was cruel and reckless. Someone is trying to manipulate our kingdom to ensure we choose the queen they want us to have, most likely so they'll have far greater influence over what we do. So many of these choices prove that whoever is behind his death is vicious. Briar was framed, and I am confident in saying there are multiple individuals involved in this atrocity. Anyone with common sense can see that." I looked sharply at Silus, who remained stoic. "We will find all who were involved and bring them to justice. The assassination was coordinated, and they didn't only kill Father. Several of the guards were slain as well, and they attempted to murder Rhielle. Captain Finbar and the Shadow Council are investigating."

"But ... why?" Elara whispered. She grabbed the front of my dark leather surcoat. "Help me understand. Cheating in the bridal competition would just infuriate Fate. Why would they risk it?"

I pulled her close, enfolding her in a tight hug. She buried her face in my shoulder as she so often had when we were younger and smaller, back in the days when she'd believed I could fix anything. Years of illness, nightmares, and loss had taught us both that I was far from invincible, and I felt as helpless to protect her now as I had when she'd woken up screaming the night her illness had manifested.

I could feel each vertebra of her spine under my hand.

She'd continued to shrink in size since that horrid night. Was I going to lose her soon as well?

I let my shadows ease out and sweep over her shadow, replenishing her magic with the remnants of my own. Her shadow darkened, but the improvement was less than it had once been.

I scanned her room, and tears pricked my eyes. She had always loved all shades of blue, and her private quarters reflected that, along with her fascination with the sea and the night. The low lights turned so many of the deep, dark shades practically black. Not even a hint of light shone through the heavy velvet curtains drawn over the windows. It was as if her chambers had been drenched in mourning and were warning me that soon I would have to bid her goodbye as well.

I held her even tighter. "We're going to find out who did this, Elara. I swear." Silently, I added, *And we'll find a way to save you too.* "They will pay, and they will never hurt anyone again. I love you."

"I love you too," she whispered hoarsely. "Just find out who really did it, and rip them to pieces." Her hands fisted my lapels. "I want them to suffer."

I held back a grin. Some thought she was weak, but I knew the true fighter she was. She and Briar had that in common. "They will. I'm already working on the plans."

"And Briar? What of her? I want to see her. How is she involved?"

At least, Elara knew her own mind and trusted her instincts enough to question what Silus had said.

I drew back enough to see her face as I shifted my hand to hold hers. "They resent her for her success in the competition, and they want to make sure that I marry the bride of their choice instead of mine and Fate's."

Should I admit my suspicions about Kaylen?

Not with Silus here.

"And you're certain she wasn't involved at all?" Her brows knitted together.

"You shouldn't ask him that." Silus stepped closer to her once more. "He's too biased to see the risk she brings to the kingdom and to us."

Anger boiled through my veins. Putting Silus in his place would only upset my sister further, but I *would* address this as soon as possible.

"Says the moron who keeps speaking out of turn as if he wants to die." Thalen patted his sword, making it clear whose side he was on.

Elara's bottom lip trembled. She didn't like it when people she cared about fought.

I had to bring the focus back to Elara. Not because I didn't want Thalen and Silus to argue—I couldn't care less if they did—but I refused to upset my sister more than she already was. "Briar is entirely *innocent* in this. The plot has always been about gaining influence in our court." Beyond what they already had.

My thoughts landed on Kaylen, and I shuddered. I suspected her to be a plant, and thinking about crowning her queen made me want to burn my kingdom to the ground.

"I ... I will start preparing the funeral." Drawing back, Elara gripped her robe tighter. "We'll have to have it for your vestment and the preparation for the coronation. We can't have a wedding before we lay Father to rest." She sniffled and blinked. "Have you given any thought to the funeral?"

I paused to get hold of my emotions before answering. "Not beyond cutting the flowers from Mother's garden for the ceremonial wreath and the enshrouding." I missed my father dearly. We'd finally been mending our relationship, which had become strained after Mother's death. Losing him hurt, and remembering Mother caused my heart to feel as if it might implode. "I agree with you regarding the timing."

"Father would like the flowers. He ... he used to love them almost as much as she did. I was always encouraging him to go there." She bit her lower lip and rubbed her eyes with her robe. "The sarcophagus Mother is buried in is large enough for two, and he wanted to be placed beside her. I have the sashes that Mother wove for both of them. And then the soulshard orbs."

Of course she would want those. Fate was not on my side at the moment.

Bracing myself, I looked her in the eye. "I'm afraid that last one isn't possible."

Thalen cleared his throat, adding to my tension.

Silus's jaw clenched.

"I try not to ask for much, but this means a lot to me." She pressed a hand to my arm. "I know it's selfish of me because those orbs mean a great deal to you as well, but they were so special to Father and Mother. He had them made just for them. Each orb had traces of both their magic and represented their strengths and skills, and the way they brought focus and peace to one another in such distinct ways. Now that they've been ... reunited, shouldn't that reminder be placed with them as well?"

I flinched. I wished my shadows could hide me. The last thing I wanted was to upset Elara more, but Briar's safety was worth the steep price. "Perhaps in time, but not now."

"You would refuse me this request?" Her brow wrinkled as she stared at me. "It would mean so much to me. It would signify that Father and Mother are together again, and be a reminder of how much they loved each other."

"The sashes will do that as well." A pang of guilt struck me.

"I don't think I even recognize you anymore." Silus grimaced and stared down at me accusingly. His withering look was one thing I admired about him when he turned it on others, but this time, he was in the wrong and speaking disrespectfully to his king's heir.

"I had to take steps to ensure Briar did not wind up dead or tortured further. And I have every intention of getting the orb back."

"She's been *tortured*?" Elara shook her head in confusion. "What—why? Father abolished interrogations involving torture. And what does that have to do with the orbs?"

"The Aurelines arrested Briar immediately and dragged her to an Aureline prison. Some of the council members involved with the bridal competition are behind framing her. We all have to be exceptionally careful." It didn't seem wise to tell her everything with Silus here. It was a cruel tragedy that, in this, I couldn't count on him as I once had, and I couldn't share everything with my sister, but it was what it was.

"So ... you gave someone our parents' soulshard orbs?" Elara's eyebrows shot upward. "Why? How do you know that they won't use them for something dreadful? Those orbs hold so much power, and if someone is hurt by them, it will be an insult to Mother! That goes against everything she stood for. And Father too." Her blue eyes sparked with anger.

The way Elara looked at me made me want to cover my face in shame. I wished I could've found another bargaining chip, but the orb was the best one I'd had. "The person I gave *one* to is involved in great treachery and must be exposed. He is connected to Father's death, and I will uncover how. I can't say much more than that. But please, trust me, Elara. It was the best option I had to secure the outcome we needed." Or that I needed. Without Briar, I was falling apart, and it wasn't just because of the vested magic.

"Why not use a false one? We have plenty of other orbs that are far less sentimental." She frowned.

"He would have identified an imitation. He has enough

magic and awareness to recognize the power in one of those orbs. It had to be tempting enough for him to take it."

"So he is a bad person?" she asked softly. When I nodded, she dropped her hands and shook her head, her distress more evident. "Then its power will make him so much crueler. Think of all the people he's going to hurt!"

"Haven't you learned?" Silus's expression twisted into disgust and worry. "Only Briar matters to him now."

Thalen spread his wings. "I'm worried about Briar too. She doesn't deserve to be where she is. And if you keep on, Vad won't be the one plucking your feathers. *I* will."

I hated the fact that whoever was behind this was causing problems in our royal circle. They were doing everything possible to break me, but I refused to let them win.

I arched a brow. "That was one of the matters I considered, and I concluded it is worth the risk. It will take him time to learn to draw from that energy. He will be dead and the orb reclaimed before that point. There's no uncertainty there."

"You can't know that." Elara stood abruptly. She pressed a hand to her heart, paced a few steps, and turned to face me. "Vad, nothing that has happened these past days has been in line with any of our plans. None of us anticipated anything remotely like this, and there's so much we still don't know! How could you give our enemy an orb?"

I climbed to my feet, my shadows spilling across the rug and circling back to Elara's. My nausea had lessened, in part because I was back in my own realm, but it spiked again as my shadows tried again to strengthen Elara's, reminding me of my limitations. "Because I deemed it best. It is not without risk, but I give you my word"—I stepped closer and pressed her hand to my heart so she could feel the steadiness and know I wasn't lying— "I will not allow him to go unpunished, and I *will* reclaim the orb. This is a necessary compromise."

"You're ... so calm." Her hand dropped away, and she hugged herself. "How can you be so calm?"

"Trust me, I've had my moments this night." I offered her a small smile and squeezed her arm. "Right now, I am what I need to be. I have a plan, and I will make sure Father's death is avenged and you are kept safe. Don't ask me to say much more than that. So far as anyone else needs to know, my bond with Briar is severed, and I will wed whichever of the brides Fate chooses."

"Except you're going to get Briar back." Her lips twitched, and her jaw worked as if she were trying to keep her emotions under control.

"Yes." Perhaps it was risky to admit. But I couldn't bring myself to lie. "You cannot tell *anyone* about this. No one outside of this room. Understood?" I looked up and stared at Silus.

He scoffed softly, a sound so subtle I could have pretended I didn't hear it, but I was in no mood to suffer fools, no matter who they were to me. "Did you wish to comment on something?" My gaze remained on him, daring him to say it aloud.

He lifted his chin. "All this talk of justice and protecting Elara is meaningless. Your first priority is Briar."

I fisted a hand, trying to hide my rage in front of Elara. Silus was very important to her, and I didn't want to upset her further.

Though I needed to pretend in most other places that I had no feelings for Briar, here, that pretense would be counterproductive. "I love Briar, and I am not willing to live without her. I refuse to leave her in prison. Don't forget, even Father approved of her."

Elara ducked her head, and her bottom lip trembled.

"Then find another way ... to save her." Silus's voice cracked. He glanced from Elara to me, eyes darkening from his own pain. "You chose to trade something sacred of your mother's for this *outsider.* You would break a precious set and deny your sister a simple favor. Do you think your father would be proud of this choice?"

I did, but before I could answer, Elara held up a hand.

She gave Silus a pained look and pressed her other hand to her chest, as if to ground herself. "That isn't a wise question to ask your friend and prince, Silus. And Father ... Father would have ground those orbs into powder or bartered them with the Void if it would have saved Mother. Sometimes, I think he would have given *me* up if he could have—" She closed her eyes, and a tear trickled from one corner. "I-I'm not happy about Vad giving Mother's orb to someone cruel. It's dangerous, but it's done. And I understand why he did it. But I need to be alone to grieve and not listen to you three bickering like children fighting over who gets the last piece of bread with jam!"

"Elara—" Silus started.

"No." She shook her head and walked past him toward the door that led to her bedchamber. "I don't want to talk anymore to any of you. But I do want to make one thing clear." She touched the door frame and turned back toward us. Her glamour faded, and I saw how chapped her lips were before it reappeared. "Vad, I'm not fully all right with what you did, but ... part of me understands. Regardless, I-I need you to know that I love you. Please don't doubt that. I just need some time alone."

"Should I send for Physician Morlo?" Silus had told me that Tai had been here earlier, but I trusted Morlo. He was practically part of the family and had tended to both of us from the time we were infants.

"No." Her tongue swept over her lips. "I just need rest and to process everything before I begin funeral arrangements."

Something was off about her manner and her stance. Something beyond the grief, or perhaps in addition to it.

I lingered at the door, my heart heavy and my bones aching as my head resumed its throbbing ache. "Elara, I love you too. I'm going to fix everything. You'll see." I placed a hand over my heart like I was making a vow. "There are good days ahead of us, little sister. Trust me."

She gave me a teary smile, then disappeared into her bedroom. The door snicked shut behind her, though the lock did not turn.

Tiredness weighed heavily on my body. It was as if all the fatigue had built up behind a wall and was now crashing over me. The list of tasks I had to complete overwhelmed me.

A wave of dizziness hit, and I steadied myself. The magic I'd used to intimidate Colm, kill the guard, and protect Briar had drained me far more than I'd anticipated. The vesting ritual's power was already waning, a disturbing sign that my time to act was significantly shorter than I'd hoped. There was no chance I could make this last a week.

Still, there was one thing I had to take care of before I left this room. As if Thalen could read my mind, he stepped to my side, and we faced Silus together.

I had something to address with him because I was tired of his shit.

Chapter Fifteen

Silus folded his arms and waited for me to speak.

I paused, not wanting to torch the centuries-long friendship the two of us had shared. Even now, he wasn't trying to be difficult. He saw himself as protecting not only Elara but me as well. The problem was, he was misguided and not treating me like the king's heir. "Why did you wake Elara when we both know she needs her rest? Was it to spite me because I left to locate Briar?"

His head jerked back. "I didn't wake her. I was in her chambers when she woke of her own accord and came out. Some of the servants were here, speaking of the king's death. I wanted you to be the one to tell her, but I definitely didn't want her to learn about it by overhearing someone who wasn't close to her. I informed her because of the circumstances."

A bit of tension eased. I had thought the worst, assuming he'd purposely tried to undermine me.

"No." Thalen tilted his hands, creating his circle of silence to dampen our voices. "Don't let him off that easy. He could've kept the servants away. He chose to tell her, despite knowing how hard it would be on her without her brother there."

"I suppose you're living your best life right now." Silus

sneered. "You must always be the center of attention, and right now, you're the golden friend."

"Did you even try to find me, Silus, before you told her?" I tilted my head and watched his facial expressions.

He shook his head, his jaw set. "There was no time. I'd stayed in her gathering room in case she needed help. You didn't see her last night. She was so ... exhausted and fragile, and I didn't want to leave her alone. She felt sick when she woke and came out here, asking what was wrong, and it wouldn't have been right to just let her overhear the servants. I didn't know where you were."

So Father's death hadn't impacted only me. She'd suffered as well. "What did you tell her?"

"You mean about Briar? Or everything?" He laughed humorlessly.

"Everything," I said sternly. I didn't have time for snide comments. I had a lot to do, but this had to be addressed.

He shifted his weight and nodded as he drew a hand over his mouth. "I told her that someone murdered your father in your mother's garden. That whoever it was had been clever. That Briar was involved but most likely as a pawn or a weakness they'd identified to keep you distracted. And that there was an investigation underway. I didn't say it was Briar's fault or that Elara should hate her. I told her how I saw it."

If only I had Briar's ability to smell lies. In all the time I had known him, Silus had never been prone to lying, but lately I wasn't sure how well I knew him—or anyone really.

My limbs weighed me down like lead, and my shadows pulsed, confirming the depths of my weariness. "I want to be clear. You are not to discuss Briar with my sister any further. I don't trust your judgment, the same as you don't trust mine. If you breach my trust in *any* way, I will prevent you from seeing my sister in any capacity. Do you understand?"

"I think your ban should include more than Briar. It should include the king's death, too, and the circumstances around it." Thalen huffed. "He wants to poison her mind."

"If you—" Silus started.

I lifted a hand and cut him off. "Elara may need someone to talk to, and both Thalen and I will be busy. I don't want her to feel alone or abandoned. But, Silus, I will find out if you so much as *hint* to my sister that Briar is the problem or was part of the assassination plan. You focus on being there for her in dealing with our father's death. One misstep, and you won't have another chance."

"Understood." Silus pressed his lips together. "I can't risk losing her. And I'm not being spiteful. I'm just as concerned for you as I am for her, but you won't listen to me."

I exhaled. He might care, but he wasn't handling this disagreement well. "She cares for you, and I'd hate to be forced to be the villain. Even though we clearly aren't seeing eye to eye right now, I don't want to hurt her in any additional ways." Now that this was settled, I looked to Thalen and nodded toward the door that led out of her chambers. "Let's go. We have much to do."

Thalen headed out the door without acknowledging Silus again.

It felt wrong not to tell Silus everything, but I had revealed more than I'd intended. He could still damage our plans if he wanted to, but I did trust that he genuinely cared for us, even though his attitude was misguided.

We left Elara's chambers and had barely made it to the conjunction of the halls when Thalen cut in front of me.

"You need to rest. If you don't go to bed, I may commit treason by assaulting the heir of the Shadow King with the Club of Swift Slumber to ensure he sleeps." Thalen jabbed his finger against my chest, then gestured toward the hall to my own room with a jerk of his thumb. "Your chambers are that way. In case you need reminding, considering it's been so long since you've slept."

I hesitated. Nausea was still roiling within my stomach, and my fingertips pricked with uncomfortable energy. "There are still tasks—"

"If it can't wait, tell me, and I'll see to it. Otherwise, let it wait." Thalen stayed directly in front of me.

More arguments rose to my lips, but another rolling wave of nausea cut through me, and my eyes nearly shuttered. "Very well. I'll rest. Inform the warden and chief interrogator about Colm's arrival and the arrangement. Make sure there are no wounded feelings, but don't reveal too much. Come wake me once the High Aureline Council has arrived or if Rhielle awakens. We need to know what she knows."

"Would you like me to see if Kaylen is available to chat? I'm certain she'd be more than happy to soothe your weary brow." He flashed a grin before swooping away with his wings spread as one of my shadows swatted at him. The shadow flickered and faded, but Thalen had his back to me at least, so he didn't see.

I'd pushed myself too far. My stomach cramped with even more nausea, and my head thundered as I made my way into my chambers. The carafe of water by my bedside was mercifully full. I drained it in a single breath, removed my boots, and dropped into bed.

MY BODY SHOOK, rousing me from slumber. I opened my eyes to find Thalen leaning over me.

"Rhielle's out of her coma. I can talk with her if you need more rest. It's only been four hours." Thalen took a step back.

"Four hours?" I grunted, my mouth tasting like salt and bile. I pushed my hair out of my face. "You're lying. It's been ...

ten minutes at most."

"Sorry. Four hours. Maybe a little more." Thalen drew back and crossed his arms. "Looks like you could use another ten."

I jolted upright, realizing I was still wearing my formal black silks from the ball. My entire being wanted to fall back into bed, but that wasn't an option. Not until Briar was back at my side. "Why don't you speak with Captain Finbar and follow up on the investigation, and then speak with the officiants about sending Elara information about the decisions needed for the funeral arrangements? While you handle that, I'll speak to Rhielle."

Thalen fought a yawn and rolled his shoulders, hinting at his own exhaustion. "That's fine. I'll find you when I'm finished."

I waited for him to leave, but he stayed in place.

I arched a brow. "Are you going to insist on accompanying me while I change?"

"Do you even have to ask?" He grinned and spread his arms. "You'll never be rid of me. At least, not until you get *your* Copper Chaos back. At which time, I will discreetly excuse myself and leave you and your shadows to her and her shadow beast."

I dragged my hand over my eyes again, barely registering the joke beyond his tone. "I need to dress. I was waiting for you to leave, but it seems you'd like to stay."

Thalen turned and rushed to the door. "I need a show from someone soon, but it's not going to be *you*." He slammed it behind him.

I rolled my eyes and went to my mirror. I dropped my glamour for a moment, needing to see how run-down I truly was.

I stumbled back a step. I'd known it'd be bad, but I hadn't been prepared for how bad.

Dark circles lay beneath my bloodshot eyes, and my skin seemed to sag. I was more than exhausted, and my appearance matched how I felt. I slid the glamour snugly back in place. I had no more time to rest and didn't need to dawdle over my true appearance.

I bathed swiftly and scrubbed my face before putting on a black tunic, a black surcoat with muted gold embellishments, onyx iron bracers, a leather belt, a dagger, and black trousers and boots.

When I entered the healing chambers, the physicians and attendants stood to attention, and one of the gray and green-clad attendants hurried forward and gestured for me to follow her. She guided me to a smaller chamber door inset between two pillars. As we passed beneath the delicate carved stone archway, I noted its protective sigils had been marked with oils, and the air smelled more of peppermint and sage than the usual medicinal herbs.

These were the recovery rooms, which meant Rhielle had already been moved from treatment. The attendant gestured toward the wooden door carved with the healing emblem of a sheaf of varied herbs encircled by a broad gold line. The attendant rapped his knuckles on the door but pressed in at once. "The prince wishes an audience."

I grimaced inwardly, wishing he had waited a moment to ensure she was ready for guests.

My attention went to the plush bed in the center of the tiny room. Small bruises spattered Rhielle's face, and a deep, thick bruise with a stitched-up horizontal gash in the center marred her throat. Her long pink hair fanned over her white pillow, and her normally fair skin held a tint of sickly yellow that contrasted with the moss-green blanket. Her hands lay laced over her abdomen, and her breaths were controlled.

Her body was near motionless on the bed, and a pale

green aura intended to restore and reverse life-draining attacks shimmered all around her.

The attendant bowed and stayed close to the door. "If you require anything, simply ring the bell." He gestured to a small inset in the wall with a matching gold bell.

"Very well," I replied, my leathery wings swaying as I moved to Rhielle's side.

My breath caught as I noted open scrapes and cuts as well as bruises on her hands and wrists. The marks were in line with someone using death magic to reverse the healing of the past several days and weaken her. It wasn't the same as draining her lifeblood but related to a similar tradition and skillset. It was a coincidence I disliked intensely. If not for Rhielle's defensive Shadow magic, she would have died. Had someone been trying to harvest her magic?

Her magenta eyes met mine, and her pupils seemed to fade marginally at the edges until they nearly blended with her irises. "Your Highness, I didn't expect a personal visit." Her brow furrowed, and she bowed her head in respect. Faint vestiges of dark purple shadows wisped around her body.

I'd never noticed them before, but they were clearly manifestations of her magic. Had the vesting of the Shadow magic granted me the ability to see them, or had her magic changed in some way? Or were they evidence of the magic working to mend her body?

My head throbbed, reminding me of my own limitations. I cleared my throat. "I am pleased to see you conscious again. Your experience must have been quite harrowing."

Needing a moment to collect my thoughts, I stared at the flames of the pillar candles burning on the table across from me and took a deep breath. The room smelled of plums and red tea, though I didn't see a telltale mug, so she'd likely been given nourishment earlier.

"It was." She clenched her jaw and glared at me. Though she'd been near death's door, it seemed she had scorned it. "Lately, almost dying has become something of a pastime."

"What can you tell me of your attacker?" I folded my arms.

"He was a cowardly asshole in a dark cloak with stronger magic than spine. Could have been a dark gray cloak; could have been black. I couldn't tell." She twitched her shoulders, then winced. "I checked my room before I went to sleep, since I'd been attacked in the night before. I thought everything was secure, and I went to sleep. Then I woke up, and before I even opened my eyes, I sensed a presence stirring by my bed. My shadow shield erupted on instinct, but something cold spread over me—something in the air. The wound in my throat opened, and it felt like every cut, scrape, and bruise I'd gotten in the past six months came back. It was ... almost too fast. It choked me. I couldn't breathe. Could hardly see anything because my eyelids froze shut. My shield only worked because I've practiced it so much it's like muscle memory."

I focused on the wound at her throat. "Was this attacker the same one who went after you before?" Captain Finbar had been investigating that as well, and to my knowledge, he had not uncovered the intruder.

"Possibly. His hands were younger than I expected. I couldn't make out much else because he attacked me with a type of paralysis. I briefly smelled something like anise. Then it faded. The magic could have been Sylvan, Shadow, or Aureline." Her brow twitched. "It didn't feel like the same poison from the first attack."

"And the wound at your throat ... it opened first?" If it was the same type of magic or the same practitioner, then it would respond the fastest to this sort of attack.

"I think so. Everything hurt though. My whole body was on fire, and I couldn't move. My shield saved me. That, and

Briar walking in. I was barely conscious, but she was trying to help. And whoever it was grabbed and drugged her next. He was taller than her by only a few inches, but if he hadn't had whatever was on that cloth, I think she could have taken him in a fight." Her lips pressed tight, and her purple-pink eyes flared with vengeful light. "On paper, she and I are rivals, but I don't give a feck about winning this competition. I know Briar didn't do anything wrong."

I gave a curt nod. She was one of Briar's friends, but there was still a possibility she had been involved. What better alibi than to be attacked? Though ... that wound at her throat was critical. Perhaps this Elias person Briar had mentioned had been used to keep Rhielle alive? Draining him could have been a treatment to save her from the blade at her throat and its poison, but then it wouldn't have left such a grievous scar. No ... that didn't seem right.

Could I trust Rhielle? Something was holding me back. I didn't want to take the risk for now.

I bowed my head and folded my dark wings tight against my back. "Thank you for your testimony. I will inform the doctors that they are to give you the best treatment. If you are not comfortable continuing in the bridal competition, I will pass on my permission for you to withdraw."

"You can do that? I thought the joint councils overseeing the bridal competition got final say." She quirked one eyebrow dramatically. The doubt on her face could not have been more apparent.

"I can make my recommendation. Whether the councils accept it remains to be seen."

Her expression flattened. "Then why don't you just claim Briar as your queen and save some innocent lives while you're at it, instead of acting like we're all expendable?" She lifted her chin. "But that isn't an option now, since you allowed the

Aurelines to take her before you even began an investigation. And you're here with me instead of doing something to protect her or clear her name.

"If you think she actually killed your father, you're just as corrupt as Kaylen, and you aren't good enough for her even if you are a fecking royal. This was sabotage, pure and simple. Whoever tried to kill me made sure to remove her, and which contestant would be evil enough to do that?" Her mouth pinched as if she had tasted a lemon, and she set her jaw. "That said, I am deeply sorry for your loss, Your Highness. But your complacency is almost worse than if you were involved in Briar's arrest. My Veralt would have set that whole garden on fire rather than let them take me, unless *I* told him to stand down."

My head jerked back. No one knew me well enough to speak so bluntly and assume it would not result in painful consequences. The mention of Veralt made me curious, though I wouldn't inquire further. Most likely a past lover, or perhaps even a current one. It wasn't uncommon for bridal candidates to have relationships before being brought here.

"What exactly have you heard?" I steeled my voice in neutrality.

"As soon as I gained consciousness, I asked about Briar." Her pupils faded at the edges again, a sign that her strength was waning despite her best efforts. "They said she killed your father in the garden. Now, I don't know what happened, but I know Briar. I thought you knew her too, but witnessing her actions in the trials seems to have given you no clarity."

She met my gaze unflinchingly, her magic shimmering around her in faint purple wisps. The look on her face demanded answers.

The way she spoke with such conviction made me want to believe her, but it was still possible that she was lying. My fingers tapped on my belt as I contemplated this. Perhaps I could give her some small comfort and see what she did with the information.

I glanced back at the heavy wooden door behind me, then stepped closer. "You must not speak of this to anyone," I said in a firm but quiet voice. "It will put Briar in danger if you do. But I am aware she did not kill my father, and I am doing all in my power to save her. For the time being and because of what is at stake, I cannot admit this elsewhere. For all intents and purposes, it must look as if I will choose another bride. But my heart is with Briar, and I will see to it that she is freed and cleared of all charges of wrongdoing."

Her eyes widened slightly before she schooled her expression into a cold mask. "Well, you better succeed. Briar doesn't deserve a weak male who can't defend his family. And I have even less tolerance for failure."

"No. She doesn't." And she wouldn't have one.

Part of me wanted to tell Rhielle the rest and seek her counsel, but that wouldn't be wise.

I turned to go, then paused and glanced back at her. "Have you noticed anything else unusual in this competition, aside from what you have said? Any signs of death magic or life draining or interference?"

"Kaylen is involved. I can't prove it. But I know it." Her gaze hardened. "I imagine you're going to have to play nice with her." She stared at me, unflinching. "We both know you're going to have to do something that'll piss me off and hurt Briar, don't we?"

Chapter Sixteen

BRIAR

My entire body ached and itched. I had no clue how long I'd been stuck in this horrendous cave, but time blurred here. Had Vad and Many-Greats forgotten me?

Drip.

Or had something happened?

Drip. Drip.

The actual assassin who had killed Vad's father could go for Vad next. It could be anyone.

Drip. Drip. Drip. Drip.

What if I never got out of this place?

Drip.

My skin crawled even more. Once upon a time, the sound of rain had calmed me, but not anymore. Between my wolf's desperation to break free and this noise, I felt damn close to insanity.

I paced around the cave, desperate to find a hint of something that promised escape. All I accomplished was reinjuring my feet and hands and remaining in agony. The only bright spot was that I received two loaves of non-moldy black bread and two waterskins a day.

I would kill for a steak, a hamburger, or some chicken. Any

meat.

My toes hit a pile of loose rocks, and I stumbled, almost dropping the half loaf of bread under my arm. I didn't want to risk leaving it for the guards to spot because I was sharing with Elias. The bread blended in with my gray wool dress, so if a guard checked in, he wouldn't see what I was doing with it unless he looked just as I was slipping it to Elias.

I bumped against the cave wall, hitting a spot where a sharp piece of rock jutted out a few inches. I grunted but held myself steady so I wouldn't fall on the scattered pebbles below.

My wolf tried to surge forward, desperate to get out of her captivity. If the dripping didn't send me over the edge, my wolf would. I'd heard the stories of what happened when we shifters caged our wolf too long, and they all ended with insanity.

The sound of feet and arms scrabbling at the stone caught my attention.

Elias was back. My heart lunged into my throat. How bad off would he be? Each time he returned from being drained, he was more quiet and shaky.

Breaths rasped against the stone.

Knowing the guards, they'd do anything to find a reason to beat me, so I needed to make sure it was Elias and not one of them pretending.

I crouched in front of the crack in the wall, steadying myself against the cold, damp stone. The hem of my wool dress dipped into the pool of water. As the damp fibers clung to my skin, I tried to ignore the itching and be grateful for the warmth the wool provided.

I tilted my head to peer through the thickest part of the crack. "Who's there?"

"Me," Elias rasped, and the scraping noises became louder and more disjointed.

A huge lump lodged in my throat when I saw him. Elias

lay face down in the tunnel with one hand outstretched and digging into the stone floor, as if he were mustering the strength to drag himself forward. His back trembled with each breath, a shiver running beneath the skin. His fingernails scraped on the stone as his fingers twitched. His skin had a grayish pallor that couldn't be blamed on the bad lighting. My heart twinged, and I clutched the bread closer to my chest.

I couldn't rely on Many-Greats or Vad to get me out. Elias was running out of time. "If you can make it to me, I saved a half loaf of bread for you again." I tried to sound a little upbeat, but my effort fell short. "We should probably file a complaint with this restaurant."

He laughed weakly, his face still turned down, and his voice muffled. "Restaurant. Such a strange word. What does it mean?"

"A place that has a long list of different meals you can choose from. When we get out of here, I'll take you to one." I tore off a chunk of the thickly crusted bread and pinched the edges to make it easier to slide through the crack.

He craned his head, then shook it weakly. "Keep it," he whispered. "Don't waste it on me."

I scoffed and pressed closer to the wall. "Don't be ridiculous. We're in this together. Besides, you need it more than I do."

He grunted as he struggled to push himself into a seated position. Blood trickled down his arms, and his loose skin jiggled under the ragged gray garments hanging loosely on his bony frame. As he settled himself, his arm centered into the peephole, and I could see that his flesh was a mass of twisted bruises and collapsed veins.

The bread I'd eaten earlier lurched into my throat, the bitter yeast drying my mouth. The tubes they'd pierced his body with to draw his lifeblood from him had left behind bloody tracks on his chest and shoulders. The four-claw tattoo on his neck had disappeared into a large bruise where someone must have grabbed him and held him in place.

"No." His throat bobbed. "Can't take much more of this. One, maybe two more sessions of draining, and I'll be ..." He stopped himself.

Words failed me. I struggled to swallow as despair crushed me, choking me, though I pushed it down. "Don't talk like that. We're both getting out of here. You'll see."

Part of my promise was selfish because I couldn't bear the thought of being trapped down here alone. My wolf was about to go insane. I needed at least one other person down here.

He tilted his head back so that it rested against the wall. "After you get out, please ... find my brother, Holn. He works for the Ignis King in the Fire Palace as a hexwright. We're estranged, but he's all the family I have left. Tell him what happened. But only if it won't put you at risk."

The request sent a chill through me. I wanted to comfort him, but the words died on my lips.

Ember's face flashed into my mind. Many-Greats had told her I was all right. But what if I died here and never got to tell her I loved her, or got to make brownies with her again? My lower lip trembled, and my wolf whined in response.

She was right. I wasn't going to give in. They wanted to break me? Fuck them. I wasn't going to let them. I'd see Ember again, and I'd hug her and Ryker so tight. I'd see Vad too, and I'd kiss him and tell him I loved him. And Elias would see Holn again.

We had to.

"I can, but it'd be better if you told him yourself." I steadied my voice and squared my shoulders. "But I don't know what's going to happen to either of us. So ... we need to do what we can to keep our strength up so we can jump at any chance we have to escape." I lined up the bread with the crack, trying not to think of the dirt and grime that would get on it by the time it reached him.

"You're relentless, you know that?" Another laugh wheezed past his lips, but he put his hand to the crack. Dried blood lined his fingernails, and his hand trembled. "Fine. If it would please you."

"It will." I pushed the chunk of bread through. The thick bread was challenging to chew. Sometimes I had to dip it in water to get it down, which made it taste worse, but at least it didn't disintegrate when I pushed it through the crack in the wall.

"You're too good to me." He drew the bread through. "No one else would do this."

"Yeah, well, I like to spoil my friends." The joke fell flat. My body ached, and I curled my hand around the rest of the heavy loaf of bread, my fingernails digging into it. The faint stale, fermented scent provided a reprieve from the filth of this place, but not much. What I wouldn't give to be back with my friends.

Drip. Drip. Drip. Drip. Drip.

The dripping of the water had me wanting to pull my hair out. Not only was it driving me crazy, but it also highlighted how uncertain time was here.

"As long as you don't invest too much in one who is doomed." He struggled to chew the mouthful and dropped his hand into his lap. "If you have a chance to escape and you can't bring me, don't you dare stay back for me."

My heart clenched, and I bit the inside of my cheek until I tasted blood. More than anything, I wanted to reassure him, but I didn't want to lie. "Elias—"

"If I find out you had a chance and you stayed behind for me, I'll curse you, girl. Or maybe I'll find a way to bring this cavern down on both of us and end our pain." He glanced at me sidelong and forced a trembling smile. "You've done me far greater kindnesses than I ever imagined receiving in this place. I can't imagine ever walking free in the fire rose gardens again with the sun on my face and the wind at my back, but ... somehow I can see you ... with Colm's head beneath your feet."

A bitter laugh bubbled in my chest, but I held it back. "I'd rip out his throat first."

I broke off another chunk of bread and passed it to him. My hands felt like they were on fire. I tried not to look at the raw sores that refused to heal.

"Yes, with your ... uh ... wuf. Isn't that what you call it?"

"Wolf." My wolf nudged at me, reminding me of her presence and that she wanted out. She paced, wearing on me, but I focused on the measure of comfort and the lukewarm spots of Ember, Ryker, and the rest of my pack in my chest. They were alive, and I wasn't ever truly alone. My fingers curled at my chest as my throat tightened.

The door above me slammed open. I jumped as the stone rang out with a deafening *thud*. "Hope you're awake, filth blood," a new voice sang.

I jammed the rest of the loaf roughly through the crack, and Elias pulled it through as best he could. They couldn't see me from this angle, so I had a moment.

Heavy footsteps drew closer to the opening in the roof of my cavern cell. Then the grate clanged open.

Not wanting them to realize where I'd been, I ran on throbbing feet to the center of the cave, just as a metal bucket tied to a coil of thick rope slithered through the opening. It clanged into the shallow puddle, sending beetles skittering away from the spray.

Two gray-armored guards peered down at me, one holding the rope and the other aiming a crossbow at me, one metal-gloved finger resting on the trigger.

Of course they'd have bad trigger discipline. These guards

lacked discipline and smarts. The only reason I hadn't managed to attempt an escape again was because they'd left me down here.

"Move your ass, grave kisser," the guard barked. "Step into the bucket. We're in a hurry."

They hadn't let me leave this cell since Vad's visit. Had Colm decided to torture me again? My entire body tensed as I stared up at the imposing silhouettes framed against the light. My wolf snarled, making it clear she agreed that we shouldn't go *anywhere* with them. "What's going on?"

"Shut your filthy mouth." The guard holding the rope spat, missing me by inches. "Someone important wants to look the king-killer in the eye. Demanded to see you personally. Now get in the damn bucket before I drag you up by your hair."

My heart skipped a beat. *A visitor?* Could Vad have come back to share a plan with me? Hope blossomed in my chest, but I forced myself to rein it in.

There was no telling who it might be—friend or foe—and my gut twinged.

My heart twisted and squeezed like it was caught in a vise. I didn't want to go with them.

"Move, or I *will* shoot," the guard warned.

I didn't have a choice. But at least I'd have another opportunity to learn the layout of the prison ... and another chance to try to escape.

I lifted my chin, refusing to allow them to believe they had broken me. My wolf growled but then whimpered, knowing that she couldn't surge forward to kill them.

Biting the inside of my cheek, I gripped the rope with my raw hands and stepped into the dingy bucket. It was barely large enough for me to fit one foot inside, and I had to balance the other foot on the rim. The coarse fibers of the rope scraped against my palms, and I held back a whimper. I didn't want them to get any enjoyment from my injuries.

The first guard began hauling me upward, the bucket swaying precariously. My cuts and sores shredded further as the bucket spun like a tilt-a-whirl, and the bread in my stomach lurched into my throat.

"Don't even think about using those teeth." Crossbow Guard pointed the bolt right in my face as my head cleared the opening. "We know what you are, and we won't allow you to bite off our noses or any other appendages."

"Shut it," Rope Guard snapped as he secured the rope on a hook in the wall. Then he reached out for me, his rough hands squeezing my arms above my elbows, and lifted me upward.

The wool of my dress cut into my skin, and I bit my cheek harder. I needed to ground myself, and that seemed like the best way.

I scanned the area for something to use as leverage to try to escape, but the closest thing was a rope that hung at Rope Guard's side, just out of reach.

He placed me on the ground, and the second guard pivoted a mere three feet from me with the bolt still ready.

"One unexpected movement, and I won't hesitate to kill you." Crossbow Guard grinned like he'd just offered me a challenge.

These two were being careful, which was problematic for me.

Rope Guard rubbed my arms, causing the wool to grate against my flesh. He removed the rope at his side and bound my wrists, knotting the scratchy rope hard, and I grunted, unable to keep the noise from coming out.

"Move." Rope Guard shoved me down the dimly lit corridor.

"Hey!" I stumbled forward and nearly struck the hall wall.

"Don't cause trouble," Crossbow Guard growled.

I placed my bound hands against the wall and stepped back.

"Come on now. Faster." Rope Guard gave a warning tug.

Stinging pricks shot down my hands, and once again, my feet scraped against the rough stone floor. Each step hurt worse than the last. As I limped down the hall, I tried to make myself appear even more pathetic. This wasn't a time for pride—it was a time for them to underestimate me.

Neither guard touched me, and Rope Guard gave me enough slack to set my own speed.

"Left," Rope Guard barked when we approached a cross-section in the dark, pockmarked hall.

"And hurry. We don't want to keep our guest waiting." Crossbow Guard gestured with his weapon.

They were taking me back to the room where I'd seen Vad, which meant I wouldn't see any more of the prison. My shoulders sagged. Every time I hoped to get ahead, it seemed I landed in an even more precarious situation. Was it even worth—

Yes.

I gritted my teeth. I wouldn't become like Elias. He and I were going to find a way out of here. Ember wouldn't allow them to break her, and I refused to break as well. We were fighters.

My heart sped faster as we approached the heavy door. No welcoming tug found me, but I caught a faint scent that I couldn't quite place.

Crossbow Guard shoved the door open, and then Rope Guard struck me between the shoulders and pushed me through. "Don't keep 'em waiting."

My shoulders hunched forward as my back absorbed the blow. I staggered into the room and narrowly caught myself against the wooden slab table with the oil lamp, jostling it. The lamp rattled loudly. The scent of jasmine and something like roses fought against the cave's smell of rot and blood. I righted myself, standing tall as the door clanged shut. The guards moved to stand against the wall, hands at their sides, but no weapons drawn.

I lifted my head to face the latest potential enemy in the room ... and blinked.

There was something about the woman in front of me. Something familiar, though I thought I'd never met her before.

She was frail, her ivory skin thin as paper with numerous cuts and bruises along the veins, as if her own blood was too violent for her body. Her cheeks were gaunt hollows carved far too sharply, much like her eyes, which had sunken in. Bloody cracks ran along the corners of her mouth and over her lips, and her black hair, which was pulled into a loose bun, had multiple thin patches, to the point that her skull was visible.

My heart broke. They had to be torturing her as well. But why would they have two prisoners meet? Although ... she was clean and dressed nicely in an indigo gown.

She moved toward me, her lips cracking even more.

I'd opened my mouth to urge her to lean against the wall and not strain herself when her delicate floral scent reached me more fully.

Elara?

My mouth went dry, and a surge of realization had me stiffening in shock.

"Hello, Briar." Her bony hand slid to the side as she tried to gently rub her bruised wrist without drawing much attention, and her wings—if they could even be called that—fluttered. They were tattered and practically skeletal, and the right side sagged despite her effort every so often to straighten and tuck them in. "After I heard what happened, I wanted to speak with you myself. It seemed wise." She tilted her head to examine me.

My gut twisted and turned over on itself like something

rotten had cracked open inside me. "I offer condolences on your father's passing, Princess Elara." I struggled to form the words around the sour dryness of my mouth. Even her eyes were glassy with barely a hint of blue, like her life force was almost gone.

Her gaze flicked toward the guards and back to me. Neither guard was looking at us, their focus seemingly on the floor. She turned away from them, angling so that, if someone came through the door, only her back would be seen. Her fingers twitched, indicating for me to move as well.

I took three steps to one side and positioned myself so my expressions couldn't be seen from the door or by the guards.

Her head inclined forward, and a soft smile spread across her face. "Condolences mean little. What I want is the truth. I came to see you for myself because I thought you were different. Someone I could trust and who would make my brother's life better. Clearly, I was *wrong*."

The words stung as the scent of rotten eggs filled my nostrils. Her expression did not match her words, and the scent had come at the end, but was I searching for anything that could provide me hope? This place had a way of messing with my mind. Her voice had trembled, but I couldn't tell if that was grief, illness, or both.

She straightened, suddenly seeming every bit the royal, her posture and demeanor almost strong again. Yet, she couldn't completely mask her ill health. She seemed a mere ghost of what she once was.

My vision blurred, and I desperately blinked back the tears. "I swear I didn't betray you or your family. I promise on my own life that I would never purposely harm you, your brother, or the king. I care for you all so much and wish I could be there beside you while you grieve."

Taking a step closer, Elara briefly brushed her cold hand against mine and said, "Even a guilty person would make that claim, but I admire your persistence."

The corners of my mouth wanted to tip up, but I forced them to remain in place. Her touch had confirmed everything that her words couldn't. I hoped she believed me, and at least I knew she didn't hate me.

However, my happiness vanished as quickly as it had come. Something was definitely not right with her. I'd already suspected something was going on with her because she never flew like the others. But if I asked about her health, the guards might listen and pass the information on to someone who might harm her or Vad. And even if I did ask, I doubted she was in any position to answer.

"I don't want my visit to be misconstrued. I'm here to hear directly from you what transpired last night." She dipped her head, and her right wing sagged again. Her brow pinched as she straightened the wing, followed by a cracking noise as if it had popped from its socket. Her expression tightened as she drew the wing back in place. "Just as you remember it." The words had a sharper, breathier quality this time.

"Last night?" My brows lifted, and I tensed. Had the guards really brought her here to ask about *this?* If they knew I was feeding Elias, why would they ask Elara to come? I'd expected them to catch me red-handed and beat the living hell out of me. "I was in my cell. Nothing happened." The stench of my own lie hit me, making me want to gag.

"No, last night, when you murdered Father." Elara pressed her lips together, and blood oozed past the cracks. "Time works differently in this place. It can seem like days, weeks, or years have passed when it's been only a short amount of time. You've been here twelve hours."

I inhaled quickly and choked on my own spit. I coughed and then swallowed hard, trying to comprehend what she'd said. "Twelve hours?" No wonder Vad hadn't returned and

Many-Greats hadn't visited me again.

Rope Guard chuckled before clearing his throat.

I wanted to roll my eyes but kept them in place. They were observing us after all.

Rolling my shoulders back, I moistened my lips and told her everything I'd told Vad. Colm's brutal, inserted memories swung at the edges of my mind, but I batted them away. For what felt like the millionth time, I recounted what had happened as clearly and simply as possible.

Elara held one hand near the base of her throat as she listened, sometimes brushing her finger over her cracked lips. When I finished, she edged forward. "He said 'lilies.' That's all?"

"That's all." I rubbed my fingers together, wishing I could reach out and comfort her. "I swear it or vow it or curse on it, or ... whatever you want me to do."

Her gaze dropped to the floor, and she shuddered. "The ball was the first time he'd served as officiant in ages. The first time he felt so good that he actually ... enjoyed himself." She drew in a deep breath. "He asked me to dance. I used to love dancing with him, but I wasn't feeling well, so ... I said another time. He suggested we walk in the garden instead, and I asked if we could do it another night after I rested. He—he said yes."

"Your father—" My heart ripped open. I understood what losing a parent felt like and knew that, if I were given the chance to see mine again, I'd do things differently. Regret hovered over me, along with the question: If I had that chance, *would* things be different?

"I should have been with him in the garden," she whispered. Naked emotion slid over her face before she caught herself and gulped in a large breath. "Or if I'd danced with him, maybe the attack wouldn't have succeeded."

I had my own what-ifs. What if Ember and I had fought against the alpha command our father had given us to run?

What if we had stayed and fought alongside our pack while they were being slaughtered? Maybe something would've changed. Those what-ifs hurt worse sometimes than what had happened.

I stepped forward, wanting to comfort her and myself.

"Stay back," Crossbow Guard growled, lifting the weapon toward me again. "Do *not* get close to the Shadow Princess."

The urge to stomp and scream surged through me. I was so damn tired of them treating me like this. I wanted to slit their throats—or let my wolf rip them out. I wasn't picky, as long as all these corrupt guards died.

"Briar," Elara said sharply, as if she knew what was going on in my head.

Suddenly, the door slammed open, and Silus slid in. Sweat beaded his brow and clung to his normally immaculate dark hair. He straightened his charcoal black surcoat and the dark-blue ascot tucked into his tunic.

The guards snapped to attention, Crossbow Guard swinging the weapon from me to Silus. Rope Guard reached for his sword, but neither moved away from the wall.

"Princess." Silus's gaze locked on Elara, and his eyes widened. "What are you doing here?" His jaw worked like there was another question he wanted to ask instead.

The air seemed to thicken, and I dug my fingers into the rope to give myself something to hold on to. Tension radiated between the two of them, all but shimmering in the air as neither looked away.

I didn't know Silus well. Every time I'd seen him, he'd been so serious and had seemed more of a stick in the mud than even Vad had at first.

His gaze traveled over Elara while his right hand fisted and curled against his trousers, as if he wanted to touch her and was holding himself in check. Tears shone in his dark eyes, and he stepped forward. "You're needed back at the palace."

She lifted her chin. "It's fine."

"Then we should take leave, Your Highness." He turned to me and flinched before schooling his expression. "If you're done speaking to the person *accused* of killing the king?"

My head jerked back a little. He'd called me the accused, not the killer. That didn't sound like the Silus I knew.

Elara turned to me, her gaze piercing through the dim light of the small chamber.

Following suit, Silus studied me in a cold, detached manner.

"I suppose there isn't much more to say." Elara sighed. "Growing up, I always wanted a little sister. I imagined I'd tell her to be brave, and to cherish the knowledge that her family and friends would stop at nothing to keep her safe. That's how family works, after all. And there is no fury like the fury that comes when someone takes one of our family from us. There would be no peace until the matter was resolved. I would tell her to keep her wings straight and her chin up and remember who she is and who she belongs to." She raised one hand as her voice shook. "I'd hoped that you would be that for me, but Fate always has her plan."

Something inside my chest had twisted when she'd said *little sister*, each word a blade with the edge turned inward. In such a short time, I'd come to care for Elara. I'd gotten a friendly vibe from her as soon as I'd arrived in Nytheria.

Her lips trembled. "But you are *not* my sister, and I was wrong about you from the start."

That blast of sulfur was the most welcome, disgusting scent I'd ever smelled. I shook my head as tears sprang to my eyes, burning and spilling over. My lips parted, but no sound came out. What could I possibly say to that? To any of this? "I hope you get a little sister like that someday." Even if it wound up not being me.

Her lips had parted as if she was about to speak again when the earth jolted.

The guards exchanged panicked glances as dust began to filter down from the ceiling. Silus ripped off his cloak and lunged at Elara. He swept the cloak around and lifted her into his arms as if she weighed nothing, while the walls groaned and the floor jumped beneath my feet.

A dull roar sounded. On the table, the oil lamp rattled and slid to the edge. I dove forward and caught it with my bound hands before it could shatter.

Then all hell broke loose.

Chapter Seventeen

A sour taste filled my mouth, and I forced myself to meet Rhielle's gaze. Everything in me rebelled against the truth in her words, and I wished I could tell her everything. "For the time being, I must play nice with everyone." I inclined my head, though my shoulders weighed heavy from this fecking game I had to play. "But eventually all games end, and all bills come due."

"Make sure to bill Kaylen her share then," Rhielle muttered. Her fingers curled over the blanket, her nails digging into the fabric as if it were Kaylen's throat.

I forced a small smile that probably didn't reach my eyes. "I hope your recovery progresses swiftly. Whatever you need, please inform the physicians and their attendants."

She huffed and lifted her chin. "I need to get out of here. Physician Karu said I'll be out of danger by tonight, but it'll be a day or two longer before I'm back to full strength."

"I'm afraid time is still required for healing." With that, I exited to the hall, closing the door behind me. I tucked my wings in tighter so that they didn't brush the walls in passing. There was one other person I wished to speak to in the Healing Hall.

As I entered the main area hall, I spotted Chief Physician Morlo speaking with a younger red-haired attendant. For as long as I had been alive, Morlo had overseen my family's health. His posture was a little more rounded now in the shoulders, and his blonde hair was less gold and more silver, and a little less shiny. He still wore it slicked back and fastened low against the nape of his neck, his appearance, as always, immaculate. He gestured to the nervous attendant in a calm manner, likely offering some form of correction, based on how he pointed to different vials of herbs and powders on the slim shelf beside him.

Once the attendant scurried away past the pillars, he turned toward me.

A small yet sad smile tugged at his narrow mouth. "Your Highness." He stopped in front of me, his hands folded before himself. "Helfir mentioned you were with Rhielle, but I did not wish to intrude. I want to offer my personal condolences and sympathy in the matter of your father." He bowed his head so low his chin pressed against the collar of his green robe. Today, in addition to the black iridescent staff in a circle embroidered on his lapel, he wore a pin that depicted a sleeping shadow beast resting beside a smaller one, his head pressed protectively over hers. Both were encircled with black roses. Morlo had chosen to honor my mother as well as my father, the pin representing them both.

My throat tightened. "May we speak in private?"

"Of course, Your Highness." Morlo gestured toward a small alcove beyond two towering carved stone pillars. "My private consultation room is this way."

I followed him into the circular chamber. The walls were lined with shelves of books, herbs, vials, and glittering crystals, the air rich with the scent of dried herbs and incense, though rosemary and sage were the strongest scents. A small round ebony table with three chairs sat in the center, lit by an elegant oil lamp with a long fluted globe, its flame low.

Morlo closed the doors. “No one will be able to hear us here. A Sylvan friend helped me carve permanent sigils into the walls and door to prevent sound from passing through, so long as the door is closed.” He crossed to the table and adjusted the wick on the lamp. The smell of rosemary and sage intensified. “How may I serve, Your Highness? May I offer you food or drink?”

“Neither. I need your counsel on two matters.” I paced five steps to the end of the room and turned. An uncomfortable idea had been building in the back of my mind, adding to my headache. “Would it be possible to detect whether someone is draining the lifeblood from someone else and using it to strengthen or heal themself? And what level of certainty can be provided for it? I don’t want hints or implications. I want proof.”

Physician Morlo’s eyes and forehead wrinkled as he *hmmm*ed. “An intriguing question, and one I never expected to be asked.”

“I wish I didn’t need to ask; nonetheless, I need an answer.”

He twisted the heavy onyx ring on his finger and then tapped it, his gaze unfocused. “If the one drawing from another’s lifeblood does not take steps to shield their participation, it should be easy enough to tell, if you know what you’re searching for. But anyone who is skilled enough to do so for their own benefit will know how to mask the signs.”

I held back a bitter laugh.

“If you can tell me the kind of fae they are draining and bring me a hair sample with the root of the person you suspect may be receiving the magic, I can determine whether they have been absorbing another’s lifeblood.” He held up one finger. “But the root is the important part of the hair, which may make it difficult to obtain."

That might be more than difficult, but I'd find a way. Anything to prove Briar's innocence and locate my father's killers. "Once you have that, how long would it take for you to determine?" I had days at most, so my plan relied on getting the results quickly.

Morlo hesitated and crossed to one of the shelves. He picked up a dark purple vial and swirled the contents. "It depends on the individual. If the person has done nothing to cover their tracks, then it is a relatively swift and simple process to prove their guilt or innocence. But if someone is using magic to mask themself, it will take more time. Perhaps two or three days."

My stomach dropped. That might be all the time I had. I needed to obtain Kaylen's hair quickly. "Test Rhielle. I'll bring you other samples as well. If there is any way to confirm this information sooner without risking the results, then please do so." Though I was relatively certain Kaylen was the true threat, I needed evidence when I went to the Shadow Council. "The fae who is being drained is a Terran. A male, if that makes any difference."

Morlo's eyebrow arched. "You have the victim? May I speak with him?"

"It isn't an option yet." I shook my head as another wave of fatigue passed over me, spiking the nausea and aching in my skull. I released a deep breath and massaged my temple. "When it is an option, I will gladly permit it."

He nodded, then strode to the opposite wall. With a soft hum, he removed another vial, this one full of shimmering black liquid with an emerald cork. As he brought it over, it caught the torchlight and glistened with iridescent flecks. "Please allow me to speak with him as soon as possible. If he hasn't been fully drained, after he has been treated, I may be able to procure additional information from him that will help me determine who has devoured his lifeblood and magic."

"Is that what that's for?" I gestured to the vial.

He chuckled. "No. This is for you." He tucked it into my palm. "You need rest, Your Highness. These past days have taken a heavy toll on you. This will help you sleep and restore your strength at a faster rate."

"But ..." I held up the vial between my thumb and forefinger, knowing that there was always a price.

"It tastes bad. And it's quite rare. You may have strange dreams, but that's a bargain, considering what you will get in return."

I considered his words, but as I stared at the vial, an unsettling memory returned to me. A few nights ago, I'd had the strangest drunken vision or dream about a silver stag. It had torn through the paintings and the walls. My stomach twisted at the memory, and I clenched the vial tighter. I recalled the stag's somber expression and its sharp antlers, which it had used to shred my family's portrait. "I see ... does it cause visions that have meaning?"

"Hard to say. It depends on what one thinks of dreams in general. Personally, I don't put much stock in dreams or visions unless they come true. In some cases, they're caused by the mind searching for answers and finding them even when they aren't truly there. The restorative rest is the important part here. Keep the vial on hand. If you can sleep without it and recover, fair enough. But you don't look as if you've had more than a few hours' rest in the past two days, and I doubt you'll get much more in the ones to come."

"I don't suppose you have something that would keep me awake and give me endless energy." My lips twisted in a faint smirk.

"I'm afraid not." He smiled, but his brow furrowed. "Do not give this to Elara though. She is not physically strong enough.

Her mind is, but ... for someone in her condition, it would be too strenuous."

"She's gotten worse. Significantly." It wasn't a question, and I watched his face intently.

He sighed, and a shadow of sadness passed over him. The lines in his face deepened. "I still do not know her true ailment, and because of that, I can offer no cure, I'm afraid. Is she resting currently?"

"She should be." I tucked the vial inside the inner black satin pocket of my surcoat. "But this loss has struck her quite deeply." I braced my hands on my belt and brought voice to an observation that terrified me. "Her glamour is masking a great deal, isn't it?"

He frowned. "Has she spoken with you about her condition?"

"Not recently."

His brow tweaked. "Well, I do not wish to speak out of turn, but I would have assumed she would tell you ... perhaps she wanted to wait until the wedding and coronation were past. Rest, food, and Shadow magic are doing more to keep her alive than any of my incantations, sigils, brews, or antidotes. But it is undeniable that she is ... *fading*."

Pain blossomed through me like poisoned blades as I caught the finality in that word. "How long?" I rasped.

Physician Morlo's expression softened with pity. "Without significant intervention? Perhaps six months. Maybe less. It's accelerated significantly in these past weeks. Given the issues with Shadow magic within our kingdom, I'm concerned that her condition will continue to worsen."

My shadows coiled tighter around me as if they could shield me from this truth. First Father, then Briar, now Elara. In some respects, even Silus. Perhaps I was doomed to lose everyone I cared about.

The kingdom's magic had to be stabilized and strengthened, but the uncertain countdown unnerved me. "Whatever it takes, please see to it that Elara receives it. Is there anything in another kingdom that might help to heal her?"

"No one has offered any additional insight into her ailment. I haven't stopped inquiring, and I will not give up." His shoulders sagged before he straightened them. "Despite all this, she is far stronger than most give her credit for. She may yet pull through, but this loss ... well, she will require additional care."

"And you're certain there is nothing we haven't tried that can be done?"

"Nothing within the bounds of what is permissible." He cocked his head and studied me. Concern flashed in his expression. "Are you considering draining the life of someone else to heal her?"

My wings bristled in response, and a tightness shot through my body. "No. Not at all." I shook my head as if to dislodge the thought. Even if I had thought of it, Elara would never forgive me, and such magic could not be forced upon another even if it could be taken forcefully from someone.

I dragged a hand over my mouth and closed my eyes, darkness sweeping over me. Through the dull thudding in my own head, I saw my sister's face. "As a child, I used to believe in the reciprocity of magic. If something was taken, something would be given. It made sense. But there is nothing that is the healing equivalent of draining one's lifeblood, is there?"

"I still believe that." Morlo clasped his hands together. "Those who committed the first abomination of draining lifeblood and magic did so centuries ago. A few of the original council members among the Aureline, Sylvan, and Ignis still live and may know more about it. I don't think Vyraetos is old enough to have been around then. At least, he would not have been on the Shadow Council." He sighed and twisted his ring. "I always thought that true healers would come from the Aurelines because their role is to provide balance, and Fate has blessed them most often with new skills to counter the harmful. It's happened several times for them and only once or twice for most of the other lines.

"The Aureline ability to infuse locations with time warps came after Terran sorcerers succeeded in collapsing ley lines to horrifying effect, disrupting magic within the soil and water. The Aureline Fae built restorative gardens that nourished the soil, changing time's passing in places to allow for more rapid growth and slowing it in others to stop damage."

"Now they use those time warping sigils and spells in their prisons," I muttered.

He inclined his head. "Sadly, all gifts can be corrupted. Redemption and transformation are far trickier. The Aurelines have changed as much as any of us. Sometimes even Fate seems crueler than she once was." He held up a hand as if to cut off that thought. "Regardless, do not despair. All of us within the healing practices are constantly seeking and learning, and sorcerers, hexwrights, and scholars never cease their attempts to uncover new methods and solve our problems and struggles. Maybe a new treatment will develop in time. If there is anything that can be done for your sister within the bounds of what is permissible, I will do it. And on that note, when Briar returns, I would like to treat her as well."

I lifted an eyebrow. It shouldn't surprise me how fast the rumors spread, but I hadn't expected him to transition to Briar so abruptly. "She is imprisoned in Firellan's Spine until the time of her execution in the formal court." Though I trusted Morlo a great deal, I couldn't bring myself to tell him of my plan. I hadn't wanted to tell even Rhielle what scraps I had. The more people who knew, the more likely an enemy would discover the truth. But Morlo knew me quite well. An explanation might not be necessary.

His murky brown eyes held mine fast, and he stepped closer. "They have tortured her?"

"Yes. Colm Ainle is the chief interrogator, but I have negotiated with him to stop and bring her here until her execution. He will be coming as well, to assist in overseeing the matter."

Morlo's face darkened, and the warmth in his eyes dimmed as he twisted his ring faster. "I see. I am quite familiar with Colm and his methods. I assume he personally oversaw her interrogation?"

I nodded, grimness tightening my muscles at the memory. "He will not do anything further to her as he understands I want her in full health, mental and physical, for my coronation and wedding. The execution of the king's assassin and everyone involved will take place afterward."

"Then, when she is brought here, I would appreciate being permitted to offer supplemental treatment to ensure that all is as you desire. After all, I have served your family for centuries. There would be some satisfaction in ensuring that ... justice is fully meted out. She healed swiftly while in the tournament, but certain remedies may be offered to better prepare her for judgment day."

"Whatever you can do." Mentally, I ran through the risks of involving Morlo and how likely it was that Colm would be suspicious. It wouldn't be hard to determine that Morlo was the family physician, but Morlo could honestly state under any binding vow that I had not said anything about rescuing Briar.

I gripped his hand. "My father always trusted you, and I know he would be grateful for how you have continued to serve our family."

"It was my privilege and honor to serve him, as it is my privilege and honor to serve you." He bowed his head. "Though this is a time of sadness, you will make a fine leader. I saw your grandfather coronated and your father as well. Having the opportunity to see you coronated and wed will be among the great honors of my life."

I smiled grimly. "It will be a day to remember, especially for myself. I should take leave to get the samples requested."

"Yes, and I need to get back to tending the injured. I will get a hair sample from Rhielle and check on Elara."

I left the Healing Hall and continued toward the Guest Hall. I had to get a piece of Kaylen's hair and pretend to be ... interested. My stomach twisted with a painful spike of nausea, adding to the discomfort of the vested magic that engulfed me.

The sound of my boots against the polished stone floor echoed in the corridor. Every step in Kaylen's direction felt like a betrayal of Briar, but I had to play this game to save her.

The ornate doors of the Guest Hall loomed before me, carved with the ancient symbols of hospitality and protection. My shadows rippled around me, more agitated by the moment. As I crossed the threshold into the hall, I noted the guards, in polished black armor, standing at attention at regular intervals. Lanterns hung over every third door and below the gold and black stained-glass windows, casting the entire space in a soft golden glow.

"It's *him*. He's here," a soft alto voice whispered behind a door to my left. "Hush now."

"Quickly, quickly," a trembling soprano responded.

Another sharper feminine voice growled, "Oh, the gall! I can't believe him. Let's get him *now*!"

CHAPTER EIGHTEEN

I squared my shoulders, dreading another confrontation so soon. I needed to focus on my plan to save Briar and not deal with distractions.

But avoiding them would only cause more theatrics.

Taking a deep breath, I turned toward the voices as the black carved door flung open. The nearest guards tightened their grips on their halberds as their attention focused on the door marked with Thalira's name.

Thalira, a tall Aquen Fae, glided out first, her hands clasped before herself. The torchlight caught on her numerous rings and bracelets and contrasted with her dark brown skin. "Your Highness," she said, respect in her deeper tone despite the sharpness in her dark eyes. "May we have a word?"

Quen, an Ignis Fae, cut in front of her. Despite not being tall enough to reach my or Thalira's shoulder, she carried far more rage in her manner than her friend. Her deep crimson eyes burned. "It's very important." She crossed her arms and tossed back her black hair.

"Please." Velessa, the soprano speaker, wrung her hands as she peeked around the door frame. Her wavy purple hair cascaded over her shoulders, moving subtly as if her air magic was at work even now. "We don't mean any offense, Your Highness, but it's about Briar."

Yuki followed close behind Velessa. The Terran Fae's green hair was perfectly straight, but her mouth was pinched. "There's no chance that Briar killed your father."

Another woman stood in the doorway now. Myantha. Her honey-gold locs hung loose as she watched the others moving toward me. Sadness filled her russet-brown eyes, and she worried her lower lip.

"We are so sorry for your loss," Velessa said as she slipped out. One arm was still in a sling from her injury the other day, bruises standing out starkly against the pale skin along her shoulder and across her hand. "It is a horrible tragedy. But—"

"There's not an ice blade's chance in the inferno that Briar was behind it," Quen growled. She snapped her arms out in challenge as she stared up at me, and I half expected fire to explode from her palms. She spat, "How could you think that she was?"

"It was a setup." Thalira kept her tone calm, as if this were all perfectly reasonable. She tapped her fingers in the air to punctuate those words. "Someone obviously wanted everyone to think she was involved, but the guards for this hall were missing that night. Most of them vanished."

"Do you think Briar killed all of them? Has she been hiding her superb assassin abilities and cold-blooded nature?" Quen scoffed and curled her upper lip. She wrinkled her nose. "Risking her life for us, but secretly maybe wanting to kill us too, so she can claim power? If you think that, you should go jump in the void."

The guards focused on me, likely waiting to see how I responded. The closest one adjusted his grip on his halberd. I gave a subtle shake of my head. No matter how little I wanted to have this conversation, it was best to get it over with. I held up my hands to calm Briar's friends down. As much as I wished that I could comfort them with promises of her return, it was far too risky. "Ladies, justice will be done. Briar is being investigated—"

"Void shit and pyre rot," Quen spat. "I don't believe a word coming out of your mouth. She's being set up. What justice is there? Justice is circumstantial, and you'll never change my mind."

"Briar saved our lives." Yuki stepped closer and looked around at the small group. "She helped so many of us when she could, even when it cost her. A person like that doesn't turn around and assassinate a king in the middle of his garden."

My wings flexed, the tips brushing against the wall as I lifted my chin. "I am aware of far more than you think. If you have specific evidence that you wish to offer aside from Briar's general character, I am willing to hear it—"

"Will you bring Briar back?" Yuki's eyes widened as if she could peer into my soul and drag a *yes* from my lips.

I almost promised I would, but that was the worst thing I could do with ears all around. I bit my tongue, fighting the urge to make that vow.

"We are more than willing to testify in her defense." Thalira stepped around Quen, her flowing, layered indigo skirts trailing over the black marble floor. As she drew closer, she reached her hand out and then drew back as if realizing she should not touch me. "Surely that will count for something."

"Yes, we'll all vouch for her." Velessa extended her hand, palm upturned. Her wooden bangle bracelets clattered up her good arm. "Please! You can't let her suffer. We'll all take vows that we believe in her innocence."

Their willingness to risk talking to me like this, let alone risking their lives, had my breath catching. I'd never witnessed such unwavering loyalty after so little time. Briar had made an impact that no one could deny.

I couldn't bring myself to silence these women. Uncomfortable as the situation was, their heartfelt pleas and even their rage warmed my spirit. Still, their clamoring voices had risen, which was problematic.

I raised one hand, stilling their outpouring of concern. "I understand your loyalty to Briar." I kept my tone low and firm. "It speaks well of her character that she has such devoted friends."

Quen raised her chin and narrowed her crimson eyes. Her red-bronze skin flushed. "We're not just her 'devoted friends.' We're witnesses to her character, and that should count for something in your so-called justice system."

"Punishing the innocent just because it's easy isn't justice." Velessa clutched my arm, and I went rigid.

I stepped away, forcing her to drop her arm. No one should be touching me but Briar, especially not another woman.

Thalira set her hands on her dark sash and shook her head.

Nodding, Myantha moved her lips, but her voice was too soft for me to catch her words.

Yuki spread her arms wide in challenge. "This isn't even close to an approximation of justice. Anyone with eyes can see that it's a setup." Her voice had grown shriller and her enunciation faster.

"Let us speak with whoever's in charge of the prison where she's being held." Thalira clenched her jaw.

Everyone started talking all at once, their voices overlapping, causing my head to pound even harder.

"Ladies, please." I rubbed my temples. "All you're accomplishing is dragging out the entire process."

The guard nearest me tilted his head as the verbal onslaught continued. Two farther down the hall stepped closer, their grips on the halberds tightening. I gave another slight shake of my head to indicate everything was still under control. At least, I hoped it would be soon because my head couldn't take much more.

A flash of white-blonde hair and silver fabric darted out from around the corner. "You all dare to speak to our prince and future king in such a manner?" Kaylen's sonorous voice rang down the hall. She glared at the five women and strode toward us. "Briar was exposed for what she was. An opportunistic and murderous wretch. She played almost everyone here. Especially you lot. Not that it was *your* fault, Your Highness." Her hooded silver eyes met mine in what I guessed she thought was a seductive expression, and she dipped her head as she curtsied. "She was quite clever with her lies. I know because I am a woman of discernment and have faced many similar cunning deceivers."

"How would you like your face to melt?" Quen demanded, starting toward Kaylen with her fists balled. Heat shot out around her as flames licked along her hands and up her wrists.

"You think you can challenge me, ash blood?" Kaylen's upper lip curled. She spread her arms, and wisps of wind formed over her palms.

Thalira stepped between Quen and Kaylen, laying a gentle hand on Quen's arm. "Not here," she murmured, though her own eyes were cold with fury. "It is a waste of energy."

Things were getting out of hand, and my patience was thin. "Ladies—"

Yuki clenched her hands into fists. "No. Given how justice is dispensed in this place, it wouldn't be wise at all."

My wings snapped out, and my shadows darkened and surged until they rose along both walls. "Enough. All of you," I barked. "I will not permit insults against this kingdom or its justice. And, Kaylen, I appreciate your concern, but your intervention is hardly necessary."

Kaylen banished the wind from her palms and clasped her hands over her heart. "Still, it is my honor to offer it. Most here do not seem to understand the gravity of this situation, or the great honor you have bestowed upon us by allowing us to be here. I wish to offer my deepest condolences for your loss. If I may be there for you in this time of trouble and offer you some comfort, it would be my honor." She cut her eyes to me.

My throat burned, and I fought the urge to retch.

"Your service is noted." My jaw flexed, and discomfort coiled at the base of my spine and neck. "I have no doubt it would be your pleasure."

A smile curled Kaylen's lips, and she dropped her gaze demurely, seizing upon the compliment like a starving shadow beast. "You flatter me, Your Highness."

The other women didn't respond nearly so well. Despite witnessing these women's participation in numerous conflicts and dangerous confrontations, I had never seen such restrained rage and hate as I now did in their faces. If I turned up dead in the middle of the night, it wouldn't be from trained assassins but from my beloved's friends, who believed in vengeance as much as loyalty. My royal Shadow guard seemed gentle in comparison.

"Now, ladies." I kept my voice even. "Please hear me."

"Unless the next words out of your mouth are that Briar is coming back exonerated, I'm uninterested." Quen wrinkled her nose like she'd never been this disgusted before.

"Forgive our boldness, but we would also accept just getting Briar back and the legalities taking time." Velessa raised her one good arm as if in surrender. "We could guard her ourselves. The evidence will prove her innocence. I assure you. Kind people don't just turn into assassins."

Kaylen scoffed louder this time and rolled her eyes. "Why are we so worried that she won't be exonerated if she's innocent?

Do we truly have so little faith in the councils and our prince to determine who is truly guilty of the crime?" She lifted her chin and stared down at them as if the black-and-gold-spiked crown already sat on her head and she upon the throne. "Although she *was* found holding the dagger over the king's broken body. Hard to imagine what innocent explanation there is for that."

"Because she was framed, you moon-faced trumpet," Quen growled, crossing her arms tighter.

Yuki scoffed at Kaylen as well, her porcelain features sneering. "Idle-winded banshee," she muttered.

This was accomplishing nothing and wasting my time and energy. "Enough," I said, sharper and deeper this time. My shadows rose along the walls. "Unless you would like to see the inside of the Shadow dungeons yourselves, do not press me further."

"Would my going to prison help Briar get out faster?" Quen demanded.

I held back a sudden laugh. I admired her spirit, though it was uncalled for. "Not at all."

Thalira whispered something in Quen's ear, and Quen folded her arms. But if looks could have killed, I would have been a smoldering pile of ash on the floor.

These ladies actually scared me a little, though I'd never admit that to anyone.

Yuki huffed and turned away. Myantha bit her lower lip and gripped her hand into a fist as she edged out farther from the door. Her pink and lavender striped dress snagged on the wooden door frame, and she paused to untangle herself.

Something jostled my right elbow. I turned.

Thalen stood behind me, his hands clasped behind his back and that crooked smile on his face. His shaggy silver white curls half covered his amber eyes, but that didn't keep me from imagining all the jokes and quips spinning in his head.

"Everything all right here?"

"Yes." I glanced at my guards.

"Never had a doubt." Thalen nodded and looped his thumbs in his belt. He leaned forward to scan my little assembly. "Tensions may be running high, but the truth has a way of coming out in time. And if we're watching someone, I think we keep an eye on that one. She's obviously trouble, yeah?" He pointed at Myantha and winked.

Myantha's eyes widened until they were completely white-rimmed, and her cheeks reddened. She stepped toward him, one hand lingering on the door frame.

"We're just worried about our friend, Th-Thalen." Her voice caught on his name, and she ducked her head before peeking back up at him and coming a little closer. "Briar is innocent. Please. We have to get her home and safe. I know you're a *good, intelligent* man. You'd never let an innocent suffer." She tugged one golden brown lock around her finger, the coil tightening with each of her nervous breaths. "Can we count on you to bring her back safely? She's a good person, and we all love her so much."

Thalen hesitated, his posture stiffening. All the women except Myantha were now glaring at him as they awaited his response.

Kaylen groaned under her breath. "These women are so annoying."

I crossed my arms, torn between amusement and irritation. This was what he got for trying to crack jokes all the time. *Yes. See how miserable it feels to be caught in this position, you silver-tongued fiend.* I could tell he hadn't expected Myantha to ask him this. Either way, I had to fight the smile that tugged at the corners of my mouth.

But it was a step too far to include Briar's friends in our plan. Even if none of them were involved, how likely was it that all of them would remain silent? It had been risky enough to bring Rhielle into my confidence, and I hadn't told her everything. Something would have to be done, or these five might go off on their own rescue and get themselves killed because Briar wouldn't be there to rein them in.

Myantha stared at Thalen like he was the only one there and stopped directly in front of him. Reaching out with her palms up, she stared up at him. "Please. It can be all I ever ask of you. Help us help Briar. Convince your prince of her innocence and bring her back."

"It wouldn't have to be the only thing you ever ask of me." His words hitched.

"So you promise?" Her face lit up.

He laughed breathlessly and took her hand, then kissed the back. His lips lingered a moment longer than necessary. "Honey Clover, I will make sure to satisfy you in every way I can."

Myantha burst into giggles and covered her mouth. Her eyes sparkled, and a rosy glow spread over her golden-brown skin.

My heart twisted all over again. What I wouldn't give to have Briar here. I'd set my own kingdom ablaze to have her back at my side.

Kaylen opened her mouth, but Velessa raised her hand. Her fingers curled in a sharp pulling motion, and then she winced. The lack of words escaping Kaylen's lips and the indignant expression that followed transformed into a rictus of silent but impotent fury when Quen stepped in front of Kaylen with a confident stance that clearly dared her to try something.

Thalira placed a hand on Myantha's shoulder as Yuki scowled, leaned in, and whispered something to Myantha that I didn't catch. But Myantha blushed and then cut her eyes back to Thalen. "I-I look forward to that and ... to our *mutual*

... satisfaction." She lifted her fingers in a small gesture. "I'm counting on you to fulfill that first promise you just gave me, so I'll owe you that favor."

Fecking void, was he about to *tell* her? I adjusted my stance, and one of my shadows swirled up, hooked on the back of his right wing, and yanked him away from her.

He stiffened, shook his head, and gave her a big smile. "Gotta be careful with promises, you know, but what I can definitively promise you is ... I'm on it, Honey Clover. There won't be any injustice happening here if I have anything to do with it, and I certainly plan to. Briar will get exactly what she deserves, as will everyone else involved, good or bad."

"Thank you ... Silver Smirk." She clasped her hands and hunched her shoulders, then ducked back.

Yuki shook her head, but there was no venom in her gaze.

Thalen straightened and stared after her like a lynx watching a rabbit, his chest rising and falling with tense breaths. Fate save him, he was already gone.

The problem was that I understood that feeling and desire.

But I'd be getting my beloved back.

I cleared my throat. "All right. Ladies, I recommend the rest of you return to your rooms. If you have any information that can assist in resolving the king's assassination, please report it to Captain Finbar as soon as possible. One of my guards will escort you to him. Do not go alone. We *cannot* speak more fully on this subject." I gave Thalen a meaningful look and used my shadow to nudge him again.

He shot me an annoyed glance and folded his arms.

I continued, "Rest assured that I have heard your statements, and I will not permit injustice to flourish in my kingdom. But even justice takes time."

"All well and good when you aren't the one falsely accused and rotting in prison," Quen muttered under her breath.

I pretended not to hear her as I gestured toward Kaylen. "I need a word with you, Kaylen. In private."

Kaylen's eyes brightened at my words, and my stomach churned. She stepped forward with practiced grace. "Of course, Your Highness," she purred, her voice oozing with eagerness. "I would be honored."

Eyebrows rising, Thalen shot me a look that was equal parts pity and amusement.

I ignored him and gestured toward a small alcove farther down the hall, where we could speak without being easily overheard but where we would not be closed off either. My shadows curled around my ankles, itching and prickling along my flesh to ensure I knew they weren't happy about this arrangement either.

The other women retreated slowly, Quen practically having to be dragged off by Thalira. Myantha lingered longest, her gaze fixed on Thalen until Yuki pulled her away. Thalen must have winked at her again or mouthed something at her, because her blush intensified yet again. Her foot caught on the door jamb, and she tripped, pitching forward in a flurry of pink and lavender striped skirts.

Thalen surged forward to catch her, stooping down to grasp her hands with one and wrapping his other arm around her waist as he lifted her easily. He whispered something to her, and she shook her head, her eyes averted.

Kaylen cleared her throat. "I am at your service, Your Highness," she said from behind me in the alcove. "What can I do for you? We can return to my room if that would be helpful."

A biting retort rose to my lips, but I swallowed it down and fought back a gag. "You have stood out in many respects, Kaylen, and you have caught a great deal of attention. This final challenge will assuredly be difficult, and I wondered if I might have a lock of your hair."

Kaylen's eyes widened with delight, her lips parting in a smile that made my skin crawl. She pressed her hands together. "My hair?" She reached up to touch her white-blonde tresses. "You wish for a lock of my hair?"

I forced false warmth into my voice. "It would be ... meaningful to me."

Her cheeks reddened, and she stepped closer—too close. I could smell her scent now, something like oversweet sugar lilies and honeysuckle. "I would be honored," she whispered, her eyes gleaming.

I drew the dagger from the sheath at my side. The ornate black hilt caught the light as I held it up between us. "May I?"

She nodded, practically vibrating with excitement. "Please." She turned her head to present the pale cascade of her hair. "Take all you desire."

I reached up, selecting a small section of hair on the back of her head. As I positioned the dagger, I deliberately caught my bracer in the strands above where I intended to cut. With a swift flick of my blade, I cut a lock, then I moved my wrist back with several other strands of blonde hair tangled in the bracer.

Kaylen let out a sharp yelp of surprise and pain, her hands flying up to her head.

"Oh dear." I gave my wrist another tug without even trying to untangle the hair. "It's stuck."

"Agh!" She glared at me and then blanked her expression. "Stop moving!" Catching herself, she swallowed hard. "Please, Your Highness. Let me fix it."

"Just a moment." A few strands had already been pulled from her scalp, but I gave another small tug as I batted her hands away. Kaylen grimaced and grunted as if she'd bitten back a curse.

"Oh no, let me help!" A melodic voice called out, and suddenly another pair of hands reached up to help untangle

Kaylen's hair. The woman's delicate fingers worked swiftly as she pressed more of the hair into my hand to ease the tension. "Here. Hold this carefully, and I'll help you untangle."

I glanced down, seeing a woman with wavy blonde hair in a feathery pink dress with darker pink wings tucked against her back. She was another bridal candidate, an Ignis Fae, though I didn't recall seeing her ever using her fire magic except for the heat blast to move stones in the fight against the crabs and leeches in the collapsing labyrinth. Her name had something to do with flowers. Lilian ... no, Calla Lily.

She chewed on her lower lip as she worked to untangle Kaylen's hair, and Kaylen whimpered. "There we are." Calla Lily darted back as soon as Kaylen was free, her steps light and silent on the marble.

Kaylen sniffed.

Quickly glancing at the strands of hair with the root along with the larger lock, I drew my hand back. Then I removed a handkerchief from inside my surcoat. "Are you all right? That must have been quite painful."

Blinking rapidly, she straightened her shoulders. "It's perfectly all right. No attention you could pay me would be unpleasant." She smiled, but it didn't reach her eyes.

I should've felt guilt for harming a woman, but I couldn't feel any remorse. I had no doubt Kaylen was part of framing Briar. I wrapped the hairs along with the lock in my handkerchief and tucked them away.

Kaylen lingered, her gaze fixed upon me as she rubbed her head.

Playing this damnable game meant I couldn't snap at her, so I indicated one of the guards at the end of the hall. "One more thing, Kaylen. Do you see that guard right there at the intersection of the halls before the Guest Banquet Hall? I want you to go to that guard and have him take you to a private room with one of my scribes and tell the scribe everything you remember about last night. Tell him it is my order, and it is to be strictly confidential."

"You don't want me to go to Captain Finbar?" She collected herself and resumed her poised stance, hands folded over her gown.

"Your report will be special. It's for my eyes only."

A frown creased her brow, but she took a few tentative steps out of the alcove and into the hall, then glanced back at me.

I gestured toward the guard once more, and she turned to oblige. Hopefully, that would keep her occupied.

Thalen was still fussing over Myantha, holding one of her hands in his as he leaned close. She was hanging on his every word. I cleared my throat loudly, and Thalen's focus snapped to me as a guilty look stole over his face. Before I could say anything, something light tapped my back.

I spun around to find Calla Lily still there. She placed a hand on my arm, her fingers curling over my wrist.

My skin crawled, and I jerked away and took two large steps back. Her touch had somehow felt even more wrong than Velessa's, and I wanted her to go away.

Her red-brown eyes widened, and she snatched back her hand as if she'd been burned. Her cheeks turned pink. I didn't acknowledge either of our responses as she stammered. "Forgive me for being so forward. I know that this must be so difficult for you. I cannot imagine how painful it is to lose a leader and a father at once. But ... they're right. Briar had nothing to do with the king's assassination. She couldn't have."

Some of my body relaxed. She was on Briar's side ... or at least pretending to be. Still, the touch continued to make me want to get away from her. "Do you have proof?" I clasped my hands behind my back and scowled at her.

She shrugged, and her head canted as she bit her lower

lip. "I'm an Ignis, but my father was Terran. He could feel the heartbeat of anyone standing within twenty feet of him if he focused, and he knew how to read those heartbeats to tell whether they were telling the truth or lying. I'm not that skilled. But ... I'm aware of more than most. Last night ... it was so odd." She wrung her hands and glanced over her shoulder. "I wasn't feeling social. It's a little overwhelming for me to be in such large crowds. So I went back to my room, took a long, hot bath, and then ... I heard footsteps enter Rhielle's room. Two sets of footsteps, and neither was Rhielle's."

"Two sets?" My eyebrows arched, and I leaned forward, wanting to catch her every word. "Do you mean two, as in the assassin and then Briar? Or two as well as Briar?"

She nodded to the last one, her eyes wide. "I ... I don't want to get anyone in trouble, but two sets of footsteps went into her room *together.* One heavy. One light. They were both so calm. Deadly calm. Then Briar came. It sounded like someone slipped, and only two sets of footsteps left. I didn't know what was going on at the time. But ... the lighter set of footsteps ... they went into Kaylen's room. They were still calm, not rushed, and I thought perhaps Briar stayed to talk with Rhielle. I know they've become good friends."

My heartbeat quickened. Briar had mentioned only one set of footsteps, and so had Rhielle, but both of them had been focused elsewhere. Was it possible there'd been a second individual in the room? It might explain how they'd managed to maneuver the bodies so swiftly. "Have you told Captain Finbar?"

She ducked her head. "I can't prove any of it, and I don't want to cause trouble. Kaylen might be innocent, even if—well, even if she *is* a horrible person. I don't know what she was doing last night. It's just ... I can't stand the thought of Briar being blamed for something she didn't do. I was considering asking

Kaylen about it, but she was so rude when I tried to strike up a conversation with her this morning that I didn't."

I needed more information. "Whose footsteps entered Kaylen's room? Could you tell?"

Her expression pinched. "They—they sounded like Kaylen's." She pressed a hand to her mouth and shook her head, her long, wavy blond hair sliding over her face. "Please, tell me what you'd like me to do. I'll do whatever would be most helpful. I don't want to cause problems, but if it weren't for Briar, I wouldn't be here."

"Report all this to Captain Finbar. Ask one of the guards to escort you. Don't tell anyone else about what you heard."

"Of course." She curtsied, holding her long, full pink skirts in both hands. "I'll do whatever I can." She started down the hall at a swift pace, then stopped and turned, looking over her shoulder. "I'm here for you, Your Highness."

Thalen appeared alongside me with the most innocent expression on his face. "Apologies. Just had to assist the young lady from falling."

"Yes, she was falling all over you," I said dryly.

"The woman has exceptional taste." He grinned crookedly. His wings fluttered a little as if to underscore his words, but I knew full well he was showing them off in hopes that Myantha was still watching ... which, based on the crack in Thalira's door, she probably was. "I heard Kaylen squeal like a stuck pig. Everything all right there?"

"We need to stop and see Physician Morlo before we continue." There was no sense in passing on what Calla Lily had said until we were in a more secure location. I took two steps toward the end of the hall, then paused. Calla Lily hadn't said anything about Briar's room, but the assassins couldn't have known that Briar would go to Rhielle's room. What if they'd left some clue in Briar's room?

My blood chilled, and my shadows coiled even tighter as I realized they might have planted evidence. My own men might have searched the room already, but I wanted to check for myself. I held up a hand, then scanned the doors for Briar's name card ... there. Her name was etched in gold on a black tile. I strode toward it at once, Thalen following.

"Physician Morlo isn't this way," he said, crooking an eyebrow at me.

"No. I—" I stopped short as I reached for the handle. The faint scent of lavender, lilacs, and earthy soil drifted to me, and the rustle of fabric sounded within.

Someone was in Briar's room.

Chapter Nineteen

Anger boiled in my veins. I raised a hand to stop Thalen. Could we possibly figure out who the killer was now and make this horrible nightmare end?

I pressed my finger to my lips and summoned my shadows. They slithered down my spine and around my ankles before sliding under the door as smooth as ink. A dull ache twinged along the back of my skull, adding to the pounding of my head, but I ignored it.

Even though I couldn't see through my shadows, I could become aware of the presence once my shadows spread deeper within her room across the slick marble floor.

Just one person.

I tapped my chest and then lifted one finger, informing Thalen of what to expect.

Easing the door open, I peered inside Briar's room. The familiar scent of her—cinnamon and ginger—filled my lungs, but my stomach twisted when the unfamiliar scent of lilacs and lavender with damp soil mixed with hers.

The room lay in partial disarray. Her simple furnishings—a wide bed with rumpled dark covers, a writing desk with scattered papers, and a dresser—showed signs of a hasty search.

The marble floor was covered with a thick black rug that muffled our footsteps as we entered. A single oil lamp burned low near the bed, casting long shadows across the walls.

Near the far wall stood a tall, older man with his back to us. His wild, dark auburn hair fell past his shoulders in unruly waves streaked with iridescent white over a heavy gray cloak of fine leather. Dark, iridescent thread secured the broad hem, and the cloak hung in neat folds along his back, suggesting it was well-kept. Multiple rings adorned the hand that gripped the left wardrobe door while he rifled through Briar's things. His head moved as if he were scanning each item of clothing up and down before moving on.

Thalen slipped forward with practiced stealth. My shadows surged ahead, twisting and elongating as they reached for the intruder. Just as they were about to snap around him, the man's aged hand flicked outward. A brilliant transparent silver shield wall erupted around him, pushing back against my shadows. They hissed and recoiled like scalded serpents, then lashed out again, wrapping around the shimmering shield.

"Unless you wish this conversation to be overheard, I recommend you close the door, Prince Vad." The man spoke without turning as he examined Briar's fighting leathers from the first competition. He had a deep, resonant voice. "We don't have much time if young Briar is to be retrieved from Firellan's Spine."

He knew about Briar. *Who is this man?*

I nodded to Thalen, who shut the door behind us with a solid *click*. My shadows remained wary, circling the shield and curling over it. My wings spread, and I tensed as I stepped forward. This man was clearly a noble, perhaps one of the High Aureline Council, but he had no authority to touch my beloved's clothing. "Who are you, and what are you doing in Briar's room? You're trespassing."

"And I don't think those clothes are your size," Thalen added, coming to stand beside me. His hand rested lazily on the handle of his dagger, but his wings twitched as if ready to shoot him forward at a moment's notice. "Nor do you have the legs or hips to pull those off, though I admire your confidence for trying."

Thalen's demeanor often made others underestimate him, but right now, I wasn't in the mood for his antics. I wanted to get to the bottom of why this man was here and alone.

With deliberate focus, the man returned the garment to the rack. He turned within the shield and fixed us both with a clear liquid-gold stare. His weathered features suggested he was beyond ancient. Deep lines cut into his brow and crinkled around those burning eyes. The front of his cloak was clasped with an ornate silver stag medallion that gleamed in the low light.

My muscles tightened as my upper lip almost curled. Yes, High Aureline Council member. One of the eldest, by the looks of him.

"Bryn Lugh, at your service." The stiffness of his posture suggested this was merely a formal statement rather than an actual offer. But I did recognize the name. He was indeed the eldest and the highest-ranking member of the High Aureline Council.

"A pleasure to formally meet you, albeit under strange circumstances. Which leads me back to my original question—what are you doing in here?" I lowered my shadows from his shield but did not remove them entirely as I faced him head-on.

He swallowed hard, the lump in his throat bobbing, but that was the only sign to indicate he was at all uneasy. Was he part of this plan to frame Briar?

"Whatever the answer is, I doubt it's in Briar's wardrobe." Thalen cocked an eyebrow.

Bryn shot Thalen a disapproving look before turning and removing a mauve dress from the wardrobe. He held it up, examined it, felt each pocket, and then hung it back up. "Despite what you may believe, Briar is an innocent woman from Earth who should never have been in the competition at all. Women like her were never meant to visit Nytheria. Fate made a bold and unusual choice." He lifted a periwinkle dress that had no sleeves but an overabundance of lace. "And those who are behind this entire conspiracy have made their own bold and unusual choice, starting with framing Briar."

I frowned as he removed yet another dress. Where had she gotten all these dresses from? She'd arrived with nothing. Of course, servants were tasked with providing clothing for the candidates as needed. If Briar had asked for all these garments, or if Elara had seen to it that she'd received them, that might account for it. But neither explanation sat well with me. Was this part of the attempt to frame her? "What exactly is your interest in Briar?"

Bryn arched an eyebrow as he set that dress aside and removed another, this one a pale yellow. He ran his hand along its sides. "I'm interested in all who are falsely accused. Is there another who has been charged with assassination whom I should rush to defend?"

"So you're just trying to free someone you deem to have been imprisoned unjustly?" Something in this room felt off, beyond the ancient man who was rifling through it. The utter disarray didn't line up with Briar, and Bryn searching the dresses didn't seem to line up with him either. My guards would never have treated the room in this fashion, so had someone else been in here? "Did you create this mess, or was it like this when you entered?" I studied his face for signs of dishonesty. Was this an Aureline test to learn my true thoughts on the matter?

"It was this way when I entered. But that isn't what should

concern you." Bryn's voice lowered as he shook the dress one more time. He scowled, then hung the dress back up.

"Do enlighten me then." I braced my hands on my belt. This Aureline Council member wasn't what I'd anticipated.

A bolt of nausea twisted through me, and I drew in a hard breath through my nose. The corresponding stab in my skull warned me that the vested Shadow magic was deteriorating fast. How much time did I have left? Three days felt like a reach, but I needed every scrap of it.

Bryn's gaze flicked over me before he snorted. "You know it already. Fate is angry, and others are working to destabilize your kingdom's magic even more than has already been done. That shortens the time you have even beyond what you and those loyal to you believe. There is far more at work here than any one individual realizes, and it must be handled swiftly, or else all will be lost."

"And the answer is in Briar's *dresses*?" Thalen cocked an eyebrow and smirked.

"Briar is innocent. She was framed to take the blame to eliminate her, and they were rather thorough." He removed a dark-blue dress that Briar had never worn from the wardrobe. It hung heavy on the left side. With an annoyed click of his tongue, he reached into the pocket. With a flash of silver, he removed a small dagger about four inches from tip to hilt. The black double-edged blade glistened on both sides with an iridescent green fluid. The hilt itself had three notches in it, and when he briskly rubbed the handle, a fae skull embossment appeared, glowing faintly from the friction.

My body froze, and a shiver ran down my spine. Someone *had* planted evidence.

I blew out a breath and moved quickly, but when I tried to take the dagger from Bryn, he moved back.

"My magic is not tainting the evidence. It protects the

integrity of the blade, but yours won't." Bryn grabbed the hem of the dress and ripped a section off, then wrapped it around the tiny handle so I could see the blade. "Here. Now you can take it."

I hesitated, confused why he would take the time to preserve the evidence. In fairness, I hadn't been thinking clearly and would've grabbed it if not for him.

He held it out to me, and I swiped it.

Thalen's brow quirked, and he folded his arms as he leaned back. "Convenient that whoever left it left such a clear marker on it. For all we know, you just put it in there to attempt to convince us that you truly believe she's innocent."

"How dare you accuse me of lying?" Bryn dropped his hand but glared. "Do you know how insulting that is, especially after I advised you not to taint the evidence?"

The truth was that neither Thalen nor I cared. "This could be a ruse to see if I truly believe Briar is guilty. How could I possibly deny it when people saw her drop the dagger used to stab my father, as well as being covered in his blood?"

I narrowed my eyes. The hilt of the blade had notches in it to serve as grips when put into its sheath. A blade like this most likely had matching partners that were meant to be kept in a harness on the thigh, across the back, or chest. Had there been such marks on the dagger used on Father?

Bryn huffed. "I thought I could speak the truth to you. Maybe I misjudged you."

I gritted my teeth and turned the dagger to study it further. I didn't know what game this elder was playing, but I didn't like him openly calling me stupid.

The metal of this blade looked similar, though not identical, to the one that had taken my father's life. It was perhaps a quarter of the size of that one. "There should be others in this set." The length of the blade was about the right size to match the wound in Rhielle's throat, which explained why it might have been countered so easily by her shadow shield. The poison itself did the dirty work. Whoever had attacked her probably hadn't even had to cut her that much but had chosen a painful stroke.

"Was the weapon used on Rhielle ever found?" Bryn hung the dress back up and resumed searching the next dress.

I inhaled raggedly. "No. Though I suspect it appeared similar to this one." I turned the blade over in my hands, careful not to nick myself. The last thing I wanted was to corrupt the evidence or inject myself with poison.

The application of poison had been done with great precision, the depth of the color showing that the blade had been dipped and allowed to dry many times. "It fought against her body's healing efforts and even all our own. It's painful and hard to stop the bleeding of someone who has been stabbed with such venom."

Bryn continued his search, his voice muffled as he leaned farther into the wardrobe. "If there is someone you trust, have them test the blade. You'll almost certainly see that the venom is the same type that was used on Rhielle. Quite the vicious poison, I might add. They'll most likely find the same poison in your father's wound if they test for it. Knowing the exact variety will allow them to cure Rhielle faster."

"So many coincidences." Thalen stooped to pick up a fallen bracelet and then knelt to look under the bed. "Too many for my taste."

The floor lurched beneath my feet. A heavy grinding rumble shook the room, and silt rained down from the ceiling tiles. Screams sounded all around us, from down the hall, along with above and below. The dagger nearly slipped from my grip as I braced myself against the wardrobe, careful not to stab myself with it. Another deep rumble shook the room, rattling the furniture and sending several of Briar's possessions tumbling to the floor. The bed frame knocked against the wall with a hollow thud as the tremors intensified.

Thalen leapt to his feet, wings flaring for balance. "What in the void—"

Books toppled from shelves, and a glass figurine shattered on the marble floor. One of the mirrors in the washroom shattered, sending fine particles of glass flying everywhere. My shadows convulsed wildly around my feet, responding to the chaos and my own startled state.

Just as quickly as it had begun, the trembling subsided, leaving the room in further disarray.

My head throbbed viciously, a sharp pain lancing from the base of my skull to my temples. I pressed my palm against my forehead, trying to steady myself as nausea rolled through my gut.

Bryn's expression darkened. Without a word, he crossed to the washbasin in the corner of the room and turned on the tap. The crimson waters rapidly changed from blood-red to a murky pink, the sugary-spicy scent wavering as well. "This is worse than I feared, and Fate is getting angrier."

I clutched at my chest, the tightness cold, sharp, and clamping ever tighter. The changing of the water ... who else had seen this now? It was a beacon to our kingdom's weakness.

My vision blurred at the edges as another surge of pain crashed through my skull.

Don't fall.

Breathe.

I had to be strong for Briar, my family, and my kingdom.

Another spasm cut through me. I doubled over, gripping the black bedpost as agony tore through me. My shadows writhed against the floor like dying things, their edges fraying and dissolving only to reform erratically. The vested magic inside me churned violently, as if trying to escape.

"Do you need to sit?" Thalen asked, moving to my side. Though he didn't touch me, he was close enough to grab me if I fell.

"I'm fine," I growled, though the lie was transparent. Blood pounded in my ears, and sweat beaded on my forehead. The pain arced tighter and tighter through my consciousness, but after three more ragged breaths, it started to ease.

The water returned to its crimson hue as Bryn stared at the swirling liquid, concern etched into his very posture. He dipped his fingers into the water again and tested it. With distaste, he flicked the droplets away. "Your coronation must happen within the next twenty-four hours, and a queen must be crowned, or else the magic will cease to flow through you at all, and the tie to this kingdom and all your people will be severed. You don't have three days, Your Highness, let alone four. Not now. Probably not even two, if I am being quite blunt about this reality. It only gets worse from here. And let me be clear on this point—if you die and Briar is still here in Nytheria, she will die horrifically as well, and I won't tolerate that."

I steadied myself and straightened, trying to swallow the sour taste that coated my tongue.

Bryn strode back into the bedroom, his boots crunching on glass fragments. "We're running out of time, especially with this game you're trying to play with me, Your Highness. Vow to me that you will protect Briar and do all that it takes to clear her name, and I will tell you my plan to get her out and allow you to assist me in rescuing her."

I didn't have time to argue anymore. "We already have a plan." I wiped the back of my hand across my mouth and squared my shoulders.

He laughed scornfully. "I knew you were lying about believing her to be the killer, thank Fate. How soon in your plan will you have Briar out of that prison?" He strode to the back of the room and examined the copper shadow beast hanging on the wall. "Three days? Two?" He set his hands on his dark gray leather belt, his fingers tapping at his sides. "I can have her out in three hours."

"Three *hours*?" I folded my arms over my chest as I regarded him, my head still spinning. He was ancient and held a great deal of power, but did he hold that much sway? "How? How do I even know I can trust you?"

With an annoyed sigh, he pinched his brow. Then he placed a hand on his chest. "I, Bryn Lugh of the Aurelines, here vow upon my life and breath to do all that is within my power to ensure Briar is returned to her home safely and swiftly, and that she comes through this alive and well so that she may lead a fulfilling and happy life with her family. I will also get her out of Firellan's Spine within three hours upon agreement to my terms." He arched one heavy brow again as if in challenge. "There. Happy? Now vow the same."

"*All* is a dangerous thing to vow." Thalen held up his hands as a flash of alarm passed through his amber eyes.

I already had my hand over my heart, my fingers digging into my surcoat. "I, Vad, son of Merrick of the Shadows, vow upon my life and breath to do all that is within my power to ensure Briar is happy and safe."

"No." Bryn's jaw and fist clenched, and he closed the distance between us. His liquid gold eyes gleamed with something almost manic, as if he were trying to compel me with his mere presence. "No, you do not vow that. You vow to get her *home,* to Earth." His voice tightened with emotion, shaking at the word *home*. "She was torn from everything, and if she remains here, she will face far greater dangers. You cannot even begin to imagine the horrors."

Anger boiled in my veins. "I will protect her with *everything*

I have." My wings flexed, and the shadows rippled behind me as I stepped up to him.

Though I towered over him by a good eight inches, he didn't even blink. "And it won't be enough. All you had wasn't enough to keep her from being taken and brutalized. You were powerless to protect her during the trials as well. And the people who want her dead take her existence personally. Briar must disappear. You may have your bargains and deals with any number of individuals, but there are far more than you think involved in this. If she remains in this realm, she will die because they will not stop trying. And while you are getting weaker, they are getting stronger. Eventually, they will succeed in killing her. And there's nothing you or anyone else can do to stop it unless we get her out of this place entirely. If you care about her even a little, you will let her go."

I parted my lips to protest as my shadows rose darker along the walls. "No. There must be some other way."

"Wait." Thalen chopped his hand in the space between us. "I understand that you want to protect someone innocent taken from Earth. But how you're going about it sounds fecking personal."

"It *is* personal." Bryn straightened his shoulders. "Setting up an innocent contender is an abomination to Fate. They are perverting Fate's decisions and not respecting her power. They're toying with magic that is not their own and using someone not of this realm to do it."

I'd been focused on Briar, mainly because of my feelings for her, but he was right. Whoever was doing this wasn't just messing with Briar—they were messing with all of us and Fate's path.

"Maybe." Thalen pursed his lips, probably trying to aggravate Bryn more.

Bryn rolled his eyes and focused on me. "You cannot even

begin to know what she will suffer if she remains. More than that, she doesn't belong here. She has a home and family on Earth. A sister and a brother-in-law. A *pack*. In time, she will have nieces and nephews. Can you give her all that? I think not."

The idea of losing Briar had me wanting to rip my heart out. I tensed, and a growl rose in my chest. "I can give her *everything* she will ever want or need, and I will see to it that she can visit her sister. *I* will be her family." The words slipped out. It was as if he had known my feelings for Briar all along, and that troubled me. Worse than that, even I could hear that desperate note that tinged my words, and I knew he could use them against me.

But it was his words that disturbed me most as they settled into my mind. Could I truly ever give Briar all that she deserved?

His brow softened, and he spoke more calmly. "If you love her, then you must let her go. It isn't safe for her anywhere in Nytheria. She was dragged here against her will to a realm she knows nothing of and into a role she neither wanted nor prepared for." His fingers brushed the medallion, and he glanced down at it. His brow tightened. "She has endured more than enough, and she is not your future queen. She cannot be. Not unless you want her to die because of it. I will not help you if you are not willing to make this vow, and her death will be on your head."

Panic and desperation clawed at my insides and my throat. "What gives you the right to say that? She has performed admirably and under great duress. She has inspired great loyalty." And I *loved* her. She was my heart, my beloved. I couldn't imagine a life without her, and I had given her a choice ...

Thalen paced back to my side and cast a challenging look at Bryn. "Shouldn't you all 'let Fate decide?' You know ... not interfere, and let things be what they are. This feels an awful lot like not allowing Fate to do what Fate wills."

"Fate has decided. It is our duty to go along with it, but there are some who are rebelling and trying to prevent it from happening." He clenched his jaw, and the corner of his mouth twitched.

Thalen's brow quirked. "If you can defy Fate, is it really Fate?"

I wasn't interested in a philosophical debate, and every fiber in me knew that Briar was meant to be here and at my side. "If Briar wants to be with me, I will never deny her that. I can give her *everything*. I can protect her. We'll bring her back and crown her queen. That will solve everything."

Bryn's gaze snapped back to me. "Except it won't. You'll give her everything you *can*. It isn't the same, and it won't keep her safe from harm. It doesn't take into consideration what is needed."

She needed to be with *me*.

The hollow sensation in my chest expanded with every breath. Was it accurate to say Briar needed me, or ... was it I who needed her?

What life could there possibly be for me without her?

Perhaps I should not be thinking of my own life. To be near her and with her was a physical need, but there was nothing to say that it was the same for her. What did *Briar* need? My throat tightened again. I'd tried to give her a choice back in the observatory, but what if that hadn't been enough? What if she'd felt that she had to accept me, regardless?

He stepped closer, his demeanor almost gentle despite the hardness in his eyes. "I know you love her. Even if you denied it, I wouldn't believe you. You might as well pretend you can keep the moon from rising with just your words. As you love her, you must do what is best for her. I can make sure that she is brought back, given what she needs, and ultimately taken to safety, all before the night is out and fulfilling what Fate demands." His jaw tightened for a breath. "I have already vowed that I will protect her and help you. If you love her, how can you possibly reject my help? All I ask is that you make your own vow."

My lungs stopped working. The thought of her not being here made life feel empty. But if he could free her ... at least she'd live. "What is this plan? Tell me first."

He glanced toward the door. Then he canted his head. "No. You see ... my vow's fulfillment is in some respects contingent upon your agreement. If you do not make the vow, I cannot guarantee that I will succeed. But I will give it all my efforts. If you want me bound, then you must vow as well. Can you live with the risk of her remaining there? Do you not love her enough to do anything for her?"

Those final questions pierced my soul. My head spun, and pure agony devoured me. Loving Briar meant doing what was best for *her*. She deserved a rich, beautiful life. Was there not some way that we could share that life? Blood thundered in my ears.

"With all due respect, sir, you're full of it." Thalen glared at Bryn and glanced at me. His wings twitched and tightened as he flexed them. "If Prince Vad—"

"Three hours." Bryn held up three wrinkled fingers, the thick rings catching the light. "Three hours with a plan to get her back to her home before midnight, safe with her sister and her pack. Precisely where she wanted to be from the beginning. If you truly love her, this isn't even a choice. How long will it take you to get her back and ensure that this place is safe for her until all of this can be resolved?"

Thalen cast an apologetic look at me. "It'll be at least a day and a half before the prison here is deemed ready, unless there's a way to expedite that."

A muscle in Bryn's jaw jumped. "At this point, seconds count, Your Highness. Firellan's Spine is worse than you know. Simply being in that place will drain her mind, her body, her spirit—everything. Even the terrain is hostile. It is far worse than you have been led to believe in the bowels of that dungeon. There is no better way for you to ensure her safety. I am aware you most likely made some deal with Colm Ainle. A wise choice, but it is not without flaws. Others not under his command could enter and harm her. Ainle is not as clever as he likes to believe."

My knees weakened. How could he possibly know?

He raised an eyebrow in open challenge. "I am also aware you gave him something of great value. If the rumors are true, it was something quite dear to you, as well as powerful. He isn't the most discreet individual. No matter the bargain you made, it is not safe for her there. You must take this vow. My method will not require delays or additional councils or permit any petitions. It is already enshrined in our laws and customs."

"Briar wouldn't want you to make her go back." Thalen gripped my arm. "Vad, you can't just decide this for her. She should have the say."

"Even if it means she suffers longer?" Bryn tapped his finger on the medallion as he fixed Thalen with his heavy stare. "Even if it means she will die?" He scoffed, shaking his head. "If you truly love her, Your Highness, then you will make this vow and prove it. True love is not selfish. It does not think of its own desires. It thinks of the one who is loved. What does *she* need? Does she need to waste away in a place where time does not follow our laws? Where, at every moment, her energy and magic are sapped by their cruelty? Even now, she will struggle to recover from all they have done. Your plan requires that she suffer longer and puts her life at risk. Mine reduces that harm."

His words cut deep, speaking to my fear and the knowledge that I failed her. The nausea and throbbing in my skull warned me that what power I had was failing fast. What good would I be to her? "Three hours ... and she won't be harmed?"

"I have sworn it." Bryn's piercing eyes held knowledge.

I opened my mouth, but my tongue didn't move. Everything inside me was fighting against this vow, but if my beloved died due to my selfishness ... that would haunt me even in the afterlife.

Clenching my right hand into a fist and pressing it against my side, I gritted. "I, Vad, son of Merrick of the Shadows, vow upon my life and breath to do all that is within my power to ensure Briar is happy and safe and that she gets ... *home*."

The spiraling agony that lanced through my chest and down my spine wasn't magic of any sort, and I realized something was wrong.

Chapter Twenty

My magic surged, fighting against some sort of foreign presence. I had no clue what it was, but as the vow locked into place, it was *furious.* I clenched my jaw and hissed through my teeth.

I shouldn't have made the vow.

The magic retreated, as if my acknowledgment and punishment had been enough for now. It seemed as if Fate had personally struck me, telling me that I'd interfered with her plan. I wanted to retch.

Thalen frowned. His lips pressed into a tight line as he pulled in his wings.

Bryn inclined his head forward. "You have chosen wisely, Your Highness."

No, I hadn't.

I'd just made the worst decision of my entire existence. Briar was the perfect woman for me, and now I'd thrown away any chance for us to be together, as well as my own happiness, in hopes that I could protect her.

Another searing bolt of pain and nausea lanced through me, sharpening my breath. "Tell me what your fecking plan is."

Bryn closed the wardrobe and took a measured step

forward. "Simple. The third trial begins in six hours. All living candidates must be present, no matter their health or condition."

My entire body went rigid while my blood roared in my veins. "That better be a joke. You cannot seriously intend to put her in a *third* trial after what she's endured in that scaffing prison. You just told me that your plan will keep her from suffering! Those trials are nothing but suffering and death." I squinted to the point where I could see only Bryn's weathered face. My wings flared as my muscles coiled tight and my shadows loomed.

"That's entirely nonsensical." Thalen's wings snapped out, and his hand fisted in his hair. "No. No, you can't have the third trial."

Bryn huffed, and his transparent silver shield strengthened, glimmering faintly. He remained motionless. "Briar will be brought here for the third trial. She will enter the third trial. So long as she follows instructions once she is inside, she will not have to actually compete in the third trial. Remember, I made a vow to you as well."

"She won't follow instructions if anyone else is at risk." Thalen crossed his arms. "Did you see what happened in the last two? If not for her ..." He paled even more as he trailed off.

"Briar is not fit to fight," I snarled. A muscle ticked in my jaw. "She needs time to rest and recover. I might as well bring her back here and declare her my queen and deal with the fallout."

"Yes, then we don't have to have another trial." Thalen clapped his hands together.

"If you do that, you will fail and doom her." Bryn's tone sharpened. "There is no time. If they even suspect that you're considering circumventing the final trial, individuals with whom you have not made any bargain will kill her."

My breath caught. "Do you know who's behind all this?"

"No, but they will do whatever it takes to keep her from becoming your queen. The laws and customs are clear. The three tests must be performed, even if you've already crowned a queen." Bryn wrinkled his nose. "To defy the trials is to spit in the face of Fate."

I bit back my retort. Fate hadn't been kind to me of late, but in that moment, I could see his commitment to her.

Lifting a hand, Bryn clicked his tongue. "These enemies will assume that she will not survive the test, and they will also take steps to ensure she does not make it through. They'll want to make it appear as if Fate struck her down to prove, once and for all, she was guilty. But we will counter them so their plans fail."

I clenched my hands, wanting to fly from this room and whisk Briar away from the prison at once. Of course these monsters wanted her dead, and they wouldn't stop until she was.

"Well, that sounds great and all, but we have no idea what the trial is." Thalen arched a brow. "So do you plan on sharing?"

"If the two of you would be quiet, I will inform you." He looked down his nose.

Thalen snorted and opened his mouth, but I smacked him in the back of the head. He glared at me, but I gave him a stern expression.

That was enough for Bryn, because he finally continued, "The contestants will meet in the Ascension Hall as in the previous two trials. From there, each woman will be portaled alone to a single chamber. Unlike the first two trials, this one will take place in the Shadow Kingdom, which is how we're going to save Briar."

My kingdom? That surprised me. Holding a trial in the land of the ruler-to-be wasn't unprecedented, but it wasn't common either. Most trials were held in neutral territory to prevent corruption.

Clearly, the Aureline were as corrupt as, if not more than, any other fae.

"Its purpose is to reveal the character of the candidate, and it is closed to outside viewers, also unlike the first two. You'll be able to see the candidates enter, and should they survive, you will be able to see them exit." Bryn shrugged. "What happens inside that chamber remains inside that chamber. If a candidate does not reappear, all will assume she died. A body won't be expected ... this particular environment is an especially harsh one."

Of course it was. I wanted to ram my head into the wall. I suspected they'd lure Briar into the most dangerous part somehow. Her heart and the way she cared were both a strength and a liability.

"You can't force them to go through the third trial," Thalen rasped, looking from Bryn to me. "It isn't right or fair. Not just for Briar but for others who aren't fully healthy. L-like Rhielle—"

"If Rhielle is alive when the competition starts, she will participate," Bryn said sternly.

I lifted my hands. "I already informed Rhielle that I would speak with the joint council about her participation, given—"

"There are *no* exceptions. Fate cannot be mocked any further." Bryn jabbed his finger in the air. "What must happen is simple. The three trials must conclude. We get Briar here, and then we get her out and to her home. I will see to that myself while you go to your coronation and choose your queen."

The words were a blow that rocked me to my core. There could be no queen for me other than Briar. The hollowness in my chest expanded, my lungs tightening. My shadows surged and coiled around me as if they, too, struggled to comprehend a kingdom ... a realm without Briar as my queen.

Bryn drew closer, his eyes flashing like lightning, and gestured to the top of my head. "You will accept your crown and choose someone else as the Shadow Queen, Your Highness, or your kingdom will fall. And from there, things will only get worse."

"There has to be another way." My wings tightened and flexed as I tried to think of something—anything. If we could catch the people behind this, then there would be no risk to Briar at all for taking the throne alongside me.

Wagging his finger in my face, Bryn glared at me. "If you defy Fate enough, Fate will strike back. You and so many of these leaders and council members do not even come close to perceiving how fecking fed up Fate is with all of you. Do *not* draw Fate's ire, Your Highness. Your father already risked it. But even he had the good sense to not scorn all tradition *and* Fate. No one keeps Fate from having her say."

I firmly believed Briar was meant to rule alongside me. The awful sensation that had hit me when I'd made that vow—it couldn't be coincidence.

"You cannot stand in the way of the third trial, and if you wish to protect Briar, your duty is simple. Assist in rescuing Briar, and let her go. Allow the trials to conclude, and either accept the will of the shared council, or make your second choice." Bryn scowled. "She isn't an option, Your Highness."

My chest constricted to the point that I couldn't breathe. There was no one else for me. No one but Briar. There was no second, third, or fourth choice. There was only one. My beloved.

Still, Briar being alive was the most important thing to me, and I'd made that damn vow, even if it had been the wrong decision. "I will let her go," I gritted out, the words bitter on my tongue. "But I won't ask her to go through another trial. If you can get Briar back here within three hours, then do it, but she must have time to recover—"

"My authority allows me to do only so much, and you don't have days to waste." Bryn's face reddened. "The third trial is a proof of judgment. It's said that Fate herself will strike down anyone who kills the family of the one who seeks a bride. No one will question why her body is not found. All she has to do is stay in the opening circle in the third trial, and we will get her out. It will look as if she died in the trial, and all threats will be eliminated."

"Then people will assume she is guilty of killing my father." I clenched my fists. No, this didn't sit well with me. Her innocence had to be known. I wanted her name cleared for everyone to see.

Bryn flung out his arms and stalked back toward the washroom. "What others believe of Briar is far less important than her safety and well-being! Better to be living and scorned by people you will never see again than dead and exonerated. And she will survive the trial so long as she retains the sense her mother gave her."

"The Shadow Council will have to—"

"I have already spoken with Vyraetos. He also disagreed initially, and he wanted us to have the funeral before the coronation and the wedding. That will no longer be possible with the way the magic is decaying. His loyalty to your family is commendable, even if his foresight is short. But after this earthquake and the dimming of the water, he cannot deny it any further." Bryn swept his left arm across the room and turned the tap on once more. As crimson water spilled out, he leaned close. "Who knows how long the destabilization will continue. Your enemies have been advancing faster than they should."

Panic clawed my insides. "Is it possible they're using life-draining magic to enhance their powers and manipulate this entire situation for their own purposes?"

His head snapped in my direction. "What?" Bryn straightened and crossed to the doorway. He set his hands on the door frame as he peered out, scowling at me from beneath heavy eyebrows. "What do you mean?"

I set my hands on my belt. "There's a prisoner on the other side of Briar's cell wall in Firellan's Spine. His name is Elias. He's a Terran Fae with four bear claw tattoos on his throat, and Briar says they've been draining him slowly. If there's any way to get him out, she wants him rescued too." The image of how she'd looked last night when I'd visited her shredded my heart. Even suffering, she'd been thinking of others. If anyone deserved happiness, it was her ... even if it had to be without me.

Bryn grunted. He pushed his wild auburn hair back and paced. "Are they draining others?"

"Are you seriously asking him that?" Thalen's forehead lined. "He barely got that much from Briar, seeing as the guards were watching and trying to listen in. They didn't have a romantic stroll and talk."

Maybe I should've scolded him, but I agreed with his assessment. The question had been ridiculous. Still, I bit out, "He probably isn't the only one. They don't seem like the sort who would do just one thing if it's working."

Releasing a sharp breath, Bryn drew a hand over his mouth. His fingers curled under his chin as he tapped his thumb against his lips. "This is worse than I feared. Much worse. Well, this plan is the priority. Briar must come first—"

"I thought you said this was about *innocents*. You're not concerned about this other innocent?" The edge in Thalen's voice made it clear he wasn't teasing.

Bryn glared at him, the wrinkles in his face deepening. "I didn't say I wouldn't help him, little imp. But there must always be priorities. Or would you rather I cast Briar and the looming destruction of your kingdom aside to save someone who may or may not be connected to this abomination?"

"I was just saying ..." Thalen shrugged.

I glanced around, once again noting how much damage had been done to Briar's room. If Briar formally won the bridal competition, the magic would transform this room into a wedding bower for her bridal preparations, as if Fate herself were congratulating the winner. And that wardrobe would reveal a stunning gown that represented the bride. Briar deserved that and more, not to be viewed as a treacherous outsider who'd slain an ailing king.

My chest tightened even more. But clearing her name wasn't nearly so important as saving her life. "We need to set matters in place to get her here as soon as possible."

The three of us planned. We settled on our roles, and I bound Thalen to silence on Briar's imminent rescue.

Once settled, Thalen and I started for the Healing Hall once again. Servants and guests whispered in worried tones about the earthquake. But no one mentioned the changing water color, and I prayed no one had noticed it.

When we neared our destination, a black-winged guard hurried toward us. His obsidian armor gleamed in the low light, and he bowed while striking a fist to his chest. "Your Highness, I have good news—you no longer need to worry. The princess has been found."

I froze mid-stride, scowling. "Found? What do you mean, 'found'?" I blinked a few times, thinking I must have misheard him.

Thalen cocked his head. "Was someone going to tell us she was missing? Seems like we're missing a step or two."

The guard's expression shifted to confusion. "We ... we've been trying to locate you for the past hour, Your Highness. Silus informed the royal guard that she was missing, and he could not find you. But they have returned."

My jaw locked so tight my molars ached. My wings flared out as I crossed in front of the shorter man. "What happened? Is she hurt? Where did she go?"

The guard bowed again, his charcoal wings tightening against his armored back. "They've returned to the royal family's quarters, Your Highness. They appeared unharmed."

Without hesitation, I strode through the corridor toward the royal quarters. What had Elara been doing? Where had she gone with Silus? Dread pooled in my gut as a suspicion blossomed in my mind. She wouldn't have gone to Firellan's Spine, would she? No ... I hadn't told her that's where Briar was being kept. So, where?

Thalen trotted alongside me. "I'm sure there's a reasonable explanation. Perhaps she needed something for the funeral. Or a quick snog."

"Silus wouldn't have informed the guard if they were going to do that." And frankly, I didn't want to think about Silus and Elara kissing and caressing each other. She was my *little sister.*

"Well, I think we can write off the likelihood that it's something nefarious." Thalen patted my shoulder. "Also, ease up, or you're going to crack your teeth before the coronation."

I shoved his hand off and kept moving. My shadows coiled around my ankles, and I quickened my pace, nearly colliding with a servant, who flattened herself against the wall.

The pain in my head intensified with each step, but I pushed through it. In three hours, Briar would be back in the Shadow Kingdom. In six hours, she'd be safe forever. Every fiber within me tightened and burned at that thought.

Safe ... without *me.*

The hollow ache within me screamed for any choice but that, but I ignored it. I just had to survive until she was safe, and then I could sift through the remnants of my own life.

As I approached Elara's chamber door, I caught a faint

whiff of rot and dried blood, like Firellan's Spine. Then I heard voices from within.

"—have to tell him, Elara." Silus's voice was low, urgent. "This changes everything. He has a right to know."

"No." Elara's voice moved away from the door as she likely paced toward the back of the room. "It's not the right time. Can't you see how much he's already dealing with? I promise you, I'm *fine*." Her voice hardened.

Seizing the handle, I thrust the door open. Silus stood in the center of the room, facing a blue silk screen in the back, arms outstretched in exasperation. He twisted around and saw me, his face blanching.

I fixed him with a stony glare before looking toward the blue silk screen, which I guessed Elara was currently standing behind. "What exactly am I not supposed to know, and where were you? A fecking guard just informed me that you were found after being missing. And what in the void are you doing back there, Elara?"

"Don't you take that tone with me, *Vad Dacian Nocthar*! These are my quarters. You may be king soon, but I will *always* be your sister."

I jerked back at the use of my full name, then scowled. "If there's something you aren't telling me, you need to tell me *now, Elara Ravenne Isolde*. It is *not* too much trouble, and I will *always* have time for you."

"Great. Then have time for me after the coronation and your fecking wedding," Elara snapped, stepping out from behind the screen. She wore a simple indigo gown with a high neck and long sleeves fastened at the wrists, but she also wore a large black cloak that was far too big for her.

Was that *Silus's* cloak?

Thalen beamed. "I love it when siblings start throwing out family names like they're insults."

Elara narrowed her eyes at him, and I shot him my own glare.

He lifted his hands and had the decency to look at the floor.

I spun back on Elara. "Where were you?"

"I went to visit Briar." She folded her arms with exaggerated slowness while staring me straight in the eye as if daring me to react.

"How did you know where she was?" I demanded. I hadn't told Silus, and I certainly hadn't told Elara.

"You have your sources, I have mine." She broadened her stance, daring me to keep pressing. The fire in her deep-blue eyes brought me some measure of comfort, even if it was aggravating for her to be pulling it out now.

"It was Vyraetos, wasn't it?" I scoffed, then flicked a glance at Silus, barely containing my snarl.

Silus raised his hands in surrender. "I tried to find you. I did. And when I couldn't, I believed it was best for me to follow her so she wasn't there alone."

His words placated me somewhat. And the guard had said Silus had tried to locate me. Still, the agitation remained knotted within me. Elara could have been hurt or killed. "I can't believe you went there alone. It's no place for any decent person."

"Briar's there, so I went." She kept her arms folded and her posture immaculate.

My shadows slid along beside hers, offering strength.

Her upper lip curled a little, but she didn't push me aside. "I'm perfectly fine. I feel wonderful. If you were unable to be king, I would easily and happily take on the crown myself."

Silus's breath hissed through his teeth. "You should *not* have gone."

She cut her eyes at him. "Do not tell me what I should and shouldn't do, unless you are actually in a position to enforce such an order."

Thalen's eyes widened as an impish grin curved at his lips. "Are you suggesting you would like to be in a position where Silus can make demands on you?"

My eyebrows shot up, and Elara jerked back, her mouth falling open and her cheeks turning scarlet. Silus went rigid, his right hand curling into a fist against his immaculately pressed trousers.

One of my shadows yanked hard on Thalen's wing, making him stagger. "Enough," I snapped. "What were you doing there, Elara?"

Elara cleared her throat. "I needed to see her for myself and hear what she had to say."

My muscles tightened. The urge to ask after Briar and demand every scrap of information rose in me like an insatiable flood. "Did you learn anything of value?"

"The earthquake in Firellan's Spine happened at approximately the same time as here. That's just further proof that what's happening here is impacting more than just our kingdom. I also saw the condition they're keeping her in," she responded, lifting one eyebrow. "But if you're not interested in that, we can skip it."

Fecking void. I stood upright. "How are they keeping her?"

"She wore some ill-fitting wool gown that was damp, especially at the hem. The only good thing I can say about it is that it wasn't moldy. When the material moved up and exposed some of her skin, I could see that she had a rash.

"They'd given her no shoes, and her feet were bleeding. She smelled like that awful black bread, blood, and bad water. From the state of her hands, it looked like she'd been clawing at the rocks, but it didn't seem like she was being tortured, beyond being kept in that place. Some of her sores are infected. But ... she's strong. Best to get her out sooner rather than later, I'd say." She pursed her lips and glared, and then said, "Anything you'd like to add, Silas?"

He cleared his throat and adjusted his stance, folding his arms across his chest. Still, he didn't say anything.

"*Do* you have something to add?" I let iciness fill my voice.

Silus lifted a brow, and I could practically see a sarcastic response forming in his mind, but he licked his lips instead. "While I do think she is a pawn and that there are matters for concern—"

Elara cleared her throat.

He glanced at her, and his expression softened. "I do not believe Briar is evil, nor is she weak. She does not deserve to be there."

A little bit of relief eased some of the weight I carried. I'd accept this small concession from him and hope that he continued to see that he'd misjudged her.

But then my annoyance returned. "Was that what you didn't want to tell me, Elara? How does this change everything?"

Her eyes narrowed, her expression pinching. "Saying it changes everything was overdramatic on my part."

Silus sighed as his grip on his arms tightened. "Her glamour failed. It sapped her dry while we were in the prison. Her condition has worsened significantly, and she is in a bad state."

"Silus!" Elara's eyes widened.

He angled himself once more toward her, his voice tight. "Be angry with me all you like. But if there were an arrow headed for you, I would intercept it and take the blow myself. Do you think there is any realm in which I could permit you to suffer in silence when intervention might help? If protecting you earns me your ire, then so be it. But do not ever expect me to stand idly by when you are at risk, *Elara*."

Spots of color emerged on her cheeks despite the glamour. She twitched her shoulders as if she wasn't sure what to say.

"Noted." She moved her hands to her waist, bracing herself as she looked at both Silus and Thalen. "I ... love you both, but I want to discuss this matter with my brother in private."

Thalen spread his arms and inclined his head. "As you wish, Shadow Princess, though it feels wrong to deny you both my scintillating wit. However, I do need food ... and alcohol. Silus?"

Expression somber, Silus's gaze flicked from Elara to me. "I could use something too."

Elara watched them go, not turning to look at me until the door sealed shut and a few breaths had passed. She said, "You don't need to worry about me. I promise I'm fine."

"Are you? Really?" I stepped closer to her, wanting to banish her glamour. But that would be a violation that would be hard to forgive, and I didn't need anything further to come between us. "Will you let me see you without your glamour?"

She lifted her chin, wearing the same stubborn expression she'd had as a child when she wouldn't move out of a doorway so I could pass, despite being half my height. "Not now. I look worse than I am, and I'd rather no one see me looking like this. I have my vanity, after all." She set her jaw as she arched her eyebrow once more in the manner she did when she was feeling defiant but also a little self-conscious. "And don't be mad at Silus for any of this. He had no idea I was going. We exchanged a great many words on the subject once it was safe, and he scolded me more than any noble should scold a princess. Even if he is like family."

I grunted, still not pleased but somewhat mollified. "I'm surprised you left so swiftly."

She cleared her throat. "In truth, Silus carried me out as soon as the earthquake struck. It is difficult to argue with someone when they have just ... picked you up like you weigh nothing." Her cheeks reddened a little more.

"I'm glad he had the sense to get you out quickly."

"He's a good friend." She rubbed the back of her neck before her hand trailed away.

My eyebrow rose slightly, but I didn't comment on her reaction. "Who all has seen you without your glamour?"

"Three of the guards in Firellan's Spine. Colm saw me when I arrived, and it wasn't so bad. Then Briar, of course. Before Silus picked me up, he put his cloak over me. As soon as I was back, the Shadow magic started replenishing for me. I had no idea that the prison would make me lose control so swiftly. It's a dreadful place." She ran her hand along the cloak that covered her shoulders.

My throat tightened. Even though I wanted to believe she was all right, that wasn't the only piece of evidence against her. "Regardless ... I spoke with Physician Morlo."

She stiffened, then shook her head. "I know what he told you, and you know how much I love and appreciate him, but he isn't a prophet. I had this same conversation with Silus. Part of the reason my condition has worsened so much is what was happening with Father and his death. Once you're coronated and the magic vests, I'll start improving."

I tilted my head and studied her. "Are you in pain, Elara?"

She stepped closer. "It isn't comfortable, but you know what that's like," she said firmly.

When I refused to concede the point, she sighed and drew back. "Vad, there are dozens of matters of far greater importance. I'm not going to fall over dead in the next two days or even the next two months. You wait and see. I'm certain that, after the coronation and the final vestment of the magic and stabilization of our kingdom, I *will* improve. I intend to be there for both your coronation and your wedding."

Emotions battled inside me, making me feel caught in my own personal war. "I love you, and I'm proud of you. You fight so damn hard. Not many know what you're capable of."

"Guess that strength and fight run in the family." Her eyes glistened, and she smiled sadly. "I'm proud of you too. It must feel like your world is falling apart right now, but I promise you, *I'm* not going to fall apart."

I rested my forehead on hers and hugged her again, trying not to react to how small and bony she was but focusing instead on her spirit.

She returned the embrace, pulling me in close. "Besides, you know I intend to see those who murdered our father and framed Briar suffer. Do you think there is even the smallest of chances that I would risk not seeing that bloody justice done? I will be there in all black with daggers for earrings and a heart that thrills to the sounds of their screams."

"If anything changes, you tell me." I drew back and squeezed her hand. The fine bones shifted beneath my grip, and I let go at once, though she didn't complain.

"I will. Don't worry about me." She peered at me with that stubborn look but also a little more of a smile. "You'll have to endure my presence for centuries to come."

I scowled at her, fighting my own smile. "Well, if there can be centuries, I suppose I can accept that. But know I will always worry for you."

If Briar had been able to stay with us, they would have become fast friends. The urge to tell her about the plan to save Briar rose within me, but I held back. Letting Briar go would be hard enough. I didn't want to ask that of Elara. Besides, I suspected she'd be angry that I'd vowed to let my beloved leave.

Kissing the top of her head, I took my leave. Now the real planning would begin.

Approximately five and a half hours later

IT WAS REMARKABLE how much had changed and yet how much looked the same. I strode onto the rail-less balcony of the black-and-gold Ascension Hall, leathery wings spread and shadows dark and heavy. The air was thick with tension, a palpable force that shortened my breaths. My shadows coiled restlessly around my ankles as I scanned the hall for any sign of Briar. She would be arriving soon if Bryn's plan had worked.

My stomach twisted. I hadn't heard an update, and I hoped to Fate that Bryn was able to pull it off.

Time had passed swiftly and lagged all at once, each second tipping me closer to madness and doom as if I were a dead man walking. Without Briar, I might as well be.

A brief conversation with Vyraetos confirmed much of what I had discovered, as well as his reluctant agreement with Bryn. I retrieved the blade and took it to Physician Morlo, along with the hair sample.

Rhielle's hair sample had swiftly proven she had not drained any magic, element, or blood from another. He assured me that if the venom was indeed a match, he could administer a direct antidote that would be even more powerful. Rhielle was both perturbed to hear the news of the third trial and relieved to hear of the antidote, but her focus also went to Briar, and she proposed a solution to one of our problems with the rescue.

Standing in the hall below me, Rhielle appeared unnaturally pale, even for her, with her arms folded tight over her chest. Velessa and Yuki stood beside her, neither attempting to talk. Based on the closeness, it looked as if they had chosen their positions so that, if Rhielle needed to lean on them, she could. Of course, she kept her back ramrod straight. The only sign of weakness was that she kept her gaze focused on the opposing wall, unblinking and barely acknowledging the others.

Thalira spoke in soft tones with Calla Lily, who looked like she was on the verge of tears, and Quen, who had an even more sour expression on her face than she had the last time I saw her. Siray, one of the other Ignis Fae, stood in the corner with her arms crossed and her head down in an uncharacteristic fashion. Ceana was on the other side of the room, her hand to her head and knotted in her dark blue hair. Kaylen stood alone in the center of the room, shoulders back and posture immaculate.

All of the women wore simple but elegant long-sleeved gowns with thigh-high slits and slim-fitted trousers beneath them, as well as thick-soled boots.

To my right stood most members of the assembled councils, the Aureline Council members in gray and the Shadow Council members in black. The High Aureline Council had not yet joined us. As best I could tell, all of the Aurelines present were part of the joint council. They had their hoods up and their heads down, which made spotting the two who had stopped me in the garden at Father's death far trickier. But we would soon find out exactly who they were. Thalen had particular skills in tracking people down. Soon enough, all would be unveiled.

But where was Thalen?

I glanced to my left again. Elara stood in her usual spot, hands loosely clasped and gaze soft but neutral as she peered down at the candidates. She had changed into a midnight blue gown with black embellishments and a lace neck. The sleeves reached to her elbows, and veils flowed from the rest.

Silus stood directly behind her, arms at his sides. His attention seemed focused on some general point below, but I knew full well he was watching her from his periphery.

I crossed my arms and surveyed the area below us again. The black winged guards stood at attention at regular intervals around the room. Golden torchlight flickered and danced across the sleek marble and made the shadows dance. Mine remained still.

The door behind me scraped open, causing me to turn.

Thalen entered, his stride unusually quick, his brow furrowed, and his smile forced. The left edge of his mouth twitched as if he was struggling to hold his pleasant expression, and his gaze settled on the main entrance to the hall as Thalira motioned to someone I hadn't yet seen. Myantha slipped in and hurried over to Thalira. But then she looked up at Thalen.

Thalen's shoulders tensed, and his smile wavered, but he mouthed a single word.

She rubbed her arms nervously, then ducked her head. A tremor shook her hands before she tucked them against herself.

A surge of realization cut through me. Myantha had barely survived the last two trials. I had no comfort to offer either. In this trial, the candidates would truly be alone against whatever elements were present in the testing chamber. Some part of me longed for my initial dull coldness of not giving a feck about what happened to any of them. But life was not easy.

Why did this scaffing abomination of a trial have to continue? I wanted to reject it entirely and announce that Briar was my queen, though just thinking of breaking the vow made my skin bristle and discomfort rise. But I could endure that. It was the knowledge that to keep Briar here was to doom her that gave me the strength to let her go.

No one was in a playful mood. Thalen didn't even glance in my direction as he remained close to the edge, arms folded and gaze unabashedly fixed on Myantha.

Where was Briar? Bryn had mentioned that this trial was time sensitive, and it could not be delayed.

The heavy tramp of booted footsteps approached. A familiar aching tug sent me closer to the edge of the balcony. I wanted to crane my neck to see her, but instead, I straightened my shoulders.

The tug became a yank, intensifying a hundredfold.

Then she stepped into view.

Pure rage flamed through me. *This is unacceptable.*

Chapter Twenty-One

My heart raced as wisps of light gray Aureline magic swirled around me. Hysteria choked me, but I focused on what Many-Greats had said when he'd half-portaled into the cave for the second time. I would be part of the third trial with the rest of the bridal contestants, and he'd make sure my friends survived so long as they listened to instructions. Everything would work out for all of us, as long as we didn't leave our circles until the end of the trial. When I'd refused to leave without Elias, he'd assured me he would take care of him as well.

The gigantic set of double doors leading into the Ascension Hall appeared in front of me. The smooth, cool floor soothed my feet, but that didn't quiet the ringing in my ears or the way my body coiled. Through it all, the *yank* in my chest had me wanting to shove the black marble doors open to find Vad.

I had no idea what I was going to face inside. And the thought of people looking at me as if I was the king's actual killer ripped me in two. I never would've done that to the king. He'd been a good man.

The Aureline guards opened the doors and gripped my arms hard at the elbows. A second later, they dragged me over the threshold into the Ascension Hall as if I were fighting them.

My bare feet slid on the slick marble, but the pain wasn't anything like being scraped by the horrible, coarse rock in the prison. The heavy wool dress still grated on my skin, warm but uncomfortable and scratchy. My wolf snarled as I tried to stand up straight once again. I needed my pride intact.

"Keep moving," the guard on my right growled low, yanking me forward.

I stumbled but caught myself as I bit back a growl. My wolf was close to the surface now, desperate after being caged for so long. I held her back, barely, but I wasn't sure how long I could.

"Briar!" Thalira called out. "By the waters, what have they done to you?" The rings on her fingers glinted as she reached toward me, her soft black hair falling around her shoulders.

Myantha pressed her hands to her mouth, horrified, while Calla Lily hid her face in Velessa's good shoulder, her other arm still in a sling. Yuki's usually calm features were twisted with anger.

Glowering, Quen started toward me. "Let her go, you callow-souled brutes!" She balled her fists. Her eyes met mine, fierce and determined despite the wetness gathering in them.

The guard on my left unsheathed his sword and pointed it at my friends. "Stay back. No one approaches the prisoner."

Quen bared her teeth. "Void rot."

My insides tensed, and my mouth dried. "Please don't put yourself in danger for me. It's fine."

"We're in the trial *with* her." Yuki approached. "If she's gonna kill us, we'll take that chance. We're all about to get sent in to face our deaths again. So, hands off our friend." She stopped beside Quen.

"I *said* back off," the guard demanded.

My heart expanded as my vision blurred. I hadn't realized how desperately I'd missed them until this moment. I couldn't let any of them get hurt because of me.

"Disqualify them all for insubordination." Kaylen sneered and tossed a mocking laugh my way. "If they're here to support the assassin, then none of them are fit to—"

"Oh, for feck's sake, let her friends hug her," Siray shouted from the back of the room. She set her hands on her waist, her expression pinched. "She's never been a threat to any of them, unlike some who love only themselves. She may be a fool, but she's got a decent spirit."

Kaylen arched an eyebrow. "It isn't a matter of friendship. The best woman will win. The one whom Fate herself deems worthy. Ceana, tell her."

There was no response, causing Kaylen to glance at Ceana, who stood there examining her nails.

Upper lip curling, Siray lifted her chin in challenge at Kaylen. "Looks like Ceana agrees with *me* now."

Rhielle moved from behind Thalira. Her gaze softened when it met mine, and she flicked her attention to Vad and then back to me. She had to be trying to tell me something, but when I followed her gaze, my eyes locked with Vad's, and my head spun.

Each time I saw him, the urge to be with him grew stronger. I would've sworn we were fated mates, but that wasn't possible in this realm.

"That's fine with me," Kaylen shouted. "I'll be the one who wins—"

"Order! There will be order!" Vyraetos's voice boomed through the huge marble room. "We will have the reading of the rules."

Everyone fell silent, and Vad turned to face Vyraetos, his leathery wings spread wide. "The rules will not be read yet."

Vyraetos's brows lifted. "Your Highness, it's time—"

"Whoever saw to the transfer of the prisoner back to this chamber, explain why the prisoner isn't dressed like all the other candidates." He tore his focus from me to glare at the guards standing on either side of me.

My breath hitched, and heat coiled inside me. The urge to run to him and throw my arms around his neck surged through me. All I wanted to do was bury my face in his shoulder and breathe in that heavy masculine scent of leather, smoke, and citrus.

"Are we putting our thumbs on the scales of justice?" Vad challenged. "Accused or not, assassin or not, if she competes, she receives the same treatment as the other candidates. Whatever Fate wills will be, and we shall not permit any accusations of creating a needlessly unfair environment."

My knees weakened, and I bit my lip to stop myself from speaking. The man afraid of love had transformed in front of me.

Vyraetos inclined his head forward. "That matter was overseen by the Aurelines. The Shadows would prefer that all candidates be outfitted equally. Therefore, unless a compelling reason is provided by the Aurelines, the proceedings will temporarily halt."

One of the Aureline Council members edged forward and said something in a voice so soft I couldn't catch it. My wolf magic was weak from being caged, and I couldn't hear as well as I could before.

Elara frowned, and Thalen scoffed.

Vad's stance stiffened, and his expression darkened. "No." He snapped his fingers and pointed to someone I couldn't see. "Go fetch her attire and boots that fit."

The Aureline Council member spoke up a little louder, her voice shaking. "We understand, Your Highness. But the trial begins at a set time. We cannot delay it."

"Then pray they move fast." Vad sneered. "Or you will bear the full punishment for this error—unless the source of this decision is presented. Send Briar through last if you must, but you will *not* put her at more of a disadvantage than any other contestant. When Fate judges her, it will be at her full capacity, and not because someone weighed things against her."

I kept my chin up, eyes forward, though I could feel the weight of all those stares. The only people whose reactions had surprised me were Siray and Ceana. Ceana refused to look at me, staring down at her blue fingernails. Siray had an expression of almost grudging respect, though I wondered if that was because she was angry with Kaylen after the second trial.

Vyraetos cleared his throat as the rapid footsteps of someone leaving the hall sounded. He spoke in the same measured tone. "Now then, we can of course proceed with the explanation and rules. This is the third and final trial. Due to unusual circumstances, the High Aureline Council has ordered that it is Fate's will for all members to participate. It is known that Fate will strike down anyone who has attempted to kill or succeeded in killing a member of the royal family for whom the trials are being held." He met each woman's eye. "This final trial will test the candidates separately."

The hairs on the nape of my neck rose. They were separating us, and there was no doubt they intended to kill me and make it look as if Fate had wielded justice.

"This trial will assess the character of our future queen." Vyraetos steepled his hands. "None of you will be told how to win the challenge. There are no special rules to be disclosed. If you survive, you will be free and will receive favors and gifts from the Shadow Kingdom in honor of your service.

"When your trial begins, you will be placed in a chamber alone. No one will see what happens while you are there. You must choose the best course of action based on the situation provided for you. But there is one small mercy."

He hesitated a beat, then lifted his index finger to draw attention to his point. "Upon entry, you will be standing in a sigil. So long as you remain within the confines of that sigil, you will not be harmed. You can step out momentarily and then step back in and still be protected. So, if you do not wish to be queen, you do not have to step out of the circle ... unless circumstances or your own choices compel you. If you stay out of your circle too long, it will vanish, so make your decisions wisely."

I wanted to laugh. The last time we'd had circles and shields, all sorts of monsters had attacked us. I doubted the reality of the trial would be even remotely as easy as he made it seem.

"The test will conclude at a point of completion known only to Fate, and the exit will open at that time, unless you complete the challenge sooner. To complete it, you must simply cross the chamber and step into the corresponding sigil at the far end of your chamber," Vyraetos continued, standing taller and leaning over, showing his face more directly. "Bear in mind. Just because you step onto the final sigil does not mean you have won. The exit door will allow you to depart within minutes after you do, but it is only if the sigil flashes gold and glows that you will know you are the first to finish and are Fate's choice according to this trial."

He paused. "If the sigil only glows white, that simply acknowledges that you completed your part in the trial. If you remain in the first sigil for the entire trial, then once it is over, a door will appear on the far side of the chamber near the second sigil. At that point, a gong will sound, and the danger will cease, making it safe for you to cross the obstacles, walk to the second sigil, and pass through the exit doors. Remember that, in the end, despite whatever recommendations we on the shared council make or what Fate herself reveals, it will be Prince Vad who chooses his queen."

My mouth dried, and I clenched my teeth. The thought of him being with someone else made me sick.

"The trial will start after you are transported inside your chamber and the gong sounds. When your name is called, please step into the center of the shadow beast sigil on the floor. Siray, you are first."

The tall Ignis Fae strode into the sigil, intentionally shoving her shoulder against Kaylen as she passed. Kaylen glared at her and muttered something, but Siray just tossed her sleek black hair and stepped into the sigil. Shadows swept over her, and she vanished.

"Velessa," Vyraetos continued.

Squeezing Velessa's good arm, Thalira whispered something to her, and Yuki and Quen joined, giving Velessa a hug.

Velessa's wide lilac eyes met mine, and I mouthed at her, *Stay in the circle.* Her arm didn't seem to have improved much since the second trial.

Stay safe, she mouthed back as she stepped inside, and the shadows swallowed her whole.

Even more pressure weighed on me, and I hoped Many-Greats was right and my friends would be fine.

One by one, Vyraetos called out a name. Yuki steeled herself and walked in with her back straight as a poker. Myantha scrubbed a hand over her face as she entered, then she glanced at her friends and then at me. She mouthed something to me that I couldn't make out, but her final glance was up at the balcony.

I followed her gaze to find Thalen with his brow furrowed.

Kaylen didn't spare me a glance and stepped inside as primly as if she were entering a limousine sent to chauffeur her to her dreams. Ceana sulked over, not looking at anyone.

Rapid footsteps pattered toward the tall marble double doors. As Ceana vanished in the shadows, a skinny fae with long pointed ears dashed in. He held a folded dark pink garment and a pair of red-brown boots to his chest. As he skidded to a stop in front of me, he looked between the guards. They grumbled with disapproval but released my arms. As the blood flowed more easily through my arms and my elbows ached, I smiled kindly at the servant.

Vyraetos called out, "Rhielle."

My head jerked in her direction as she strode forward, arms still folded.

The scar across her throat was a vivid purple and heavily bruised. "Just want to say feck every single last one of you who supported this." She tossed me a tight-lipped smile and stepped into the sigil.

"Briar," Vyraetos announced.

My insides tightened at the sound of my name, and on instinct, I stepped forward. The eyes of everyone in the room followed as I moved toward the sigil, clutching the garment and boots.

"Win this thing, Briar!" Quen's voice rang out, fierce and determined. "Show them what you're made of! I know you didn't kill the king. We all do."

Despite myself, I looked up at Vad. His dark, leathery wings flexed, and his steely gray eyes were fixed on me, intense and unreadable to anyone who didn't know what lay beneath that stern exterior. But I knew. I recognized the tension in his jaw, the almost imperceptible softening around his eyes that he reserved only for me.

Soon I'd be out of this mess, and I could be in his arms, breathing in his scent, feeling the steady beat of his heart against mine. No more accusations, no more hiding, no more pretending. The thought sent a warm current through my veins, melting away some of the icy fear and desolation that had formed during my imprisonment.

The shadows swept up around me, and my stomach lurched as the ground fell out from under my feet. My arms tightened around the dress and boots.

Then the shadows vanished, and I found myself in a cavern. I stood in the center of a white circle carved directly into the floor, its edges smooth and cut with precision. At its heart lay a symbol I didn't recognize: two slender swords crossed behind a chalice, all three etched in a fine silvery line that caught the light and shimmered faintly. A solid wall curved behind me and snaked out on either side of me, creating an elevated protective alcove that descended into a larger chamber beyond.

Orbs of golden light floated high above me, eerily similar to those in the first trial. Their glow cast shifting shadows across the broken terrain, but some of the shadows twitched too slow or too fast to be natural. Something lurked out there and would most likely be triggered once the gong sounded.

A massive, uneven mountain of rubble loomed in the center of the space, its shape jagged and chaotic, like someone had poured the contents of the world into one place and let it rot. Boulders jutted out at crooked angles. Veins of sand spilled between slick banks of clay and mud. Segments of gravel butted against smoother sheets of slate. And in its heart, half-swallowed by the stone at the very top, sat a crumbling well, its lip cracked and the paths to it rising at odd intervals.

The floor beneath me wasn't any kinder. It rose behind me onto an elevated ledge that went right up against the solid curving wall. In front of me, it slanted downward in a relatively steep embankment that ended at the base of the mountain. The cracked marble fought against rough, unworked rock in a jagged patchwork, as if the chamber itself couldn't decide what it was. Strange symbols pulsed faintly along the surface, all ancient and unreadable but vibrating in a way that made the hairs along my arms rise.

Magic thrummed in the air, filling my ears with a buzz just shy of causing pain. The sensation coiled around my throat and chest. What was wrong with this air? I grimaced and rubbed my throat. Already, my mouth was drying, and my eyes had started to burn.

The air smelled wrong. Ozone and upturned earth, but beneath that, something sickly sweet, like poison disguised with flowers. And then another note—a dry, sun-warmed scent—hay, or straw perhaps?

I curled my toes against the stone, still barefoot. It was cold in here. Many-Greats had told me to stay in the circle. It was large enough to sit in and stretch out my legs, but my wolf chomped and growled, begging me to let her out.

My skin crawled and itched, and the burning air stung even more. I needed to change out of this wool gown into the softer pink one. As I set down the clothing to change, I noticed the boot laces had been bound together. Assholes.

My wolf pushed harder to the front. Shifting while badly injured was dangerous, and I knew that the spells and torture at the prison had done a number on me. But—my wolf wasn't having it.

I lost control, and she relished it.

Pain ripped down my spine as if someone had lashed me with a whip. My arms spasmed, the muscles seizing so hard I cried out. My skin tingled, and my fingers twisted and cracked as the bones realigned far more slowly than usual. Wool ripped as I tossed the dress and boots away. My back arched, and my body contorted, each *pop* a wrenching pull that left me gasping.

Fuck! What was wrong? This wasn't how shifting was supposed to feel. It had never hurt like this before.

The forced shift on top of my partly healed wounds had

to be why.

I collapsed forward, my fingers pressing at the edge of the carved and painted sigil circle. My skin felt like it was peeling away as my bones ground against each other. My wolf howled in panic. Something was wrong. She pushed against me, frantic and clawing.

A wind picked up, stirring dust and grit into the air and circling me. I choked and squeezed my eyes shut as tears spilled down my cheeks. *Stay in the circle. Just stay in the circle.*

What was making this shift take so long? Had I messed up?

Bile coated my tongue, and I gagged.

Was Fate doing this? Or had the real traitors laid a trap?

Another searing burst of pain exploded down my spine, and I screamed. My arms twitched again as my hands became half-formed paws and shifted back and forth between human and beast. I couldn't hold the shape. My body burned and twisted. I howled, long and raw, as the magic inside me writhed like it was being torn apart. Fur sprouted along my back and arms.

The gong sounded.

Shit! Not now!

Its toll was deep and resonant, loud enough to rattle my ribs. The air shifted again, sharpening like broken glass. I tasted copper and something foul, like mold and hot dirt and garbage.

I pressed my forehead to the floor and tried to breathe. The pain dulled, then spiked again, crawling under my skin in waves. The magic surged again, pulling the shift forward with another violent jolt. My legs bent in the wrong direction, and I yelled, my throat raw. My vision went black at the edges.

Red eyes opened in the darkness around the mountain, some seemingly in the air itself.

I froze, half-shifted and shaking as my body fought to

continue, my wolf form pulling at my human shape.

Stay in the circle. That was all I had to do. For however long this took. Then the rescue would happen.

A new sound cut through my pain-filled haze—the unmistakable splash and gurgle of water. My ears, now partially pointed and sensitive, twitched toward the mountain. The well. Water was bubbling and rushing at intervals. Was there perhaps some sort of pool beneath the well, and a spring or a pump that was drawing on it?

My throat constricted painfully. How long had it been since I'd had water? The prison guards had given me enough to survive, but never enough to satisfy, and I'd shared what I had with Elias. My tongue felt swollen, my lips cracked. The sound of water filling the ancient well sent a desperate wave of need through me.

"Water," I gasped, the word barely audible.

The shift surged forward again, my body twisting as fur rippled across my skin in waves. I bit down another scream as my spine realigned with a series of sickening cracks. The thirst intensified with each spasm, my wolf's instincts amplifying the need.

My wolf pushed even harder, and my spine popped into place as fur finally rolled over my body. My claws cracked out of my fingers, and my snout formed, wet and burning. The final wave hit like fire in my lungs.

I collapsed on my side, panting, still in the circle. Barely.

The wind howled louder above me, dry and gritty now, cutting at my skin like a thousand tiny blades.

My wolf rejoiced at being free once more as I lay on my side and gulped in the air. My tail brushed the edge of the circle.

I blinked, finding that my eyes burned just as much in wolf form as in human. How long until the rescue?

Movement flashed at the edge of my vision. The sound of

feet hitting the ground echoed to my right. I jerked my head in that direction and saw someone tall, wearing all black. The attacker swiped a black blade in the direction of my neck.

I lunged, and my teeth sank into flesh, bone crunching. Blood flooded my mouth, coppery and sweet as the man screamed in agony and dropped his weapon. He tried to jerk his arm from my mouth, but I bit to the bone and held on.

A part of me hated doing it, but this man had come here to kill me. I'd be foolish to let him get away.

Jerking my head, I ripped a large piece of his flesh and pushed him out of the circle. I glanced at the dagger, wanting to hide it in case I needed it later, and noticed an iridescent green color on the blade.

"You *bitch*!" the attacker spat, his face red, before charging at me again.

All regret left me. He wanted me dead at all costs, and he was just like the guards who'd beaten and mistreated me.

He didn't have control of his right hand after the damage I inflicted, so I jumped onto his chest and knocked him to the ground on his back, then chomped on his other forearm. The bone gave way with a sickening crack. I bore down with my jaws, savage satisfaction flooding through me as tendons and muscles tore beneath my teeth.

The assassin's scream echoed off the cavern walls, high and desperate. "Let go! Let go! I was just following orders." He struck at my back with his legs but missed.

I snarled and bit deeper and twisted.

"Let go, you bitch! Don't you know mercy?"

Mercy? Like the mercy shown to me in that prison cell? Like the mercy shown to the king?

I released his mangled arm and pulled back, lips curled over my teeth in a snarl that rumbled from deep in my chest. Blood dripped from my muzzle as I crouched low, my claws digging into his chest.

Fog rose around him, and he shuddered as he tried to pull a silver pendant from his tunic. Soft silver light shone from the vial of liquid set inside, and the chain strained as he held it fast. "Get back!" he screamed hoarsely.

Tired of this game, I lunged and sank my teeth into his neck. He whimpered as I jerked my head to the side, ripping out his throat.

I pulled back, and the chain of his pendant snagged on my teeth. The vial struck the stone. It shattered, and a bright floral scent like freesia sparked in the air, then dissipated. He went limp, and the ground around us swelled and seethed with shadows and dark fog like an oncoming tide, curling and rolling. A stinging sensation cut across my hindquarters and tail, where it touched me.

Yelping, I darted out of the fog, smelling burnt fur.

I jumped back into my circle and scanned the area, looking for the next attack. Luckily, there was no fog here. But the body of the assassin was swallowed up by it. Dark particles from the fog spread over his body, covering him more and more until something jerked the body back into the darkness. Heavy, sloppy crunching sounds followed, as if massive jaws were devouring him. Then more red eyes opened, blinked slowly, and slithered away.

What the hell was *that*? I panted, and even in wolf form, I couldn't see anything through the haze. My back legs still stung.

Cold fear flowed through my body.

What kind of a nightmare was this third trial?

The fog swept around the circle and moved, gathering farther away as the water continued to run in the well, making my mouth drier than ever.

If this was all I'd have to deal with, I could endure.

I paced the two steps I could, back and forth in the circle, taking deep breaths, trying to calm my rising anxiety.

Where was the promised rescue? Many-Greats hadn't told me what to expect. Just that I would know it when I saw it. Great. Well, I also knew when I wasn't seeing it. What fresh horrors were waiting for me in this hellhole?

"Help!" A woman who sounded eerily familiar screamed in the dark. My ears snapped forward, and the fur on my back lifted.

Then it hit me who it was.

Ember.

Chapter Twenty-Two

Terror locked me in place. I shook my head, trying to bring myself back to reality and the task at hand. It must be an illusion, because Ember couldn't be here.

But it sounded exactly like my sister.

My mouth was so dry I could no longer swallow. But that wasn't what worried me in that moment. Every nerve in me tightened, and I couldn't push the echo of her voice from my head.

Vyraetos had said that we might feel compelled to go running out of the circle in this trial. One way to lure me was to use the voice of someone important to me.

It was working. I wanted to bolt out of the circle and search for Ember.

The real dilemma was that I knew my sister. She'd already nearly died protecting me. I had no doubt that, if anyone could find a way to this realm, she'd be the one.

But she wasn't here, right? Many-Greats had told her I was safe. He would do anything in his power to keep her from coming here.

Still ... what if whoever was behind all this had gone through the portal and grabbed her to hurt me? That sounded like a sadistic thing they'd do, especially that asshole in charge of the guards at the prison.

"Briar, please!" she whimpered. "If you're out there, I need you."

No. Ember wouldn't ask me to come out there to help her in an environment like this. It had to be a trap.

"It's Ryker." She sobbed loudly. "He's hurt. He rushed to attack the man who tried to kill you, but something dark swooped over him."

My heart skipped, and my hackles rose. That was what had happened to the guy I'd just killed.

If Ember were truly here, I couldn't live with myself if I didn't help. I crouched and lunged onto the stretch of stone leading toward the mountain. I sniffed the air, searching for any hint of her scent to help me locate her faster.

My paws struck uneven stone as I cleared the circle, a jolt of heat running down my spine. Thank Fate that my wounds had healed, because that horrible shift could've done the opposite and ripped them apart.

I barreled up the mountain, focusing on my surroundings. If this was a trap, I wanted to be smart about it.

The terrain was worse than it had looked, the layers unsteady under my paws. Pillars of stone and boulders jutted out at odd angles, but just as many sat on sand or soil, likely unstable despite their size.

Slate cracked under my weight, and sand slid beneath it. My claws scraped for purchase as I dug in and climbed. I skirted a line of wet clay, ears twitching toward the trickling sounds of water.

"Ryker! Stay with me." Ember's voice was higher on the mountain, coming from the same direction as the water.

The red eyes in the fog turned in my direction. They blinked out, and the fog rolled toward me. Its slow, relentless pace quickened with each moment.

I tugged at the pack link. *Ember, I'm almost there.* The link was barely warm, as it had been ever since I got here, but then Ember's voice cut over me, slicing into my very soul.

"Be careful, I'm trying to pull him somewhere to shield him from the fog."

I forced myself to go faster as panic clawed at my throat and mind, threatening to undo me. I wasn't sure how we were going to hide from the fog, but I couldn't leave them out here to die.

Yet, I still couldn't catch their scent, and her voice wasn't getting closer.

The slope steepened, and I jumped from one jutting rock to the next. A stone gave out from under me. With a yelp, I slipped and dug in my claws to grip the edge of the newly formed crater.

I dangled, trying to find the energy to lift myself up. Even though I'd shifted, my wolf and I hadn't eaten any protein in what felt like weeks.

A sob echoed around me.

I had to get myself out of this mess and help them.

I scrabbled my paws farther up on the stone, despite my screaming muscles, and managed to drag myself to safety.

The fog hissed behind me, moving faster than I'd expected. My paws slipped again on a slick patch of shale, and I barely avoided tumbling back down the slope. I righted myself more easily this time and linked, *Are you two hidden yet? There's something in the fog, and it's getting close. Get higher, and I'll find you."*

Ember's voice echoed again, weaker this time. "Briar, please ... don't let me down *again*."

I froze, and reality smacked me in the snout.

Ember would *never* say that. I tugged once more at the pack link, realizing that nothing about it had changed at all.

The realization hit me like a punch to the gut. This was a trick, and now I was far away from the circle, if it was even still there.

Bastards!

I pivoted on the next ledge and started down the slope, moving fast along the rock face.

The fog surged toward me, rolling thicker and faster. It had grown so much that it now surrounded the entire base of this side of the mountain and was oozing upward on the rock face.

Turning hard on a bank of gravel, I kicked up a dust cloud behind me as I darted across a ridge.

The circle was hundreds of feet away. The fog lay between it and me, moving steadily closer. At least four sets of red eyes opened and shut.

A chill ran down my spine. Was this a single creature, or multiple?

I leaped again, determined to get higher than the fog. The well at the peak looked to be the highest point.

The sand under me slipped, sucking at my paws. I turned too fast and slid, skidding across the uneven terrain. My side hit stone, and I scrambled back up, breath wheezing. My legs stung and ached, but I kept moving.

If I couldn't get back to the circle, I would either have to run and evade the fog, or I would have to get to the other side and finish the trial. Many-Greats had said to stay inside the circle until the end, and by that point, the rescue should be underway. Perhaps sooner.

Another scream tore through the air. "Briar, help me! Please! We're going to die." More voices rose up, screaming and howling. Voices of my family and packmates.

My blood chilled, and my stomach twisted. I chanted internally, *That isn't Ember! That isn't your pack. The voices aren't real!*

However, if I did want to see Ember again, I had to survive and get the hell out of here.

A whistle, like something flying through the air, barreled toward me. I ducked, huddling against the ground, as something long, thin, and dark landed in front of me and clanged against a chunk of granite.

Hot pain sliced across my left foreleg, and blood trickled down the limb. My eyes snapped to the left, and a deep growl rose in my chest.

Two figures in black stood on a dark slate ledge lower down on the mountain, just outside the thicker parts of the fog. Gray, wisping magic spiraled around them as if they'd teleported in. Their clothing was simple and well-fitted, complete with glowing silver pendants hanging by silver chains. One held a sword while the other held a bow.

The one with the bow lowered it, and the silver pendants around their necks glinted in the golden light from the orbs above.

"Give up now, bitch, and you'll die fast," Arrow Assassin shouted, his baritone echoing off the rocks. He plucked another arrow from his quiver and nocked it.

The second assassin charged in my direction, the sword gripped tightly in his hand. The tip of the blade had the same iridescent green coating as the first assassin's dagger. "Coming for you, filth blood. Make this harder than it has to be, and you'll suffer like you wouldn't believe."

The fog curled around them, but it parted as Sword Assassin jogged in my direction. The first assassin who had attacked me hadn't been touched by the fog until the end—after I'd shattered his pendant.

Arrow Assassin laughed, and his bow creaked as he drew it taut. "The folgan is almost all around the mountain now. No one can get away from it until that gong sounds. And before you got here, one of our associates made sure you wouldn't have any of the tools. You're doomed, girl, so why don't you just come here and make it easier on all of us?"

Jumping onto another ledge, Sword Assassin's boots slid half a step, but his pace remained steady. He adjusted his grip on the sword hilt and laughed.

I huffed. He had better balance than I'd hoped. Veering hard left, I ducked into a narrow run of broken stone, using the natural terrain as cover. Another arrow hissed through the air and skipped off a rock behind me.

I leaped across a chasm and landed on a sharply angled slab of stone. My claws clicked and slid as I forced myself upward.

A deep, wet clicking noise, like jaws opening and closing, sounded. Fog spilled over the ledge above me, bubbling and building. Three more pairs of eyes opened and then shut ... and surged forward.

Shit! It was going to cut me off.

I refused to die, especially after surviving that prison for as long as I had.

To my left, the mountain terrain formed an island of rock with larger blocks of stone and natural pillars amid the sand and clay.

My heart lurched. I could use them for cover.

Maybe the folgan couldn't cross the chasm because of all the empty space below it. If I could jump the almost fifteen-foot narrowest section, I should be home free.

Summoning all my strength and ignoring the burning in my foreleg, I ran and leaped. I shot through the air and struck a boulder on the other side.

An arrow shot past me into the rock near my paw. The relative safety of the natural pillars was only a few feet away. The folgan, or whatever the hell it was, rolled down from the top left of the ledge at an angle and poured into the chasm surrounding the island. It wasn't crossing.

Oh, thank Fate!

"*NEEEE-iiih.*" A terrified whine rose above the whipping wind. The agonized sound cut into me.

I leaped onto another ledge formed of numerous jagged rock columns protruding like broken teeth. The edge crumbled, bits of rock and sand sliding down into the rising fog. Fear clawed through me as I scrambled to stronger, higher ground. Some of the naturally formed pillars blocked Arrow Assassin from reaching me.

"*Mmmrrhh—neeehh.*" A throatier, broken sound whinnied through the dry air. I spun and peered through the stone pillars.

A delicate unicorn foal with a pearly gray horn was scrambling up the mountainside toward the spot where I'd just been, its gray coat streaked with dirt and blood. Its spindly legs trembled with each frantic step while the fog monster continued to build behind it. The fog filled every crack and crevice as the unicorn continued to move closer and closer. Some of its blood oozed down into the chasm.

Another arrow whistled past my ear. Veering away, I ducked behind a line of rough boulders and natural pillars and peeked back out.

Below me, the unicorn squealed and redoubled its efforts to escape, slipping on the loose gravel. Its charcoal hoofs kicked out the stones, and it slid back.

Would it be able to jump the chasm? My wolf strength had propelled me far, but this unicorn barely looked old enough to run.

Another arrow snapped past and embedded itself in the rock pile ahead of the unicorn. The foal screamed again, high and wild. It almost fell, and the fog reached for it from behind while also seeping in from the top left.

Now, almost half of the ledge was covered.

I bared my teeth at Arrow Assassin and scanned the mountain for any advantage. There was more sand and soil here than I'd expected, and it looked like there was more the higher it went.

"Focus!" Sword Assassin shouted above the wails, his voice close. "At least wound the bitch again before you start going for the unicorn. She's acting like she didn't feel it at all."

Arrow Assassin laughed coldly. Rocks shifted under his feet as he jumped to a closer ledge and pulled out another arrow. "Relax. I already got her once. We kill her and the unicorn and remove the horn. Double prize. Double gold."

I wanted to vomit. They wanted to kill this unicorn for its horn? Not on my fucking watch.

The foal raced to the edge of the chasm. Its white-rimmed eyes rolled as it tossed its head, a panicked squeal escaping its gray muzzle. The dim golden light caught on its iridescent pearl-gray horn.

From about thirty feet away, Sword Assassin moved up behind the unicorn.

The foal peered over the edge of the chasm, then reared up on its hind legs. Its nostrils flared as it snorted and squealed. "*NEEEE-iiih.*"

Rage boiled inside me. I could jump back there and end Sword Assassin once and for all, but the monster was taking up more and more space on the ledge. Even if most of it had disappeared into the depths of the chasm, it'd still reach the unicorn, because there was nowhere else for the unicorn to go.

Then I had a plan.

I raced to one of the looser pillars situated at the edge of the platform. The pale gray and beige rock was already tilting toward the chasm. If it fell right, it'd be a bridge. Growling, I rammed my shoulder into the stone, teeth clenched. Then I slid down and dug at the base, my claws hooking into the clay, gravel, and silt.

From the broad ledge I'd just abandoned, Sword Assassin chuckled. He adjusted his grip on the sword and gestured toward the chasm and then me.

The pillar shifted, but not enough. I backed up and charged again, hitting it harder with my shoulder and striking at the weakened foundation point. Pain lanced through my side, but the pillar groaned. The unicorn bleated again and moved back and forth along the edge as if it wanted to jump.

The monster oozed closer. Two sets of eyes opened and closed. It moved faster as its focus intensified.

Come on!

I thrust my shoulder into the pillar once more, and hot blood spattered out of the wound on my foreleg. A shower of gravel spilled as the rough stone column shifted free and tumbled. It crashed over the ledge, landing just low enough to form a narrow bridge across the chasm.

The little unicorn blinked at it, then bolted across.

Crack. THUD. Crack.

The pillar shifted against the rock ledge, dropping a little farther. The unicorn foal stumbled but caught its footing and ran faster. Silt rained down from where the pillar's end had settled on the stone.

"Hey," Sword Assassin snarled. He raced up from the back of the ledge, forcing the monster's fog to part. "The unicorn's ours."

I growled, and another arrow hit the rock behind me, spraying grit. I pressed my body flat to the ledge, noticing even more blood dripping from my leg. It hadn't clotted. My wolf healing wasn't working. They must have done something to their weapons.

Arrow Assassin moved to a ledge almost directly across from me. He whipped out another arrow and smirked.

My blood chilled, and I inched back.

Sword Assassin placed one foot on the end of the pillar I'd knocked over. His boot crunched on the rough, curved stone, and he shook it to test its stability.

My breath snagged. The coppery scent of my own blood mingled with the smell of ozone, burning fur, and rot. Dust and small rocks rained down on me, and I twisted around to see the unicorn peering at me from above. It tilted its head and snorted, stomping its right hoof against the stone as if trying to get my attention. Then its focus snapped back to Sword Assassin, who was still testing his weight on the pillar. It stamped both hooves as it reared and drove down again and again.

"*HRRRFFF—chh—chh.*" It exhaled forcefully through flared nostrils and tossed its head.

Sword Assassin laughed. "You really think you can do something? Go ahead and make your distress calls all you want. I'd love to kill your herd too."

Was the foal trying to call to its family for help? I snarled, snapping my jaws.

"Got it." Arrow Assassin nocked an arrow and shot it. This time, it sliced across the back of the unicorn's hindquarters, making it squeal and veer away. The foal vanished from sight and screamed in terror. Something slick and heavy splashed, and the cries intensified. Arrow Assassin laughed heartily until a tremor shook the mountain.

The well at the top cracked, and crimson water leaked out, cutting through clay and earth in a slow trickle that threatened to worsen.

"Fecking void." Sword Assassin froze halfway across the pillar, his breath sharpening.

"Relax. We've still got time." Arrow Assassin slung his bow over his back and climbed the embankment. "I'll take care of her."

They still had time? What was going on with the water?

My hackles rose, and I growled again. My teeth ached to sink into their flesh and snap their bones. Ripping out their throats was too good for creatures like this.

Snarling, I lunged to the base of the pillar and dug, trying to position myself so that Arrow Assassin couldn't get a shot at me. If I could get the bridge pillar to drop, Sword Assassin might fall to his death, and then I could focus on Arrow.

Chunks of dirt and clay fell into the chasm as the monster surged forward and slid down into the darkness. The pillar jolted down and shifted. Sword Assassin's eyes widened, and he swung his arms to keep his balance.

The ground began to shake.

My breath caught. Could this be another earthquake?

Stones ground and rattled, and a horrible, tearing sound vibrated through the chamber. Silt sifted between the pillars and the ledge, and a crack formed in the large platform on the other side of the chasm.

A few of the pillars rocked and wobbled. Then one collapsed and crashed forward, cracking on the dark stone and then rolling into the abyss.

Sword Assassin's pillar shifted further, and he screamed and pressed his body flat to the stone.

A loud, pained shriek above me, and more rocks rolled down the edge. I glanced in Arrow Assassin's direction just as stones slid from above and covered him.

Thank Fate. Maybe she didn't completely hate me after all.

The ground calmed, and I went back to my end of the pillar. Sword Assassin had managed to stay on.

I growled, daring him to continue across, and then dug once more.

He spat over the side. "Stop digging!"

Yeah, that only made me dig faster.

Beyond the rock ridge, the terrified cries of the foal bounced off the stone walls.

Sharp pain sliced across my right shoulder. I howled and jerked back from the pillar.

A green-coated blade stuck out of the rubble. My stomach twisted as more hot blood leaked down my shoulder, blending into the blood on my foreleg.

I had to move fast, or I might bleed out.

Sword Assassin snarled, holding his sword in one hand while his other fumbled down the front of his tailored jacket.

My heart galloped. I was running out of time.

I jammed my forelegs against the pillar's end and shoved hard, causing it to crack and groan against the stone.

The stone shifted, and Sword Assassin let out a scream and flailed.

"Noln!" He slammed his hand down in time to keep from losing the sword, but his ice-blue eyes were wild with terror, and his breathing was ragged.

I snarled, letting drool drip from my teeth, and snapped my jaws. The monster had slid up against the base of the pillar on his side, but now it just oozed down into the chasm.

I glanced over my shoulder, then leaped back into digging at the base of the pillar. One of these assholes had to go, and now, before they could team up on me again.

Sword Assassin bared his teeth at me and inched forward, trying to finish crossing.

I was running out of time. I dug more frantically, dirt and rock hitting my eyes. Still, I pushed through, and finally the pillar groaned and sank lower.

The assassin flung his sword, and it struck the rock beside me with a clank, then spun off into the chasm. It disappeared from sight, and adrenaline fueled me even more.

The pillar trembled and shook as he struggled to crawl

across.

I shoved the end of the pillar with both forepaws. He was almost an arm's length from me.

He got into a crouch with his arms still wrapped around the stone. Then he jumped ... and his stomach hit the edge of the wall. He grunted as his lower body dropped, and he caught the ledge with his fingertips. His boots found traction below, and he boosted himself a few inches upward and flung his arms over the edge. He froze when he saw me, and then his right arm slid out of sight.

I went for his hand.

Just before I reached him, his right hand shot up, holding a small, dark dagger, aimed right at me.

Chapter Twenty-Three

BRIAR

I jerked back, but not soon enough, and the blade sliced my right foreleg up to my shoulder.

My jaws snapped shut, and I twisted in agony. Sharp pain radiated from the new wound, and all four of my legs buckled. I slid against the ledge's back wall as my vision blurred.

The world spun, and I blinked, fighting to orient myself. My head pounded. Grunts rang in my ears, and I forced my eyes open and struggled to my feet as Sword Assassin hauled himself up.

His rough breathing stirred the debris, and he strained and moved slowly, as if he wasn't worried about me attacking him again.

Summoning my remaining strength, I lunged forward and seized him by the throat. The chain of the pendant hooked around my teeth, and I clamped hard and worked my jaw to thrash at his skin.

Fragrant blood poured into my mouth as he let out a wet, gurgling scream. His fingernails scraped the stone as he tried to reach his remaining daggers, but his front was pressed against the stone.

I loosened my grip just enough to bite deeper. Men like

him didn't deserve to live. My vision turned red, and everything narrowed in on his pulse and weakening struggles. My legs shook beneath me, and my shoulder and forelegs throbbed.

But I didn't let go.

He twitched and went limp. I jerked my head to the side, ripping out his throat.

Blood pooled, and his eyes glazed over as he transitioned into death.

Now I needed his necklace to survive the monster.

It would be easiest to wear it instead of fighting off an attacker while holding the pendant in my mouth.

Lowering my head, I nosed the long chain into position and hoped this plan worked. I'd never tried to remove a necklace and place it on myself in wolf form.

Luckily, the chain was long and came free of him easily enough, and I maneuvered it and pressed my face down along his chest to thread my muzzle and head through the loop. His blood smeared the side of my face, but I ignored it. The pendant was the most important thing.

I managed to get it around my neck, and a shimmering sensation passed over me, sending shivers down my spine.

More plaintive cries from the unicorn foal ripped through the air as the wind whipped around me. My body throbbed, and my legs struggled to keep me standing.

Whatever they had laced their weapons with was affecting me, and the only thing I knew to do was keep going until the rescue finally happened.

Where the fuck was Many-Greats?

I spun to face the area where Arrow Assassin had been taken. The rocks were still in the same place, so that counted for something. He could be unconscious.

The unicorn wailed again, causing me to look higher, but I couldn't see it.

However, crimson water was pouring from the cracked well faster than before. Clay and soil crumbled along the slope as the water carved a path through the terrain, making multiple streams.

My chest tightened. How long before a mudslide added to my growing list of problems?

I clambered up, doing my best to be quiet. If the assassin was conscious, I wanted to surprise him. But each time I moved a leg, rocks tumbled free and pebbles dropped into the chasm.

My head spun, and the scent of my blood and the disturbed soil filled my nostrils. I couldn't catch the scent of the assassin or the unicorn. But I could hear the foal panicking, its desperate cries coming shorter and faster.

With each pant, my mouth dried even more. The sound of rushing water only made me thirstier, but I couldn't focus on that. I had two missions to complete before even thinking about drinking something.

The cuts on my forelegs and shoulders pulsed, stinging and bleeding as if something in the wounds was rejecting my healing abilities. Blood spattered on the rocks in a constant reminder that my wounds were not on the mend.

Arrow Assassin lay about thirty feet away with a large rock on his torso. His bow rested on the ground beside him, still strung. He groaned and shifted, his boots scraping against loose shale. His right arm was pinned at the elbow, but his left groped blindly, reaching for the bow.

I had to move quickly before he could shoot at me or the unicorn.

My lips peeled back, and I launched forward. Every muscle in my body screamed in discomfort, but I didn't slow down.

That bastard was working with the people who had tortured me, hunted me, and destroyed my life. They'd sent him to finish me off.

I refused to go down without a fight.

"Fecking abyss," he muttered as he wrenched his arm free.

I pushed myself harder, trying to reach him. But then he nocked an arrow to the bow, drew it, and released it right at me.

I dropped to the left of the coarse ridge for shelter, but the space was too shallow. The *whoosh* of the arrow sounded like death's hand reaching for me. White hot and agonizing pain sliced my side, then metal *ping*ed behind me, and I twisted in time to see the arrow falling between two boulders.

Hot blood poured out of the new wound on my side, adding to my ongoing blood loss problem.

Bastard!

Rocks clattered, and clumsy, uneven footsteps sounded. I leaned to the left and saw him running in the opposite direction, up to higher ground and toward a protective rock.

I swallowed hard. He had to be getting into a better position to take me out.

I shoved my weight onto my back legs and almost stumbled from the pounding in my head. Heart racing, I tried to focus on the ground because, if I didn't get my shit together, my likelihood of surviving would be reduced significantly.

Forcing myself forward, I dug my claws into rock and followed his blood trail. The wall curved ahead, obscuring my sight.

Not wanting to rush and do something stupid, I took a breath to survey the situation.

The rubble that circled the area had gaps I could see through and that he could probably shoot through. I edged a little to the right and peeked through a smaller opening and saw a stone path that dropped off into a steep embankment and led down into a basin of what looked like bubbling quicksand.

My stomach revolted. Death by quicksand was one of the worst ways to die, or that's what Gage, one of my packmates, had once told me.

At the narrowest point, the basin was maybe eighteen feet across, but what I saw next shook my entire world.

The unicorn was up there near him.

He shot it in the flank, and the unicorn fell backward ... and dropped into the quicksand.

I had to save it. I needed the assassin's attention on me.

I moved past the small opening and poked my head around the curve of the wall.

Immediately, another arrow whipped toward me. I jerked my head back, and it hit the stone where I'd just been, sparking before dropping with a clatter.

Adrenaline spiked within me, making it easier to think clearly.

Moving back to the small gap, I scanned the area until I located the assassin sagging against a gray rock shelf, his lower half obscured as he whipped out another arrow and nocked it. Blood dripped from his right arm, and I noted the silver chain hanging around his neck. The pendant was under his shirt.

He stood, unsteady, and his hands shook. "You wanna save the unicorn, bitch? He doesn't have much time before he goes under." He pointed down the slanted wall to the quicksand.

I bared my teeth, but the burning in my paw and side surged again, bringing tears to my eyes. My heart was beating fast as it fought what I thought must be venom, pulsing in sync with the pain from the cut in my foreleg. My head swam, my vision blurred, and I was so *damn* thirsty.

If I ran around the stone lip of the basin, I might lose my balance and slide down, and the assassin would see me coming.

The ground rumbled again, vibrating every single bone in my body. A chunk of the ridge Arrow Assassin was leaning against broke off and plunged down into the mire. He scrambled away, trying not to fall with it.

That was my chance.

I crouched and lunged across the chasm. His eyes widened as he grasped his bow and drew back an arrow while trying to aim, but he had no chance. In less than a breath, my claws struck his stomach, smashing him to the left. He swung the bow back my way and loosed the arrow, and it cut across my chest.

Everything inside me screamed to just give up. But I'd rather die fighting than at the hands of the people who'd tried to break me. I batted the arrow to the ground and smashed into him again, my front paws colliding with his chest. Every injury I had burned, wrenching a howl from between my teeth, and the two of us tumbled back away from the edge of the embankment, limbs tangling.

Squeals from the unicorn had me glancing over. The quicksand was up to its neck. The foal fought desperately to get to the shore.

A fist punched me in the snout, snapping my head back. My face exploded in pain, but I pushed through and sank my teeth into the man's arm.

He screamed as he used his free hand to search for the fallen arrow.

It was time to end this. Black dots clouded my vision, and I adjusted my hold on his arm, shifting my head just as metal flashed in front of my face. He whipped the arrow by with his free hand, missing me and jamming the pin-sharp point into his own leg.

If my mouth hadn't been so dry, I'd probably have laughed, but not when so much was at stake. I lunged forward and sank my teeth into his neck, just as I had with Sword Assassin. Each of them deserved a real wolf killing for everything they'd done.

He gurgled as blood filled my mouth. He clearly had something to say, but unluckily for him, I had no desire to hear it. I wanted him gone, and for the first time, I didn't care about taking a life.

Jerking my head to the side, I ripped out his throat. I backed a few steps, watching him try to grip it and stop the bleeding with one hand.

I yanked my wolf back, wanting to say something to him before he fully died. She tried to fight me—she'd been caged so long—but I yanked her back harder. Shifting while bleeding this much wasn't smart, but I didn't give a damn. I was dead either way, and I'd need to be in human form to save the unicorn.

She huffed but receded, and soon my bones cracked back into my human form. The hot, dry wind chafed my bare body, and the cuts from the blades bled faster. Kneeling and snarling in pain, I grabbed him by the shoulders and growled in his ear. "Which do you think will kill you first? Bleeding out? Or the quicksand?"

He choked as blood dripped from the corners of his mouth and frothy red saliva formed at his lips. They moved, but gurgling and gasping was his only response.

This was too easy a death for him.

I yanked the arrow from his leg and pushed him off the boulder, straight over the edge. He sailed headfirst into the quicksand with a heavy *plop*.

I waited for the satisfaction, and though it didn't come, neither did any guilt. It was as if killing him meant nothing. He wasn't the one who'd forced me into this. He was just some knight who hadn't done his job.

I took a breath and studied the opening to ensure another assassin hadn't appeared.

A whine drew my attention back to the baby unicorn, which continued to work its legs as if swimming slowly. I kept hold of the arrow and raced around the basin's edge to get closer to it, taking care not to trip.

"Come here, little one." The unicorn was still almost a

dozen feet away.

The unicorn's dark gray mane whipped back and forth as it shook its head, and another panicked squeal escaped. Its nostrils flared wide, and it wheezed, its chest heaving. There was no way to reach it from here.

Not without rope.

Wait. I didn't have rope, but I did have that dress. If I wanted to retrieve it as quickly as possible, I needed to shift back into animal form.

I hated to leave the arrow behind. It was my only weapon. But if I didn't, the unicorn would die.

And that was something I couldn't live with.

Setting the arrow carefully on a nearby rock ledge, I held up my hands. "Just hang on. I'll be right back."

I tugged at my wolf, but she lay inside me as if she didn't have the strength to get up.

Realization slammed into me like a boulder. I was too injured to shift again, which meant my time was running out.

I jolted forward, and the pendant dangling from my neck bounced into an arrow wound. Blood coated the pendant and trailed down my body, but I continued to run.

As I rushed back to the original circle where I'd entered the chamber, the unicorn's cries grew more frantic, breaking my heart a little more. It didn't understand that I'd be coming back ... I hoped it would soon.

My injured feet pounded the stone, causing my injuries to open further. My vision narrowed, my head spun, and my feet throbbed worse than ever. Still, I jumped from the basin and down the path. When I glanced up at the well, crimson water was gushing out stronger than before.

What *had* they done to that well? Those two had said something was going on with it. Apparently, I'd pissed off whoever was behind this so much that they didn't want there to be any chance of me surviving this trial.

Torrents of water were pushing out the dirt in broader streams, forming multiple grooves in the sides of the rubble pile and exposing jagged blocks of stone stacked precariously on top of one another. My gut twisted in warning. This was bad. Really bad. Especially if the volume of water kept intensifying.

The monster continued to steam and pulse over the edge of the cliff face. It parted itself when I jumped over the chasm, bubbling and curling. Only one red eye opened, and it shut almost immediately.

Thank Fate, the pendant worked for me as well.

Blood slicked the stones behind me, but I didn't stop. If I did, I doubted I'd be able to run anymore. I jumped from ledge to ledge, picking my way down the rubble mountain while avoiding the sand and gravel that could slow me exponentially.

My breath came in short, shallow bursts, and my hearing narrowed to the pulse of blood and the distant screams of the foal.

Just a few minutes more. Hopefully, the foal could survive that long. I wished I could pack link with it to soothe it.

As I maneuvered around a slate boulder, I glimpsed the entrance sigil. My circle was still there, but the light was duller, the dark pink of the gown and the red-brown of the boots distinct against the darkness. I could still hide in the circle until the end of the trial.

I could hear Many-Greats scolding me. *It's just an animal. Leave it.*

But this was about more than an animal. It was more about what these horrible people did to innocent beings in this world.

Rage boiled within me, and I embraced it. There was no way in hell I was going to abandon the baby unicorn and let these assholes win. If I could save it, could the baby unicorn fit with me in the circle?

When the circle appeared in front of me, I nearly cried. I ran to the boots and dress and snatched them into my arms. I could carry the boots by the laces, which now made me thank whoever had knotted them together, though I doubted they'd meant for me to be appreciative.

I ran as quickly as possible back up the mountain. The gush of water had grown even stronger, and my stomach twisted with fear as my pace turned into a slow jog. Each time I glanced up, it seemed like there was more water, and the foal's cries grew louder.

By the time I reached the basin, the unicorn had moved a little closer to the edge of the quicksand. Its panicked voice was hoarse, but when it saw me, its eyes brightened.

My knees nearly buckled, but I caught myself.

Fate help me. How much longer can I keep going? I rubbed one hand over my bleeding chest, wincing at the sting. *At least, let me live long enough to save the foal.*

Gritting my teeth, I picked up the arrow and used it to cut the gown into pieces. Pink thread snapped as the fabric gave way. I triple-knotted the sections together, layering them as I glanced up at the foal. "It's all right. I'm gonna get you out. Just stop struggling."

The unicorn tossed its head again, but its panicked breaths slowed.

I picked up the makeshift rope and attached it to one of the boots to help it go farther. Heart in throat, I tossed it.

The colorful rope shot out over the quicksand and wrapped loosely around the foal's neck, the boot thudding against its cheek. The unicorn startled and jerked its head back with another squeal.

"Grab it!" I gasped. It was getting harder to speak. "I'll pull you out."

Whether it understood me or just acted on instinct, the foal twisted its head and bit down on the knotted dress. I wrapped the rope tight around my hands and began to pull.

My arms ached, my body throbbed, and my head wanted to split in two. My wolf had gone quieter than I ever remembered her being.

The ground trembled, and a heavy tearing sound groaned through the air. Something cracked.

I glanced up to find that the water from the well was surging even faster. A large chunk of mud and earth slid down the side of the well facing the entrance sigil. More crumbling chunks rolled down after it.

Fuck!

Muscles burning, I braced my feet on the rock and heaved. The makeshift rope dug into the raw cut in my hand. Sweat and blood stung my eyes, and the world wobbled around me. Everything tunneled to the rhythm of my arms and feet: yank, slide, brace, and yank again.

The foal scrabbled for traction, hanging on to the rope with its mouth and pulling itself forward. It twisted and winced as if the pressure was increasing on it as well.

Above us, the hiss of water intensified. It poured from the well as if some spell had turned it into a fire hydrant. Another strange, aching groan vibrated through the air, and the water turned an ugly shade of pink.

Black dots swam in front of my eyes. Gritting my teeth, I pulled harder. "Come on!"

With a great sucking *POP*, the unicorn foal came free, and I fell hard on my butt. It stumbled up the stone embankment. The sky swam above me, and I gasped in another shallow breath.

The unicorn trotted up beside me, its hoofbeats light and shaky. It thrust its head under my arm and jostled me. Its breath whooshed against me, and it whickered in my ear.

"Have to—have to go." I struggled to stand.

I managed to get one foot under me and pushed hard, using the unicorn's surprisingly sturdy neck for leverage. Then I was up, but barely, hunched over and reeling as the world continued to shake around us.

Rock dust fell in stinging showers, and the rumble built from a shiver to a growl. My teeth clacked as the mountain convulsed. The unicorn whinnied, high and terrified, as water geysered from the cracked well like an erupting volcano, turning the entire far slope into a landslide.

Mud, boulders, and broken slabs careened down the mountainside in a red-black river. The far end of the mountain sheared away, an entire segment breaking off and plummeting toward the entrance sigil.

"Go," I rasped, pushing the unicorn away. "Save yourself."

The foal shook its head, keeping its position against me. I gripped the venom-tipped arrow just as the ground under my feet dropped, pitching me sideways. Still, the unicorn went with me, helping me to keep moving forward.

Shoving the foal ahead of me, I dodged the first volley of falling rocks. The pendant bounced on my chest as I ran, and its energy thrummed into my skin.

A massive crack split the ground ahead. The foal skidded to a halt as stones tumbled into the new abyss.

"Jump!" I hurled myself at the unicorn and hooked one arm around its neck, and together, we leaped.

We landed hard on the other side. My knees screamed with pain as they hit the stone floor, and I whimpered. The mountain behind us peeled away in a roar, a shelf of clay, sand, granite, dirt, and slate crumpling as the well at the top caved in. Now-red water and debris rained down, sliding toward the chamber entrance.

Adrenaline spiked in my veins, urging me forward. We

had to keep moving.

The ground heaved with every step, and the air thickened with dust. Down the other side of the mountain, to the left of the base, I saw an alcove similar to the one at the entrance. Stone jutted out on either side of it, providing possible shelter.

Or a tomb.

Slim chances are better than none.

I cut left, and the unicorn and I lunged onto the next shaking ledge below. I held the arrow tight as its hoofs clattered. We skidded down to the next one, and the ledge we'd just been on split open and cracked apart on either side.

"Move!" I gasped, tugging on the foal's mane. My voice came in shreds now. My lungs were raw. Each breath scorched and tasted of copper and grit.

The foal balked before stumbling with me toward the alcove. I didn't dare look back as the earth vibrated harder beneath our feet. I knew what was coming. Just because it was smaller than the main landslide didn't mean it wouldn't kill us if it hit us full on.

The embankment steepened into a high shelf, but there wasn't enough time for us to reach it, and there wasn't anything to hide behind up there if the debris rose that far.

With a pained grunt, I fisted my hand in the foal's mane and dragged it into the alcove. The space was barely big enough for us both, but its back curved over our heads like a thick stone shell.

One arm wrapped tight around the foal's neck, I crouched beside it and turned our faces toward the wall. It sounded as if a freight train was barreling down on us, the whole world shaking.

Rock, soil, clay, and marble struck the alcove and shot in alongside us. I could scarcely breathe as the foal screamed again and pressed hard against me.

Sand and soil, hot and coarse, poured onto us from the side and shoved me against the rough wall, my cheek grinding against stone as I struggled to catch a breath.

Then everything went still.

Light from the golden orbs highlighted heavy dust. My vision blurred. Though my lungs pulled hard, I struggled to get a full breath, and my limbs felt like lead.

Somehow, I was still alive. Somehow. That counted for something, though I felt pretty damn miserable.

The foal nuzzled into my side, its heart thudding fast and frantic.

Slowly, I took in the state of the place. We were mostly buried in the runoff of sand, dirt, silt, and small rocks. The slide had shot all the way up to the top of the embankment, covering some of it with debris. But if an exit was going to form back there, it should still appear.

My eyes grew heavy, and I struggled to lift my head. *We have to ... have to get out.*

The full force of the rockslide had missed us, but the mass that *had* poured in was enough to pin me.

The unicorn foal wriggled and beat my body as it worked its way free. "*Mmmrrrhhh* ..."

Groaning, I slid farther down, my eyelids so heavy.

The foal stumbled out and found its footing, then turned and started pawing at the ground as if trying to dig me out.

I choked and coughed, wishing I could get an arm free. Bile rose in the back of my throat. I had to keep moving.

The foal whinnied again, then nuzzled my cheek. Despite the dried blood and mud on its coat, its fur was so soft. If I were in a safe place, I might have cuddled with it.

My nerves spiked. If they sent more assassins, I'd be dead meat. I tried once more to move, and pain burned through my left thigh. A whimper escaped me, then I froze.

The arrow.

I hadn't let go of the arrow.

The foal stiffened and spun around, laying its gray ears flat against its head. It bared its teeth and stamped its hooves, the vibrations running through me.

Alarm spiked through me. I tried to wriggle my way out, but my left arm was trapped, and my right was barely moving.

The foal tossed its head and backed up. I winced, then froze as I saw a dark mass oozing into the corner.

The fog monster.

One set of red eyes opened. The pupils dilated as they caught sight of me, then five more sets of eyes opened.

The creature moved forward faster.

Fuck! I looked down for the pendant to make sure it was visible, then froze. The pendant was gone.

"Run," I wheezed. "Go on. Get out." If the foal jumped, it could get past the fog monster. Or if it ran up the embankment, maybe it could hide.

The foal squealed again, stamping and pacing, but not abandoning me.

The fog monster rolled closer as it slid over gravel, soil, and sand.

No, he couldn't die this way. He had to stay alive and find his herd.

Thud. Thud. THUD.

A large chunk of the wall across from me crashed inward as a goliath of a man strode across the piece he'd plowed through. He had a wild mass of red hair and a black eye patch over his left eye, and a white pendant hanging from a silver chain around his neck.

My heart thudded. *Another assassin.* I had to break free or die by his hand.

"Well, hello, trouble—you ready for me?" he boomed.

Chapter Twenty-Four

My eyes widened as adrenaline surged through me. I jerked my right hand, trying to free it to no avail. The dirt and rocks might as well have been cement.

Grinning, the massive man strode toward me, his heavy black boots crunching over the dirt and soil. Unlike the other assassins, he wore a V-neck white shirt with long frilled sleeves. A worn black leather cloak covered his shoulders, and that, combined with the eye patch and the loose black and white striped pants tucked into his heavy black boots, made him look like an enormous fae pirate.

Was he even a fae? I'd never seen one like him here.

The fog monster halted when the pale light of his pendant cut across the loose soil. "Off with you now," he said gruffly, shooing it away as if it were a stray dog begging for scraps. He scuffed one boot into the dirt and sent a spray of debris in its direction.

The red eyes blinked, and it curled back and away.

They had a happy killer who liked to dress up? Who the fuck were these people? "Stay away from the unicorn and me, or you'll regret it," I seethed, using one of the only things that I had left to survive—my mouth.

The foal stamped its hoofs again, but its challenging whinny was softer and more hesitant, as if it didn't know what to think of this stranger.

My head was still spinning, and my sense of smell wasn't working, but I bared my teeth at him. "Come one step closer, and I'll launch myself at your face. I killed all three of your friends." I hated the way my voice cracked, but I snapped my teeth, the best attempt at defiance I had left.

He placed his hands on his waist, his dark brown eye blazing with delight as he canted his head. "Love to see you try, trouble. I bet if you were in better condition right now, you'd give me a good run. But those weren't my friends you killed. I'm your rescue. The old one told you I was coming, right?"

Many-Greats? My heart leaped as my eyes widened. I remembered his warning against mentioning him or my Aureline heritage. "The—the auburn-haired old man with gold eyes?" What was Many-Greats' real name?

He snapped his fingers and pointed. "That's the one. Smells like lilacs. Bryn Lugh of the Aureline High Council."

On the Aureline *High Council*? The ones who were making us go through this nightmare? My blood turned hot ... well, what was left of it. Still, it was enough to have me trying to twist my right arm free with effort once more. "If he's on the council, why the hell did I have to go through this?"

He chuckled as he raked his hand through his shaggy red hair. "Can't say I know the answer to that. Not really my business. Veralt's the name, and you're Briar. And I'm here to get you out."

My rage dimmed as I blinked slowly, my thoughts murky. Veralt? That name was familiar. Where had I heard it? I'd deal with Many-Greats later. He'd probably show up in my bedroom on some random night again soon. That was his preferred method of visiting me.

He stooped down and began digging me out of the dirt. "Hey there, trouble. You're not looking so good. Wake up now. Gonna get you out safe, all doctored up, and on your way home, yeah?"

"Okay." I winced as his hand grazed one of the cuts.

The unicorn stood there watching, tense, like it was still unsure if it liked the pirate or not.

"Any broken bones?" he asked.

"Maybe. There's an arrow in my leg." I bit the inside of my lip as another wave of pain crashed over me. "My cuts won't stop bleeding."

"Hey, stay with me. Deep breaths." He crouched beside me. "We're going to get you out. You're gonna be just fine." He reached into his pocket and removed a silver pendant like the one I'd lost and that he and the assassins wore. He lifted my tangled, matted hair and gently fastened the silver chain around my neck. As soon as he did, that thrum of energy passed through me.

"What's it doing?" I murmured weakly.

"It'll slow the bleed-out and boost your healing. Also repels certain kinds of monsters, provides light, and boosts teleportation spells. Very helpful in situations like this." He lowered my hair. "Now, you brace yourself, and when you're ready, tell me, and I'll dig you out. You need to stay conscious if at all possible, so talk to me if you need to."

The foal circled him, edging closer then edging back.

Veralt stroked the foal's head with one massive hand and scratched around its horn. "Easy there, sugar. She's gonna be fine. You'll see." He clicked his tongue and then looked at me. His good eye softened as his brow furrowed with heavy lines. "I think you made a friend here. Now, while you're getting your breath, how about we take care of something else?"

He reached behind himself under the cloak and removed

a large waterskin. A leather bag swung along with it, secured by the same strap. He unclipped the waterskin, unfastened it, and pressed it to my lips.

I gasped as he helped me drink the water. The sweet, clean flavor exploded over my tongue and eased the dry ache of my throat. My head pounded relentlessly, but I choked while swallowing greedily.

"There we go. Drink all you want." He adjusted it so as not to overwhelm me, his hand shifting on the waterskin.

He drew it back after I'd had a few swallows, poured some in the palm of his hand, and offered it to the foal with one hand while he pressed the waterskin back to my lips with the other. I wanted to bless him and thank him and cry all at once.

The foal sniffed his hand and then licked up the water. He repeated this, alternating between giving me and the foal the most delicious water that had ever existed. Once we'd both had enough, he set the waterskin aside and laid out his cloak.

"I can't guarantee this next part won't hurt, so bear with me," he said, kneeling beside me and digging. Bit by bit, he removed the sand and dirt, working my naked body free. Within minutes, he had my torso uncovered.

I tried to cover my breasts with my arms, wincing a little. The cuts on my chest, shoulders, and forearm continued to drip blood. A shudder coursed down my back, screaming that he needed to go away. "This feels wrong."

He scooped the dirt from along my thigh. "Yeah, fair enough. Can't say I'm enjoying it either. But if it makes you feel any better, there's no one for me but Rhielle. She is my fate, my stars, my cosmic force. The only reason I'm here is because of her. You're, like ... her kid sister or something. But I'll get you covered up here in just a moment."

I blinked. *Rhielle? That's why I know his name.* The way Rhielle had smiled at me before we'd entered this trial now made sense, but how had they managed this? "You're Rhielle's Veralt?"

A huge smile spread across his face. "Guilty as charged, happy when with her, and no longer considering regicide 'cause I don't have to worry about my woman getting snatched away by some prince." Leaning in closer, he resumed removing the dirt, his touch respectful and swift. "Only reason I didn't burn this void-doomed palace and competition down is 'cause Rhielle told me we'd find a way to be together and it wasn't worth anyone getting executed or banished. She said Fate wouldn't give her to someone else, not when Rhielle had made her own choice. And it's a good thing too. I can't stand the Aurelines, and I'm not much fond of anyone telling me what to do unless they're the love of my life. My conscience and my woman are the only beings that rule me."

Knowing that he was Rhielle's lover didn't necessarily make me feel comfortable, but it did ease some of my distress. If I hadn't been so miserable and in so much pain, I would have had dozens more questions for him.

He worked at a steady pace, making conversation and spouting endless praise for Rhielle. After he'd dug me out enough, he picked me up like I weighed nothing. "Watch your leg then. I'll try not to jostle you. If it hurts, tell me."

"Everything hurts." I bit back a pained gasp as the pressure shifted in my leg and the arrow cut deeper. Blood trickled from the wound.

He grunted in sympathy. "True, true. If it hurts worse than before, then let me know." He placed me on the cloak and wrapped it around me, taking care to leave my left leg out.

"What kind of shot did he get on you to hit you like that?" he asked, brow tight with concern. "Good thing it missed the arteries, or not even that pendant could delay your death."

I dropped my head as I sucked in a deep breath, my fingers

digging into his leather cloak. "I was carrying it when we got caught in the rockslide. I picked it up on the mountain so I could have a sample of the venom."

"Scaffing void! If you just wanted to take one so you could have a sample for the doctor, you could've carried it in less painful ways, trouble." He winked as he wrapped me up and continued, "Remind me to get you what we like to call a bag." He reached into his pocket and pulled out a small glittering blue orb. He tapped it with his index finger and traced a sigil on it. Humming a few notes of a jaunty song, he stood, walked a few paces into the chamber, and then hurled it.

The golden light caught on the blue orb as it spun in the air. Then it vanished from sight. He clapped his hands together and turned back toward me. "All right then, trouble, we've got a few minutes before that explodes and makes it seem like you were never rescued."

"You're blowing the place up?" My eyes widened as he hefted me into his massive arms. That sense of wrongness intensified. He shouldn't be the one holding me. My very being screamed and ached for Vad, and my wolf agreed.

"Sure am. In my line of work, knowing how to make that happen is delicate and delightful. Little bit of Shadow magic. Little bit of Ignis magic. Little bit of Terran magic. Little bit of Aureline too." He hummed in satisfaction and took a step toward the opening in the broken wall. Then he stopped short. A slow grin spread over his face.

"What?" I frowned, not sure if him being so happy was good or bad.

His smile broadened even more. "Just one more thing before we get out of here." He carried me up to the top of the embankment and kicked off some of the dirt and debris that covered the second sigil carved into the floor without any paint or chalk to mark its path. The emblem in this one was of two blades with a full goblet sitting between them. "You fought hard, and you finished. Might as well log it."

"I don't give a fuck that I finished," I grumbled, hugging myself tighter and trying to avoid pressing against him.

"Yeah, well, Rhielle would want it known you finished. When you don't come out, the baddies will think the collapse happened after you finished. Your door isn't supposed to open for a long time anyway, and after I trigger another rockslide in here, no one will be asking questions."

"You're sure we have time for this?" I glanced around the chamber. How long did magical bombs take to explode? "And what about the unicorn?"

"Sure am. At least as long as you don't make this difficult." He lowered me until my feet touched the sigil without putting any weight on them. "We'll be out of these tunnels by the time it goes, and Sugar will be going with us. Don't worry."

Energy surged through me, buzzing lightly. Gold light flared and lit up the whole sigil. The pulse made my blood thrum faster, and then my head throbbed even more.

Veralt laughed, his deep voice echoing off the stone walls. "You're the first! You won, trouble. Oh, that'll stick in the craws of those Fate-twisting bastards! I love it!"

Amid my throbbing head and the twisting nausea, I struggled to form a coherent thought. My fingers and toes tingled as if they were falling asleep, and a numbness crept from the very tips.

The foal trotted beside Veralt, who carried me as easily as if I were a child. The faint light from his silver pendant illuminated the rocky tunnel, revealing nothing but jagged gray rocks.

My vision hazed even more, and I struggled to breathe. "Hey, trouble," he said with a concerned rumble. "Talk to me. Don't go falling asleep now. You got a name for this unicorn?"

I fought to keep my eyes open. Sounds faded in and out, the darkness in the tunnel deepening. "N-no. Not yet."

"Well, you'll want to think of something special." He kept talking, but his voice turned into a droning series of syllables that faded in and out.

The magic in the amulet that slowed the bleeding and the effects of the venom wasn't going to be enough. I was going to die. The numbness in my fingers and toes had crept up to my wrists and ankles. My head sagged back.

The world shook and bounced. Vaguely, I realized Veralt was running. His mouth moved, but I couldn't hear him anymore. Part of me longed for sleep, but it wasn't safe. This wasn't right. I couldn't sleep now.

My wolf whined and nudged me. I was fading—slipping away. Cold fear spiked through me. Not like this. It couldn't end like this.

A sexy, deep baritone voice sliced through the haze. "Give her to me *now*!"

I fought to open my eyelids as the tugging in my chest screamed for me to wake up.

Vad.

His name rose to the tip of my tongue, but my lips barely had the strength to part. Was he here, or was this a dream?

Something cold wrapped around me and pressed under the cloak and then into my wounds. His shadows. I remembered their touch from the prison. At first, I stiffened, but then some of the pain lessened. Vad folded me closer to his broad chest, and his warmth engulfed me. His heartbeat thudded against my ear, so fast it seemed that he had been running.

A warm and satisfying humming buzz pulsed through my body. *Yes*. I breathed out, relief flooding through me amid the exhaustion and the pain. My eyelids slid shut as the world faded, and one single thought remained: I was safe.

"Briar," Vad pleaded. "Stay with me. I need you awake."

Chapter Twenty-Five

My shoulders ached with tension as I knelt at the bedside, watching over Briar. I wasn't moving until she woke, and I could beg Fate to let her pull through this with no permanent injuries or scars. If I had found a quicker way ... if I'd demanded the trials not be finished, she wouldn't be in this condition tonight.

Until her eyes opened, I wouldn't leave this spot, come void or high water. I wanted to soak in all the minutes we had left together before she was sent home.

The darkness in my bedchamber mirrored my mood and gave my shadows the room to pulse and curl. They had coiled around the bed protectively, a few tendrils near her and against her. But I held them back from fully touching her, not sure if they would make her chances of recovery better or worse.

At this point, it seemed anything I did led to something worse.

She lay in the center of my bed, scrubbed clean and bandaged, her copper curls fanned against the obsidian sheets. Physician Morlo had attended to her personally, along with one associate he said he trusted with his life.

They had scrubbed her clean, stitched her long cuts, bandaged her, and, after examining the arrow that had been stuck in her thigh, provided the antidote to reverse the effects of the venom. The bastards who'd tried to kill her had dipped it in a venom that kept blood from clotting. It was the same type that had been used on Rhielle and likely my father.

Morlo had insisted that, based on what he had seen of Briar in the other trials, she would be up soon and with enough strength to attend the coronation and wedding. He'd said it with confidence and pride shining from his eyes, as if he was watching his own family members getting their happily ever after. He'd promised to return to check on her as soon as he completed the next round of tests on the hair sample. He'd said, "Briar suits you well. I haven't often thought this, but ... it seems that you were made for one another. It reminds me of your father and mother. It's a beautiful thing."

It is ... was.

And that had reinforced how stupid I'd been to make the vow. Understanding had struck me that, now that I had her, I had to let her go. Still, I could only acknowledge his words, unable to tell him that Briar was going home.

The tugging in my chest increased as I remembered what it had been like when my parents were together, and the pain the memories brought was enough to make me bite back a groan. My parents' love had been doomed, and perhaps mine was as well. The only way to save Briar was to deny our connection and send her back. I couldn't even argue with Bryn after she'd almost died yet again.

My room was decorated in black with touches of gold. Lying among the silk sheets in my massive bed, Briar looked like a brilliant wildfire gem in a setting of onyx. The black put her presence front and center in the room.

Like she was meant to stay here by my side.

I bowed my head and pressed her freckled knuckles to my lips. My beloved. Always mine in my heart for eternity. No one else could replace her, nor would I want anyone to. Our time together had been brief, but it would remain the best part of my existence, always.

Where we touched, a buzzing sprang to life under my skin, and something in my chest yanked me toward her, like a desperate need to be closer to her. In such a short amount of time, my kingdom and realm had collapsed in on itself, compressed into the shape of *this* wonderful woman.

Gently, I placed my hand over hers and breathed her in, savoring the scent of cinnamon and ginger, along with the warmth of the hazelnut red tea.

Brushing her hair from her brow, I memorized the rhythm of her breathing and craved far more contact with her. The only thing holding me back was not wanting to harm her anymore, especially with the injuries all over her body.

Time usually didn't mean much to me, not when I was immortal. But right now it was a paradox because I both wanted her to wake so I could talk to her and apologize, and didn't want her to wake because, when she did, I'd have to let her go.

Bryn promised that he and one of his most trusted attendants would be waiting for us two hours from now in one of the secret passages. I'd been annoyed and surprised to discover Bryn even knew about them, which I needed to follow up on later. It seemed he intended to use the old portaling doorways to get Briar home, though I wondered how he had managed to restore them. They hadn't been in operation since my grandfather's time.

More questions for another time. Right now, I just wanted—no, *needed*—to focus on Briar.

I kissed her palm and was surprised to find that her injuries had already scabbed over. I ached to pull her into my arms and kiss my way down her neck.

She stirred, her lashes fluttering.

My heart leaped, and my breath hitched. "Briar?"

Those beautiful green eyes opened, and my heart melted. In my mind, I chanted, *Anything for you, my love, so long as you are safe.* I had to keep repeating it so I remembered there was no way to keep her at my side now.

"Vad." My name fell from her lips.

It cut so deep I had to restrain a pained breath.

I brought her hands to my lips, kissing them again. My eyelids slid shut while I committed all of this to memory. "How are you feeling?" I rasped, then swallowed hard.

"A lot better than I expected." She sat up slowly, and the blankets slid down.

My breath hitched in my throat.

The simple, pale-blue nightgown Morlo and his attendant had dressed her in hinted at her figure and clung to her breasts, the scooped neckline offering a tantalizing peek of cleavage. My fingers itched to peel it off her and examine her for myself and verify her well-being, but respect stayed my hand.

"Good," I said hoarsely. "Are you hungry or thirsty?" I gestured toward the ebony bedside table and the carved carafe filled to the brim with spring water. "There's water there, and I can get you something more substantive."

"Just thirsty right now." She picked up the carafe and drank deeply, holding it with both hands. When she set it aside, her eyes met mine, and she ducked her head, blushing a little.

That sweet shyness made my heart clench. How could any one person be so perfect? I drew my hands back as well as my shadows, trying to give her as much space as she might need.

"What about the foal? And Veralt? Do you know anything about Elias?" She tilted her head, and her mass of loose copper curls slid over one half-bared, deliciously beautiful shoulder.

My mouth went dry. I wished to explore that skin with my lips and tongue. Trying to regain my composure, I cleared my throat. "Elias's rescue is in progress. The foal is safe in the stables with one of the gentler mares. Veralt is with Rhielle."

Her lips curled into a soft smile. "I bet they're happy."

A pang of jealousy lashed through me. Had she found Veralt attractive? He had certainly found her so, no matter how much he'd insisted that Rhielle was his cosmic force. I'd wanted to cut his eyes out and his hands off. But he'd gotten her out of the trial and bought me enough time to handle the councils during the final trial so that it didn't look as if I was completely derelict in my duty. For that—and so long as he never touched Briar again—I would reward him handsomely.

"I'm sure they are." I curled my shadows in tighter and fought the urge to touch her again. My wings itched and flexed, though I kept them drawn against my back. "I am so glad you're all right, Briar. I couldn't see you at all until Veralt split open that wall." My throat thickened. As horrifying as it had been to see her get hurt in the last two trials, it had been a separate and, in some cases, worse horror to see and know nothing until the end.

I struggled to speak around the tightness in my chest. It built with each moment. "The sight of you like that ..." My voice broke, and I ducked my head. Everything within me burned and seethed, raging that they had dared to treat her that way. "Veralt said that you killed all the assassins who came for you. Well done."

She shook her head, her brow creasing as she fisted the sheets. "They weren't the ones who made all this happen. They were just hired to kill me."

"They deserved far worse," I growled. Her killing them was a mercy compared to how I would have butchered them. "But what matters is that you're safe. Physician Morlo said you would recover swiftly, but he did leave behind a jar of bath salts and dried herbs to help. He wants you to soak in a bath for at least half an hour. And then ... you're going *home*."

I tried to hide the brokenness in my voice and forced a smile to my lips, though most likely it was little more than a grimace. I sought comfort in the knowledge that she would be with her sister and her pack again. All those whom she loved, and she would continue to be loved here in the Shadow Kingdom for so long as I lived and beyond that, if I had any will.

The bond of the vow pressed in upon me, warning me not to break it.

Her shoulders stiffened, and she straightened. "Home?"

"Yes. I'm sending you back to Earth to live with your sister." I met her gaze, and it took every ounce of strength I had not to rip those words back.

"For a visit, or forever?" Her brow furrowed, and her eyes blazed with questions.

"Not a visit." I couldn't force out the word *forever*. My lips refused.

That stubborn set of her mouth and the way a muscle ticked in her jaw would have made me smile if not for what we were talking about. I would miss that. I would miss everything about her.

Her nostrils flared. "Why?"

I lifted one brow. I'd expected maybe some sadness, perhaps some grief or curiosity. But if I knew anything about her ... that was rage.

She jerked her chin up. "Do you not *want* me anymore?"

Scaffing void, no! My mouth dropped open, but thankfully, I caught myself before I could say that aloud.

Feck.

I should've known this wouldn't be easy, but she'd wanted to go home during the entire time of the first and second trials. "I had to get you out as soon as possible. And one of the Aureline High Council members said he could do it within three hours.

But the only way he would was if I made a binding vow to help him send you home."

Her eyes glowed eerily as she stared at me and spat out, "So you made the choice for me?"

For once, I realized there was no right answer. I'd never experienced a situation where I loved someone so dearly, and yet every choice I made caused them more distress and pain. "I had to make a vow to free you. The vow required that you go home. You'll get to be with your sister and the other wolves again."

"Didn't you ask me to be your queen? Or did Doucheface implant that memory in my head?" She pushed herself out of bed and stalked away. One hand thrust into her hair, and she spun back around. "And now, you just ... took that away?"

My head jerked back. "Briar, I *had* to get you out of that prison, and this was the quickest way possible. The longer you stayed imprisoned, the worse it would be for you there. Time moves quickly there, so getting you out was a priority. To do that, I had to make an unbreakable vow." I set my hands on my belt, resisting the urge to pull her to my chest and wrap her in my shadows and wings. "I protected you the best way possible—by getting you out of there."

"Did you even try to compromise, or did the bastards who set me up change your mind about me?" Her bottom lip trembled, but her chin remained lifted in defiance. "You know what? It doesn't matter. Clearly, off to Earth I go." She spun and moved away from me.

My blood heated. Her accusation stung. I sprang up and gently seized her arm. "Stop right now. At least let me explain." When she looked at me, I couldn't bring myself to let her go.

"Go on then." Her words were sharp. "Explain. Though I'm pretty sure you can't add much more to that."

I scowled, still holding her arm and trying not to look

anywhere but in her eyes. "I can easily justify it. Briar, you were being *tortured*. Did you expect me to just let you rot in there when I had a viable alternative?" I'd done this because I *loved* her. Couldn't she see that?

Some part of me was thrilled at the realization that she didn't want to go. She wanted to be with *me*.

"Going home or not was my choice, and you took it from me!" She set her hands on her waist and stepped closer.

"How could I let you stay in that place for even a moment longer than necessary?" My insides twisted, and my shadows curled around her, two tendrils wrapping around her ankles. I tugged them back, exasperated that my own body and magic seemed to have only one impulse when it came to her.

"Briar," I said, my voice low. "Please. Understand. I was trying to get you out of there as swiftly as I could. From our perspective, you weren't even gone a full day. Think of all the horrible things they did to you in that short amount of time and how much they distorted the timeline from your perspective. It was going to take me another full day here, perhaps two, to get you out. The councilman promised to free you within three hours, but I had to pay his price. I'd already failed you by letting you be taken. I couldn't let you suffer any more than you already had."

"I could have waited for you longer—" she started.

"We had no way of knowing how much time was passing for you in there. And despite the vow I bound Colm to, the council member confirmed there were others involved who were also trying to kill you. Not to mention the sheer horrors that infest that place. The time warping alone can twist the mind permanently. It would have been, at most, three days for me to get you home in my time, but, Briar—" My voice cracked again, my throat hoarse with emotion. I leaned in closer, taking her hands in mine and bringing them to my lips. "Briar, it could have been *years* for you. And I will give *anything* to keep you safe. You didn't deserve any of this, and you never asked for it."

"No, but you asked me to be your queen, and you said you loved me. I would've tried to find another way."

"I do! I love you more than anything. I love you more than my own life and my kingdom and my throne. You mean more to me than my own happiness, so I swore that vow to make sure you were happy and safe and could go home."

A tear rolled down her cheek.

I shouldn't be touching her. I knew I shouldn't. But I caressed her cheek with the back of my knuckles, wiping the tear away before sliding my finger under her chin and letting my thumb brush her perfect, kissable lips.

Her lips pressed into a tight line, and she shook her head. "I would have waited for you. I would have found my own way out. I'm still willing to fight for *us*. There is no happiness for me without you."

Those words struck me deep, and it took what little self-restraint I had left to not pounce on her and devour her. There was no way around this. I had to see it through.

I stroked her jawline with my thumb and said, "You are the most remarkable woman I have ever known. Your spirit and courage, as much as your kindness and compassion, are unlike any other, and I will *never* forget you. When you return home, you take my heart with you. It will always be yours. But you deserve far more than I can give you. And you'll see ... you're ..." I wanted to retch even as I formed the words, but I forced them out. "You're going to find someone else to ... make you happy, Briar. To give you all you deserve. Some man out there is going to be the most lucky and Fate-blessed man to ever walk through time and history."

She grabbed hold of my surcoat collar and jerked my face down until my lips were right over hers. "Listen to me. I will always love my sister and my pack, and I *do* want to see them again. But my home isn't back on Earth anymore. My *home* is with you. Don't you get that?" Her gaze softened, then she stood on her tiptoes and kissed me on the cheek. A buzz jolted deep within me.

My breath hitched, and the shadows trembled around me. A low, needful groan rose from my throat.

She walked toward the bathroom with elegant grace, her hair loose against her back and the nightgown sliding down one of her shoulders. For half a breath, I thought she might look back at me.

She stepped inside and closed the door with a solid *click*. Rushing water soon followed.

I fell back a step and covered my mouth, resisting the urge to send my shadows in to check on her. My cheek burned where her lips had touched it, and my thoughts returned to those wonderful moments in the observatory and on the ballroom floor. I craved that and more.

So much more.

All that diverted blood flow made it harder to think. A slow thought pushed up within my mind. She had said something important. Her home ... was with me?

My throat tightened, and I looked to the door, hunger and need pouring through me like liquid fire. If her home was with me ... then ...

My restraint snapped, and I rushed to the door.

Chapter Twenty-Six

Steam rose from the crimson waters that filled the enormous black marble bath dominating the center of the black bathroom.

Frustration bubbled inside me. I understood why Vad had done it, even though I didn't want to admit it to him. I'd have done the same in his position, but that didn't make it right.

I grabbed a tall jar marked with my name in chalk and dumped the entire contents into the water, and the room exploded with the scents of chamomile, sandalwood, roses, and lemons. The herbs and salt swirled in the dark waters.

How could he? And how could the person I had to assume was Many-Greats require such a vow to help me? It was a good thing he hadn't popped up in this room, or I'd have ripped into him.

Huffing, I stripped off the nightgown, relieved that my injuries had healed so much already. I was just a little sore, and my wolf magic had kicked in, full swing.

Small black stitches ran along my chest and arms where the long, venomous cuts had been made, but the wounds looked as if they had all but closed. A large bandage was wrapped around my thigh where the arrow wound had been, which made sense. The arrowhead had been buried deep, and I shuddered even imagining the damage it had probably done. At least my natural healing seemed to have resumed.

The water was so hot, I almost recoiled when I dipped in one foot, but I needed to feel something other than this emotional pain that seemed to be drowning me.

I sank into the water, and it sloshed over me, the deep heat sinking into my bones. The tub was deep enough that I didn't have to lean back to fully immerse myself, and it was long enough that I could easily stretch out.

Though I didn't want to relax, my muscles unknotted with every second in the bath. The doctor's recommendation was apparently right and doing something good for my body.

I pressed my forehead to my knees and tried to slow my breathing. The inside of my skull was a mass of anger, hurt, frustration, and confusion. What was I supposed to do or say? To get me out of prison, Vad had made a vow to send me back to Earth.

It wasn't that I'd wanted to stay in that horrible place. My breath knotted in my chest as I remembered the constant cold, the torture, and the terror. My fingers and toes ached at the memory, and my breath hitched.

No, I was safe now.

Those bastards would pay.

And I didn't care what Many-Greats had made Vad vow. I wasn't going back to Earth and leaving Vad behind. My home was here, in this beautiful yet treacherous place. Not only was Vad here, but I needed vengeance.

My heart seized. If Vad didn't crown me, who would he marry and make his queen? Panic clawed at me, and my skin crawled.

The door banged open, striking the far wall and vibrating.

I yelped, covering my breasts with my hands.

Vad stood in the doorway, wings outstretched and bristling,

and his shadows swirling around him. His hungry gaze latched onto me, his pupils wide and his breathing ragged. "What did you say about your home?"

That look in his eye made my core tighten, and my heart restarted. I lifted my chin and raised an eyebrow. "You mean where I said my home really is?"

He nodded and stepped across the threshold. His wings folded in so that he could enter, but as soon as he was inside, they flared out again. "Yes," he growled.

I sat up straighter, water droplets rolling down my neck and across the tops of my breasts. "Well ... my home would be with the man I love, but according to you, that's not you, is it? And apparently, you're okay with crowning and marrying someone else."

Another low growl rumbled in his chest. "I never said I didn't love you, and, no, I don't want to crown anyone but you."

"You just told me you took a vow to send me away—"

"To your *home*. I didn't specify Earth." Vad stopped at the edge of the tub and raised his hands, pausing as the shadows coiled around him and circled the tub.

"What?" Still glaring at him, I flicked one of his shadow tendrils away. The cold wrapped around my finger briefly, but it retreated. An icy chill coiled down my spine, and the memory of him cradling me swept back in.

A ragged breath shook Vad's broad frame as he stared down at me. His hands clenched at his sides. "Do you mean it, Briar?"

"Mean what? That I love you? Yes, I do, or I'd be thrilled to be going back to my sister." My voice was steady, but my pulse raced as I leaned back, the water's edge lapping softly against my skin. My fingers curled against my thigh as I tried not to notice just how masculine he was and how his black tunic and tight black trousers left little to the imagination.

He narrowed his eyes and looked at me as if he wanted to eat me whole. "That home is with me?" His low voice sounded raw and filled with need.

The air between us grew heavy, the rich, fragrant scent of the water rising with the steam and a hint of spice. There was a challenge in his gaze along with desperate hunger, confirming he wanted me as much as I wanted him. "Yes, you're my ho—"

He lunged forward and grabbed my face with both hands, shaking as he thrust his mouth over mine. I responded, the sudden buzz of our connection making my head spin. If he were a wolf, I would have no doubt that we were fated mates.

His tongue pressed between my lips, and his hands moved to my neck and tangled in my hair.

Pulling back slightly, he let out a hasty breath. "Is this all right? If not, I don't want to disrespect you further."

"If you stop, I will take what's mine," I growled, my wolf slipping out as she moved forward. "I want all of you, Vad. My body is physically craving you, so much so that I wonder if it's possible that we're fated mates."

"Fated mates?" His brows creased. "What is that?"

"Supernatural beings on Earth believe that some souls get separated by Fate, and if they are fortunate enough to locate each other, their souls sense one another." The yanking in my chest intensified as my wolf became restless. "I've never felt anything like my draw to you before."

"We don't have fated mates here," Vad rasped, "But if I could have one, I would definitely choose you."

He pushed me against the far wall of the tub, and my back slapped against the marble. I'd never believed I'd love to be dominated, but when he climbed inside fully clothed and straddled me, pinning me to the wall, need knotted inside me.

His hardness pressed against my stomach, and I barely had time to draw a breath before his mouth was on mine again.

His tongue swept in, tangling with mine, tasting like smoke and blackberries with a bit of spice.

Desperate, I gripped his surcoat, wanting to see him bare-chested. His free hand slipped under the water and brushed the side of my breast.

"You're still an asshole for making that vow without talking to me," I rasped. "Good intentions or not. I don't ever want to be separated from you again."

He grinned as his fingertips glided over my nipple. "I will always protect you, but perhaps I can make it up to you." His lips found the corner of my jaw, then the hollow of my throat.

I arched my back, wanting him to keep going. He was moving way too slow for the need building up inside me. "Well, I still haven't forgiven you."

"Hmmm." His tongue slid over my collarbone and lower, catching a bead of water at the top curve of my breast.

My body was on fire, and I needed to feel his skin on mine. I placed my hands on the front of his tunic, gripping each side of the collar. Then I ripped it apart, causing him to freeze. I touched his chest, tracing the scars that crisscrossed it, before sliding lower to the curves of his abs, making his body shudder.

"My love, I'm struggling to go slow and be careful with your injuries. Your allure and eager response though—I'm—"

"You mean, I shouldn't do this?" I asked innocently as I moved my right hand to his dick and stroked him over the fabric.

He groaned and jerked his hips.

My heart skipped a beat as I realized how huge and hard his shaft was. I wasn't sure it would fit inside me, but dammit, I was more than willing to try.

Hissing, his lips returned to mine, and he slid one hand between my legs, which I spread open for him eagerly.

"You know, it's really not cool that you're all dressed and

I'm naked," I said breathlessly.

"Do you want me naked, Briar?" He moved back enough for me to see the glint in his stormy-gray eyes. "Whatever shall we do?" His wings flexed out again, and his shadows rose along the sides of the tub as he grinned.

"Well, if you're dressed, then I should be too." I bit my lip and pretended I was going to stand.

"No need for that, my love. Putting your clothes on before I finish worshiping this body will not do." He kissed his way down my neck to my chest. "Let's see if you can handle what's next."

I'd had no control during my whole time here, but I was taking it back for now. I placed my hands on his chest and shoved him toward the other end of the tub.

He set his hands on the side of the tub and shoved himself up so that he stood, towering over me. His wings pulsed and flexed again, sending droplets of water raining all over the bathroom.

I ducked my head, remaining seated, though I held up my hands to shield myself from the spray. My breathing quickened.

He ripped off his boots, socks, belt, and pants and tossed them across the room one at a time. They struck the wall with loud *slaps* and formed a pile beside the sink.

I licked my lips, enjoying the sculpted V of his pelvis, his hipbones, and his dick. For a moment, he let me look, savoring my anticipation. My wolf howled eagerly in my head, urging me to jump him. I moved forward, wanting to taste him, when he took a step back.

"Let me see you, too. Out of the water, or else I'll drain it."

Heat stole across my cheeks, but my legs moved of their own accord. I slid up onto the lip of the bathtub, my arms over my breasts and one hand between my legs.

"Little tease," he growled. One of his shadows curled along

my shoulders and caressed me. "I said I want to see my queen."

The ache between my legs intensified, and the yanking in my chest nearly had me crawling to him.

"Let me see you," he said, his gaze fixed on me, hungry and wild.

More heat spread through my body, and I knew I had to be blushing. But slowly, I moved my hands and set them at my sides, curling against the marble bath.

His breath sharpened. "Fecking void, how are you even real, Briar? You're too perfect."

He leaned forward and palmed one of my breasts, thumb circling the nipple, and the sensation sent a jolt of heat through my core. He gripped my ass and lifted me so my legs wrapped around his waist, and I rocked against him involuntarily and moaned as his hardness rubbed between my lips.

"Never has there been a woman so perfect," he breathed huskily. "I want to tear out the eyes of anyone who has ever looked upon you. What did I ever do to deserve someone like you in my life?"

My heart warmed at hearing how much he cared for me. I swallowed hard and looked up at him. "I could ask the same thing."

"I want you, and my shadows want you too. I want you again and again until your voice shatters and my legs give out and I can barely hold myself up." He lowered his head and licked where his thumb had just been.

My head jerked back. Part of me wanted to tease him, but the rest of me just wanted to be with him and satisfy the ache that now practically consumed me. I rocked against him once more.

"Not quite yet." He slid his fingers between us and circled as his teeth gently raked my nipple.

I gasped and tried to reach down to touch him, but he

caught my free arm. "Not until you're ready."

"Oh, believe me, I ..." I started, but his fingers and mouth cut off every thought aside from pleasure. His fingers slipped inside me while his thumb circled, and he kept my wrists locked within his other hands. Then his teeth and tongue sent me over the edge.

My body quivered and clenched around him as he continued to caress me. I didn't know how long the sensations lasted before I came down, but somehow my body craved him even more.

"I was foolish. I wouldn't be able to live without you, especially now that you've fallen apart for me." He began the onslaught again, but that wouldn't cut it.

My wolf surged forward, tired of waiting for the one thing I desired.

I yanked his hand away and rasped, "I want you, *now.*" And rubbed against him even harder than before.

He grunted, then spread my legs wider. My entire body opened, welcoming him.

"Fate," he rasped, placing his forehead against mine. "You feel so ready, but I don't want to—"

"I'm good." I licked my lips, tasting my sweat and his. "Please, make love to me."

"You feel tight. I don't want to hurt you." His forehead lined.

I huffed a shaky laugh. "I can take anything you dish out. I dare you. I'll tell you if it gets to be too much." I thrust against him again.

His smile curled higher on the right side. "We shall see." Then he pressed into me.

The entire world fell apart as he entered me. I spread my legs wider as his lips captured mine. My hands gripped his back, feeling the base where his wings connected near his shoulder blades.

"I will always adore and worship you," he promised as he thrust faster and faster. As my fingers rubbed the base of his wings, he shuddered.

Everything tightened inside me as the friction built up even more. All I could focus on was his body, how he felt, and his scent as he kept taking me higher.

Cold tendrils brushed my body as his wings surrounded me, and his movements became frantic. As he kissed me, his shadows caressed my breasts and had me tightening in pleasure.

As the pressure came close to exploding, a sudden urge took me by surprise. I tried to ignore it, but it became uncontrollable. I moaned as the cold sent me over the edge and I shattered in pleasure.

Without my intent, my teeth lengthened, and I sank them into the smooth, pale skin on the side of his throat. His taste—sweet and salty, wild and metallic—exploded in my mouth, and my growl became a moan of delight. My essence opened up and spilled outward.

"Feck." He gently pushed back my head and stared at me.

"I'm sorry." I licked my lips, craving the taste of his blood once more.

His eyes darkened, and his own fangs extended. The sight had me leaning my head back as more pleasure surged through my body. Claws formed on his hands, and he gripped the back of my head, guiding me to expose my neck. With a deeper rumbling snarl, he bit at the juncture of my neck and shoulder.

I gasped, arching in closer as my wolf howled with delight. I could feel something pour into me, adding to my ecstasy as I saw stars. The orgasm that ripped through me was the strongest one by far.

His touch went from buzzing to electric.

He pounded into me, and soon his own body quivered

from his release. He pulled back just enough to soothe the spot with his tongue.

Kissing my lips gently, he collapsed forward, caging me between his arms and wings. His hands trembled where they gripped my shoulders.

"I've never experienced anything like that before." He peppered kisses on my cheek. "And sharing blood ... I never imagined it could be so erotic. I should've known you would be exquisite, and now I'll crave you at all times."

My happiness felt stronger, almost as if my emotions had somehow doubled. "Good. Because I'm already craving you again. I love you, Vad, but don't allow anything to attempt to come between us again. I want to be here with you. No matter the cost."

He kissed my forehead, then my cheek, then every inch of skin he could reach, with a desperate reverence that made my chest ache.

"I can't vow that I won't make a stupid decision again if it means keeping you safe." He leaned his forehead against mine and continued, "Thank Fate I'm your home. Maybe she doesn't despise me completely after all. From here on out, no one will touch you other than me. I will not stand idly by and allow anyone to take you from me. I will kill anyone who tries to harm you again. I messed up before, and I will never be powerless to protect you *ever* again."

My heart raced. I'd never felt this safe before.

"But we have a coronation to attend, which will allow you to be by my side at all times."

The future sounded perfect.

The water lapped around us as he finally withdrew, and we both cleaned up. Then he carried me, dripping, out of the bathroom and toward the massive bed. "I need to make sure one last time, before you can't change your mind. Will this truly make you happy, then, beloved? Being queen of this place and holding my heart while you share my throne and bed?"

I beamed and snuggled closer, smoothing his dark hair back from his face. "Well, I'll share your bed, but I'm not sharing the blankets. The blankets are mine."

"Are they now?" His eyebrows arched, and he laughed. "You intend to leave me in the cold?" He tossed me onto the bed.

I struck the mattress and bounced. "Well ... your shadows are cold, so ... maybe that's where you belong." I grabbed the blanket on both sides and prepared to cocoon myself.

He swatted the blanket out of my hands and then pinned my wrists over my head. He settled on top of me and glared down at me. "I do not like to sleep uncovered. It seems this must be our new sleeping arrangement." His wings folded down against his spine, and two of the shadows folded the blanket over us.

I giggled and kicked as his teeth grazed my neck. "The blankets." I gasped, turning my head so he had more access. "Mine." I couldn't even form a full sentence.

"And I get to keep you." He kissed me again, taking his time now.

I returned the kiss, nipping at his lower lip and running my fingers through his hair.

He rolled his hips against mine, and his hard dick hit just the right spot.

I wrapped my legs around his waist, making him chuckle.

"If we do use this sleeping arrangement, I don't think either of us will get much sleep. There is one other thing we need to discuss, but ..." He rolled his hips against mine as a wicked grin appeared on his face. "But I have a certain problem."

Laughing, I rolled against him. "I might be able to help you with that."

"You're the only one who can."

His shadows coiled around me, and we connected all over again.

~

A DOOR SCRAPED open, and footsteps woke me from my half-dozing state. I bolted upright, pulling the blankets over Vad's and my naked bodies.

Oh, Fate. Please don't let it be him.

Chapter Twenty-Seven

I gritted my teeth. If that was Many-Greats barging into another damn bedroom again, he'd get to experience my true wrath, especially with Vad here with me. He couldn't just barge into the future king's private areas like that!

"Stay here." Vad bolted up.

By the time I realized what he was doing, he had taken a robe out of his wardrobe, flung it on, and bounded to the door. "What do you want?" he demanded as he pulled the door shut behind him.

Wait. If that was Many-Greats—

Hearty laughter followed on the other side, which confirmed the visitor was definitely *not* Many-Greats.

Someone pounded on the door. "You cheeky little minx! You just *had* to make sure Kaylen didn't pull in the win, didn't you?" Thalen called from the other side of the door.

Vad made a low grumble, so I tapped into my wolf magic. "If you even think about going in there, I will *kill* you."

Something sizzled inside me for a second, and a rush of frustration washed over me that didn't feel like my own.

Strange.

My wolf hearing flickered out as the strange sensations

took front and center.

"How'd you do it, Chaos?" Thalen called out, ignoring Vad.

What in the world was Thalen talking about? I wrapped the blanket around myself, padded to the bedroom door, and cracked it to peek out.

Thalen stood in front of Vad with his arms folded and his expression bright. "Are you *serious?*"

Giving him a push toward the outer door, Vad shook his head and said, "Get out and inform him that her *home* is with *me,* thus the terms of the vow are fulfilled, and she remains here. She is my queen."

"Really?" Thalen gave Vad a huge smile. "Can I hug the bride?" His gaze slid back to the door, and he froze when he caught me peeking through the crack. "Copper Chaos! You're staying." He then bowed dramatically. "I am at your service, my queen."

Vad smacked his shoulder and then held a hand over Thalen's eyes. "You do *not* need to be looking at her right now."

"She's completely covered by a door." Thalen shook off Vad's hand and gestured toward me as if it should be obvious.

"*Go.* You can talk to her later," Vad rasped, pushing him once again toward the outer door.

"Fine. I'll go, but only because the sooner it's done, the sooner I get to see the looks on all those scaffing windbags and Fate twisters when they see who you're really crowning." Thalen tapped his brow as he stepped back. "See you soon, Your Majesties."

Vad returned inside, shaking his head. He shrugged the robe off, letting it drop to the floor. "I did not intend for us to be interrupted so soon. He was just providing me with updates on various matters, one of which I think will especially please you. Elias has been retrieved, and he is recovering in a safe location."

My heart leaped as relief flooded me. "So he's going to be all right?"

"'All right' may be a flexible term, but he is receiving the best care possible. You can visit him after the ceremonies." He sighed and dragged a hand through his hair, then scanned me in a way that made me want him inside me once more.

He groaned, "Feck, why do you have to be such a temptation? There's much to be done, and it would be wise for us to start the preparation process. We'll have all night to delight in one another."

"But ..." I walked alongside him and teasingly stroked his beautifully sculpted lower abs down to just above his dick. "What if you have another problem before the coronation and wedding?"

He caught my wrist but didn't move it. "We'll just have to savor the anticipation." He grimaced as he moved my hand away, as if doing so pained him. "But I am pleased to hear that the sigil turned gold for you. That means you are unequivocally Fate's winner in the trials, and I want to take you back to your guest room so that you can see your prize."

I nuzzled into him, not in the mood to be separated. The hard planes of his body pressed against me, and his wonderful smoky, spicy scent filled my nostrils. "You mean I won a prize other than you?"

He growled again, then kissed my forehead. "*I* am the true winner."

"And I don't want to leave you for a moment. We've been separated long enough. If we go out, people will see us, and they'll want to talk." The thought of staying in bed and sharing our bodies with each other thrilled me. I understood that, for royalty's sake, the coronation and the wedding were required, but maybe we could work something out where we got ready in here instead of having to be apart.

"I have a solution." He smiled and trapped me between his body and the wall.

If he was trying to calm me down, he wasn't doing a great job. My wolf whined with the urge to be even closer to him.

Vad leaned in and put his hands on either side of my head. "There are ways to allow for faster transportation throughout the palace and realms without walking. Spells and charms alike can help. Some people embed the sigils into jewelry or bracers or something similar. Some make it temporary. That room obviously won't be your regular quarters anymore, of course."

"Oh? Whose room am I staying in?" I smiled.

He narrowed his eyes and grinned. "My woman sleeps in my bed with me." A low growl curled from his throat and set me on fire. "Which is why it is now known as *our* bed."

"Even if I want to sleep somewhere else because someone doesn't want me to have all the blankets?" I cocked my head and pouted.

"I assure you, my queen, I will always keep you at the perfect temperature. So long as I have any say, we will never sleep apart." He kissed my chin, then my nose, then my lips. "And rest assured, my body will always be at your disposal." He kissed me and pulled back a little with a groan. "Now ... as I was saying, I'm having Thalen put a charm in your former room so that I can whisk you there."

"Why on earth would I want to go back to that room?" I tugged at his hair and whispered against his ear, "I like what's in this room far better."

He shuddered. "These chambers will be far less grand in your absence." He kissed me slowly then pulled back. "After Thalen places the charm, I can take you directly to your room through the shadows and my magic rather than having to pass through the halls and risk you being seen."

"Clever. But how am I to get back to *our* room without

being seen, hmm? And that still doesn't answer why I would want to be in there without you."

"If you would let me finish, I would tell you." He smirked and took my hands in his. His thumb caressed the backs of my hands. "In a bridal competition such as this, Fate's ultimate winner will have her bedchamber transformed to celebrate her victory. Fate even provides the gown in which you are to be coronated and married. It will be uniquely designed and tailored to you, and it will not be wearable by anyone else."

My heart skipped as my chest expanded, and I squeezed his hands tighter. "Fate really designs a dress? Through magic?" No one had ever designed a dress for me. I got my clothes from thrift stores and bargain sales. "What if you decided not to pick me? What would happen?"

"It's a beautiful honor, and I wouldn't think of depriving you of it. If I had not chosen you as queen, you would still have received the dress because Fate blesses the one she chooses. As for how you will get back, you'll take this." He opened the wardrobe and reached inside.

I could just make out that the shelf had numerous small boxes.

When he drew his hand out, he held a small box with the lid up and a small gold ring with a black stone nestled inside. "This will bring you here. As you learn to use the magic, you'll be able to enter other open rooms in the royal family quarters as well as other restricted spaces throughout the palace. But let's keep it simple. When you want to use it, press any of your fingers against the stone and visualize yourself in this room. The magic will see to the rest." He slid the ring onto my pinky finger and beamed. "By Fate, this looks like it was always meant to be yours."

"Guess I'll have to be careful not to lose it then." I lifted a brow. "Otherwise, we might wind up with more surprise guests in your living room or, even worse, in our bedroom."

He smirked, then nuzzled me before stepping away. "Yes, well, that would be exceptionally unfortunate for anyone who tried. I don't share what's mine. I'm not even fond of others seeing you at all, unless all they are capable of is admiration. But, to your point, the ring isn't something to concern yourself about. It is bound to you now. It will work only inside the castle and without risk to you. Beyond that, it may take some building of your skills. For instance, you won't be able to use it to come straight back after we visit your sister. We'll have to go to a portal for that."

"Can we see Ember soon?" I bit the inside of my cheek as I watched him walk away, feeling the chill of his absence. "I don't want to stay there forever, but I do miss her. She's protected me from so much, and we've always been there for each other."

"Very soon." He picked up his robe and wrapped it around me, his hands lingering to massage my shoulders in lazy strokes and then sliding down to briefly cup my breasts. His throaty groan confirmed how hard it was for him to pull free, and I knew well that that wasn't the only thing hard now.

Smiling, I burrowed into the soft fabric and inhaled his scent. If I couldn't have his body around me, this was the closest thing to heaven.

Vad dressed, but he didn't bother to tuck in his shirt. He didn't even put on boots. Instead, after pulling on a shirt and pants, he crossed into the bathroom and returned with a small vial of blue-green oil and deposited it into his pocket. He bowed and extended a hand to me as if we were about to dance. "Allow me to escort you."

"Just don't let me go." I dropped into a half curtsy, and he swept me closer.

"Never," he whispered into my ear, his voice so low I felt it more than heard it. The heat of his breath stole mine, as did the light tickling of his jaw against the sensitive skin behind my ear and along the side of my neck.

Smoky shadow wisps curled around us. Some actually stroked me when darkness swept over us, while his arm secured itself tightly around my waist.

The scent of cinnamon, ginger, smoke, leather, and something rather like roses and lilies reached me in a glorious, conflicting mass of scents. I blinked as we appeared in my trial room, and my eyes widened.

My mouth dropped open. Vad hadn't been joking about Fate changing it.

The whole room had been transformed into an elegant black bridal suite. The bed was gone, and in its place was a massive vanity. Three full-length mirrors were situated in front of a small stool, and a black velvet settee and a broad, flat ottoman completed the space. In the very center of the room, sitting on an embroidered black-and-copper rug, stood a large octagonal box that was as tall as Vad.

The copper wolf mask still hung on the wall but was now framed by a large arch of black and white flowers with a few copper dahlias woven in. Beneath it was a small table holding a chilled bottle of some beverage, two flute glasses, and an assortment of tasty bites. My stomach grumbled at the sight of what looked like little brownie squares, blackberry trifle on shortbread, sausages stuffed with herbal cheese, and little shish kabobs of grilled meat and veggies. My mouth watered, and my wolf whimpered at the sight of meat.

"Is that safe?" I placed a hand on Vad's arm. Though I didn't like refusing good food, just diving in didn't seem like the smartest course since we had no way of telling whether anyone had tampered with it. So many things had gone wrong already. It was a hard thing to resist when my stomach cramped again, and my wolf tugged at me once more in complaint.

Vad sighed and looked over the spread. "Fair enough. Probably best if we don't partake. Fate may have provided the food initially, but it's always possible someone came in and messed with it since I haven't secured the room." He kissed the top of my head. "Do you want me to get you something? I could select it for you myself and bring it straight here."

"That seems likely to raise suspicions." I cast another look around the suite and found myself smiling. I felt almost ... giddy, even without being able to eat the food.

"Not if I do it properly." He booped me on the nose, winked, then stepped back. He then removed a small vial of oil and poured some on his finger.

The scent of sandalwood and sesame oil flared through the room. With a satisfied grunt and a flourish, he marked a sign on the door. "No one other than family is now permitted to enter. It's not just blood family, so right now it does include Thalen, but he won't come barging in on you. Neither will Elara, as she is going to be far too busy preparing for the coronation and wedding. You'll be safe. After this is finished, if there is someone whom you view as close as family and wish to add them to the marking."

Some weight lifted from my shoulders. I hadn't realized the magnitude of all the things I had endured and how much it had all been pressing on me. "That's a relief."

"I'm glad." He brushed a strand of hair behind my ear and asked, "Is there anything special you want to eat? I was thinking of some sort of meat and sweets since I'm sure you had neither in that void of a prison."

My stomach rumbled loudly, causing him to laugh.

The way he threw his head back was the most carefree I'd ever seen him, and my heart skipped a beat.

"I take that as your approval." Shadows swept around him. "And, my love, please wait until after I bring food and leave for the second time before you open the doors to see your dress. I'm not supposed to see it before the coronation and wedding." Then he vanished.

My entire body felt lighter, and my cheeks ached, making me realize that I was smiling so widely.

I turned to find that the bathroom had been likewise transformed. A range of oils and bath salts had been placed near the tub, and both the vanity and the wash basin held an assortment of oils, salves, and powders.

Opening one of the drawers at the bottom of the vanity, my stomach swooped. A pair of iridescent, pearly white sneakers with thick soles had Shadow written on one, and the other said Queen.

Laughter bubbled from deep within. Fate had thought of everything, and I loved that she was just as petty as I.

In a swirling twist of smoky shadows, Vad returned, holding a silver tray of small dishes and two bottles, one green and one dark purple. He set the tray on the vanity and gestured. "Blackberry crostinis, blood sausage croquettes, bone marrow in onion, elk jerky with smoked salt and goat cheese, fig bites with seared venison, ashmoon quail eggs, and venison bites. Then to drink, this is sparkling water from the mountains, and this is another bottle of copper mead, similar to the one Fate provided."

"You didn't have to do that." My mouth watered, and my gaze fixed on the meats. I rushed over and picked up one of the fried balls he'd said was a blood sausage croquette. It had been days since I had had anything other than that horrible dry black bread.

As soon as I sank my teeth into it, the savory iron flavor exploded over my tongue with a rich medley of peppery spices and a hint of something like nutmeg. "Mmmm."

His smile broadened as I devoured another. "I had a

feeling you needed red meat. Our wedding dinner will include a great number of delicious grilled, seared, and fried meats, all for you." He set the tray down on the table, then kissed the top of my head.

I purred happily and hugged him as I finished chewing. A few crumbs fell onto his tunic and rolled off.

"Eat all you wish, my love," he whispered. "I need you at full strength tonight. My mind brims with all the things I want to do with you."

Need curled in my stomach, and I rubbed against him. "So does mine." Considering how I felt for him, I struggled to believe that this realm didn't have fated mates. I would've sworn he was mine if it did.

His chest rumbled, making me want to jump him.

Instead of pulling me closer, he stepped back and stared at me with hungry eyes. "Finish your preparations, beloved. Nourish yourself. Then return to my chambers in an hour, and I will personally escort you to the coronation."

With that, he vanished once more in smoke.

My stomach somersaulted, and I shivered, wishing the hour would fly by. After all that time in hell, I couldn't believe how I was feeling right now.

I popped another meaty appetizer into my mouth, enjoying the smoky, savory, spiced saltiness of what he'd brought me. It drove all memory of the dark, bitter bread from my mind. As I finished up, my gaze returned to the octagonal box.

It had to hold the wedding dress. I couldn't see any locks or fasteners on it. After wiping my hands clean, I brushed my fingertips along the cool wood, searching for the way to open it.

The walls of the octagonal box fell away and vanished, leaving behind a stunning wedding gown. My breath caught in my throat as I stared at the glistening fabric. When Vad had said that Fate would create a dress perfect for me, I'd expected something simple and plain. Probably black. Especially with the decor she had chosen for the bridal suite.

But this ... this dress ... it was as if Fate had reached into my mind and plucked a secret fantasy that I hadn't dared to dream until right this moment. Situated on a headless ebony mannequin, the floor-length gown was all shifting shades of rose, gold, and pale blue, like the colors couldn't make up their mind. The skirts spilled across the floor in waves, each one edged with little sparks that caught the light—beads, maybe ... or stardust. I covered my mouth in awe as I circled it.

The bodice cradled the breasts with a low V and sculpted off the shoulder straps for the sleeves. The whole dress was scattered with tiny crystal beads that shimmered as I moved around it. Layers of silk—no, something finer than silk—overlapped at the hips, curling like petals caught mid-breeze. If I tilted my head, I saw the faint outlines of butterflies worked into the sheen, similar to the butterfly tattoo that still pulsed on my hand, but in rose gold, pale lavender, and ice blue.

For good measure, I cleaned up in the bathroom once again, washing myself and enjoying the soaps and soft fragrances. The cinnamon vanilla smelled the best, and I used the matching oil to scent my hair. In less than an hour, I'd be Vad's queen and bride. The thought had my stomach somersaulting.

As I stepped into the dress, the fabric responded to my touch, yielding easily and then wrapping around me as if drawn on by invisible hands. My skin prickled. The dress fit like a glove, the cool fabric swiftly warming to the perfect temperature and supporting my breasts, putting every curve on display.

I trailed a hand over the shimmering skirt and half-laughed, half-sighed. A giddiness spread through me as if this were a dream.

But then reality crashed over me.

Ember wasn't here, nor were my parents. Granted, having

my parents here was impossible, as they'd passed. But when I was a little girl, I'd always dreamed of my parents knowing and approving of the man I loved and mated with. However, not having Ember and the rest of my packmates here to stand beside me and be part of this memory didn't feel right. The last memory I had of Ember was of her panicked face when the fae had taken me from Earth.

As if the ground were impacted by my memory, the floor beneath me shook with a hollow, gut-punch thud.

I yelped and stumbled as the palace came alive, moving in an unnatural way. The huge mirrors rattled in their frames. Glass bottles in the bathroom clanked and crashed. The bottle of mead fell from the table and shattered, filling the air with the sweet, ripe scent of spiced honey and apricots as the amber liquid poured onto the rug. The remnants of the meal Vad had brought me and the tray of appetizers Fate had provided fell as well. The dishes clattered and rolled while a few smashed.

Shrieks from the other contestants came from the hall.

The trio of mirrors rocked forward, and I lunged at them, barely catching them before they fell. Silt and dust rained down from the ceiling as everything continued to rattle. Then, just as fast as it had come, the shaking stopped.

My heart raced as I trembled. There'd been earthquakes in the prison and during the last trial, but this one had lasted longer and been stronger. Whatever was going on, my gut warned me that it was worsening.

Taking deep breaths, I tried to calm my racing heart. I had to focus. The earthquake had stopped, and though Ember wasn't here now, Vad had promised he'd take me to Earth to visit her soon.

I straightened the mirrors with care and then stepped back just as something damp brushed against my ankle. I frowned, realizing I had stepped in some of the copper mead that now soaked the floor. Lifting my skirts, I stepped off the rug and laughed bitterly. New dress, and it was stained within minutes of me wearing it.

That sounded about right.

I hoped Vad hadn't gotten injured during the earthquake. I understood him not wanting to see me in the dress prior, but worry nudged at me.

As I stooped to blot the fabric dry with a handkerchief, the smell of lilacs, earth, and roses flashed into the room.

My blood boiled as I spun around and saw gray wisps spiraling around Many-Greats. He wore dark charcoal garments, as if he intended to blend into the shadows.

I straightened and crossed my arms, glaring at him. "Why am I not surprised you'd show up where I've been sleeping? Can't you just portal outside the door and knock like a decent person?"

Many-Greats scowled. "I warned you, young lady. I didn't want it to come to this, but you have left me with no choice. I told you that you can't marry him, and the vow he gave me was meant to protect you. I'm doing this for your own good."

So it was *him*.

Bastard.

My fists clenched as I stepped toward him. "You're the one who tried to force Vad to let me g—"

He twisted his hand, and a shard of silver light pierced me in the throat. A cold paralysis spread over me, and my voice vanished. Icy fear spiked through me. *What had he done?* My legs locked ... and I collapsed.

He caught me before I could fall to the ground and draped me over the ottoman. "I didn't want to have to do this, but you have to go home to your sister."

Crossing to the mark Vad had made on the door, Many-Greats smeared the outer rim of the sigil, changing its form.

No!

What is he doing? This can't be happening!

My mind screamed, and my wolf howled. My eyelids tried to open wider, but they became heavier with each breath. My wolf tried to surge forward, but my vision darkened. Something thick and suffocating wrapped around me as if cutting me off from everything.

Many-Greats moved in front of me. "Why couldn't you or that fool of a prince just listen? I was clear with you, Briar. You have no concept of what you being with him would do." He picked me up, his arms shockingly strong. "You'll thank me when you're home with Ember."

The door creaked open, giving me enough of an adrenaline burst to peek.

Let it be Vad, please.

It wasn't him. Instead, Calla Lily stood in the doorway in a pale pink dress, her leathery pink wings tucked against her back.

Relief surged through me. Surely she had to see that something was wrong. I fought to twitch my fingers or give some sign, but honestly, the sight of a young woman being physically carried off by someone had to raise questions even among the fae.

Calla Lily gasped and covered her mouth. "Oh, no! What's this?"

"None of your concern. She fell ill. I'm helping her." Many-Greats lied as easily as he breathed, despite the sulfur stench hitting me. "Either fetch a physician or go. I'd recommend the latter. I hold a position of great authority on the High Aureline Council, and I can assure you my connections are far better than yours."

Calla Lily stepped all the way inside and closed the door. A sly smile tugged at her mouth, twisting into something ugly.

"Oh, I know exactly who you are, old man, and I've got you right where I want you."

My stomach curdled, and dread spiraled through me. My consciousness hung on by a thread. Many-Greats' grip on me tightened.

Lifting her chin, Calla Lily laughed low in her throat. Her red-brown eyes gleamed with delight. "Let's talk about what happens next, shall we? I think it's safe to say you owe me big now."

Chapter Twenty-Eight

Terror and hot rage bolted through me, and I nearly fell into the railing of the Ceremonial Hall's dais. My heart squeezed, and my hand clutched at my chest. *What in the fecking void was that?* A single panicked thought seared through my mind: *Briar.*

Vyraetos placed his hand on my shoulder. "Are you all right, Your Highness?"

We'd just endured yet another earthquake, and yet the old man was steadier on his feet than I was. I straightened and kept gripping the marble railing. "Yes," I forced out. A bitter taste coated my tongue. The odd sensation in my chest twisted, then vanished.

I wanted to portal to Briar at once, but I was at the front of the Ceremonial Hall, which had been charmed and sigiled against using any such magic. I needed to go to the sigil on the other side of the doors to be able to use my magic. My shadows coiled uneasily around my ankles, lashing out and pressing up against the walls.

The sensation vanished, but the dread refused to leave. It weighed on me more heavily than anything I'd experienced before, and my chest seemed cold. Was it the earthquake? Perhaps, but none of the others had done this to me. Even the previous symptoms of the weakening magic had not been this bad.

The Ceremonial Hall had fared better than expected. The quake had shifted things more than it had shattered, but it had lasted longer than the previous ones.

Nausea churned within me, and my head thundered. My grip on the magic of this kingdom was slipping, and it soured within me. The coronation and wedding couldn't happen soon enough.

Vyraetos gave a mournful shake of his head. "A pity the vesting didn't hold longer. It's good that this will be over and done with so soon. It cannot be hidden any longer."

"Agreed." I scanned the hall as the servants milled about, frantically adjusting and reordering furnishings and décor. The long red carpet running down the center of the hall from the towering onyx double doors to the front dais had been pushed partly aside in places where black benches had scooted into it, and unlit black torches lay across it.

A pair of servants moved through the two broad seating sections on either side of the carpet, checking for damage. We had less than half an hour before people would start arriving, and I had to finish overseeing the final preparations, then dress in my royal raiment and return to greet the essential dignitaries and council members.

The black and gold marble dais had several hairline fractures, but the orchestra box had escaped mostly unscathed. Luckily, the two high-backed thrones on the smaller dais were simply slightly askew.

The only thing that had remained perfectly in place was the massive shadow beast banner that hung from the ceiling and above the thrones. The shadow beast's red eye looked out over the grand hall with cunning and wisdom, the weaving itself so vivid that it looked real.

An unsettling sensation passed through me, my stomach twisting again, and the sense of urgency intensified.

"Do whatever is necessary to finalize preparations then." I set my hands on my belt and lowered my head, fighting a grimace. Another spasm passed through me, and my veins burned. Feck. This was getting bad, and I didn't know how to stop it.

"Colm Ainle will almost assuredly inquire again about the execution." Vyraetos clasped his hands behind his back. "I have thus far kept him at bay by telling him that all plans have been placed on hold because we've been forced to advance the coronation so swiftly and because we don't yet know the identities of the co-conspirators, so his expertise is unneeded."

"He doesn't have to be pleased right now. He just has to stay out of the way," I muttered. "Make sure there are extra guards present here. Loyal ones. Captain Finbar will be in attendance as well." Briar coming onto the dais and kneeling to receive the crown and take vows would create a scene. I'd already warned Thalen to be ready with his circle of silence, and he had promised to use it to excellent effect.

I wished more than anything that I could visit Briar right this moment. Generally speaking, it wasn't considered wise for a groom to see his bride in her full regalia before a wedding, but after all that had happened, I didn't care about tradition. As soon as I was out of this damnably long hall, I'd portal to her room and make sure she was all right.

I continued down the staircase, pushing down the sensation of nausea. My shadows coiled tighter around me.

Attendants darted up to me with last-minute questions even as I quickened my pace. I answered brusquely. The black armored winged guards at the massive double doors stood to attention and opened them for me as I approached. Almost there. Just a few feet more until I could be with Briar once more.

To the void with bad luck!

I'd barely reached the threshold, though, when Calla Lily ran up to me, her eyes wide and tears streaming down her cheeks. She clasped a folded piece of parchment in one hand. "Your Highness," she sobbed. "Your Highness, I'm so sorry." She handed me the letter.

The two guards at the door looked to me, their grips tightening on their spears as they angled them in her direction.

I didn't take the letter and drew back a step to stop her before she could even attempt to touch me. I scowled. "What's going on?" I tried to keep my voice level, but I wanted her to leave so I could reach my beloved.

She covered her mouth with one hand, then tried to hand me the folded parchment again. "Forgive me, Your Highness." She continued to keep her hand outstretched with trembling fingers and clearly wasn't going to leave until I acknowledged whatever the letter held.

My frown deepened as I snatched the letter away, avoiding brushing her fingers. It weighed more than I expected, the wax seal nothing more than a blob of white candlewax. But the paper smelled like cinnamon and ginger, and my stomach dropped. Dread rose within me.

I opened it carefully.

The onyx ring slipped out and onto my palm, and my heart chilled. The black inked letters, written in a hasty, sprawling script with little hearts over any letter with a dot, blurred on the page.

Vad,

I'm sorry to tell you this way, and I hope you can forgive me. Please know that this decision was not made lightly.

As much as I thought I cared about you, I've realized my

priorities were wrong.

I belong to another life, one that comes with my own duties and expectations. I'm both upset and ashamed that it took me this long to remember who truly has my loyalty.

You were a dream and a lie. My sister needs me. The pack needs me. I have to go back, and I'm leaving right now. Don't try to find me, ever.

I've decided to keep the dress. I couldn't bear to part with it after everything, and it will remind me of you, of our moments, and of the way you looked at me like I was a rare unicorn. I will treasure it even as I return to the world that needs me.

I want to reiterate to the fullest measure that you shouldn't come looking for me. That would only cause more complications and pain, and you deserve peace. You deserve a queen who is strong and certain of her place beside you. You must trust the will of the councils. They know what is best for the kingdom, and they will tell you who has been chosen.

As for us—–there never truly was an "us," was there? It was always something ... brief. Temporary. An escapade of sorts. But I will think of it—-of you—-fondly.

Goodbye, Vad. Do not grieve. This is for the best.

With sincere warmth and a wish for you to thrive,

Briar

My mind spun, and I stumbled. No.

No!

My heart ripped apart to where I couldn't feel it anymore.

This was *wrong*. It didn't make sense at all. She'd wanted us both to visit her sister. Why would she do this, and why wouldn't she tell me to my face?

Though my mouth went dry, I forced myself to swallow and steadied my grip on the letter. I peered at Calla Lily over the parchment and fixed her with a stern glare. "You speak of this to no one under pain of death, do you understand?" Misunderstanding or not, I didn't want anyone to know that Briar was still alive yet. "Who else knows of this?"

She bowed her head, still trembling. "She only told me."

That was odd. Why Calla Lily? I shook my head and gestured toward the hall beyond the great doors as Thalen approached. "Go."

"I'm so sorry, Your Highness," she said, bowing her head. Turning, she fled.

Thalen spread his arms, and his wings mirrored the movement, catching the golden torchlight on his silver feathers as he continued toward me. "Breaking more hearts?"

I thrust the letter at him and drew a hand over my mouth. I wanted to vomit, but my stomach cramped around nothing. This wasn't happening. It made no sense. How could it be real?

Thalen's eyes widened as he read the letter. His fingers crumbled the edge of the page. "This isn't from her, Vad."

One of the attendants approached me, wearing a dark gray uniform, his blonde hair swept back and tied in a low ponytail. "Your Highness, the princess wishes to inform you that she awaits your presence in the welcome alcove so that you may both greet the arriving dignitaries and royals. Two delegations have already arrived."

Feck. I still had to get dressed. A tight breath hissed through my teeth. We were running out of time. "Tell her I will be there in a few minutes." I massaged my temples and motioned for Thalen to come with me. He lowered the letter and folded it, but his posture tightened, his smile flattening into a scowl.

"This *isn't* her," Thalen said again.

"Then who is it?" I gritted my teeth.

He shook his head grimly. "I don't know, but this doesn't even sound like her. She'd never say you were a lie and to not come look for her once, let alone twice. Maybe someone got to her and threatened her?"

"How?" I demanded, shifting my weight back. My shadows boiled, and I ached to explode in a maddening display of rage and terror. "No one could enter her room if they weren't family, and she has no family here. Elara wouldn't have told her anything remotely like the contents of that letter. If the entire palace fell down, an orb of protection would remain around that room, so long as the sigil remained. Even if the earthquake damaged the door, how would *anyone* have gotten in there in time to convince her to go away?"

I pressed a hand to my head, everything inside me shattering. I could barely think through the splitting headache that now swept over me and the way my body felt as if I'd lost a part of myself.

"Let's go to her room," I commanded, grabbing his hand and portaling us both there.

We landed in the center of the room, which had been torn apart by either the earthquake or someone who had gotten to her. A sour taste filled my mouth as my worst fear turned true.

She wasn't here.

My gaze went to the sigil I'd made to protect her.

I stumbled, and my breath caught. Someone *had* altered it ... or had I drawn it wrong? My head spun, and I inhaled deeply. There was no other distinctive scent in the room.

No. I knew I'd drawn it correctly, and Briar wouldn't know how to change it. Even if she'd agreed to go home, she wouldn't have left without talking to me. She wasn't a coward. Someone had forced her to leave.

I wanted to search for her, but everyone would notice, especially with diplomats and dignitaries arriving.

That didn't matter. The tug in my chest intensified, urging me to rip the palace apart to find her.

Thalen moved around the room ... and froze. "She hasn't been gone long, Vad. The trail is fresh."

The floor tilted under my feet, and I stumbled toward the door as more nausea rolled through me. Blood pounded in my ears. I had to get to her. If she was leaving, I had to see with my own eyes and hear with my own ears, and if someone had taken her, I was going to rip them apart.

Thalen grabbed my arm. "Hey! Where are you going? You've got to go down and be the prince, soon to be the king."

"Get out of my way!" I shook free and shoved him back.

He struck the wall and leaped back up, wings flaring out as he cut in front of me. He flung his hands up, and a blast of icy wind slammed into my face.

I staggered back, grunting and swearing as my boots slid across shattered glass and ceramics. My shadows flared up and hooked toward him. "Feck you, Thalen! I'm going to find her and get her back."

"No, listen!" He kept his hands up, and his wings blocked the door entirely. "You have to calm down *for Briar.*"

My blistering rage quieted, and a pang of awareness struck me. But I lunged for Thalen anyway.

He shoved me back again, the wind knocking the mannequin over. "You're not thinking straight! Everyone will know something is going on because the coronation will be happening without a prince to become king! No matter whether Briar left on her own or someone kidnapped her, you'll be offering them a huge, gaping weakness. And if they kill you or take you down, you know they'll go after Briar next just as a matter of principle. Not to mention, everyone will see you if you go searching for her now, and if someone *has* taken her, they'll be informed. Let me go get her."

His words cut into me. My wings flexed as I clenched my fists, struggling to form thoughts through the maelstrom. If going after Briar would make her situation more precarious, then I couldn't. Somehow, I had to pull myself together.

Thalen's jaw set. "If you go looking for her, you'll lose her."

Fear strangled me. "*Fine.*" I dragged a hand through my hair, hollowness gaping within me. I couldn't lose control, but my restraint hung by a thread. "Go look for her. Check the tunnels that used to lead to the old portaling doors. The ones where we were supposed to meet Bryn Lugh. If she's been abducted, kill the abductors. If she's leaving, tell her—tell her that this is her choice. If what the letter said is true, I will accept it. I will love her no matter what happens. But ... ask her to come back just so that I can crown her queen. She can leave after that. I ..." I struggled to force out the words, but I meant them as much as they ached and stung. "I won't stop her. But there is no other queen for me, and I won't crown another.

"However, if she's been taken against her will, there's no body count too large."

Thalen's brow tweaked, and he lowered his hands. "If she's been abducted, don't you want us to take prisoners to interrogate—"

"No. Kill them. Kill them all. I'm tired of people taking her and thinking they can get away with it," I snarled. "We aren't wasting time with prisoners."

"You know she didn't leave you. She *loves* you."

My mind twisted as I agonized over the possibilities.

Loving me didn't mean she hadn't wanted to go back home. Hadn't I been prepared to let her go because I loved her? Or ... perhaps what she would have to sacrifice to be with me was too much. Maybe this person had said something to her that made her see things differently ... or maybe she'd been taken against her will. "Do it. Don't argue with her about her decision if it's what she says she wants." I'd talk with her anyway. I'd beg her to stay. And if, even after I pleaded, she wanted to go, I'd let her.

The thought of her not being my wife and queen broke me. I couldn't believe that the gorgeous, vibrant woman who had lain in my arms and bit me would simply choose to run like this. It didn't feel like Briar at all.

Dread spooled within me as Thalen bolted away and I portaled back to my chambers. It was like existing in a nauseating dream. The edges of my vision darkened.

She *had* to have been abducted. Between her telling Calla Lily, of all people, that she was leaving, and writing a letter? None of that was like her.

But how had someone gotten in? I *knew* I had drawn that sigil correctly.

My mind felt scrambled, and the hollow sensation intensified and spread through me. Had she shown signs of unhappiness or hesitation, and I'd missed them? What could have changed so fast? She'd been so upset when I had vowed to send her home—meaning Earth.

Thinking someone had kidnapped her against her will again made me see red.

Thalen was one of the best trackers I knew. If anyone could find her, he could. And I would get my vengeance on whoever was to blame.

Time passed in a blur. Somehow, I dressed in layers of silk and leather and fur, fastened my cufflinks, straightened the seams, and ensured every line was in its proper place and form.

Meeting Elara and greeting the select royals and dignitaries who wished to give their condolences and congratulations to us before the coronation went by in a haze.

Briar had to come back soon. Surely Thalen would catch her.

The Ceremonial Hall filled swiftly as the guests arrived. I paced inside the small chamber to the right of the dais, waiting for any sign of Briar and Thalen before the three blasts of the heraldic trumpet. A tug. A letter. Something!

A knock sounded, and a soft voice spoke on the other side. "The bride is in her chambers now, Your Highness. All is prepared."

I lunged toward the door and flung it open. The attendant drew back with terrified green eyes. "Your Highness?" She bowed her head once more.

"She's there? Is there any message?" I demanded. My wings flexed as my shadows stretched out. I didn't even try to draw them back. My heart galloped, but something still felt *wrong*.

However, even if Briar had come back to say no to forever, she was safe and would be crowned my queen.

"N-no message. She just ran up," the attendant stammered.

The heraldic trumpet blasted three times, piercing my skull. With a ragged sigh, I lowered my head, then drew myself up and closed the door. I'd find out soon whether Briar was returning to me as my queen or as my queen and my love. Whatever came next, I would honor her choice. Even if it destroyed me.

I strode onto the dais as the music swelled, choral voices interlacing in ancient harmonies as the drums beat and the strings sang. Practically every seat in the hall was filled.

Vyraetos stood before the coronation pedestal, which now held two crowns. The Shadow King's crown was forged from star metal and obsidian, all sharp angles and harsh lines with jagged peaks like the mountains at night.

At the center point was the head of the enchanted spear used by the first Shadow King to slay the ghost dragon that had tried to destroy our magic eons ago. The Shadow Queen's was smaller and more delicate, shaped with dark silver and midnight iron, braided together with thorns at the sides until it all came together in a central weaving shaped to resemble a full moon with roses.

My shadows hummed in anticipation, and the icy burn of my magic flowed through me.

Elara waited for me at the foot of the dais, her manner calm and a look of soft happiness upon her face. Her glamour had returned to full strength, and she wore a floor-length indigo gown with silver beads woven throughout like starlight in a midnight sky. Silus stood at attention in the first row, but Thalen wasn't there. My brow furrowed. If Thalen had gotten Briar back for the coronation, had she asked him to remain with her? Or was he trying to convince her to stay?

Physician Morlo was missing as well. His seat farther down the bench from Thalen and Silus was startlingly empty. Perhaps something had happened to delay him?

Briar's friends were among the assembled guests. They all sat near the front in fine garments. Veralt sat beside Rhielle with his broad arm flung around her shoulders. Calla Lily leaned over and whispered something to Rhielle from her seat at the end, and Rhielle shook her head with a sly smile before glancing at Veralt. He shrugged and responded. Whatever he'd said, Quen seemed to approve, and Yuki and Velessa whispered back and forth until Thalira motioned for them to stop. Myantha watched the front with wide eyes and rapt attention.

Flanking the sides of the dais were the members of the councils. On one side was the joint council of Aureline and Shadow, who had assisted with the trials. The rest of the Shadow

Council stood on the opposite side. They watched me from beneath their hoods, and my skin itched from the knowledge that at least some were still traitors yet to be exposed.

My nerves remained raw, my heart hammering. The discomfort within me intensified, and I wanted to crawl out of my skin. Briar was in the next room, but there was no tug of awareness. Did I always feel that tug when she was near, or only sometimes? But if she were here, why did I still feel like I was on the verge of breaking?

I barely registered Vyraetos picking up the Shadow King's crown and approaching me. He spoke of our people's sacred history and sacred duty, of how our magic flowed through the king and into the kingdom. His voice droned on and on, and I fought to keep my eyes away from the door that hid Briar from me. Everything within me tightened, and blood thundered in my ears.

Soon.

Vyraetos placed the crown upon my head. "Behold your king. Long live the king!"

His voice sounded as if it were coming from far away. Blood rolled down the sides of my face from where the points of the crown had pierced my skull, but I barely felt it. I could scarcely breathe as I kept my gaze fixed on the door.

"The trials have been given, the tests made. A queen has been searched for, tested, and seen. Behold now the one whom Fate, the councils, and the king himself have chosen." Vyraetos gestured toward the door on the left side of the dais.

Silently, the black wooden door opened beneath the arch of black and white roses, lilies, and other flowers. My breath caught, and my hands twitched as I forced myself to remain in place.

A shimmering blue skirt ghosted at the entrance, and then—Kaylen stepped out to greet me, dressed as a bride.

Chapter Twenty-Nine

Nausea roiled through my stomach, and when I tried to open my eyes, I couldn't, not even a little. My head pounded, and my entire body ached like I'd been in a horrible fight and knocked unconscious.

What the *hell* was going on?

My heartbeat quickened, and adrenaline pumped through my body. My arms and legs dangled, limp and useless, and my wrists were bound together by what felt like thick rope. Something pressed into my side.

Cold realization settled over me. What the *fuck*? I was slung over a shoulder and being jostled with every step.

Breathing in, I realized the air was so strong that I could taste its dry, stale, salty flavor.

Where am I?

I shook my head, but the sensation made me feel worse. The world was a smeared, shadowy swirl I was struggling to bring into focus. The wedding dress rustled with each step, and my abductor kept an arm banded tightly over my thighs.

Move.

I had to move.

My eyelids slid shut again. I tried pulling on my wolf, but

she didn't respond. All I felt was heat and nausea.

"Come on. Pick up the pace. I hate this place," a gruff voice ahead of me said. "Gives me the creeps. It's like something's waking up, and I don't want to be here when it does."

"Stop," the man carrying me said sharply. "Bryn Lugh said he gave her enough to put out a male timber wolf on steroids. He said that means she's down. Whatever that is. No way this little thing is waking up any time soon, and I'm not running. She's thin but sturdy."

Bastard. I'd show him.

Spite gave me an extra edge of energy. My limbs barely responded, but pins and needles stitched their way down to my fingertips. The heat burned hotter, allowing me to curl my hand into a half-fist.

I pried my eyes open and caught a glimpse of the floor—gray, coarse stone littered with dust. Boots. I was being carried over the shoulder of someone in a simple gray uniform without any insignia I could spot. His stride was methodical but urgent. A thick belt wrapped around his waist.

I listened, trying to orient myself, but it felt like a lost cause.

Ahead of us, more footsteps echoed.

I inhaled again, catching a whiff of old sweat and something sharper underneath—blood? My stomach clenched.

This time, I glimpsed the second person. Based on the gold light following him, I guessed he was holding a torch. Perhaps a weapon as well. With my luck, he had more than one. The man carrying me also had a dagger in a black sheath hanging on his belt. With my hands bound together, I could scrape my fingers on it. I just needed to reach a little farther down, and I could grab it.

My wolf remained asleep. I nudged her, trying to rouse her as I blinked, fighting for my vision to clear. She started to stir, but not much.

Come on! Wake up.

We turned a corner, the torchlight flickering. I tried to take in my surroundings and noted we were in an unfinished corridor that looked as if it had been carved out of rock, most of the stone unfinished and rough.

A puff of fresh air reached me, smelling brighter and cleaner. I flexed both hands, clenching and unclenching until the pins and needles intensified, then dissolved into heat.

Finally, my vision cleared.

The corridor opened into a larger, finished stone chamber. Charcoal black marble tiles covered most of the floor, though some were cracked and sat askew, probably due to the earthquake. The dark marble tiles on the walls had cracked and chipped as well, some panels falling away entirely and revealing the same coarse stone as in the corridor. It was hard to see clearly from my position, but there seemed to be several stone doorways standing in a line at the back of the room. Pale light filtered through one, but I couldn't see a door. I sucked a few more breaths through my nose, the stench of sweat and blood almost grounding.

The longer I took to get free, the harder it would be to get back to Vad. I had to move. Time was running out.

Strange fire burned through me, heating my entire body as the world seemed to churn around me.

The man carrying me paused and grunted. "Check to make sure it's going to the right place. He'll kill us if we send her to the wrong realm." His grip loosened as he adjusted the arm over my thighs.

As his grip loosened, I flexed my abdominal muscles and slipped forward just enough. My fingers wrapped around the hilt of the dagger before he noticed, and I yanked it up and jammed the blade into his lower back.

He roared and jerked. I slid off his shoulder, keeping

the dagger in hand, and hit the ground hard on my side, the iridescent folds of the wedding gown tangling around my legs. He crouched next to me, face twisted, and I shoved the dagger into him again—this time under his ribs. He crashed forward as I twisted away and ripped out the blade. Blood poured onto the marble, seeping into the cracks and pooling around the corpse.

I rolled out of the way, panting, the dagger still in my grip. My head was pounding, but I forced myself to stand up.

The second man stared, his hazel eyes wide with shock. He lifted his sword. "How in the void are you even standing?"

I bared my teeth at him as fiery rage poured through my veins. "You tried to take me from *him*!"

"You don't—" The man's eyes bugged out, and several small silver lines hissed through the air and into his chest, slicing clean through him. He pitched forward, face-first, into the pool of his own blood with a sickening squelch.

I spun around, dagger lifted, ready to attack.

And stopped short.

Thalen?

He stood beneath the raw stone opening of the corridor. "What're you thinking, Chaos? Taking all the fun for yourself?" He *tsk*ed and furrowed his brow in a mock pretense of annoyance.

"Thalen!" I staggered forward and hugged him. "I'm so glad to see you!"

"As you should be, Chaos. I'm pretty happy to see you too." He hugged me fiercely, the strength of his grip belying his casual teasing tone.

He pulled back, his hands on my shoulders. "We don't have time to chit-chat. If you still want to marry Vad, we've got to get you back to the Ceremonial Hall." He guided me back through the raw stone archway and back into the rough-hewn corridor. "I'm assuming this wasn't a consensual passage through the portal?" He launched into a run.

"No!" I ran alongside him. Heated energy surged through me, burning through whatever it was Many-Greats had done to me. Multiple paths branched off from the one we ran along, and our footsteps thundered and echoed off the stone walls and low ceiling. "Many-Greats kidnapped me!" He'd warned me never to reveal our relationship, but fuck that. He'd given up his right to any secrets. Now wasn't the time to talk about it though.

"Not sure who in the void that is, but feck him." Thalen pointed to a turn ahead and gripped my arm. "Vad's about to go out of his head. If you wanted to go home, he said he'd understand, but he wants you to be his queen, even if you do go back to Earth. He's never going to have another. Between you and me, I think he's about half a thread short of snapping and wrecking the whole coronation and wedding."

My chest warmed. That was possibly one of the sweetest things I'd ever heard. He was as crazy for me as I was for him. I might have laughed if it weren't for the intense energy surging through me and the deep, pressing need to get to him.

Panic worked inside me, along with a rage that didn't quite feel like my own. It twisted in my stomach and pounded in my skull. "Can we portal there?"

"Not until we're past the sigils and spells," he said grimly. "No one's supposed to be down here—period. It was sealed off and enchanted. We won't be able to portal at all until we're past the first seal. Keep your eyes peeled in case there's anyone else down here. The air smells too fresh. We might have company."

My body tensed. I needed to get to Vad, not fight more enemies.

VAD

RAGE POURED THROUGH me, vibrating in my veins as I

stared at the wretched abomination who dared to stand in my bride's place.

"You are *not* my bride!" I roared. My shadows exploded out as my fangs lengthened and my claws emerged. My wings flared out, striking the air and joining with my shadows. I cast a furious look over the shocked and terrified assembly.

Good. They should fear me. If I couldn't have Briar, then I'd wreck this all to the void and kill anyone who tried to replace my beloved.

I gestured, refusing to look at Kaylen again. "That *vile* and *selfish* creature is not my bride. She won none of the trials, and she is not Fate's choice, but most of all, she is not *my* choice. Get that fecking wench out of my sight!"

Kaylen fell back, paling. The iridescent blue gown seemed dark against her pallor. "I-I was chosen," she said, her hand lifting to her collarbone. A bright flush appeared on her cheeks and collarbone as she drew back.

"Get out!" I bellowed, slashing my arm out. My shadows lashed, some striking the railing and others knocking down the flowers that hung at intervals. The sweet scent of roses and lilies intensified. I craved Briar's scent, my lungs filling with the desperate need to smell that warm cinnamon ginger.

Everyone fell deathly silent, staring with lined faces of worry, mouths open with shock, and expressions frozen in terror.

Blood dripped down the sides of my face. "You are not worthy of the crown. You are not worthy of my family. You are not worthy to be queen," I snarled, stepping toward her.

Kaylen drew back, silver eyes shining with fear. "But—"

I cut her off with a vicious sweep of my hand. "Even if the council did, I did *not* choose you!" I advanced another step, my shadows writhing around me like living serpents. "You think you can steal what belongs to another? You think you can take her place? You think you want me? Will you want me when my shadows rip you to pieces and pour out your lifeblood on the seal of the Shadow Kingdom?"

A hand tugged at my arm, and I twisted around to see Elara. She shook her head with wide eyes. "Vad, please calm—"

I jerked my arm free. "She deserves death."

"The Shadow King is correct that Kaylen is not the choice of the councils." Bryn's voice rang out across the Ceremonial Hall, sounding more tremulous than I'd ever heard it. He moved out from the benches into the center aisle.

Unlike the council members in the front, he was not wearing a hood that obscured his face, and his usually wild hair had been neatly combed back.

Kaylen gasped. "What? But—"

Bryn silenced her with a look, and her shoulders sagged as if he had struck her. Two of the wingless Aureline guards approached her. Where had they even come from? My guards approached more slowly, seeming to exchange looks as if to ask who took precedence.

He'd better have Briar, or I would slit his throat here, happily.

"The Aureline choice is in accordance with the winner of the trials. There was an error in formalities and procedures, for which we are truly apologetic, but Fate's choice is ... Calla Lily." Bryn gestured to his right.

My stomach twisted, and I froze again in pure rage. More blood dripped into my eyes. He had to be behind this.

Calla Lily rose, one hand rising to her chest as she demurely curtsied. "I am at the service of the Shadow Kingdom."

The feck she was. My shadows expanded, searching for Briar and for vengeance.

The council members exchanged glances, most looking between one another, though a few simply stared straight ahead.

"Calla Lily not only survived all three of the challenges, but she was the gold winner of the third and final trial, in which character was tested." Bryn didn't glance at Calla Lilly and sounded as if he'd rehearsed the line over and over again.

"Liar!" Veralt stood, towering over the seated guests. "That pink-winged girlie didn't win shit in the last competition. That was Briar, through and through. She won it fair and square, and there were folk sent in there to try to kill her too."

Briar's friends jumped to their feet around him.

Shocked murmurs rippled out among the crowd. "The king's assassin?"

"The girl from the other world?"

"The outsider?"

"The weird shadow-beast woman?"

Bryn paled. "I do not know who you are or why you think you have the authority to speak against the will of the High Aureline Council, as well as the Aureline Council members who participated in the oversight of the bridal competition." None of the Aureline Council members at the front moved.

I wanted Bryn's blood. Had he been involved in my father's death as well? Rage boiled within me, seething as my shadows lashed out. The stone railing cracked, and one of the spokes shattered.

Calla Lily's gaze darted around the room as she took a half step toward me. "I am Fate's choice as well as the choice of the Aurelines involved in this test, and I am willing to serve. I mean no harm."

"No *harm*?" Something hot flared inside me that I didn't understand, and my shadows gripped the railings harder and tighter. More spokes shattered and splintered, exploding outward.

Vyraetos held out his hands, looking around with pure confusion on his aged features. "No one informed the Shadow

Council that Calla Lily was the winner. To my knowledge, there was no determined winner because of the disruption with the earthquake. Is this not so?"

Bryn cleared his throat. "It was clarified—"

"You are part of this conspiracy!" I snarled. It would mean instant war if I murdered a member of the High Aureline Council, but I didn't care. Not anymore. "Are you among the traitors who sought to destroy my beloved and frame her for the murder of my father? Were you involved in his death?" Darkness loomed within the hall. My madness was on full display as my claws lengthened. They cut into my palms, but I didn't care.

He had fooled me and taken Briar from me. That sin alone meant death.

Bryn fell back, and his liquid gold eyes widened even more.

Elara gripped my arm again. "Vad—" Panic filled her voice. "Vad, please—"

I looked at my sister, a desperate plan forming in my mind. I could pass the crown and the throne to her. Let the magic transfer to her. Then I'd find Briar. I'd give all this up for her. Every shred. Every moment. Nothing mattered as much as Briar did.

The doors at the end of the Ceremonial Hall slammed open, striking the walls and shaking as the guards barely ducked out of the way in time.

Vad.

My heart stopped. Briar's voice had sounded in my head, and something yanked in my chest.

I sucked in a breath.

There she was in the Ceremonial Hall, at the start of the red carpet, standing between the heavy doors. Her copper hair was loose and wild about her shoulders, framing her face. Those green eyes met mine from across the room.

My beloved.

My queen.

My all.

She was a vision, despite the dirt and dust and blood smeared across the iridescent gown that Fate had made for her. Anyone viewing her now would see the difference between her dress and the others and would know that she was the one Fate had marked. This woman was not just my queen. She alone held my entire heart.

"Briar," I whispered. "You're here."

Bryn's eyes widened as he looked from Briar to me, and he stretched out a hand. His face went deathly pale. "No!"

But I ignored him. *Nothing* would keep her from me ever again. It was time to claim her once and for all.

I turned and grabbed the queen's crown.

Trying to block me from Briar, Bryn said, "No, you don't understand. She's an Aur—"

Velessa sprang up on her bench and raised her hand in a grasping motion, silencing him as Veralt picked him up and moved him out of the center aisle, Yuki flanking the giant.

Three wingless Aureline guards started toward Briar, but Rhielle's shadows swept in front of them. Her pupils faded away entirely as her shadows sealed them in. Quen, Thalira, and Myantha raced down the aisle toward two more guards, parting them and letting Briar through as she ran toward me.

The thorns on the queen's crown pricked my palms and fingers, but I held it tightly and leaped off the dais, then raced toward Briar amid the screaming guests.

When she had almost reached Briar, Myantha tripped and went sprawling onto the carpet. A dagger with a green-coated blade spun from her pocket. Thalen paled, and then he grabbed her and pulled her away, holding her hands at the wrists.

Quen and Thalira cut off two more guards from reaching Briar with a water whip and a heated blast that sent one flying.

When I finally stood in front of her, I asked, "Do you wish to be my queen and my love?" The question seemed to come both from my voice and my mind at once.

Her eyes shone as she stared up at me. The most incredible being in all of creation and existence. "Yes. I never wanted to leave. Now and forever, I'm yours. Always."

My heart expanded and felt fuller than ever before as I lifted the queen's crown and placed it on her head. The blood from my hands dripped onto her hair, and the thorns pricked her scalp, though I tried to be gentle. The crown was a heavy burden, like the duty to our kingdom, but she was a queen and the strongest person I'd ever known. She could more than handle it.

Blood now dripped down her cheeks as well. I seized her in my arms and pressed my lips to hers. The comforting jolt had me melting into her, refusing to ever let her go again.

I had to have her. Hold her. Breathe her in.

Her sweet cinnamon and ginger scent was not marred by the smell of blood, and I clasped her tight against my chest and savored her. She was my home and my world. Nothing mattered right now except holding her.

You're my everything, her voice said in my head.

I didn't know how this was happening, but I never wanted it to stop. I wanted her to be a part of me always. *I love you more than the realm.*

The screams intensified, and then Briar stumbled in my arms.

"Earthquake!" she exclaimed.

The ground shook, and I tightened my arms around Briar, refusing for her to ever be harmed again. The vibrations caused my feet to stumble, and one of the huge chandeliers above the guests dropped and shattered.

Pieces of glass cut into my arms as I wrapped my wings

around us both.

"Fire," someone yelled, as feet pounded and wings flapped frantically.

"My water magic isn't working!" another responded. Cries arose from others, saying their magic was impacted, followed by an odd, rushing sensation that poured through my veins and screamed in the air around us.

Then the torches went out.

All light vanished, and the screaming cries turned to whimpers and then silence.

I lifted my head to see if it was over, and my gaze caught on the shadow beast banner above the dais. The beast glared down at us, its red eye molten and glowing.

The banner collapsed, rustling as it vanished from sight. In its place, a ghostly stag loomed ... and the world split apart.

Bryn yelled brokenly, "You don't know what you've done!"

Also by Jen L. Grey

Of Fae and Wolf Trilogy
Bonded to the Fallen Shadow King
Claimed by Shadow and Blood
Forged by Heart and Claws

Rejected Fate Trilogy
Betrayed Mate

Fated To Darkness
The King of Frost and Shadows
The Court of Thorns and Wings
The Kingdom of Flames and Ash

The Forbidden Mate Trilogy
Wolf Mate
Wolf Bitten
Wolf Touched

Standalone Romantasy
Of Shadows and Fae

Twisted Fate Trilogy
Destined Mate
Eclipsed Heart
Chosen Destiny

The Marked Dragon Prince Trilogy
Ruthless Mate
Marked Dragon
Hidden Fate

Shadow City: Silver Wolf Trilogy
Broken Mate
Rising Darkness
Silver Moon

Shadow City: Royal Vampire Trilogy
Cursed Mate
Shadow Bitten
Demon Blood

Shadow City: Demon Wolf Trilogy
Ruined Mate
Shattered Curse
Fated Souls

Shadow City: Dark Angel Trilogy
Fallen Mate
Demon Marked
Dark Prince
Fatal Secrets

Shadow City: Silver Mate
Shattered Wolf
Fated Hearts
Ruthless Moon

The Wolf Born Trilogy
Hidden Mate
Blood Secrets
Awakened Magic

The Hidden King Trilogy
Dragon Mate
Dragon Heir
Dragon Queen

The Marked Wolf Trilogy
Moon Kissed
Chosen Wolf
Broken Curse

Wolf Moon Academy Trilogy
Shadow Mate
Blood Legacy
Rising Fate

The Royal Heir Trilogy
Wolves' Queen
Wolf Unleashed
Wolf's Claim

Bloodshed Academy Trilogy
Year One
Year Two
Year Three

The Half-Breed Prison Duology
(Same World As Bloodshed Academy)
Hunted
Cursed

The Artifact Reaper Series
Reaper: The Beginning
Reaper of Earth
Reaper of Wings
Reaper of Flames
Reaper of Water

Stones of Amaria (Shared World)
Kingdom of Storms
Kingdom of Shadows
Kingdom of Ruins
Kingdom of Fire

The Pearson Prophecy
Dawning Ascent
Enlightened Ascent
Reigning Ascent

Stand Alones
Death's Angel
Rising Alpha

ABOUT THE AUTHOR

Jen L. Grey is an *USA Today* Bestselling Author of romantasy and paranormal romance. In her stories, you'll find angsty fated mate stories with tons of action.

Jen lives in Tennessee with her husband, two daughters, and three Australian Shepherds. When she isn't writing, you'll find her with a nitro cold brew in hand while chauffeuring her children around town or watching television.

Learn more at: jenlgrey.com